NOT YOUR *Sweetheart*

A HOLIDAY COLLABORATION FEATURING 13 BESTSELLING AUTHORS

WINTER TRAVERS, SHANNON MYERS, SAPPHIRE KNIGHT, MORGAN JANE MITCHELL, LIBERTY PARKER, KATHRYN C. KELLY, GAIL HARIS, E.M. SHUE, DAWN SULLIVAN, D. VESSA, ANDI RHODES, AVELYN PAIGE, ALEX GRAYSON

Not Your Sweetheart

COPYRIGHT © 2025 BY SAPPHIRE KNIGHT

WALL STREET JOURNAL & USA TODAY BESTSELLING AUTHOR

COVER DESIGN: CT COVER CREATIONS

EDITING: SHELBY LIMON

PROOFREADING: SHELBY LIMON

FORMATTING: SAPPHIRE KNIGHT

THIS BOOK IS A WORK OF FICTION. THE NAMES, CHARACTERS, PLACES, AND INCIDENTS ARE PRODUCTS OF THE WRITER'S IMAGINATION OR HAVE BEEN USED FICTITIOUSLY AND ARE NOT TO BE CONSTRUED AS REAL. ANY RESEMBLANCE TO PERSONS, LIVING OR DEAD, ACTUAL EVENTS, LOCALES OR ORGANIZATIONS IS ENTIRELY COINCIDENTAL. ALL RIGHTS ARE RESERVED. THIS BOOK IS INTENDED FOR THE PURCHASER OF THIS E-BOOK ONLY. NO PART OF THIS BOOK MAY BE REPRODUCED OR TRANSMITTED IN ANY FORM OR BY ANY MEANS, GRAPHIC, ELECTRONIC, OR MECHANICAL, INCLUDING PHOTOCOPYING, RECORDING, TAPING, OR BY ANY INFORMATION STORAGE RETRIEVAL SYSTEM SUCH AS ANYTHING WITH AI IS EXPRESSLY PROHIBITED, WITHOUT THE EXPRESS WRITTEN PERMISSION OF THE AUTHOR. ALL SONGS, SONG TITLES, AND LYRICS CONTAINED IN THIS BOOK ARE THE PROPERTY OF THE RESPECTIVE SONGWRITERS AND COPYRIGHT HOLDERS.

THESE WORDS ARE COPYRIGHTED PROPERTY, AND YOU WILL BE PUNISHED TO THE FULLEST EXTENT OF THE LAW.

Contents

Frequently Used Terms

Story 1

Chapter 1

Chapter 2

Chapter 3

Chapter 4

Chapter 5

Chapter 6

Chapter 7

Chapter 8

Chapter 9

Chapter 10

Chapter 11

Chapter 12

Chapter 13

Chapter 14

Chapter 15

Epilogue

Story 2

Chapter 1

Chapter 2

Chapter 3

Chapter 4

Chapter 5

Chapter 6

Chapter 7

Chapter 8

Chapter 9

Chapter 10

Chapter 11

Chapter 12

Chapter 13

Chapter 14

Chapter 15

Chapter 16

Chapter 17

Chapter 18

Epilogue

About The Authors

Acknowledgements

Frequently Used Terms

mo chroí agus mo anam – my heart and soul

bailigh leat – fuck off

bòidheach – beautiful

mo ghrá – my love

ceann an teaghlaigh – head of the family

feck – fuck

shite – shit

arse – ass

Jaysus – Jesus

eejit – idiot

da – dad

granda – grandfather

tá mé i ngrá leat – I am in love with you

bellezze – Italian for beauties

The Faction – Irish Mafia

clan – Irish family

~ Nyx & Greer ~

Chapter 1

Avelyn Paige

Greer

MY BROTHER IS DEAD.

The words echo in the empty corners of my mind, bouncing around like a moth caught in a bulb's warm embrace, scrambling for freedom but finding none. I can still feel the weight of that phone pressed against my ear, its plastic cold against my skin contrasting sharply with the heat radiating from my mother's voice. Hysterical, yet *trembling*. Her cries ring with an urgency that slices through my carefully constructed existence, each syllable sharpening my reality into something jagged.

I remember the moment—I was sprawled on my bed in my off-campus apartment, surrounded by textbooks as I crammed for an exam, the soft whisper of afternoon sunlight filtering through the curtains, illuminating dust motes as they danced lazily in the air. I thought it was just another call to catch up, to hear about mundane things like laundry mishaps or Dad's latest attempts at grilling without setting fire to the backyard. But then there was panic. Every word rushed out like it was trying to flee from her lips, each one crashing into me like tidal waves over rough, pointed rocks.

"Greer!" she yelled, punctuated by choked sobs that twisted the fabric of her voice. "You have to come home! You have to..."

I froze. Time suspended itself around me, drawing taut like a string about to snap. "Mom?" I barely whispered, unsure if I wanted to hear what came next or if I was hoping she'd suddenly be reminded of something bright and soothing instead—a memory of when we used to build blanket forts on rainy afternoons or how he'd spin me around until I couldn't breathe from laughter.

Then she handed the phone over to Dad. His voice cracked slightly, like an old record, already slipping into a place where sound ceases to matter. "Greer," he said, each word layered with sorrow so thick it felt tangible. "Rowan is... dead."

Dead.

The word slammed into me with brutal finality, as though it had emerged from the depths of some unfathomable abyss to swallow whole every shred of reason I clung to. Time slowed; I found myself suspended in that moment—the world around me collapsing into muted chaos while I spiraled deeper into confusion.

"What do you mean dead?" The question wrinkled my brow with disbelief; it tasted foreign on my tongue, like unripe fruit too sour to digest. My heart pounded furiously against my ribs as if trying to escape this nightmare.

"We don't know all the details yet," he spoke, and even though his voice trembled, it contained a strange stoicism that left me feeling utterly hollow. "He was—he was shot last night."

Shot. The truth cut deeper than any blade could wield. Images of Rowan drifted through my mind: him laughing over shared secrets on our porch swing or crouched over our late grandfather's guitar, playing melodies he created just for me. He had always been the spark—wild and untamed. A wildness that took him on a very different path. A dangerous one that I had told him on more than one occasion would get him killed.

Now, he was gone.

Forever.

My warning held a sickening truth to it, and fuck, I wish I hadn't been right. Now, a week later, it still doesn't seem real. I stand before a full-length mirror, my fingers trembling as they adjust the delicate necklace Rowan had given me—a silver locket shaped like a feather. It glimmers against my warm ivory skin, just like those long-forgotten summer mornings when we'd sit outside with an orange juice in hand, dreaming of living on the beach in a shack without a care in the world. But that was before everything changed, before he became Crow and fell into shadows I still struggle to understand.

He wasn't only my brother, but growing up, he was my best friend. We were thick as thieves. Closer than any typical sibling duo, and now a piece of me is missing.

Downstairs, the muffled voices of my parents spiral around me, a chaotic symphony of anger and despair. My father's voice rises, its sharpness cutting through the tension. "How can I show my face there? He chose that life—that *gang*! I can't be a part of any of it." His words are fueled by bitterness, heavy with regret that stains his soul like spilled ink on fresh paper. "The Bishop already looks down his nose at me. If I step foot into that funeral home, what kind of message does that send?" "He's our son, Robert. Not some stranger off the streets. If the Bishop cannot offer grace and understanding in our grief, he shouldn't be Bishop at all." Mom's voice trembles beneath his roar, pleading yet steel-like.

The silence that follows is deafening. I imagine them standing on either side of our old oak kitchen table, tension crackling between them like electricity. My heart aches for Rowan, for all he was and could have been—the good times overshadowed by his choices and entanglements with a world we hardly understood. With a shaky breath, I pull my hair into a loose bun, letting a few strands fall delicately around my face like soft tendrils of forgotten dreams. Who am I to fight against the tide of their grief? An echoing silence fills me as I remember Rowan's laughter—how easy it had been for him to make friends out of strangers while I hid behind walls painted with skepticism. Now, I'm left holding fragments of his existence—broken pieces we all failed to stitch back together.

I cross the room, my feet moving as if on autopilot, drawn to the closet where my black dress hangs. It's a simple thing, a vintage piece I found at that secondhand store on campus. I slip into it, feeling the coolness of the fabric against my warm skin; it clings just right, accentuating curves that have so often felt like barriers rather than blessings. I reach for the black kitten heels borrowed from my friend Carrie from college and slide them on with a sense of borrowed confidence. They add a subtle click to each step I take on the hardwood floors, echoing softly in the room.

I glance over my shoulder at the mirror and see a stranger staring back at me. My once bright green eyes now have flecks of gold, searching for warmth but only finding shadows of despair. With a sigh, I gather my phone from the bedside table and tuck it into the small black purse my mother lent me last night.

Leaving my room, I navigate the creaky wooden staircase with cautious steps, the dim moonlight filtering through the curtains and casting eerie shadows on the walls. Each footfall echoes in the now-silent house as I descend towards the unknown heartache brewing in the kitchen. A lump forms in my throat, constricting it with each passing moment, yet I push myself to straighten up, bracing for the emotional storm about to engulf me.

The door slams behind me as I enter, sending a shiver down my spine. And then I find her—my mother, hunched over our old Formica table, her body shaking with silent sobs.

"Mom?" My question is tentative, fragile against the thick atmosphere.

She flinches at the sound of my voice, her shoulders jerking as if jolted by some unseen force. I take a step toward her, eyes searching for some sign of recognition amid the tears that glisten like glass on her cheeks. She wipes them fervently, as though erasing a story she never wanted to write.

"Did you hear us?" The question trembles from her lips, laden with an anxious weight that hangs in the air between us.

"I did," I reply quietly, as the truth settles within me—heavy and dense. There's no point in pretending I didn't know about their argument. The neighbors probably heard it, too. Dad's voice tends to carry, thanks to his years of preaching.

Her voice cracks as she continues, "I don't understand why he won't come." Each word strikes like a drumbeat in the stillness of the room, punctuating our collective despair. I can see the way her fingers grip the edge of the table, knuckles white against its worn surface—a desperate anchor in her turbulent sea of emotions.

"Mom," I whisper, willing my voice to be steady, "he'll be back." I glance at the clock on the wall, a constant reminder of the minutes slipping away. The hands are reluctant, moving almost as if they're weighing the gravity of the situation instead of marking time. "He just... needs a moment."

Frankly, we all do. It had taken the detectives working his case five days before they released Rowan's body to the funeral home. Despite the number of calls Mom had placed, they have told us nothing regarding Rowan's murder. Part of me wonders if they were going to investigate it at all or would they just chalk it up to another gangbanger getting what is coming to them.

I shift to comfort Mom as the door creaks open and Dad steps inside, his shoulders stooped under an invisible weight. He meets our gazes one at a time—Mom's first, then mine. "I pulled the car up," he says quietly, but I manage to pick up on the hints of regret slipping through his words like whispers carried on the wind. My breath catches as his eyes flicker over my mother's tear-streaked face—there's guilt simmering beneath his hardened exterior. "We should leave soon," he adds awkwardly.

Mom nods slowly—a motion that seems weighted down by everything left unsaid. She picks up her purse from the kitchen counter, passing my father in silence, then opens the door and steps outside. Dad follows closely behind her, leaving me to bring up the rear and lock the door. By the time I make it outside, Mom is already in the front seat, securely buckled in, and Dad is waiting at the open passenger door for me. As I slide into the car, the stale scent of leather wraps around me, mingling with the faint traces of Dad's cologne. He takes his place in the driver's seat, and I can't help but glance at his face in the rearview mirror. His eyes are fixed on the empty road ahead, and I wonder if he even notices the thickness of the silence settling like a dense fog in the cramped space between us. The engine hums softly as we pull out of the driveway, tires crunching on gravel that seems oddly significant; each pebble somehow manages to echo our collective reluctance to face what lies ahead. The streets whiz by in a blur of color—familiar houses and storefronts distort under the speed, just as my thoughts twist and turn through fragmented memories of laughter and chaos from times more innocent.

This is grief. The notion slams into me as my emotions bubble up, everything seemingly too loud, too bright, and just too much.

An uneasy tension hums beneath my skin as we approach the funeral home, its facade unassuming, yet marked by an unmistakable gravity. A few cars are already parked haphazardly outside—strangers bearing witness to our loss, but none familiar enough to offer a semblance of comfort. Dad parks near the front and kills the engine before he sets out to open the door for Mom first, then me. I peer at the building in front of us. It's a small chapel, unlike the sprawling sanctuary of my father's church.

We step inside the building, and the scent of lilies is overpowering—a cloying sweetness that's almost suffocating in a sense. It drapes itself over me in a blanket I've never wanted but am forced to wear regardless.

A tall man clad in a dark suit approaches, his name tag reading 'Mr. Hargrove.' He extends his hand toward my father, who shakes it with a stiffness that speaks volumes of unprocessed emotions lying just beneath the surface. "This way, please," Mr. Hargrove orders gently, his tone steady as he guides us through the narrow corridor lined with framed pictures—each frame holding faces frozen in moments once vibrant and full of life.

I wonder if they're all dead too.

Following closely behind my parents, I measure their steps against my own wavering resolve and glance at Mom's profile. I take in her tightly pressed lips and narrowed eyes, betraying how hard she's working to hold herself together. However, I know that beneath her carefully composed exterior lies a shattered heart trying to piece itself back in place. As we reach the main room, an expanse dominated by a simple wood-closed casket at its center captures my attention—a monument marking not only death but all that has shifted in our world.

Dad's voice breaks through my thoughts as he murmurs something to Mr. Hargrove about the service he's left up to Mom and me to plan—words that seem to evaporate in the air before reaching my ears.

My focus shifts toward Mom again as she stands rooted in place, staring ahead with glassy eyes that betray her internal battle. "Mom, would you like to go see him?" I ask softly, my voice a mere whisper.

She shakes her head, admitting, "No, Greer. I can't." The small movement seems to take every bit of strength she possesses, as if she's trying to fight against some unseen force.

The ache in my chest deepens as the distance between us widens. I tuck a loose strand of hair behind my ear and take a hesitant step toward the casket. Each footfall feels laden with an unutterable sorrow, as if the very ground beneath me resonates with the memories of a life cut short.

"Hey, Rowan," I murmur, my breath hitching slightly as I find rasping words lodged in my throat once I make it to his resting place.

I swallow hard and lean closer, lowering my voice to barely more than a hush that feels as fragile as gossamer threads spun by careful hands. My fingers tremble as they brush against the cool wood of the casket, and I can almost convince myself that he can hear me, that somehow, my words might weave back through the veil between us. "Do you remember those late-night talks we used to have?" I smile sadly at the thought, imagining his mischievous grin lighting up his face as he threw his head back in laughter. "We dreamt together about what life would be like after high school—how we'd escape this town and build something better... something real." My voice wavers as nostalgia washes over me like a wave crashing against rocky shores. "But then everything shifted for you, didn't it?"

I press my palm against the surface beneath my fingers, wishing desperately for signs of warmth—some evidence that he's still somewhere out there beyond this world. "I just wish things had been different; I wish they hadn't gotten hold of you." A tear slips free and traces a path down my cheek as I allow myself to be raw and exposed in this moment. "I want you to know... no matter what decisions you made or where life took you... I loved you, Row. *I still do.* And I'll miss you until the last breath leaves my body." The honesty hangs thickly in the air; it's liberating, yet painful—a double-edged sword piercing through layers of regret and sorrow intertwined with love.

The funeral director's voice cuts through my reverie, a soft yet firm reminder of the finality unfolding around me. "Ms. Ellis, calling hours are about to begin." I blink away the new wave of encroaching sadness, allowing a fragile sense of composure to settle over me now that I've had a few last moments with my brother alone.

My parents approach, wearing solemn expressions, their grief cracking like old porcelain under pressure. My mother's delicate hand reaches for mine, fingers trembling as she intertwines them with her own. "Are you okay, sweetheart?" she questions, her voice barely above a whisper.

No. I'm anything but okay. I nod, though my heart is heavy and hard—a stone lodged deep in my chest. The sound of approaching footsteps pulls me from my despair, and instinctively, I straighten my posture, unsure of how I'll handle the influx of visitors.

Each face that steps across the threshold is merely an echo of a moment lost in time, faces I recognize but haven't seen in years. Members of my parents' church and some of Mom's cousins filter into the room, their expressions fluctuating between solemnity and sympathy. One by one, they shake my hand or hug me, murmuring their condolences on the loss of my brother as they pass me by to speak to my parents. A few friends from high school trickle through the line, disappearing as quickly as they arrived. The only solace is that none of my brother's gang members bother to show up. Considering it was his association with *them* that got him killed, I wouldn't have shown up either. Their absence is one less worry for my parents.

As the scheduled calling hours end, the crowd thins, leaving only my second cousins lingering behind for the brief non-religious service that my mother and I had planned. Unlike my parents, Rowan and I were not devout followers, much to my father's disappointment. I have had more than enough organized religion to tide me over for the rest of my life.

The funeral director approaches us as one of his assistants shuts the doors to the viewing room. "Our service will begin momentarily if you'd like to take your seats."

My father clears his throat, ushering my mother into one of the open chairs in the front row and motions for me to take the open seat on her right. I settle into my place, the wood hard and unyielding beneath me. Considering the exorbitant fees they charge for funerals, you'd think they could at least invest in chairs that wouldn't leave your back and ass aching from sitting on it more than a few minutes.

The funeral director steps forward while an instrumental hymn that my brother would have hated plays quietly around us. The music finally fades, and as the funeral director begins to speak, the doors slowly open, the quiet creak from the movement drawing my attention away from my spiraling thoughts. A figure stands there, silhouetted against the muted light spilling in from the hallway.

My breath hitches in my throat as recognition crashes over me like a tidal wave—*Nyx Bennett.*

He's different now, yet achingly familiar. His dark hair spills down to his shoulders, held back in a loose knot, leaving his angular features bare for all to see. But it's those gray eyes—stormy, but piercing—that hold me captive. I want nothing more than to turn away, to focus on something—anything—else but him. *I can't.* Nyx steps further inside, and our eyes lock.

Why is he here? Why now, when the one person who needed him the most is dead?

Chapter 2

Winter Travers

Nyx

THE SCENT OF LILIES and polished wood hits me as I step into the room. It's too bright for a funeral—sunlight filters through the stained-glass windows, casting warm colors on faces that look anything but warm. I stay near the back, far enough to avoid any real interaction, yet close enough to take in the scene.

It seems like every eye in the room glances at me, but none burn hotter than Greer's. I feel her gaze before I see her. It's been years since I last saw her, yet I know it's her without even looking. The weight of her stare pulls at me, and finally, I lift my eyes.

She's sitting near the front, just to the side of the casket. Her chestnut hair is pinned back, but a few loose strands frame her face. Her green eyes—gold flecks catching the light—lock onto mine, and for a moment, I swear she's about to come charging across the room to confront me. She doesn't, though. She just stares, her lips pressed into a thin line, and her expression unreadable.

She's grown up. I mean, I knew she had, but *damn*. She's not the girl I remember tagging along behind Rowan and me, her laughter chasing us down the street. She's a woman now, curves and confidence, though I can see the pain. The grief is there, even if she's trying to hide it.

I look away first. It's easier to focus on the guy at the front. Some suit. He's droning on about Rowan's life, skimming over the real story. The sanitized version of Rowan. The one where he was just a guy who had a tough break, not someone neck-deep in gang shit with the Iron Palms.

I cross my arms over my chest, leaning back against the wall. My jaw tightens as I listen. It feels wrong. All of it. Rowan was no saint, but he wasn't a mere cautionary tale either. He was my best friend once. Years ago.

And two weeks ago, he called me.

"Hey, Nyx," his voice crackled through the line, low and hesitant. "It's Rowan. You got a second to talk?"

Hearing his voice had been like a punch to the gut. Eight years of silence, and then, out of nowhere, here he was.

"Rowan?" I blinked, caught off guard. "Yeah. Yeah, I've always got time for you."

The words came easy, but the truth was more complicated. We hadn't spoken in so long, not since I joined the department and he joined the Iron Palms. We didn't have a falling out, but the gap between us became too wide to cross.

"I don't have much time," he muttered, the tension in his voice unmistakable. "Life's been... it's been a lot lately. How's life treating you?"

"Crazy, but good," I said, trying to sound casual. "Can't really complain."

He laughed, a dry sound. "Good. That's good. Listen, Nyx, I need to ask you something."

My gut told me this wasn't going to be a normal conversation. Rowan didn't call me out of the blue to just catch up after all these years.

"What's up?"

"It's about Greer." His voice dropped, and my chest tightened. "Things are happening, and I don't know what the future holds. Can you promise me something?"

"Rowan..." I warned, already uneasy.

"Promise me you'll look out for her if something happens to me."

"What the hell are you talking about?"

"I can't explain, Nyx. You know why. But I need to know she's got someone. Someone who'll really be there for her when I can't be."

"You're being dramatic," I said, trying to brush it off. "Nothing's going to happen to you."

He sighed, the sound heavy with resignation. "I'm doing everything I can, but shit's messy. Just promise me."

"Fine. If it'll get you to calm down, I promise I'll keep an eye on Greer."

"No, Nyx. Not good enough. You're going to need to be in her life. Whatever it takes."

"Rowan—"

"Promise me," he snapped, his voice sharp. "Fucking promise."

I swallowed hard, knowing there was no talking him down. "Fine. I promise."

"Good," he said, his tone softening. "You really need to be there. She's probably going to tell you to fuck off, but you can't let her brush you off. She can't be alone if I'm gone. Do whatever you need to stay right next to her."

I laughed, trying to lighten the mood. "What, you want me to marry her too?"

"Yeah," he said, dead serious. "That's probably what it'll take."

The guy in the suit at the front keeps talking, droning on about Rowan's "legacy" as if he actually knew him. His voice is monotone, professional, and detached. He talks about Rowan's smile, his generosity, his "kind soul," skimming right past the truth—the gang ties, the danger, the double life.

I can't stop myself from scoffing under my breath. Kind soul? Sure. Rowan had a good heart, but he also had blood on his hands. The Iron Palms don't recruit saints, and they sure as hell don't let members stay clean. The man glances in my direction, but I keep my face blank. He moves on quickly, his words as empty as the many chairs.

From the back of the room, I scan the crowd again. Rowan's parents sit near the front, next to Greer. His mom is staring down at her hands, a crumpled tissue in her lap. His dad has his arm around her shoulders, his face a mask of stone. It doesn't crack, even when the suit mentions Rowan's "troubled youth."

Greer is a different story. Her spine is straight, her head held high, but her fingers clutch the edge of the pew like it's the only thing keeping her tethered. Her green eyes—so much like Rowan's—stare straight ahead.

I recognize a few other faces scattered through the room. Some cousins I remember from childhood birthday parties and barbecues. Their aunts and uncles I haven't seen in years. The rest of the people are strangers to me, likely here out of obligation or curiosity.

What I don't see—or don't recognize—are any Iron Palms members.

Rowan was deep with them; there's no way they aren't here somewhere. Maybe in the crowd, maybe outside, but they're close. I can feel it.

And that's the problem. They're *always* close.

Two weeks ago, after my call with Rowan, I dug into the Iron Palms, looking for anything that could help. I was working undercover, trying to get into the Blood Saints, the rival gang to the Iron Palms, and what I found made my stomach churn.

Rowan wasn't just involved with them—he was a key player, and the shit he'd gotten into was bad.

Deals gone wrong.

Debts that couldn't be paid.

And worst of all, a target painted squarely on Greer's back.

Rowan had been right to worry. The blowback from his actions isn't going to stop at him. It's going to hit Greer like a freight train, and she won't see it coming.

So, I came up with a plan. A desperate, half-baked, last-resort kind of plan. One I never thought I'd have to use.

Marry her.

I had been joking when I said it to Rowan on the phone, but as the days passed since he died, it stopped feeling like a joke. Tying Greer to me legally, officially, can shield her in ways I can't from the outside. It will put distance between her and the Palms, making her untouchable in their world. At least, that's what I keep telling myself to justify it.

Now, standing here at Rowan's funeral, that plan isn't just an idea anymore. It's the only option. The *only* way to keep my promise.

The suit finally wraps up his speech, and people begin filing past the casket. Some linger, whispering prayers or brushing their fingers over the wood. Rowan's mom stands, leaning heavily on Robert's arm as they approach the front, but they don't stop at the casket. Greer follows behind them, her movements stiff, controlled.

I stay put, watching. My hands clench at my sides as I track Greer's every step. She doesn't look at the casket for long, just a quick glance before she turns away. Her face is set, her expression unreadable, but I notice the tension in her shoulders.

When the line thins, I push off the wall and make my way to her. She's standing off to the side now, arms crossed, avoiding eye contact with anyone who tries to offer condolences. She spots me before I'm halfway across the room, her gaze narrowing, to the point I can practically hear the gears turning in her head.

"Nyx," she says as I approach, her voice cold. "What are you doing here?"

"I've come to pay my respects," I reply simply.

She snorts, crossing her arms tighter. "Respect? Since when do you care?"

I take a deep breath, trying to keep my tone calm. "You know that's not fair, Greer. Rowan was my best friend."

"*Was*," she echoes bitterly. "Not is. You left him, Nyx. *You left us.*"

The accusation stings more than I want to admit. "I didn't leave," I argue, my voice low. "I made a choice. One I *had* to make." Rowan and I couldn't have been friends, being on opposite sides of the law.

"And look how that turned out," she snaps. Her green eyes glint with anger, but there's pain behind the emotion. "He's dead, Nyx. And you're here, what? To absolve yourself?"

"No," I state firmly. "I'm here because I made him a promise."

She blinks, caught off guard. "What are you talking about?"

I glance around the room. Too many faces, too many ears, too many risks. "Let's find somewhere quieter to talk," I suggest, lowering my voice.

She narrows her eyes, hesitating for a beat before nodding. "Fine."

I step closer, gently wrapping my fingers around her arm, just above her elbow. Her skin is warm beneath my touch, and I'm careful not to grip too tightly. She lets me guide her through the maze of mourners. Her tension is palpable.

At the end of a dim hallway, I find a small room with a frosted glass door. A bronze plaque reads *'Prayer Room.'* I push it open, leading her inside. It's quiet here, the walls lined with bookshelves holding dusty Bibles and hymnals. A few chairs and a small kneeling bench are scattered around, but I don't sit. Neither does she.

I close the door behind us, the latch clicking softly. The air feels heavier now, intimate, *charged*. Greer stands in the middle of the room, arms still crossed, her stance defiant.

"Well?" she demands, her voice cutting through the stillness.

I hesitate, the weight of Rowan's words pressing down on me. "Two weeks ago," I begin, my voice low, "Rowan called me. Out of the blue. He told me he was in trouble. He asked me to look out for you if anything happened to him."

Her jaw tightens, her eyes narrowing into slits. "I don't need you to look out for me."

"I know you think that," I say, stepping closer, my tone calm but firm. "But you don't know what's coming, Greer. The shit Rowan was involved in—it's going to spill over. Onto you."

Her expression hardens, and she takes a step forward, her voice dropping to a hiss. "Don't you dare try to scare me, Nyx. I've been through enough."

"I'm not saying this to scare you," I explain, my voice steady. "I'm trying to protect you."

She lets out a bitter laugh, her arms falling to her sides as her fingers curl into fists. "Protect me? And how exactly do you plan to do that?"

I take a deep breath, bracing myself. "By marrying you." Might as well just rip the damn Band-Aid off. The sooner we get past her being pissed and telling me no, the better off we will be.

Her laughter dies instantly, replaced by stunned silence. She stares at me, her eyes wide, disbelief etched into every line of her face. "Excuse me?"

"You heard me," I say, meeting her gaze head-on. "If we're married, it'll give me the leverage I need to keep you safe. The Iron Palms won't touch you if you're tied to me."

She takes a step back, shaking her head like she's trying to clear it. "You're insane."

"Maybe," I admit. "However, I'm also right."

Her hands ball tighter, and for a moment, I think she might take a swing at me. "You think I'm just going to roll over and let you make decisions for me? You think I need you to save me?"

"No," I say. "I think you need someone in your corner. Someone who knows what's coming and how to stop it."

"This is ridiculous," she snaps.

"Maybe," I say again, my voice quiet but firm. "But I'm the best shot you've got."

Greer moves toward the door, her hand gripping the handle like it's the only thing keeping her steady. She pauses, glancing back at me over her shoulder. Her stare glints with defiance, but there's a crack in her armor, one that's barely visible.

"I don't need you or anything you're offering, Nyx," she declares, her voice sharp and biting. "I've done just fine without you the past eight years, and I'll continue to be fine without you."

She gives me one last look, a mixture of anger, pain, and something I can't quite place, before stepping out of the room. The door swings open behind her, left ajar, and the sound of her heels clicking down the hallway fades quickly.

I stand there for a moment, staring at the empty doorway, my fists clenching and unclenching at my sides. She might not want my help now, but she's going to find out she'll need it eventually.

I only hope it won't take her too long to realize it—before it's too late.

Chapter 3

Dawn Sullivan

Greer

How dare he? I seethe to myself as I stalk down the hall toward the front of the funeral home looking for my parents. After all of these years, he thinks he can come back into my life, spout some crap about me being in danger, and then expect me to *marry* him to stay safe? How exactly would marrying him protect me from the Iron Palms if they came after me anyway? And why does he care? I'm no one to him now.

Just... no.

Hell no.

What planet is he living on? Obviously, not the same one I am, because there is no way I am going to exchange wedding vows with the bastard. If I ever do get married, it will be to someone I love and trust—not someone who thinks they can just waltz back into my life after being gone for years and put a ring on my finger.

Nyx left us. Walked out of our lives with no warning. Here one day, gone the next. Oh, he stopped by our house late the night before he decided to leave town. Showed up right before midnight. He came to let us know he was moving out of state so he could go to college. Said he was going to better his life. That he wanted to be a cop, and he couldn't be friends with my brother anymore because Rowan was going down the wrong road.

Gangbangers and cops don't mix.

I sigh. To be fair, Nyx didn't actually say they couldn't stay friends, but he never once picked up the phone to call Rowan after he drove away that night. I would have known. My brother would have told me.

Although, he didn't tell me he reached out to Nyx two weeks ago. He never said a word about thinking I might need protection from his gang of 'brothers.'

Why would he call Nyx? And why would the Iron Palms come after me? I'm nobody to them. My brother may have been a part of their gang, but I only know one other person who's a member. A man Rowan brought around a couple of times, which means he trusted him. He would never introduce me to someone if he even remotely thought they would harm me. I was his baby sister, and he had always been really protective of me. I'm not sure what the guy's name was or anything else about him. Tracker or Tracer, or something like that. I frown as I try to remember.

Trickster. It was Trickster.

I'm not a threat to anyone. I'm a journalism major with a minor in photography, and I have an internship at the local newspaper where I go to college in the city a mere forty-five minutes away from the place where I grew up. I have a small, one-bedroom rundown apartment there that I sometimes worry I won't be able to pay rent on. I live on ramen noodles and mac and cheese, like a lot of other college students I know. I'm a senior this year, so hopefully once I graduate, I can get on full-time where I'm interning now and stop having to worry so much about money.

I grit my teeth as I walk into the entryway, where I find my mother waiting by the door. She looks so alone. Her head is bowed, eyes closed, with her hands clasped tightly together in front of her.

Not wanting to startle her, I clear my throat. Her head comes up quickly, tired, sad eyes meeting mine. "Greer, there you are."

I paste on a small, fake smile as I walk over to her. "Sorry, I was talking with Nyx."

My mother nods, and her gaze goes beyond me. I turn to see Nyx standing just a few feet away, a dark scowl painted on his handsome features. He's glaring at me, and I have to fight the urge to flip him the bird as I glance back over at my mom. "Where's Dad?"

"He's getting the car."

Of course, he is. He came, did his time, and ran as quickly as he could. With the type of pull the Bishop has on him, I'm glad we got him to show up in the first place, let alone stick around. I was so out of it all day for the service that time escaped me.

I nod. "Let's go."

As we walk out the door, I refuse to look back at Nyx, even though I can feel his eyes on me the entire time. Dad pulls up, headlights momentarily blinding us, and I open the front passenger door, then help Mom inside. As I close it, I stiffen when the feeling of being watched washes over me. It's a different sensation than when Nyx's eyes were on me. This one makes my skin crawl, and I begin to tremble with newfound fear.

My heart races as I slowly lift my head and look around the parking lot. Standing off to the side, only a short distance away under a streetlight, are three dangerous-looking men. The light illuminates them, making it so I can see them more clearly, but I don't recognize their faces. What I do recognize is the large tattoo on the bald guy's neck. It's the same one that my brother has on his chest.

It would seem the Iron Palms have shown up to my brother's funeral after all. My hand shakes slightly as I reach down to open my own door.

One of them gives me a smirk and steps my way just as the door behind me opens and Nyx walks out. I glance back at him, but his gaze is locked on the three men who are now glaring in our direction.

"Get in the car, Greer," Nyx growls as he reaches me. He gently takes my hand from the door handle and opens the back door, waiting until I'm seated inside before leaning in and slipping a piece of paper in my hand. Very quietly, he says, "Call me, please. I know you think you can handle this on your own, but you need to let me help. I made a promise to Rowan, and I'm not going anywhere."

I find his words hard to believe. Past actions have shown differently. But I nod and slip the paper into my purse. Right now, all I want to do is get back to my parents' house where I'll feel safe again. I didn't take what Nyx was telling me seriously until I noticed Rowan's gang members standing there, looking as if they were waiting for me.

Why would they be after me? Rowan always claimed the gang was like a family—his brothers, ones that would do anything for each other. What changed? What did my brother do?

A couple of hours later, I stand by my bedroom window, my hand resting on the cool glass as I stare out into the darkness and remember back to that night so long ago. The night Nyx severed ties with my brother, leaving both Rowan and me behind.

"What do you mean you're leaving, Nyx? You can't go, man. You're my best friend. We have plans."

I stand at the top of the stairs, looking down at my brother as he reaches out to grab Nyx's arm.

Nyx shakes him off and moves back. "I can't stay here. I have to get out of this town. I want to make something of my life, Ro. Not just be another gangbanger on the streets."

"What the fuck is that supposed to mean?" Rowan demands, his hands curling into fists at his sides. "You think I'm nobody? That I'm some loser who won't *ever amount to anything?"*

"I didn't say that," Nyx snaps, shaking his head. "The Iron Palms are pushing us both hard to join, and I've decided it isn't the kind of life I want."

"What do you want then?"

Nyx hesitates, his jaw hardening. Even from far away, I can read the determination in his eyes as he says, "I'm going to be a cop."

I gasp, my hand going to cover my mouth as I watch Ro take a menacing step toward him and growl, "You fucking what?"

Nyx stands his ground, glaring at Rowan. "I'm going to school for criminal justice, then I'll be going through the academy."

"Why the hell would you want to do something like that? Dammit, Nyx. We have everything planned out. We're supposed to be joining the Palms. You're going to finally get the family you've always wanted. Brothers. Someone to have your back when you need it besides me."

My brother told me before how Nyx's mom left him and his dad when Nyx was ten years old. He basically raised himself after that. He has no siblings, and his dad works during the day and is at the bar all night, so he's never around.

Nyx shoves a hand through his dark hair, a tormented expression on his face. "I can't, Ro. I'm sorry, but... I just can't. I don't need brothers like that. Who fight, steal, and kill. I can't live my life like that."

"But I thought we were brothers, for life, remember?" Rowan mentions, and my breath hitches at the pain in his voice.

I've never heard him sound so hurt and dejected.

"We are." Nyx reaches for him, but Rowan flinches and moves back away from him. "Come with me, man. There's still time. Apply at the college I'm going to. Go through the academy with me. We'll get an apartment together after..."

"No." Rowan is shaking his head adamantly. "No, it's not what we talked about, Nyx. It isn't what I want. I'm joining the Iron Palms. That's the plan, has always been the plan. I'm doing it, with or without you."

Nyx's arm falls back to his side, and tears fill my eyes at the agony on his face.

"Then, I guess I don't have any brothers," he admits quietly, turning and walking to the door. He opens it, glancing back at Rowan before looking up to where I stand. "If you need anything, either of you, call me."

Rowan stays silent, and so do I.

Nyx takes a deep breath before turning and walking through the door and out of our lives.

I sigh as I slowly allow the curtain to fall back into place, covering the outside from my view. While I'm still angry with Nyx and the way he's stormed back into my life like a wrecking ball, I'm also worried about the Iron Palms coming after me and my family. Because there is no doubt in my mind they were there for me at the funeral home tonight, and my parents were with me. They could have been hurt.

I shudder as I remember the look on the man's face who'd taken a step toward our car before Nyx came out the door and over to my side. It was evil, full of intention. He was coming for me and probably would have taken me if Nyx hadn't been there. I have no idea what his plans were for me, but I know they weren't good.

I've made it a point to check all of our doors and windows, and I locked them as soon as we got home. I've done several rounds from each window to make sure no one has been standing outside watching the house, but I haven't seen anyone so far. It doesn't mean they haven't been there, though. However, I choose to believe if they are, they'll show themselves as they so eagerly did at the funeral home.

Picking up my phone, I scowl as I find Nyx's name in my contact list. I added him earlier when I got back to the house, already knowing I was going to reach out to him, even though no part of me wants to. But I'm also not in any hurry to die.

Swearing softly, I close my eyes and count to ten before typing the text and sending it.

Me: Meet me at the coffee shop two blocks from my parents' house tomorrow at one p.m.

I'm going home tomorrow, but I will meet up with Nyx on my way out of town. I sure as hell won't be telling him there are wedding bells in our future, but he seems to know something about my brother's death, and I want whatever information he has. I refuse to sit back and wait for any info the law decides to share with us when they get around to finish working my brother's case. They haven't been very forthcoming so far.

I don't need them, though. I'm going to school for journalism. What kind of journalist will I be if I can't hunt down a story myself? No, I won't be waiting on the police. I'll be finding out what happened to my brother myself.

Nyx: I'll be there.

I don't reply. I have nothing else to say right now. It can all wait until tomorrow when I'll see him in person.

I'm just nodding off to sleep when a thought hits me. It's one I realize I do not know the answer to, but I suddenly want to.

Did Nyx do what he said he was going to? Did he become a cop?

Chapter 4

E.M. Shue

Nyx

I'VE BEEN STANDING IN this darkened alley for a couple hours now, waiting for Greer. I want to be here to make sure that we beat the Iron Palms, and my team is in place prior. In my gut, I knew the gang would be here. I suspect they've already bugged or mirrored her phone and know about our meeting today. Their hope is to intercept her before I get to her.

My team isn't going to allow that.

Rowan knew of two things by asking me to protect Greer. I couldn't tell him no. She's one of the reasons I walked away all those years ago; he must have suspected. I had to leave when she came between the two of us. She had the power to destroy our friendship with a mere look. She'd always held that power, but in the end, I could barely fight it. I was hanging on by a thread... and I wasn't willing to go to prison or destroy my brother for her. The other reason being I'm the meanest person on the street, and Rowan knew it. I have a reputation no one crosses.

The power to destroy people.

The funny thing is, most men the streets claim I've killed are in a hole somewhere, wishing they'd never gotten into business with me. They're alive, but barely. The others, well, I'll plead the Fifth on.

What Rowan and Greer aren't aware of, and what only a few people are, is a couple weeks before I made the decision to walk away from everything and become a lawman, I saw something *bad*.

I watched one of the gang initiations or jump-ins. They raped a girl not much older than Greer was at the time. It freaked me the fuck out, and I couldn't do it. All I could picture was Greer screaming and crying, not the other girl there. In that moment, I made a decision I don't regret and never will. I went to the police the same night and turned in the same men I believed would become my brothers.

Best decision I ever made. I made a call not long after I was recruited, and those men, those shitbag rapists, all were found dead in their cells later. My reputation started before anyone ever knew about it.

My life took a dramatic turn when I left for college. I had so many plans, and they all went out the window before I applied to the academy. My little stunt with the gang got back to certain people within various agencies, and I was recruited. The night I showed up at Rowan's house and informed him I was leaving, I wanted him to come with me. It killed me inside to witness the betrayal burning in his eyes when I told him I wasn't going to follow him but instead go to the academy. To his credit, he never let the Iron Palms in on my plans. *He still protected me.* It all played into my backstory and gave me the credibility most undercovers lack—authenticity.

I was going to become a gangbanger, just not for the Iron Palms.

Now, everyone important knows me as Nyx. The others, well, I have the reputation as one of the *meanest* gun dealers around, also known as *The Armorer*. No one crosses me and lives. I don't allow it to happen because if I did, I wouldn't be where I am today. It's not only how I'm going to be able to get into the Blood Saints but also be able to scare the Iron Palms into leaving Greer alone.

She must marry me and be mine; there's no other option.

Part of me isn't upset by the turn of events; the other doesn't want to bring her into my life at all. Being the spouse of a deep undercover ATF agent isn't easy. The Bureau of Alcohol, Tobacco, Firearms and Explosives, along with my own ambition, has molded me into the man I am now. I know more about guns and ammo than most people do in their entire lifetime.

I live a life that I never dreamed of, in a luxurious house and all, but it's a front.

All smoke and mirrors.

According to the ATF, it is, anyway. They aren't aware I'm slowly stashing money away for my personal rainy day. I'd take that pass now and run with Greer if I had to, but I don't need to. My reputation alone is what's going to save her, along with my highly skilled team.

My chain of command doesn't want me to do this. However, I've already informed them that if they don't want me to tank a case we've been working on for years, they have to let it happen. I will protect Greer. Now that my handler knows who Greer is interning with, they want to keep a close eye on her too. They certainly don't want any more women kidnapped and trafficked by the gangs either.

It's a bad image for the Bureau.

I didn't keep in contact with Greer and Rowan, and I hate that fact. I also knew back then that if I did, it'd shine a spotlight on them, being both good and bad. It was imperative my superiors didn't look into Rowan before I had the chance to.

I certainly didn't want anyone else looking at Greer. Period. Yeah, I'm a selfish, jealous bastard. I knew what she had planned for her future too, and keeping my secrets private keeps me alive.

"Boss, she's coming in," my second in command, Ace, calls through my earpiece. I watch her for a moment. She's more beautiful than I remember. I knew she'd be gorgeous, but she's stunning in her quiet, curvy beauty.

I just need to keep her from hating me before this day is through. The plan is in motion now that she's on scene, and it won't stop until my point is proven. Last night, it took everything in me not to steal her away when I saw those pricks thinking of taking her from her parents.

Greer's dressed in a vintage jumpsuit, putting all those sexy curves on display, with the cinched waist and off-center neckline. I can practically hear the click of the black boots over the noise of the city as she stomps toward the coffee shop. She wants my help and is keen to know what I do, but she won't say yes to my proposal. I'm not giving her a choice any longer, and I clock the reason to the three people coming up behind her as she pulls open the coffee shop door.

The Iron Palms aren't going to let her go.

They want to know what she knows, too. Which, if I'm right, is nothing. Rowan wouldn't have knowingly put his younger sister, or anyone in his family, in the middle of the shitstorm coming his way. The fact the gang plainly wants her bothers me, and I need to find out what that's all about. Do they plan to traffic her? Did Rowan do something so bad that she's being punished for it too? Or did she just catch the wrong person's eye? But why not the whole family and only her?

The fact Ro introduced her to a man like Trickster still bugs me, badly. I drop my earpiece into my pocket, striding across the street, stopping traffic in the process. I cut off the gangbanger before he can ever enter the shop.

Scoffing at him, I lift my chin before I shoo him off with a wave of my hand, silently ordering him to *get the fuck out of my way*. I'm not scared of him and he's not of me, but he's *young*. He's not sure who I am, but he'll learn. He lifts his shirt to show me he's packing, threatening without words, and I tip up my lips in a sinister smile as I shake my head at him. I'm not going to stoop to this fucktard's level merely to prove a point. I'm packing, alright. I have enough weapons on me to put this pissant in the grave a couple times over, but I can't play with him today. I have more important things to deal with.

My woman, to be exact.

"It's your lucky day, douche canoe, and you'll live." I chuckle before I step into the shop, closing the door behind me.

I instantly clock her at the counter, drawn to her any time she's near. Greer's busy ordering some frou-frou drink, I'm sure, so I weave around people to get to her. As she reaches into her bag, I put my hand over hers, taking in her cherry blossom scent now that the overpowering lilies from the service aren't suffocating me anymore.

"I have this, sweetheart." I order a black coffee and a bottle of water for myself, then slip a few bills to the barista. We head for the table that Greer picked right by the front window. Before she can take the closest seat, I pull out the opposite, gesturing for her to sit. I strategically put her in the seat with her back to the door, and I take the one facing it. It's a mistake, allowing her to choose the table next to the window, but it's hard for me to deny her and make her move when I need her on board with marrying me.

The gangbanger from earlier is standing nearby, watching us. Greer stares back at him, dumbfounded. My hand reaches out, lightly resting on top of hers as I say, "Sit down and ignore him, babe. He'll go away sooner. It's like a gnat; the more attention you give it, the more it bugs you."

"I'm not your babe," she declares, pinning her green eyes full of fire on me. Her ire makes the gold flecks in them appear almost molten, and I can't help but smile at her. "What are you smiling at, Nyx? What about this whole situation is funny?"

I really can't help myself now, and I laugh because I missed this curvy bombshell spitfire. I like when she gets all defensive and upset; it proves she has fire and isn't as cold as some people think she can be. She's got a backbone, one I admire.

Another Iron Palm walks up, and they start to argue. That's it. I've had enough. I pull out my phone and send a quick message to Ace.

Me: Take care of them before I make more of a scene than I'm supposed to.

"Nyx, what did Rowan say to you when he called?" Greer starts as soon as I put my phone away in the pocket of my jacket. I stand, tugging Greer up onto her cute little heeled boots. Sliding a hand behind her neck, I tip her head back before I take her lips in a deep kiss. She fights me at first but then softens and opens for me. My tongue slides in, tasting the mix of coffee, sweet cream, and *Greer*.

I've had to stay away from her, from the sizzle I feel whenever she's close enough to touch. I never would've been able to stop with her once I started. This feeling for her swirling in my gut only serves to confirm it.

I groan as I pull back, hearing the slam of fists against the glass. We both turn to find the local cops pressing the gangbangers against the thick glass window, arresting them.

Well, that works.

I smirk in triumph.

Glancing down, Greer has my black leather jacket gripped in her fists, and I know that she might fight this in the beginning. Regardless, it's going to be one hell of a fun fight. I also know damn well I'm going to love every minute of it.

"Why?" she huffs and pauses a moment. "W-why did?" She pauses again, stuttering around whatever she's trying to get out but can't seem to find the words. "Why did you kiss me?" She finally spits it all out.

"Because I needed to know." I start to pull away, but she still has her grip on me. "I'm going to need you to let me go, babe." I meet her gaze, and she immediately releases my jacket.

"Don't call me *babe*." She sits down with a huff and takes a deep swallow of her drink before she realizes it's hot and almost spits it out at me.

I reach for the bottle of water and hand it to her. After a deep swallow, she gives it back, and I just can't help myself. I make sure to take a sip with her watching me, right over where her lips were moments before. She's momentarily entranced but immediately shakes her head.

"I have to head back to campus to finish my classes."

"I can help with that, *after* the wedding."

"I'm not marrying you, Nyx. I'm not saying it again."

"Sweetheart, those men," I wave my hand to where the Iron Palms were standing moments ago, before Ace called in the locals to have them hauled off. I don't know what Ace said because he's not exactly ATF, but he's loyal to me, and that's all that matters. "They weren't here for the coffee. Only one reason why they showed up today, and it's because they came for *you*. I stopped them. The little punk on the street showed me his gun."

"And yet you weren't scared." She cocks her head to the side, her long, shiny chestnut hair falling over her shoulder.

"Nope." I pause to see if she's going to ask me more, but she chooses to wait for me to offer her information. She doesn't understand the extent of my training. She can't intimidate or interrogate me. My watch pings, and I flick my gaze to the message from Ace. I have to get this moving along. "As soon as you're ready, we will head to my place, and then I'll take you to campus to pack. You'll stay with me."

"No, Nyx. You left. You left us. You left *me*."

And there it is.

Reaching across the table again, I take her hand in both of mine. My calloused fingers against her soft, warm palm fascinates me, the difference in tone and texture. I almost catch myself stroking hers when I realize how truly dirty my hands really are. They're probably just as dirty as her brother's, but I say it's under the guise of being legal. *Is it any different, though?*

"I had to. I made a choice, an important decision. If I stayed here, I wouldn't have been true to myself." I can't tell her the full truth yet. I don't want her to have that much power over me already.

"What did you do while you were gone?" She changes the subject, and I offer her this. I can't give her all of it right now. Not until she's married to me can I tell her half of who I really am.

"I went to college." I give the basic of replies.

"Are you a cop?"

"Not really..." It's not a lie, but it's not the truth either.

"What does that even mean?"

"Marry me and you'll find out?" The deep, quiet rumble comes from my chest. I haven't laughed like this in a long time; it has to be nerves. The show must go on, though, so I pull out the ring box from my pocket. I was prepared this time. It's all for show, but it also has a tracking chip in it just in case.

"No. Now, what did my brother say to you when he called?"

"He told me to marry you. To protect you." I give her a bit of information as I flip open the box. She peers inside and shakes her head. She's stubborn.

"So that's the only reason you want to marry me?" I watch as the hurt crosses her face.

Dropping the box on the table, I take her hand again, this time pulling it to my mouth. My lips on her skin aren't for show like the kiss started out to be earlier. *This is real.*

"No, it's all you, Greer." I kiss her hand and tug her up once more as I take the ring box and tuck her into my body. The armored SUV rolls to the curb, and Ace is at the wheel, ready and waiting. We walk out, and I clock all the enemies watching us.

God, I hope this is the right decision.

When I open the back door, she slides into the seat. I push her further across so I can sit next to her. She still hasn't spoken, but she's not arguing with me. I like it, but I'm also worried because I know she's going to let me have it soon with both barrels of her anger.

"Greer, this is Ace. If you need anything, anything at all, you ask him. Except to leave me; he won't help you with that." She nods and remains quiet. "Ace, is Brandy ready?"

"Yes," he watches behind us. "She will take them out if they try to follow."

"Good."

As we pull away from the coffee shop, I hear the blast. It doesn't faze me, so I don't bother looking, but Greer gasps and swings around. It's hard to remember she's not used to this life.

"What just happened?" she asks and turns back toward me. I take her phone from her lap and roll down the window, tossing it out. She yells at me for a moment, but I hold up a finger to stop her.

"They thought I'd allow them to follow us. *To put you in danger.* I won't take threats to you lightly. Now, they know it too."

Chapter 5

Andi Rhodes

Greer

"**D**AMN, BRANDY'S GOOD."

I whip my head back around to stare between the front seats of the SUV and out the windshield, trying to put the careening vehicles behind us out of my mind. Ace is chuckling, and Nyx is, well... He's staring at me as if waiting for me to fall apart at any moment. I won't let that happen, though. *Not now.* No, I'll wait until I'm in the privacy of my shitty apartment.

If I'm ever there again.

"Greer?"

Nyx's rich tone wraps around me like my favorite blanket, soothing my frayed nerv—

No!

Shaking my head, I remind myself that I hate this man. Unfortunately, my thoughts don't sink in because all I want to do is curl against his side and cry. Cry for Rowan, cry for the life he could've had, cry for all the pain causing my every nerve ending to burn like acid.

A gentle touch pulls me back into the moment, and I turn to see Nyx pulling his hand away.

"Sorry," he mumbles. "You're crying, and I was just…" A deep sigh falls from his lips, and he lowers his head.

"I'm fine," I snap before taking a deep breath and sitting a little straighter. He doesn't get to see me this way because the last thing I need is for him to think I'm going to give in to his cockamamie plan of marriage.

Nyx levels his gaze on me and nods. "Ace, step on it," he says without looking at him.

I'm thrown against the seat when Ace does exactly that. Fear trickles down my spine as he weaves in and out of traffic at an ungodly rate of speed, but it dissipates when I realize he really is a good driver.

"Where are you taking me?" I ask.

"I told you, my place," Nyx responds matter-of-factly. "Once I'm sure it's safe, we'll go to your apartment to get your things."

"Yeah, no thanks." I take a sip of my coffee, grateful it hasn't spilled. "I've got class in the morning, so if you don't mind, let's skip your place. In fact," I say, grinning like my world hasn't spun completely off its axis, "you can just drop me off anywhere, and I'll find my own way home."

Ace snorts, and Nyx smacks him upside the back of the head. "Sorry, man, but she's got spunk. I like her."

"See, Ace agrees with me."

"Uh, no," Ace corrects. "I said I like you. As far as agreeing with you… not even a little bit. Sweetheart, you've got no idea what's coming for you, and your best chance at surviving whatever shitstorm your brother brewed is to stick with that guy," he says, hitching a thumb over his shoulder to indicate Nyx.

"First of all, *I'm not your sweetheart*," I practically growl. "I'm no one's sweetheart, babe, honey, or whatever other stupid ass names you wanna call me. My name is Greer."

"Got it… Greer," Ace says snidely. "And second of all?"

"Secondly, I'm not going anywhere but my apartment." I shift my glare from Nyx to Ace and back again. "No. Fucking. Where."

"Damn." Nyx whistles. "I don't remember you having such a filthy mouth. A sexy one, yes, but not a filthy one." His lips flip into a grin. "I like it, though."

Groaning, I throw my hands up. "This is a joke to you, isn't it? My life has turned upside down, and you think it's funny."

In an instant, his expression hardens, and he grips my chin, forcing me to look at him. "Don't for one second think that I'm not fully aware of how far up shit's creek you are without a paddle. There isn't one thing funny about the fact that I'm throwing you a lifeline, and you're refusing to take it."

My mind flashes back to the men standing outside the funeral home and the Iron Palms' members who were shoved against the window at the coffee shop. Even without Nyx saying it, I know they were there for me. The creepy wink was a dead giveaway. But that doesn't mean I need my dead brother's former best friend to swoop in and save the day. I'm in college, a grown woman... And the Iron Palms will forget all about me with time.

Out of sight, out of mind, as the saying goes.

Sensing that Nyx isn't going to cave to my demand, I decide to try a different tactic. I let the ever-threatening tears slip past my lashes to glide down my cheeks and face him.

"Please, Nyx," I whimper, allowing my shoulders to slump. "I'm just... I'm tired, and I want to go home. Haven't I lost enough? Do I have to lose my freedom too?"

He stares at me for a long moment before his gaze softens. His jaw is still hard as granite, but it's the eyes that tell me everything I need to know: he's gonna give in.

"Ace, change of plans."

NYX

This is stupid, foolish even. I know it, and Ace knows it. Hell, deep down, Greer probably knows it, too. But all the sense in the world can't stop me from giving this woman what she wants. I'll just have to keep her safe on the fly tonight because I can't bear to break her heart any more than Rowan already has.

"Thank you."

"You can thank me if you're still alive in the morning," I tell her, trying my damndest to not let my frustration bleed into my tone.

Pulling my cell out of my pocket, I shoot off a text to my team members not in the vehicle and give them a quick rundown of the new plan. As soon as I hit send, I set the phone on my leg, knowing the responses will be fast and full of fury. It's not like me to go off the book, but sometimes the situation calls for flexibility.

"C'mon, Nyx," she pleads. "You're being overly dramatic, don't you think?"

"No, I don't think," I respond. "But I also know I can't protect you if you don't trust me, and maybe, just maybe, this will gain me a little of that."

Greer's eyes widen, the gold flecks sparking, and she lowers her head. Fidgeting with her hands, she says, "I did trust you... completely."

Dammit!

The rest of the ride to her apartment is spent in tense silence. Ace drives around the block several times to make sure we haven't been followed, and the second he parks, I throw the door open to step out into the fresh air. Being this close to Greer, feeling her rage, her anguish, her distrust... it was suffocating me.

Greer slides across the seat and exits after me. Without waiting, she walks toward the entrance of her building.

"Check the perimeter," I call to Ace as I rush to catch up with her, putting my earpiece back in as I go. "Meet us upstairs."

As soon as I got off the phone with Rowan a few weeks ago, I made it my mission to know exactly where Greer lives. I checked the security features of her building—*spoiler alert: there are none*—as well as the blueprints and security features of every building within a four-block radius. Ace and I have spent a few days memorizing every detail and know this area like the back of our hands.

The problem is, several of my team members were supposed to install cameras, alarms, and other shit before we got here. Now, we're gonna have to wing it because they aren't showing up for another few hours.

"Zone one, secure." Ace's voice comes through the comms, and he's all business. "Clearing zone two now."

I slip between the closing elevator doors and smirk at Greer when she groans her disappointment. "Might as well get used to me being around."

"No thanks," she mutters, standing as close to the wall of the conveyance as she can get without melting into the damn thing.

I shrug. "Suit yourself."

When we reach the third floor and the elevator door slides open, the hair on the back of my neck stands up. Over the years, I've learned to trust my instincts, so I slip my gun out of the holster. Greer's eyes widen as she spots the weapon at my side.

"What the hell, Nyx?"

I push past her and ease her behind me. "Something's wrong," I say.

Greer attempts to step around me, but I extend my arm to block her path. She sighs dramatically. "I'm sure you're just being overly dram—"

Gunfire explodes around us. The elevator door is already closed, so it's not a viable escape. Fortunately, there are only two apartments on this floor, and the doors are set into the wall a little, which affords us some place to duck for cover while I fire back.

"Don't move," I snarl as I shove Greer into the doorway of her only neighbor. I press the comm in my ear. "Ace, get to the apartment building now. Shots fired."

"We just want the girl," a man shouts. "Give us the girl, and we'll be on our way."

Yeah, right. And I'm the Pope.

I glance at Greer, and the sheer panic on her face pierces my heart. It also pisses me off a little because it's like she thinks I'm actually going to hand her over to the wolves.

"You wouldn't…" She shakes her head. "I mean, I can't…"

"No, I'm not giving them what they want," I assure her as bullets ricochet off the wall.

Blindly, I return fire. A pain-laced shout fills the air, and I know I've hit someone. I reload while I have the opportunity.

"Motherfucker! You're gonna pay for that."

I level my gaze on Greer, ignoring the threats being yelled by our attackers. "I need you to run for the stairs. Don't stop. Don't look back. Don't do anything but run down the stairs and outside. Got it?"

No doubt sensing I'm her only chance at survival, she nods. "But what about you?"

"I'll be right behind you, sweetheart."

"O-okay."

Greer takes off, and I move out of the doorway to provide her cover. A bullet grazes my side, pain searing through my flesh, but I ignore it and remain focused. It's not as if I haven't been shot before. As soon as I hear the door to the stairwell close, I begin to move backward until I come up against the same door. Another bullet hits me in the bicep, and I groan as I whirl around and race down the steps.

"Outside," I yell at Greer when I catch up to her on the first floor.

We race to the sidewalk, and Ace is waiting with the SUV ready to go. Greer jumps in the back while I hop in the passenger seat.

"What the fuck happened?" Ace growls.

"Ambushed."

"Oh my God," Greer says, her tone hushed as she leans forward between the seats. "You're bleeding." Ace navigates through the rundown part of town, and Greer prods at the wound on my arm. "You've gotta go to the hospital."

"Nah. I'm fine. I've got someone who can stitch it up when we get to my place."

"You've got someone? What the hell does that even mean?"

I take a deep breath and shoot a quick glance at Ace. Never before have I let someone in on the specifics of my team, but I need Greer to trust me, which means I've got to be able to trust her, too. Not to mention the whole *marriage* thing. Won't exactly go well if I keep her in the dark about everything.

"Your call, boss," Ace mutters.

"Nyx, I was just *shot* at," Greer snaps. "Either you start talking or I'm jumping out of this damn vehicle! Despite what you and Ro clearly think of me, I'm not some fragile flower who can't handle the truth."

I love her fire. Her spunk. Always have.

I've never been more grateful for it than I am right now. She's going to need it if she has any chance of getting through whatever is coming for her.

And a life with me.

"Before I spill all my secrets, I've got *one* question," I say, staring into her eyes.

"What?"

"Will you marry me?"

Chapter 6

Gail Haris

Greer

I BLINK TWICE AND then take a deep breath. He's serious about me marrying him, yet he doesn't want to open up. If I hadn't just had gang members chasing me, I'd laugh at this situation. The idea of marrying someone who won't even tell me who they are is completely ridiculous. Plus, I don't want to spend more than five minutes with Nyx, so the idea of being *married* to him is a serious problem for me.

"You won't tell me who you are unless I marry you?"

He nods but doesn't speak.

"Why would I marry someone who won't even tell me who they are?"

Nyx shakes his head. "Desperate times?"

I grit my teeth and lean forward. "I'm not *that* desperate."

He laughs. "I didn't mean it that way. Come on. You do know me." He reaches for my hand, but I pull away. *"You know me, Greer,"* he repeats. Then he sighs in frustration. "There're some things I am involved in, but those secrets I'll only share if I know you're willing to trust me."

I look him in the eyes and arch a brow in question. "Prove my loyalty?"

"Yes."

Slowly shaking my head, I speak. Though my voice is sweet, it carries a hard edge. "And why would I be loyal to someone who left me and Ro? Why would I trust you? What loyalty have *you* proven?"

Nyx glances down to the spot where he'd been grazed by the bullet, and then back to me.

"That's not my fault. I didn't ask those guys to shoot you. And I certainly didn't ask you to play the role of hero. It still doesn't prove I can trust you."

He watches me for a few seconds with eyes wide in disbelief. "I took a bullet for you!"

"You said you're fine." I roll my eyes to hide the fact I am worried about him. Not enough to agree to marriage. He isn't going to guilt me into this. I'm certainly not going to pledge my undying love to someone out of fear.

"I am, but it still counts. It shows my commitment."

"You're dedicated to keeping me alive; I'll give you that. You seem like you live a life of danger, so didn't you sign up for this?"

My heartbeat quickens at the heated fire in his eyes as he watches me. I hate him. He left us. He left me. I'm not going to allow any physical attraction to distract me from the hurt he's caused me and Ro. There was a time I would've done *anything* for Nyx. I would've married him without a second thought—it would've been a dream come true. I'd lusted after him for years. He was my older brother's best friend, and I was convinced he was the most gorgeous and wonderful person in the world.

Heat creeps over my body, remembering how vivid my fantasies had been. Never imagined he'd be begging me to marry him. And I certainly never thought I'd refuse him. Too many years have passed without a word, and now he wants to show up at my brother's funeral and expect me to welcome him back with open arms. Yet, I have a strange compulsion to lean in to him.

Nyx's jaw twitches, and then he reaches forward, snatching my hand. Electricity courses through me, lighting up all my nerve endings. I hate how he still affects me. I try to pull away, but this time he doesn't allow it. His voice is menacingly calm as he speaks. *"You're mine,* Greer. No more games or snarky remarks. Marry me."

The car stops, and I can't get out of it fast enough.

I need air.

We're in an underground garage. It's not too big—about twenty rows of various expensive vehicles. It's dimly lit, and the air is chilly. There are no other sounds, making it eerie. This must be a private complex. I guess this is our stop for today, since Nyx and Ace aren't rushing to hide me or get away. He still isn't too concerned with his wound from earlier. *I hate that I still am.*

Nyx left me once when I was no more than his best friend's little sister. It devastated me when he did and never reached out to me again. There's no way my heart will survive if I marry him and then he abandons me for a second time. If I were to marry him, my feelings would develop into something stronger and deeper. No matter how hard I fight to prevent it from happening. I might fall under the illusion that if he's willing to rescue and marry me, he might actually care.

Would we have sex?

Sex with Nyx... now that might be reason enough to marry. It was my ultimate fantasy as a horny teenager. A man of his size and all that muscle—I'd gladly let him ravish my body. Would I even be able to handle that beast of a man? Then again, just because he's a large man doesn't mean he's big everywhere, or worse, knows what to do? Oh, *what a tragedy* if he turns out to be a selfish lover. Maybe I'm getting ahead of myself.

What if we're married in name and nothing more? It might be better to only have my fantasy than to experience the real thing and be disappointed. Or worse, fall for the asshole harder than the first time around. Could I have sex with him and not get emotionally attached?

The sound of car doors opening and closing has me turning around to face Ace and Nyx. "Are you expecting sex in this marriage?" I blurt out.

Shit.

Ace snickers but quickly quiets and turns around. Nyx smirks. "I'd never force you to do anything."

Eh. That's debatable. He forced himself into my life.

"Do you expect fidelity from me?"

In a few quick strides, Nyx is towering over me. "I already told you that you're *mine*, sweetheart."

"Yes, you did. Doesn't make it true." My body is once again hyperaware of him. The heat coming off of him has desire pooling between my legs. Instead of allowing myself to focus on the ache building inside of me, I decide to poke the bear. Because why not? There's already a dangerous gang chasing after me. I should probably piss off the one guy who is trying to save me.

Putting on a brave and confident face, I tease him. "You want me to be yours just in time for Valentine's Day, but do I get to have other Valentines since this isn't a marriage for love?"

"*No.*" His voice sounds dark and dangerous. "I *don't* share."

I give him a challenging glare. He isn't backing down. I'd expected him to get annoyed and storm off. Instead, he's staring me down with a possessive look on his face. None of this makes any sense. Did my brother really call and ask him to come help me? Why wasn't I made aware of any of this before the funeral? Nyx is being so intense and passionate about this whole thing, as if he actually cares, but if he truly cared, why leave and never return?

His large hand wraps around the back of my neck, and he forces my lips to his. A surge of pleasure rushes between my legs. Nobody has ever kissed me in such a possessive manner. His claiming lips are borderline punishment and ecstasy. He's leaving no traces of doubt about who my lips belong to.

He pulls back and demands, "Tell me you're mine."

"Hell no."

A masculine growl comes from somewhere deep in his throat as his mouth seizes mine once more. His tongue slides between my lips and wages war with mine. Every single one of my senses is being consumed by Nyx. The feel of one strong hand on the back of my neck as his other expertly begins caressing the side of my body. His cologne mixed with his sweat is surprisingly an intoxicating combination. Hints of mint from his tongue. But the most satisfying are his groans of frustration from my rejecting him turning into moans of pleasure also brought on by me.

Nyx brings both hands up to cup my face as he leans his forehead against mine and pants. "Tell me..." He takes a deep breath and then continues, "...you're *mine.*"

"I hope you bleed out."

His powerful body guides me back until I'm pinned against the side of the car with his arms caging me in. I crane my neck back to stare up at him and give him access to my lips. I'm eager for more of his kiss, no matter what my words say aloud. His lips crash against mine, and I feel his desire press firmly against me, my body weeping with happiness. Two of my questions from earlier have been answered. He *is* big everywhere, and sweet Lord, he does know what to do with it. I shamelessly roll my hips, chasing that delicious friction as he hits exactly where I need him to.

This time Nyx proves what an asshole he truly is. He pulls his hips away from my eager touch and seethes. "Tell. Me. You're. Mine."

"Fine. I'll be your... *Valentine,*" I say with as much enthusiasm as I'd use if I wanted a colonoscopy.

"Fine." He closes his eyes, and when he opens them, he's perfectly composed. He takes a step back and begins walking.

Panic fills me. I wasn't done. I want more of him all riled up and taking out his frustration with his lips and tongue.

"Where the hell are you going?" I call after him.

He doesn't stop walking. "I'm going to get stitched up."

"But... but..."

Nyx spins around and walks backward. "Did you think I was going to go back to making out with you? I'm not playing games with you, Greer." He turns his back to me and is within a few feet of a large metal door where Ace is standing.

Well, I was enjoying the game we were playing.

Hungry for his touch, I chase after him. "Stop." I take his hand and spin him around. I search his eyes for the boy who used to be such a central part of my life. He has to be still in there somewhere. "If I marry you, do you promise to tell me everything? No secrets between us? I want the truth, no matter how ugly."

"Sometimes in my line of work, part of protecting you is *keeping* secrets. But if I can tell you, I will. However, if it puts your life in danger, your life will always come first. You will always come first." Nyx lowers his voice. "You've always come first, even if you don't believe me."

That's hard to swallow. All I remember is the ache in my chest from him disappearing. Is there more that I'm unaware of? I give him a nod, and then I'm pushed back into another car. Nyx takes my pants on either side and rips them down my legs, taking my underwear with them. My mouth opens to protest as the cool air hits my exposed privates, but instead, all I get out is a silent scream as his warm mouth is on me. I completely surrender myself to him. I thought he knew how to use his tongue in our kiss earlier, but his tongue on my clit has left me speechless and incapable of functioning. My body is in a heightened frenzy.

"This is mine," he mumbles against my tender flesh.

I won't argue there. If he pulled away right now, I'd murder him. I'm vaguely aware that anyone could walk up. Wait—

My eyes snap open, and I'm slapping him on top of the head like a cat. "Where's Ace? Is he watching us?"

There's nobody by the door. Where in the heck did he go?

"Calm down." Nyx takes a long lick, and I shiver. *Focus. Focus.* "He's on the other side of the door." He blows against me. "Remember what I said. This is mine. I don't share." He places an open-mouth kiss against my clit and then sucks the soul from my body. "I don't want another man to see you like this. I'd kill him."

"That's a bit dramatic."

Nyx slides two large fingers inside me. "If his eyes saw this, he'd lose them."

"He wouldn't be able to do what he does for you now if he couldn't see."

"Exactly. So I might as well kill him."

That took a dark turn, but all thoughts leave my mind as he begins to lick and work me with his fingers. I throw my head back and forget everything except

Nyx. He doesn't let up until I'm shaking and pulsing with pure pleasure, my moans echoing off the walls.

Nyx's hands gently tug my pants up, and he helps me stand since my knees are weak. His gaze is one of arrogance and satisfaction.

Whatever. I'm the one who got an orgasm, and I'm not returning the favor.

And I still haven't told him yes to marrying him. I might've nodded, but it was never an official yes.

Chapter 7

Sapphire Knight

Nyx

SHE'S INFURIATING. AND CONSUMING. Fuck, I knew it was going to be tough showing back up in her life after being gone for so long, but it wasn't like I had a motherfucking choice. She'd be dead if I wasn't here to save her.

Hero complex? No. I simply live in the dangerous world she's been fortunate enough to be oblivious to. She no longer has the option, as they've come to collect; whether she's guilty of anything or not, my dear old best friend has set his younger sister up for the fall. Unknowingly on his part, but not surprising. Ro was always headstrong and jumped into whatever he thought would be the best path. Too bad he didn't think he'd end up six feet under before he could put a better plan in place. In his defense, he always knew I'd protect Greer however I could. Still leaves a sour spot towards the fucker for putting her in this spot in the first place.

Now, she thinks she can play games. Toy with my protection and feelings for her. If she only had a real fucking clue how badly I've wanted her before it was ever appropriate. She was on the edge of being legal when it was college time, and I knew I had to get the fuck out of there before I crossed the line in my friendship with Rowan. Besides, I had bigger plans in line, and I had to see them through. Once I witnessed that chick getting fucked up, knowing my precious Greer could be next, I had to get the fucking justice deserved. I'd make the same decision over, no matter if it created a divide between us. It was the right thing to do.

Now, I have to figure out a way to bring Greer to my side. Make her see reason without giving too much up to further entangle her in the dangerous side of my life. I'm not immune to enemies; I have my share who hunt me down. Luckily enough, they never make it too close because my team is trained well, and I'm not fucking stupid. They either end up behind bars or conveniently in the ground, where they all belong in the first place.

Stupid motherfuckers thinking I'll allow anyone to hurt Greer. I'll die before I ever allow that to happen.

Licking my lips, her flavor explodes over my tongue once again, reminding me of how she squirmed, clenched, and flooded around my fingers and tongue. She's delicious, making my mouth water in anticipation of eating her juicy pussy again. It'll happen. Soon.

My fingers wind with hers as I lead her to the metal door. I bang on it a few times, and it opens, Ace grinning on the other side like the cat who got the canary. Fucker.

He hits the button five times in a row, and the elevator starts to descend. There's no down button in here on purpose, can't make it too easy on people following us. I can feel Greer's million questions filling the air without her saying a word, but I offer nothing. Choosing silence, I inhale, exhale, and wait for us to go down another level until our floor opens up. Ace glances my way, grinning wide now as the door slides to the side, revealing a short dark hallway with another door at the end, along with a few blinking dots from the multiple cameras installed.

Shooting him a glare, the expression immediately drops from his face. I'm possessive—a territorial motherfucker when it comes to Greer. I always have been. She never knew it, but I did.

Just another reason why I had to stay away from her; I'd have ended up in jail for killing the dipshit who took her virginity. This pussy is mine, and it always has been from the moment I stood outside her bedroom window the night I left town. I almost pried that window up, sneaking into her bedroom so I could be the lucky fuck to claim her first. I'd have been gentle with her, making sure all she felt was pleasure from my tongue and cock. It'd have hurt at first, sure, but I'd have made it up to her, again and again.

We were always meant to be—a fact I wasn't ready to face when I was younger, but I'm damn sure all over it now. She'll marry me. I don't care what I have to do.

"Where are we going?" she asks.

Flicking my gaze to hers, I lean in, nipping her lobe. Her body shivers, her nipples pebbling through the thin material. "So many questions, Greer. Haven't you learned by now to pick and choose wisely?"

She glares, but it's lacking the heat of true anger. She's annoyed, but her body's relaxed from coming all over my mouth. I like her this way—testy but pliable. Maybe I'll start our days by tasting her pussy each morning; it'd be hard for her to stay pissed at me for long if I do. "You're an asshole."

"But one who knows how to eat your pussy, apparently." I smirk. Ace turns to the opposite wall, trying not to laugh too loudly. He murmurs, talking into his earpiece, and the loud click from a powerful lock disengaging fills the air. The door opens from the inside, revealing Bug, another deep undercover operative. He was also my roommate through the majority of my training. We work well together, and he's one person I know I can always count on at the ATF.

"Bug, meet my girl. Greer, this is Bug."

His brows rise, but he says nothing, walking back to the shared surveillance room.

"Well, he's just great," Greer's voice is laced with sarcasm, the sound making my lips twitch, holding back my laugh. "Are you guys living in someone's basement? What is this place? A thug hangout for rejects?"

"There's an apartment on the upper level for meetings. This is a safe place. We decided it was best to stop here after what happened at your apartment."

"When? I didn't hear any of this conversation in the vehicle, and I was literally beside you."

"Bug was in comms; he suggested it, and we obviously agreed."

"*Obviously*. Thanks for sharing with the rest of the class." She rolls her eyes.

"We'll be here for the night."

"Nyx, I told you, I have class. I need to get back to campus. Besides, you're not being helpful, and I told you I plan to find out who killed my brother. Wait... if you're a cop, can't you find out what the local cops know?"

"Am I a cop?" I return, and she groans in frustration. "Again, if you marry me, I'll be able to give you more information. I will tell you, I'm as curious about his murderer as you are. Probably more."

"I'm not arguing with you over this. I can't believe you brought me to your underground bunker, and are those... Valentine decorations? In a basement dungeon?"

"Not a dungeon; do you see any bars or chains? Although, maybe a good idea to add some."

"You're ridiculous."

I shrug, pulling her to me. Her hands fly to my chest as I lean in, lightly bumping her nose with mine. "Only for you, sweetheart."

"Not your sweetheart, remember?"

"You gonna fight me on everything, forever? I'm a persistent guy. I can be patient when I need to. It's time to grow the fuck up, Greer. You're in serious danger. Rowan knew it, and so do I. He wouldn't have called me if this wasn't serious enough; he was worried you'd end up in the ground next."

Tears crest, her chin wobbling as she hisses, "How dare you! How can you say something like that after we *just* buried Ro? It's not enough I have to wade through grief, you have to be so careless with your words?"

My arms wrap around her, holding her tightly as she begins to sob against my firm chest. Her tears coating my shirt make my heart feel hollow. My words weren't nice, but she needs to realize the situation she's in. The gang won't care that she's grieving, only that she's an open target now—one they can utilize to get some of the money back they're currently out of, thanks to Rowan.

Pressing a kiss to the top of her head, I hold her, letting her use my strength for as long as she needs it. I quietly murmur against her sweet-smelling hair, "It's my worst fear, Greer. Can't you see it? You not being in this world would literally be the fucking death of me. I need you to open those beautiful eyes of yours to reality. The path you're on will be your downfall, and so help me, whether I hurt your feelings or not, I'm going to keep you safe. It's the one thing I can give you; hopefully, it'll make up for having to leave in the first place. There's so much you don't know. If you'd just trust me, marry me, you'd see."

She sniffles. "Trust you? Marry you? But I hate you."

"Love and hate, sweetheart. Are you sure you're not confusing one for the other?"

"Y-you think I love you?"

"I hope you do." I admit, wanting to confess what I've always known. What I've always felt when it comes to her.

She exhales, stepping out of my hold. "Where's the bathroom?"

Tipping my chin up, I gesture to the hall on the opposite side of the living area. "First door on the right. There are towels in the cabinet if you want to soak in the tub. Might make you feel better."

"No amount of water can smother this emptiness my brother's death has left inside, Nyx."

"I know, baby doll. Your muscles are tense, you went through some shit today. School and everything else can wait another day; you are allowed to take time to recover."

"I'm scared of free time," she admits, and I can't blame her. We seem to have our grieving method in common, wanting to keep going. To find who's responsible for this tragedy and do what we can to bring them to justice. Greer and I were made for each other, and unfortunately, the death of her brother has given me the perfect reason to finally have what I've always wanted.

"We'll figure out who did this. I promise. In the meantime, you have to let yourself go through the process. It won't be easy, but I'm here if you need me."

"Are you allowing yourself to process?" I nod. It's a lie. I'm too worried about the Palms getting to her to feel the full blow of Rowan's death on me right now. I can go through the motions later; the only thing at the front of my mind is slamming those fuckers, any way I can, and figuring out who is at the root of this entire operation.

"Okay, maybe a bath is a good idea." She gives in, and I press a tender kiss to her forehead. It's a small win, but I'll take it.

As soon as I hear the bathwater turn on, I head for the kitchen. I have the stuff here to make her favorite strawberry pancakes. I'm starving after burning through so much adrenaline. I'm pouring batter into the shape of hearts into the sizzling pan coated in butter when Bug graces me with his presence. "'Sup?"

He chin lifts in greeting. "You went to her apartment too soon. Fucked up the plan."

With a sigh, I admit, "I know. She's hard to say no to."

"Well, get used to saying it, or she'll end up dead. Hell, both of you will. Not trying to lose my partner to the fuckin' Palms, you feel me?"

Greer wasn't wrong calling us out being thugs. Bug fits the description perfectly when you look at him, but we're this way on purpose. We have to fit in; it's literally our jobs. His dark hair's been freshly buzzed, making the tattoos on his scalp more visible. He's had a pretty shitty life; his father was heavily involved with the Mexican Cartel. Bug was on the fast track to be one in the same, but when the Cartel turned their backs on his father and cut off his head along with his wife's, Bug's mom, well, Bug became motivated to bring the organization down. Hence what we've been doing: getting close to the Blood Saints.

They're the Cartel's biggest gang runners into Cali right now, which fits perfectly with me being so deep in guns. The Cartel wants me on their side, which makes the Blood Saints want me directly involved with them too. It was win-win until this shit with the Palms and Rowan popped off. Now, I'm having to balance between two big cases with the most important person in my life right beside me.

The most pressing question weighing on my mind while I flip heart-shaped pancakes isn't how to get Greer to say yes to marrying me.

It's if risking her life to get justice is truly worth it, or if taking my cash and her on the run is the real answer.

CHAPTER 8

D. Vessa

Greer

I HADN'T REALIZED HOW much weight I was carrying around until the first wave of hot water washes over my shoulders as I sink down into the tub. A long, shaky sigh escapes me. For the first time since Rowan died, I feel like I can finally breathe. I told Nyx that I'm scared of alone time because I'm too afraid of the breakdown. Since I've arrived back home, it's been non-stop staying strong for Mom. In doing that, I did my best to block the emotions out. They are still there, just more of a deep hollow void, the type you know will never be filled.

Hot tears pour down my cheeks as everything catches up to me. I know there's a lot of information that Nyx isn't telling me. Even though he abandoned us years ago, Rowan still felt comfortable enough to go to him when he knew he needed help. I guess help isn't the right word because the lifestyle he claimed to love is what *killed* him. He still trusted Nyx enough to take care of me. Is he more connected to Rowan's way of life than I originally believed?

The way he was shot today and acted like it was nothing out of the ordinary seems to point to that. He wants me to love him, but there's too much anger and resentment for it to be true right now. I'm not the same as I was when he left.

His absence marked me.

"Baby doll," Nyx's soft voice breaks me from my thoughts. "What's wrong?"

Blinking quickly, I clear the unshed tears until I can see him. I didn't hear him come in; it's how lost in my thoughts I've been. He's kneeling next to the tub, one hand resting on the edge of the porcelain and the other unsure if it should be in the water or out. His long dark hair is tied back in his signature low knot. Nyx's eyes are no longer focused on my face, they're aimed lower. I don't need to look down to know that the bubbles have long since faded away, leaving me on full display for his taking.

He drags his gaze back up to meet mine, irises full of challenge and heat. I've never been one to back down, so holding his gaze, I slowly spread my legs. The only sound that can be heard throughout the bathroom is the light splash of water.

Your move.

The desire flares in his stormy eyes, making a shiver rush down my spine. His hand moves until it's cupping my knee that's sticking out of the water. He squeezes it gently before lightly trailing a finger down my inner thigh. The slow torture seems to go on *forever*.

Nyx finally reaches the ache only he can cure. A moan escapes me as two of his fingers enter me without warning. "Is this what's wrong, Greer?" he asks, face now inches from mine. His tongue darts out, licking up a row of tears. "My girl's got a greedy pussy."

It's not what's wrong, and we both know it.

The orgasm by the car didn't even begin to make a dent in the sexual tension I've felt ever since the moment I noticed him at the funeral. No matter how much I want to hate him, my body betrays me. Pussy clenching down on his fingers, I let another long, low moan escape. My second orgasm of the day approaches rapidly, the feeling making me curl my toes. His thumb finds my clit, flicking across the sensitive bud, and that's all it takes. I'm throwing my head back in bliss and calling out his name as I ride the pleasure, eager to escape reality once more. I need a few moments to come down from the high he's offered me, but once I do, I'm greeted with a smug-looking Nyx.

"Seems like I may have found the perfect remedy for when my girl is stressed out."

I hate that he's right. I do feel less tense. The sadness still rests heavy on my heart, but being around Nyx makes me feel like everything is going to be okay. He doesn't deserve to know as much, though. At least, not yet. "Is there a reason you felt the need to barge in here?"

His eyes sweep across my face, a small smile toying on his lips at the abrupt subject change. He doesn't argue. If there's one thing Nyx has always been good at, it's reading me. He's always seemed to know what I need. "Your pancakes are ready."

"My what?"

"Pancakes. I doubt you've eaten much with everything that has happened. This is me seeing to you."

Emotion clogs my throat as I swallow, trying to come up with the right words to respond with. Since Nyx left, the only person who has looked out for me is Rowan, and even that became slightly half-assed the deeper he got in with the Iron Palms. "I don't know if you have that right anymore, Nyx. You threw it away when you left us."

His smile falls from his face, his expression hardening. "I didn't. I want to be sorry, but I'm not. There are reasons I had to do what I did back then, and I hope one day I'll get to share with you what they were. If you would have come to me in the years I was away, with any sort of problem, I would have dropped everything to help you. What you need to understand, Greer, is that I still possess the right. *I've always had it.* If you need reassurance, then have a look around. Right now, you're naked in *my* bathtub, wearing a fresh orgasm face that *I* gave you." Nyx pauses as he removes his hand from the water, sucking the same two fingers that were inside me moments before into his mouth. "Tastes like mine too."

My eyes narrow into slits. "And, let me guess, the day you'll share the reasons with me is the day I marry you." I refuse to acknowledge the rest of what he said. I don't trust my body and my mind to be on the same page. Not when all I can smell and feel is *him*.

"Now you're catching on."

"Leave," I splash water at him. "I'll be out in a minute."

Nyx retreats from the bathroom without another word. Well, I'm glad my head could shut off for all of five minutes. I'm starting to think curiosity from all of these secrets is going to outweigh the little voice telling me not to marry him.

As soon as I step out of the tub, I realize my mistake. I don't have a change of clothes. In fact, I don't have anything with me. Before I can think of a solution, there's a knock at the door. Nyx pokes his head in, gaze briefly running from the top of my head down to my toes.

"I brought you a pair of sweats and a T-shirt. They're going to be a little big, but they'll do until we can get some of your things," he offers, placing the set of clothes on the bathroom counter. He's gone before I can thank him and let him know we won't need to get any of my things because I won't be staying here for long.

I quickly toss on the clean items that no doubt belong to the man himself and fold my dirty clothes into a neat pile. I step out of the bathroom, heading toward the smell of pancakes.

"You made them pink?" I ask as I stare down at a plate full of heart-shaped pancakes.

"They're strawberry," he responds, placing a fork and butter dish down next.

My favorite.

How did he remember such a small detail?

"Thank you," I say as I pull out the closest bar stool and sit down.

Nyx nods but doesn't say anything else, allowing silence to settle over us. I wouldn't say it's uncomfortable because there's always been an ease in being around Nyx. The air's a little charged, heavy with the unanswered questions floating between us.

Clearing my throat, I break the quiet, "You can take me back to my parents' house once we're finished. I'm sure you have things you need to do."

I want nothing more than to be able to go back to my apartment. It's definitely not as glamorous as this place, but it's home. Never mind there were thugs with guns there when we stopped before. I'll eventually sneak my way in or something.

"Not happening."

"Excuse me?"

"I'm speaking the same language as you, Greer. You're a target right now. They will stop at nothing to get to you, including going through your parents if necessary. Do you truly want to drag them into this any further? Haven't they been through enough? I'm trying to be patient here because I know you've gone through a lot recently, but you need to clue the fuck in. And do it soon."

God, this man is so infuriating. "I'm not staying here."

"It's cute you think you have a choice."

"Tell me why you left."

He doesn't say anything as he studies me. Inside, I'm squirming because it's like he's looking into my soul to get what he wants. On the outside, however, I'm fuming. How dare he think he can waltz back into my life and dictate every little thing I do. And why? All because Rowan asked him to look out for me?

"Do you remember when you agreed to be my Valentine?"

"Yes..." I reluctantly admit. Where is he going with this? Oh God, this bastard is about to pull a fast one on me.

"Marry me on Valentine's Day."

I should have known he would manipulate the situation to get what he wants. He was always good at getting what he wanted when we were kids. I remember in elementary school when this girl would knock me down on the playground every day and laugh with her friends. The teacher never believed me because the girl always denied it, and I had no proof she pushed me. Sure, I had cuts and scrapes peppering my hands and knees, but you get the same injuries when you fall on your own. One day, Nyx had enough of me coming home crying about it and confronted the girl. He manipulated what she said enough until eventually she admitted to it. Now that I think about it, it doesn't surprise me he decided to pursue law enforcement. The nature has always been there.

I don't think I can live with myself if I don't find out what's going on. I hate that it's Nyx I need to go through to get it. The only thing I know for sure right now is he will take a bullet for me. As much as I hate to admit it, it might just be enough for me right now.

"Valentine's is in a week. You can't plan a wedding in one week."

"I'll take care of it."

I search his face, looking for any sign of doubt. In the end, I come up empty. His expression gives away nothing, but I can see it in his eyes.

He's scared I'm going to say no.

He really wants this.

I'm sure we'll only keep the marriage charade up until everything with the Iron Palms blows over, right? "Okay, I'll marry you on Valentine's Day," I finally give in. He's backed me into a corner.

Part of me expects him to gloat since he's getting what he wants, but he doesn't. Instead, he reaches into his back pocket, pulling out a small, black velvet box. The kind of box used to hold a ring. He slides the black velvet square across the counter in my direction. I stop it with my right hand, running my thumb over the top, feeling the velvet before slowly opening the lid.

My breath catches in my throat at the sight of the ring. I was expecting something basic, a ring everyone has. Not because Nyx is cheap, but because of how last minute this is. He couldn't have known I would eventually agree, right?

This ring, though... it was planned. The gorgeous marquise diamond is accompanied by a diamond on each side. The sparkle is unreal, and at the same time, it's exactly what I'd choose for myself.

I hold my breath as I pick it up, scared I'm going to break it or something. Sliding it on my ring finger, I let out the pent-up breath I was unknowingly holding. *It's a perfect fit.* The marquise diamond almost takes up my entire knuckle.

"This is way too much," I try to reason with him, but I don't close the lid of the box nor remove the ring. I can't stop staring at the diamond sparkling in the light.

"Do you not like it?"

"You know I do. It's the most stunning thing I've ever seen. But what about when it's safe to go back to my place? My apartment isn't in the worst area, but people definitely aren't walking around with giant rocks on their fingers."

"Doesn't matter because your time there is done. You'll be with me from now on."

Uh, what? "I think you might have had a conversation with yourself in your head because I didn't agree to those terms."

"This is the last straw with you playing dumb. The next time you do it, I'm going to tie you to my bed and torture you until you're about to fall over the edge… but I'll stop there. You'll be a giant ball of achy need. Only once you become compliant will I let you finally fall. But don't worry, sweetheart. I'll catch you." The bastard has the audacity to wink.

"Don't you dare call me dumb, Nyx." I hiss, ignoring the way my body is responding to what he said.

"I didn't say you're dumb. I said to stop playing dumb, Greer. What kind of husband and wife live separately?"

I open my mouth to prove him wrong, but I come up empty. All of the married couples I know that have lived separately were only doing it because they were in the process of separating. "I think some celebrities do," I reply lamely, not ready to give in completely.

"Not good enough. My ring is on your finger, your ass is in my bed."

Did I just make a deal with the devil?

Chapter 5

Andi Rhodes

Nyx

TOMORROW, GREER AND I will be exchanging vows.

A Valentine's Day wedding.

I'm not a romantic guy, far from it given my profession and lifestyle, but for Greer, I'm going to give it a shot. I'm not sure what her childhood dreams were when it came to professing nuptials, but I figure going the traditional route with our vows will be what's best for both parties involved. I told her I'd take care of everything, and I have. Thank fuck I have a team standing behind me because she was right about one aspect—throwing a wedding together in a week has been a pain in the ass.

I make a mental checklist and notice two things:

One—Her dress is hanging in the bridal suite, waiting for her arrival.

Two—Her bouquet, a mixture of blooming wildflowers the florist did an excellent job of entwining together, is already here as well. It's sitting on the top shelf of the mini-fridge in the corner that has been pre-stocked with water and fresh fruit.

"Everything's ready for tomorrow," Bug informs me, placing a hand on my shoulder. "She's going to be safe, Nyx. After you exchange your vows, she'll be untouchable."

"Will she, though?" I have doubts since the Iron Palms haven't given up in their attempts to snatch her. I keep getting reports that her parents' house is incessantly having drive-bys. Her school has an influx of gangbangers walking the campus—they aren't attempting to blend in at this point, as they wear their colors for all to see. An intimidation tactic. The campus police have kicked them off the grounds, but they keep showing up like the pests they are. The situation is being monitored, but other than having them escorted off the premises and followed by local law enforcement, our proverbial hands are tied.

Needless to say, the last week has been trying. Between the barbs Greer tosses my way and dealing with keeping her busy so she doesn't get bored... has been a testament to my will. She's temporarily taking her classes online, logging into her school's portal so she can be a part of lectures she can't miss and needs a participation grade for.

I even took the bull by the horns and went to speak with her parents. Our conversation didn't go as planned. I thought they'd be happy, if not content, over the fact we're tying the knot. Apparently, the reputation I've garnered doesn't sit well with them. They all but spit on the years they've known me by kicking me out of the house and refusing to attend the wedding. I didn't get the blessing I sought, and Greer was devastated when I sat her down to tell her they wouldn't be there to support her. As Bug and I jump into the car to head back to the safety of the bunker, my mind drifts to mine and Greer's earlier conversation.

"Sweetheart?" I start, sitting across from her on the sofa. Her books are sprawled out on the coffee table, her long hair piled up on her head in a haphazard bun. She has a pen stuck behind her ear with a highlighter in hand, making up the sexiest student I've ever seen. "Got a second for a break so we can talk?"

She huffs at the affectionate nickname I've given her but doesn't argue with my use of it, a clear indication she's exhausted and not in an argumentative mood. My fingers are crossed it works to my advantage. "Yeah, I need a second." She tosses the highlighter on top of her notebook, looking up at me. "The words are starting to blur together anyway. What do you want to talk about?" She rubs the spot between her eyes over the bridge of her nose. She's been cracking open the books a lot lately. Morning, noon, and night she has one of her textbooks in front of her.

Deciding it's better to lay it out there rather than beat around the bush, I'm upfront with her. "Went to see your folks today. Talked to them about the wedding."

A humming noise leaves her lips before she inquires, "How did that go?"

I slant my head to the side and admit, "Not as well as I thought it would." I'm still livid at the way they reacted, treating me as if I were a viper invading the lion's den. Growing up, they were my pseudo-parents, and the fact they looked at me as if I were no better than shit on the sidewalk has my fingers twitching.

"Honestly, Nyx." She stops and sighs. "What do you expect? You didn't only abandon Ro and me, but them too. They're hurt; they missed you."

"They aren't hurt, Greer."

"Then what are they? My parents loved you once upon a time. You know that. They treated you like one of their own."

If she'd slapped me across the face, it wouldn't wound me as much as her words do. My head hangs, shame washing over me, but everything I did... every decision and sacrifice I made, I had to for her. And Ro, but most of all, for me.

"Not fair, Greer. One day, you'll understand why I've made the choices I have."

"The day will come when I marry you, right?"

"As soon as we consummate our marriage, absolutely. I need to know you're all in, Greer. As much as you want it to, this can't be only a marriage of convenience."

"You're asking for a lot, Nyx."

"I'm only asking for what's right," I say through clenched teeth.

"But this is for my safety. Isn't it? It's not us being in love with each other. We haven't dated. Hell, we hardly know one another anymore. It's the reason I don't know a damn thing about your life." She crosses her arms, shooting me a narrow-eyed stare.

Not wanting this to turn into an argument where we'll say things we can't take back, I clear my throat and tell her, "Anyway. Thought you'd want to know they aren't going to be in attendance. Do you have any friends you want to call who can help you get dressed and do all the other bridal shit women like to do?"

She vehemently shakes her head in denial. "Nope. We'll just have to hope and pray I can snap or zip everything up so I'm not walking down the aisle half-dressed."

"Not going to happen," I decree, gnashing my teeth. "I have women on my team who can help you out. I'll make sure they're on standby."

"Yeah. You do that. This is your show anyway." She reaches out and drags her book back in front of her, dismissing me.

I'm brought back to the present as I remember to ask about the few people I have to outsource for everything to run smoothly for our special day. "Has the hairdresser and makeup artist checked in, Bug?"

"They did," he confirms. "Both will be there at eight sharp to help Greer."

Nodding, I ask, "Did Vanessa and Brandy say if they're going to be there to help my woman with her dress and shoes?"

He smirks before responding, "Sure did."

"What has you smug over there?" Even though I ask, I'm not sure if I actually want to know the answer or not. Things between me and Vanessa have been *strenuous*. She's believed since day one there is something possibly brewing between us. It's all one-sided on her part; I don't feel a motherfucking thing for her. She damn sure better not be devising a plan to shove a wedge between me and Greer. There're already issues there; we don't need anything added from another source.

"You know how Vanessa is. She has to play the 'pity me' card. She's the victim, and you're the villain. You've shunned her and all the other bullshit she spews when she wants attention."

"Take her off Greer's detail. I don't want any of her fantasy shit mentioned to Greer. Nothing ever happened between the two of us, and I don't want my future wife believing otherwise."

"Thought you'd say so. It's already been taken care of. I put her on the Lopez duty to get her away from the team. She'll be shoveling shit from the bottom of the ranks until she straightens herself out."

"Good call. Thanks for looking out for me, man," I reply, scooting down in my seat on the passenger side of the SUV. "Vanessa's been a thorn in my side for a while; it may be time to put her on another team completely."

"Thought you'd say that too." He smirks, his eyes flicking in my direction for a beat before he trains them back on the road. "She's being transferred tonight. Hazard is taking her."

A malicious chuckle escapes me. Hazard is in charge of taking down a prostitution ring. There's been rumblings of a new skin trader around, kidnapping ladies of the night and selling them off for profit. It's common knowledge these women aren't reported as missing. They're deemed throwaways, and their friends are reluctant to go to the cops and report their absence.

"Good riddance," I comment, waving my hand through the air. Greer is the most important thing in my life, and protecting her against everything, even other women who live in a fantasy world, is my utmost priority.

"You ready for tomorrow?" he asks, changing the subject.

Glancing back over at him, I confess, "Been ready for this since I was eighteen. I've been drawn to her from the day we met. It didn't bother me when she followed me and Ro around like it would most other kids at that age. Actually, I used to encourage it. Inside, I always knew she belonged to me; I just never thought it'd happen."

"Well, it's happening now. For better or for worse."

"Amen to that." Other men would be offended if their woman shot fire and brimstone their way, but I enjoy it when she gets feisty and stands up for herself. Not many women are willing to go toe-to-toe with me. It makes my dick hard when she does.

Pounding on the wooden slab, I demand, "Open the door, Greer."

"Not happening, Nyx. You wanted the whole wedding thing, not me. So if we're doing this, then we're going to follow tradition and do it the *right* way."

"What the fuck are you talking about, woman? We have things to discuss." My fists double down on the door, banging on it with a heavy dose of my strength. It rattles on the jamb but doesn't seem to have the effect on her I want it to. Am I throwing a bit of a tantrum from being locked out and kept away from her? Maybe.

"Well, then we'll be talking with this door between us. A groom isn't supposed to see his bride the night before the wedding! It's bad luck, and if you ask me, we have enough already. Let's not add any flames to the fire, huh?"

"You're being obstinate, Greer. Nothing about you and me is bad luck, and you know it."

"Ha!" she huffs out a laugh. "Whatever you have to say to me, say it now, or it'll have to wait until after we say *I do*. I plan on soaking in the tub and pampering myself tonight."

Damn woman thinks she's won this round, but I've got news for her. There's no door that can stand between us. I have the key to every lock in this place. Even if I didn't, I'd break the damn thing down and charge inside. I'm done playing games that keep us apart.

She wants to do this the hard way, then I'm down. I like a challenge; I live for them.

"Fine," I reply, wearing a smirk. "Have it your way. I'll see you at the altar."

"See ya," she sings, wholeheartedly believing she's won this round. I hear the faint sounds of her feet as she shuffles away from the door. I decide to give her a few minutes to get situated in the tub before I make my grand entrance and remind her I'm not a man who can be easily swayed and set aside. If there's something I want, I take it.

She's just painted a red bullseye on herself.

When thirty minutes have passed, I figure she should be nice and relaxed by now, soaking in some bubbles. I'd placed the bottle on the edge of the bathtub earlier with her in mind, but now it's time for me to make my move while proving my point.

Taking the keyring out of my pocket, I quietly slip the right key into the notch, disengaging it. When it clicks, I tiptoe into the room. I silently shut the door with the heel of my foot, not wanting anyone to barge in on us. I'm sure she'll be screaming her disdain once she discovers I've gone against her wishes, so I lock it behind me.

Making myself at home, I strip down to my boxers and traipse my way into the bathroom. Leaning against the counter, I take Greer in. She's lounged back in the porcelain tub, eyes closed, with my blue pair of earbuds tucked into her ears. My gaze scans downward, taking in her pert nipples. They're exposed above the water, and I lick my lips at the sight.

It's time to assert my dominance. I'm not a man to be trifled with, and the sooner she's reminded of that, the better things will go between us. "Sweetheart?" I call out, raising my voice so she'll hear me over the music she's listening to. "You and I need to have a talk."

Chapter 10

Shannon Myers

Greer

I LET MY HEAD fall back against the tub, trying to focus on the hot water lapping against my body and the music blasting in my earbuds. Ro's playlist. He spent hours curating it while visiting me at my apartment one rainy afternoon, convinced it would be the thing that turned me on to the West Coast hip-hop scene. Much to his disappointment, it didn't. But on nights like tonight, it makes me feel close to my brother and reminds me of a time when it felt like my life was mine.

Despite my best efforts, my thoughts drift back to a certain six foot three roadblock, and the music in my ears fades to background noise. I close my eyes and sink lower into the water, but I can't escape Nyx. Not even in my own head.

He's like a shadow, always lurking at the edges of my consciousness. I may have locked him out of the room, but my mind's apparently shown him where I keep the spare key.

The slut.

It's not fair that he still has this power over me after all these years. That one look from him can set my skin on fire and make my heart race like I'm a teenager again.

This is dangerous territory. *Nyx* is dangerous territory.

But God help me, I want to explore every treacherous inch of him. I squeeze my thighs together, fighting a surge of heat that has nothing to do with the bathwater before giving in to temptation.

Keeping my eyes closed, I slide a hand down my belly, trying to conjure up some Hollywood heartthrob as I ghost my fingers over my sensitive flesh. However, it's Nyx's stormy gray eyes that keep flashing behind my eyelids. It's his rough, calloused hands I imagine touching me, and his name threatening to spill from my lips.

Damn him.

A soft exhale slips free, and heat pools in my lower belly as I stroke my clit in excruciatingly slow circles. I bring myself to the edge before backing off, over and over again, denying myself the release I so desperately need for reasons I don't want to explore.

"Sweetheart, you and I need to have a talk."

The sound of Nyx's voice sends my heart lurching, and I hastily pull my hand from between my legs, caught between panic and desire. He's leaning against the counter with a cocky smirk. I like the look a hell of a lot more than I'm willing to admit.

"What are you—how did you get in here?" I tug the earbuds out, tossing them aside, briefly losing my train of thought at the unmistakable evidence of his arousal, clearly outlined in the boxer briefs clinging to his muscular thighs. "I—I locked the door!"

He chuckles, the sound rumbling deep in his chest. "You forget who I am. There isn't a lock on the planet that can keep me out." His eyes darken as they roam over the curves of my body, lingering on the swell of my breasts. "Especially not when it comes to you."

Annoyance flares within me, mingling with the lingering heat of my arousal. Determined to maintain control, I sit up in the water, folding my arms over my chest to shield myself from his intrusive gaze.

"Get out, Nyx," I warn, trying to suppress the quiver in my voice. "I mean it. I'll scream."

His laughter dies away, and he pushes off the counter, stalking toward me with that infuriating swagger. "Oh, sweetheart," he says, clicking his tongue against his teeth. "Do you remember what I said would happen if you continued to act like a child?"

"What are you going to do?" I arch my brow, daring him to take another step closer. "Continue to keep me locked up in your secret dungeon? Refuse to tell me anything about where the hell you've been for the past eight years?"

Despite my fierce determination to win this battle, there's a small part of me wanting to see Nyx ditch his cool exterior and lose control. He's always been my weakness, no matter how much I've tried to deny it. Is it so wrong that I want to be his?

With a low growl, he reaches down to grip my upper arms, hauling me out of the bathtub and over his shoulder.

"Put me down," I demand, trying to ignore the flex of his ass as he carries me across the bathroom. A challenging task, given that I'm almost at eye level with it. "Seriously, I'm too heavy."

He freezes, his intense gray eyes meeting mine in the mirror over the counter. "What did you just say?"

My pulse quickens at the warning in his voice, and I swallow. "I said I'm too heavy."

His palm comes down against my wet ass cheek with a reverberating *smack*. "That's my future wife you're talking about."

"Ow! What the hell, Nyx?" I jerk against the sting and inadvertently grind my clit against his heated skin. My breath catches at the sensation, and I press my thighs together, fighting the moan threatening to slip past my lips.

It's as if my body knows he has a claim on me, even though the rest of me refuses to acknowledge it.

When we reach the bedroom, he gently lowers me onto the bed before straddling my thighs. Water droplets from my body cascade over the hard planes of his chest as he reaches across me for something on the nightstand.

"What are you doing?" I ask, the words coming out much huskier than I intend. I catch a glimpse of silky fabric before he's pinning my arms above my head.

"What does it look like I'm doing?" he murmurs, looping the material around my wrists before securing them to the headboard. "Making good on my promise."

"Nyx, wait—" I start, but he silences me with a searing kiss that steals my breath and scatters my thoughts. I'm lost. All the pent-up desire, the years of longing and hurt and confusion—it all comes out in this kiss. When he pulls back, I'm panting, my body thrumming with need.

"I warned you. No more games, Greer," he says, his voice low and rough. "I'm done playing."

It's hard to keep up my bravado when I'm bound and naked before him, but I do my best. "And if I don't want to stop playing?"

"Then I'll show you exactly what you're missing."

I try to summon some biting retort, but the words die on my tongue as his thumb traces my bottom lip. Before I can think better of it, I swipe my tongue against it while gazing up at him through my lashes.

He slips it past my parted lips, and I instinctively hollow my cheeks before swirling my tongue around the calloused digit.

"That's it, sweetheart," he says, skimming his free hand down the column of my throat and over my collarbones before cupping my heavy breast in his palm.

"Don't call me that," I mumble around his finger, even as my nipples tighten and I arch into his touch.

Nyx's eyes darken as he withdraws his thumb, trailing it between my breasts and down my stomach, leaving a glistening trail. "What should I call you then? My little brat? My stubborn, beautiful bride?" His hand dips lower, ghosting over my stomach. "Or maybe... *mine*."

I shiver at his words, desire pooling hot and heavy between my thighs. "I'm not yours," I whisper, but there's no real conviction behind it.

He chuckles, the sound vibrating through me. "Your body says otherwise, sweetheart." His fingers brush against my inner thigh, so close to where I need him. "You're soaked for me."

I can't help the soft moan that escapes as his knuckles brush against my sensitive flesh. "Doesn't mean anything."

"No?" Nyx asks, raising a dark eyebrow. "Then you won't mind if I stop..."

His hand starts to pull away, and I catch it between my thighs with a whimpered, "Don't."

A triumphant smirk crosses his face. "What's that, sweetheart?"

I grind my molars together, torn between my ego and my desperate need for his touch. "Don't... stop," I finally manage.

"That wasn't so hard, was it?" He lowers his head, his hot breath fanning over my damp flesh. His tongue flicks out, barely grazing my clit, and I jerk against my restraints, my hips canting up to reach him. The silk holds firm, keeping me at his mercy.

As soon as his mouth closes around the bundle of nerves, I arch off the bed with a strangled cry, his talented tongue quickly working me into a frenzy. He alternates between broad strokes and pinpoint precision, but it's not enough. Just when I think I can't take any more, he slides two thick fingers inside me, curling them as he continues his relentless assault on my clit. My body is a livewire, every nerve ending crackling with electricity while he keeps me hovering on the edge.

"Please," I beg, making no attempt to hide the neediness in my voice. "Nyx, I need to come..."

He lifts his head, his stubble glistening with my arousal. "Not yet. Not until you agree to stop fighting me at every turn."

"What?" I pant, struggling to focus as his fingers continue their maddening rhythm inside me. "That's not fair!"

"Life's not fair, baby," he says, punctuating his words with a particularly firm thrust of his fingers. "Just like I'm not the man you would have chosen to marry but the only one who can keep you safe. And make no mistake, I'll protect you until my last breath, Greer. All I'm asking is for you to let me."

His words land with all the subtlety of a bomb detonating.

Not the man I would have chosen... Is that what he thinks?

"You idiot," I choke out with a shaky laugh. "You're exactly the man I saw myself marrying."

Nyx goes completely still. "What?"

"God, I had the biggest crush on you when we were teenagers," I confess, my cheeks burning. "I had so many dirty fantasies about you. You have no idea."

His eyes darken with desire, but there's a vulnerability there I've never seen before. "Tell me," he demands softly.

I bite my lip, suddenly shy despite our current position. "On the nights you'd sleep over, I used to imagine you waiting until everyone was asleep before sneaking out of Rowan's room and into mine. You'd pin me to the bed and give me my first kiss before..." I trail off, my face flaming.

"Before what?" Nyx prompts, his fingers resuming their torturous rhythm inside me.

Admitting it feels like surrendering a piece of myself I've held onto for so long, but the words tumble out before I can stop them. "Before you'd peel my pajamas off so you could touch me everywhere. I lost so much sleep thinking about how your hands would feel against my body, about how you'd tease me until I was begging for it."

"And then?" he growls.

"Then you'd finally slide inside me, slowly stretching my body to fit you," I whisper, lost in the fantasy and the feel of his fingers moving inside me. "You'd hold your hand over my mouth so we didn't wake the house up before taking me hard and making me come over and over again."

"Jesus, Greer," Nyx groans, his control visibly slipping.

"I was saving myself for you... before you left, I mean." I bite my lip. "You must have known. It was obvious to everyone—"

Even Rowan, who was often oblivious to the emotional states of the opposite sex, knew. He said it was the way I looked at Nyx, like he was the hero in some fairy tale who'd come to rescue me from my boring life.

My lips part, but I can't draw in a breath as some of the pieces start to shift into place.

Rowan reached out to Nyx after eight years of silence and asked him to marry me. Not just to protect me from the Iron Palms but because he saw what I'd been blind to this entire time.

It was never just a crush.

I love Nyx.

I want to deny it—to lock it away and maintain my carefully constructed walls. But I can't. Not anymore. The realization hits me like a freight train, tearing through my defenses and leaving me breathless and raw.

Tears prick my eyes as the weight of it all crashes down on me. "I don't want to fight you anymore," I whisper as a tear slides down my cheek. "You're right. I've been pushing you away and acting like a brat because *I'm scared*. Scared of how much I still feel for you after all these years apart."

"Greer..."

I shake my head, needing to get the words out. Needing him to know how deep my feelings run, even if he doesn't feel the same. "You've always been there, protecting me. Keeping me safe. When you left, I wanted to hate you, but I couldn't because I..." My voice catches, and I have to swallow hard before I can continue. "I love you, Nyx. I never stopped."

He searches my face, a myriad of emotions flickering across his features before he releases my bindings and gathers me into his arms.

"Mine," he breathes against my hair, using the pads of his thumbs to brush away the tears that have escaped. "The night I left town, I stood outside your bedroom window for hours. I wanted nothing more than to pry it open and claim you. To be your first. I didn't understand then what it really meant."

His confession stirs something deep inside me. I picture him standing in the shadows while I lay awake in my bed, feet apart and wrestling with the same desires.

"And what's that?" I whisper, needing to hear him say it.

"We were always meant to be," he says, pressing my palm against the bloody heart tattoo on his chest. The skin there is warm, his heartbeat strong and steady beneath my fingers. "You've had my heart since day one, Greer."

Chapter 11

Shannon Myers

Greer

MY FINGERS TRACE THE scripted letters wrapped around the heart tattoo on Nyx. Memento Mori.

Remember, you must die.

Icy fingers of dread skim my spine like piano keys, and I pull him closer, suddenly feeling like we're on borrowed time. Like this fragile moment could disappear in an instant. I shudder and press myself closer to him, seeking his warmth to chase away the sudden chill that's settled in my bones.

"Make love to me," I whisper against his skin, desperate to feel something other than fear and grief.

Nyx lowers me back onto the bed, trailing open-mouthed kisses along my jaw and down my neck. My nipples harden into points, the beaded pink tips begging to be in his mouth.

"Please—"

He presses a kiss to my sternum before his mouth closes around my nipple, his tongue swirling and teasing the stiff peak. He uses his fingers on my other breast, and every pull sends jolts of pleasure straight to my weeping core.

"Nyx," I moan, reaching up to free his hair from the low knot, anchoring my fingers in the wavy strands as he lavishes attention on my breasts.

He releases my nipple with a wet pop, looking up at me with dark, hungry eyes. "I'm going to worship every fucking inch of you," he growls.

True to his word, he takes his time exploring my body with reverent touches and scorching kisses. By the time he settles between my thighs, I'm a breathless, quivering mess. The first swipe of his tongue against my slick folds has me crying out, hips bucking off the bed. Nyx grips my thighs, holding me open as he devours me like a man starved.

"Right there." I tighten my grip on his hair as he sucks greedily at my clit, the coil of pleasure winding tighter and tighter in my lower belly. "I'm close—"

When I'm teetering on the edge, he pulls back, tugging his boxer briefs down and freeing his impressive erection. My mouth goes dry at the sight of him, thick, hard, and ready.

He positions himself between my thighs, the blunt head of his cock nudging against my entrance. "Are you sure?" he grits out, his voice straining with the effort of holding back.

I wrap my legs around his waist, drawing him closer. "I need you. Only you."

"Look at me," he commands as he pushes inside me with agonizing slowness. I force my heavy-lidded eyes to meet his intense gaze. "I love you, Greer. I always have."

My nails sink into his broad shoulders. "I love you," I repeat, my voice breaking as he stretches and fills me beyond anything I ever dreamed about. My body welcomes the burn like it was built to take him.

Nyx's hips snap forward, burying himself to the hilt. I let out a rough exhale at the sudden fullness, my inner walls fluttering around him. He stills, giving me time to adjust, his forehead pressed against mine.

"You feel fucking perfect," he murmurs, pulling back slowly before thrusting deep again. "Like you were always made to be mine."

"Maybe I was." I roll my hips to meet his next thrust, drawing a guttural groan from his lips.

We move together, finding a rhythm that feels as natural as breathing. I'm hyper-aware of every touch, every sensation—the slide of his skin against mine, the way his muscles flex beneath my fingertips, the taste of salt on his neck as I drag my tongue along his pulse point.

"Harder," I plead, digging my heels into his lower back. "I'm so close."

Nyx growls, hitching my leg higher over his hip and driving into me with a powerful thrust. The change in angle has him hitting that perfect spot inside me, and I throw my head back with a keening cry.

"That's it, sweetheart," he pants against my neck. "Come for me." His hand snakes between our bodies, his thumb finding my clit and circling it with practiced precision, sending shockwaves of pleasure through my body.

"I love you," I breathe, my body seizing as the pressure builds to an unbearable crescendo. "God, Nyx, I love—" The words die on my tongue as ecstasy crashes over me in waves. My inner walls clamp down and pulse around him as I come with a hoarse cry, my nails raking down his back.

"Fuck. Say it again," he demands, his muscles tensing beneath my hands.

"I love you, Nyx Bennett," I murmur, pressing my lips to his throat.

His thrusts become more erratic, his powerful body trembling above me, trying to hold back his release. "Let go, baby. I've got you." With a final, deep thrust, he comes undone, spilling himself inside me with a guttural moan that vibrates through my entire body. "I love you, Greer," he pants, burying his face in my neck. "So fucking much."

We lay tangled together, breathless and slick with sweat, letting the aftershocks of our shared climax ripple through us. I've never felt so thoroughly claimed, so utterly consumed by another person. It's both terrifying and exhilarating all at once. He presses a tender kiss to my collarbone before rolling onto his back, draping my boneless body across his chest. I nestle into him with a soft sigh, grounded by the steady thump of his heartbeat beneath my ear.

I trace idle patterns on his skin, slowly coming to terms with the magnitude of this moment. The walls I've built up over the last eight years have crumbled, leaving me raw and defenseless.

For the first time in perhaps my entire life, I feel... complete.

I'm on the verge of dozing off when the shrill ring of Nyx's phone shatters the comfortable stillness. He tenses beneath me, and I know without asking that our little break from reality is over. Disappointment washes over me, and I cling to him a little tighter. "Don't answer it."

"You know I have to, sweetheart," he says, already extricating himself from my grip. His expression hardens as he reads the screen, and a knot forms in my stomach. "I'll be right back." He tugs his boxers back on and slips out of the bedroom, his voice a low murmur as he answers the call.

Minutes tick by, and the euphoria of our lovemaking begins to fade, replaced by a gnawing sense of unease. Even after everything we've just shared, there's still so much about Nyx's life that remains a mystery to me.

What if this is all temporary? What if we're right back where we started by the time the sun comes up?

His expression is unreadable when he finally returns, but the tension in his shoulders tells me that the person on the other end of the line wasn't calling with good news.

"Let me guess. Duty calls?"

Nyx nods, already reaching for his discarded clothes. "I have to go."

"Wait. Right now?" I bolt upright, clutching the sheet to my chest. "It's the middle of the damn night."

"I know, and I'm sorry." He doesn't meet my eyes as he says it, and the unsettled feeling in my belly only worsens.

"Can you at least tell me where you're going?" I ask, hating how small my voice sounds.

He pauses in the middle of pulling on his slacks. "You know I can't, Greer. Not until—"

"Not until we're married," I finish, trying to keep the hurt out of my voice. More secrets. More half-truths. "When will you be back?"

"As soon as I can. I promise."

I wrap the sheet around my body and pad over to where he's doing up the buttons on his shirt. "Don't be too long," I say softly, lifting onto my tiptoes to kiss the side of his mouth. "You wouldn't want to miss our wedding."

Nyx's gray eyes widen slightly at the gesture, and I notice a flicker of the vulnerability from earlier. He cups my face in his hands, pressing his forehead to mine. "I'll be back before you know it," he murmurs, his lips brushing against mine in a tender kiss. "Try to get some sleep, okay?"

I nod, fighting the urge to wrap my body around his so he can't leave me. "Just—just be safe," I whisper, my eyes stinging with the threat of tears.

He stares down at me with an intensity that steals my breath away. "I love you, too." Then he's gone, leaving me alone with his release running down the inside of my thigh and the scent of him branded on my skin.

* * *

A sharp knock jolts me awake. Disoriented, I blink against the sunlight streaming through the ballistic-resistant glass and reach for Nyx. It takes a moment for my sleep-addled brain to register the cold and empty sheets on his side of the bed, but when it does, my stomach drops.

He never came back.

The knocking continues, more insistent this time. I push down my growing alarm and force myself out of bed, wincing at the pleasant ache between my thighs. "Just a minute!" I call out, hastily throwing on a robe before shuffling to the door.

There's a small team of women waiting in the hall and an overly caffeinated Brandy. "Rise and shine, bride-to-be!" she chirps, far too cheerful for this ungodly hour. "We've got a busy day ahead of us."

I rub the sleep from my eyes and stifle a yawn, still trying to process why they're here. "What time is it?"

"Just after eight," a woman with neon pink hair says before extending her hand with a smile. "I'm Noah. I'll be doing your makeup."

"Greer," I reply, shaking her hand before turning to introduce myself to the other woman—a tall, curvy blonde named Kat, who's apparently here to style my hair. I nod, my head moving up and down like a bobblehead doll, trying to act as though I've known this was the plan all along and not something I'm just learning about before stepping back to allow them inside.

Brandy presses a to-go coffee into my hand. "Drink up, babe. We need to get going if we're going to have you ready by noon," she instructs before clapping her hands together. "Alright. Let's set up here. I'm thinking the island will give us the most room..."

Noon.

My heart does a little somersault in my chest.

In just a few hours, I'll be *Mrs. Nyx Bennett*.

While she bustles about the room, giving orders, I scan the living room for any sign that Nyx returned while I was sleeping. Everything is exactly as we left it last night. The realization has the uneasy feeling in the pit of my stomach intensifying, and I set the coffee aside, fighting a sudden wave of nausea.

"You good?" Brandy asks, studying me through narrowed eyes.

"Yeah," I lie, trying to keep my tone casual. "Have you, um, have you seen Nyx around this morning?"

She frowns. "Not since yesterday. Why? You two have another fight?"

"No, nothing like that," I rush to say. "I just... haven't seen him this morning."

"Maybe he's taking care of last-minute details?" she guesses, lifting her shoulder in a half-shrug. "You know how meticulous Nyx is about security. Besides, it's bad luck to see the bride before the wedding. Everyone knows that."

I take a deep breath, trying to quell my rising anxiety. Nyx is fine. I'm fine. Everything is fine. Maybe if I say it enough times, I'll eventually believe it.

Noah guides me into a chair at the kitchen island. "So, how are we feeling?" she asks, pulling various products from her makeup case and holding them up against my skin. "Nervous? Excited?"

"A little of both," I admit, fidgeting with the belt of my robe and forcing a smile that doesn't quite reach my eyes.

"Pre-wedding jitters are totally normal. You're going to make an absolutely stunning bride, and getting married on Valentine's Day is super romantic," she gushes while applying a cream to my face.

The next several hours pass in a blur of hairspray, makeup brushes, and celebrity gossip. When I finally step in front of the full-length mirror in the bedroom, I barely recognize myself. Kat has transformed my bedhead into loose waves, pinning half of it up in an elegant twist while letting the rest cascade down my back. Noah keeps my makeup subtle yet glamorous with a smoky eye and a soft pink lip stain. There's a warm, dewy glow to my skin enhancing my features without overwhelming them.

It's the dress that takes my breath away.

A blush-toned, rustic gown with a sculptured off-the-shoulder bodice, dainty sleeves, and a romantic, almost ethereal skirt. I run my hands over the delicate fabric, marveling at how perfectly it hugs my curves. It's exactly what I would have chosen for myself.

For a guy who's always claimed not to be the romantic type, my groom certainly has a knack for it.

Brandy lets out a low whistle from behind me. "Nyx is gonna lose his damn mind when he sees you."

At the mention of his name, my stomach does another nervous flip. I try to ignore the worry swirling in my gut and focus instead on the beautiful woman staring back at me in the mirror. This is the happiest day of my life. I refuse to let my paranoia ruin it.

"Ooh, before I forget. I have something for you!" she exclaims, digging through her purse before holding up a red velvet box. "I know your family isn't here, so I took care of your something borrowed."

She pulls out a gorgeous pink pearl necklace. "It was my grandmother's. She wore it on her wedding day."

"It's beautiful," I murmur as she works to fasten it around my neck, wincing when she catches my skin several times in the process.

"Sorry, sorry. It's this stupid antique clasp. Almost got it and... ta-da!" She spreads her arms wide and takes a little bow.

"And here's your bouquet," Kat says, handing me a stunning arrangement of wildflowers. "There's your something blue."

I inhale the sweet scent of the flowers, swallowing hard against the sudden lump forming in my throat. "Thank you, guys. For everything."

"No! Don't ruin your makeup!" Noah flutters in front of me, dramatically fanning my eyes. "Blink, blink, blink, and think of something ridiculous."

Something ridiculous... something ridiculous...

My mind immediately goes to Ro and Nyx's disastrous attempt to bake cookies for a class fundraiser in high school. I remember thinking Mom was going to kill them both when she walked in and saw the state of her kitchen. The scent of burnt sugar and chocolate lingered in the house for weeks after. A watery laugh bubbles up at the memory, and Noah breathes a sigh of relief.

"Crisis averted."

Brandy runs through the checklist, ticking items off on her fingers before pausing. "Wait. We're missing something old."

I sit down on the edge of the bed and rifle through the contents of my purse before finding the note buried in one of the interior pockets. The paper is yellowed and creased from years of being folded and unfolded, but the messy scrawl is unmistakable.

"Got it. A letter Nyx wrote me when we were kids." I carefully tuck it down into my bouquet.

"Aww..." Kat scrunches her nose and presses a hand to her chest. "That is the sweetest thing ever!"

I don't have the heart to tell her it's just a hastily scribbled note he left on our kitchen table letting me know where he and Ro were so I could meet them when I got off the bus. Nothing romantic, but a reminder that even then, he was looking out for me.

Brandy checks her phone. "We need to get moving."

My heart skips a beat. This is really happening.

I take one last look in the mirror before following her out to a nondescript black SUV similar to the one I rode in after leaving the coffee shop a few weeks ago. God, it feels like a lifetime has passed since then.

As we pull away from the safe house, I realize I have no idea where we're going. Nyx assured me it wasn't a church, which I was grateful for. Wouldn't want to do anything to upset the Bishop and ruin Dad's pristine image. Other than that, though, he's been highly secretive about the location—more for security reasons than romantic ones, I'm sure.

"Can you tell me where we're going, or is it classified like everything else?" I tease Brandy while fussing with the necklace. The clasp keeps poking against the back of my neck, almost like the metal is rusted.

Her eyes meet mine in the rearview mirror. "Sorry, babe. My lips are sealed."

I nod, sinking back into the leather seat. The air feels stifling despite the AC blasting, and I tug at the bodice of my dress, which seems to be growing tighter by the second. "Can you turn the air up? I'm burning up back here."

"Sure thing." She reaches for the controls, but it does little to alleviate my growing discomfort. The buildings outside the tinted windows start to blur together, and I blink hard, trying to clear my vision.

"I don't... I don't feel so good," I mumble, my tongue heavy and uncooperative in my mouth. A light sheen of sweat breaks out across my face, and I swallow hard, feeling like I might throw up. Everything is spinning, but through the haze, I can tell we're heading away from the city, not toward it.

"Bran...dy," I slur, struggling to keep my eyes open. "Where... going?"

Her face swims in and out of focus as she turns to look at me, her expression unreadable. "Don't fight it, Greer. Just relax."

Panic claws its way up my throat. I've been drugged.

I fumble for the door handle with numb fingers, but it won't budge.

Locked.

Trapped.

The world tilts sideways, and I slump against the seat, unable to keep myself upright. Brandy's lips are moving, but I can't make out the words over the rushing in my ears.

Remember, you must die.

This isn't my wedding day.

It's my funeral.

Chapter 12

Kathryn C. Kelly

Nyx

SHADES OF RED AND pink accented with green foliage add a romantic flair to the otherwise drab hall. Soft, warm lighting with LED candles and fairy lights creates an intimate atmosphere that, surprisingly, I revel in. Cascading red and pink roses, lush greenery, and draping crystal garlands adorn the arch where we'll exchange our vows. Since Greer doesn't have many friends, there are only a limited number of white chairs, all decorated with satin ribbons, alternating between red and pink.

I glance down the aisle where rose petals adorn a pristine white runner bordered by small arrangements of roses and greenery in short crystal vases. Bug sits in the first row next to Cathy and Robert, though I avoid their gazes like the fucking plague. Instead of thanking me for leaving my bed—leaving *Greer*—they're trying to incinerate me with resentful looks.

I refuse to point out *again* that I didn't get them into this predicament. Rowan did. I'm trying to clean it up by not only honoring his wishes—and finally giving in to the inevitable—but by saving *their* lives. I gave them the choice of accompanying me to my wedding to their daughter or going to a safe house until the Iron Palms were extinguished. I knew they'd be motivated to take my advice with the recent drive-by on their house that the local PD did little to prevent. They're terrified the harassment hasn't stopped but still remain stubborn about me and Greer.

Cathy wants to see her only daughter get married, and Robert doesn't wish to be separated from her. So, here we all are. Somehow, Noah was able to get a dress to the hall for Cathy to wear. Robert grudgingly changed into the suit Ace had found for him. Not the tuxedos Ace, Bug, and I are wearing, but it'll do.

Pastor Ellis sits rigidly in his seat, his jaw clenched so tightly I'm surprised his teeth don't resemble Chiclets. I'm certain his thoughts aren't particularly holy right now. Cathy fidgets nervously, a dainty lace handkerchief in hand. All in all, I admire their fortitude after the night they've had.

If Mac hadn't been monitoring their place, Greer would've had to bury her parents mere weeks after she lost her brother. Anger surges in me, and I clench my fists.

Drawing in a deep breath and glancing at Cathy and Robert, all safe and sound, I remind myself that Greer is fine, too. Brandy is a helluva driver and a crack shot. It's why I chose her as Greer's driver. She won't allow anything to happen to her.

I stand next to Ace, eagerly anticipating the moment Greer is finally mine legally. She stole my heart years ago, and apparently, I stole hers too. How fitting we marry on the most romantic day of the year.

You should be here, Ro.

The unexpected thought cuts through my happiness. As boys, we had so many plans that should've happened together. We had hopes and dreams. Did I feed into becoming an Iron Palm with him? Yeah, certainly. Once I discovered their true nature, I couldn't do it. I never told Rowan what I witnessed. Then, I might've had to come to terms with how he responded to that news. Yet, in the end, he joined the gang, and I refused to think about how he was jumped in.

I don't want to equate Rowan with *rapist*, but the Iron Palms were bad motherfuckers who had absolutely no regard for women. They were commodities. Runaways and prostitutes were easier to abuse, traffic, and murder, but they absolutely did not give a fuck. They'd sell their mamas if it came to it.

I shift uncomfortably, in turns cursing Rowan and mourning him. Mourning Cathy and Robert, for that matter. They didn't know what I said the last night before I fled to make a better life for myself, but both Rowan and Greer did. Somehow, *I* was still the bad guy, even though I would've given anything for Rowan to course-correct and set his life on a different trajectory.

He made his choice, however heinous—or not—and I made mine.

Memento Mori. The words written in script and wrapped around the bloody heart tattoo are part and parcel of who I am. *Remember, you must die.*

We all have that road to travel, but the headspace I was in when I got that tattoo was one of... *reflection*. Greer was uppermost in my mind. As always. Perhaps even Rowan. From the time I walked away, I was fated to return to her. I knew changes had to be made before I came for Greer. To claim her, the man I've become, *The Armorer*, had to die. Or so I told myself. He hasn't been put to rest, and yet, today, the woman I've loved since we were kids will become my wife.

I wonder if Rowan had to die for it all to become a reality. Guilt threatens to rise up. I didn't want Rowan dead. I wanted the man he'd become to die.

Stop.

Death has no place on the day I'm finally marrying the woman of my dreams. I won't allow it because it will affect Greer. I'll extinguish *anything* threatening her happiness or her life.

The doors at the front of the room fly open, with Kat and Noah rushing in. Because of Vanessa's transfer, I'm one person down, so Kat and Noah will double as flutist and photographer, respectively. They look lovely in their dresses, with baby's breath entwined in their hair, even though they seem to be rushing not to be late.

I glance toward the door. There's still no sign of my bride-to-be. Has she dipped out on me?

No, not after last night.

She offered me a mirror into her soul and, in turn, I bore mine to her. Her profession of love was heart-wrenching, gut-clenching, and eye-opening. She shattered me, then in turn, put all the pieces back together with the sweet balm of her love.

She would *not* run. So where the fuck is she? Pursing my lips, I count to ten. Wait until Kat opens her flute case and Noah pulls out her camera. Still, no doors open, where Brandy should be peeking inside at this point to give me the thumbs up so the ceremony can begin.

"Where's Greer?" I demand after a full two fucking minutes have passed and she's still a no-show.

"She and Brandy left before us," Kat explains, casting a worried glance to the same doors I've been staring at.

Noah's brows scrunch together. "We thought we were late," she confesses. "They should've beaten us here."

Alarm prickles my nerve endings; I squint between Kat and Noah, always as loyal to me as Brandy. Something isn't adding up. With a frustrated sigh, I grab my phone from my inside pocket and pull up the app linked to the tracker in Greer's ring.

It's moving *away* from the city, straight toward the outskirts. *Fuck*. It's heading toward the Iron Palms' base.

A terror I've never known immediately seizes me, pain twisting my gut while all the air threatens to leave my lungs. I have to fight to hold my shit together, but where Greer is concerned, there are no limits. "Brandy went rogue," I snarl, bits and pieces of my sanity, my humanity, falling away. "She's taking Greer to the Iron Palms."

I don't recognize my own voice or the need to kill. Usually, I take motherfuckers out because of necessity. I had a job to do and they stood in the way.

Now, it's personal. They have my Greer, and I want to spill buckets and buckets of blood. Starting with Brandy.

"Kat, Noah, stay with Cathy and Robert," I order.

"Where's Greer?" Cathy's voice wobbles.

Robert's shock is palpable with his deer-in-headlights expression, as if he can't believe what's happening.

I warned each one of the Ellises, starting with Rowan and ending with Cathy and Robert when I wanted their blessings to marry Greer. No one believed me. Now, it might've cost Greer her life.

What the fuck did you do, Ro?

Greer

My fingers tremble as I use the last of my strength to yank the necklace away. The substance has to be there, and I don't know if it is meant to subdue me or kill me.

With the 'something borrowed' removed, I no longer have the overwhelming feeling of closing my eyes and never waking. I'm still groggy as hell, and my limbs are heavy, but awareness is seeping into my brain again.

Brandy's words are clear, carrying from the front. "I'm here. Yeah, yeah, yeah. She can't resist. Uh-huh. *Byeee.*"

The drawn-out 'bye' annoys me. Hysterical laughter bubbles up, but I have the presence of mind to bite it down. If there's any chance I can escape the Iron Palms, I have to play this smart. Giving away the fact I'm awake and coherent isn't smart. Where else is she taking me *but* to them?

We turn on a screech, jostling me around in the backseat. *Bitch.* Brandy slams on the brakes, and I squeak, rolling onto the floor. In the next beat, the door to the SUV flies open. A hand digs into my lovely hair, jerking me forward.

Ouch. Did this motherfucker *really* ruin my bridal do?

I'm tossed away, landing on my knees with my hair swirling around me. The sound of ripping fabric hurts me to my soul, making me want to throw hands. The thought in the middle of everything happening is hilarious and tragic, and I can't hold back the snort of laughter escaping. I'm sprawled out on my back, staring at the lovely evening sky with an artist's palette of purples, pinks, and oranges when someone kicks my thigh.

"Get up, *bitch*." The new female voice shocks me.

I lift my head. The rest of me is still a little too heavy to bother with, though it's lessening.

A tall, voluptuous woman with ink-dark hair stands near me, her hazel eyes narrowed. "You thought I'd let you steal him from me?"

"Who?" I demand, laying back against the asphalt again. Because, yeah, we're outside, and I'm on the ground trying to recover.

She kicks me again. "Nyx!"

"C'mon, Vanessa, you promised me you wouldn't hurt her. Just keep her long enough to miss the wedding," Brandy speaks up. "She's done nothing to you."

"Says *you*," Vanessa sneers. "Because of her, Nyx broke it off with me."

"Ha!" I burst, laughing hysterically again. "Unless you know another Nyx, you're a liar." I lift my hand, wagging a condescending finger at her. "He wouldn't have done that to you or to me, dummy."

Dummy? Why not, bitch? Cuz, hey, *mano a mano*. A few other choice words cross my mind.

"Nyx is mine," Vanessa screams, losing her shit. "And he'll remember that when you don't show up for the wedding. You've been such a difficult fucking snipe; he'll think you ran away. He's *mine*."

"Yeah, in your fucking dreams," I retort, still drugged because I am decidedly calm about a woman abducting me on my wedding day and claiming *my* man as hers. At the least, she needs a beatdown. "Nyx belongs to me," I state with the utmost confidence, my hand landing heavily on my chest to back up my words. "He's mine and I'm his, so fuck you."

"You're nothing to him. Zero. It was good between us until you came along. Once you leave, it will be good again."

Pish-posh. I giggle at that bit of nonsense, but it seems fitting. My head is still swirling. For some reason, I break out into my rendition of *'Que Sera, Sera'* an incredibly old song from one of my father's favorite movies. The sentiment is true: whatever will be, will be.

"Shut up!" Vanessa screeches after a few minutes of suffering through my singing. "You sound like a braying horse." Her nasally tone is grating on my nerves; this chick is like nails on a chalkboard. She needs her nose broken; it'd probably help her out.

I lift my head long enough to make a disgusted face at her. Oh wow. Much of the fog has lifted from my brain. *And it's about damn time.*

I roll to my side, dragging myself onto all fours. I'm as shaky as a newborn colt, but I need to look her in the eye while she *tries* to hand me a dish of other-woman-drama on what will be the happiest day of my life. Brandy runs to my side to try and help me up, but I push her hands away and glare at her.

"Don't feel guilty now. I'm here because of you," I retort, and she has the grace to look ashamed at my words. I finally stand up, flipping her off in the process. Surprise hits me at how tall and gorgeous Vanessa is.

In the distance, motorcycles roar. The same uneasiness filling me drops onto Brandy's face, but I'm in no condition to drive if I manage to get away. Furthermore, as I glance around, I realize we're in an abandoned parking lot, surrounded by fields of trash and overgrown weeds. Unless someone tipped them off, the Iron Palms don't know my location.

"When did Nyx break it off with you? Not that it matters," I forge on before she answers. "I know he hasn't been a monk. He obviously had a life before we reconnected."

"I called him late last night to see why he hadn't come over," Vanessa bites out. "He left *you* and came to me to eat my pussy and have his cock sucked. He waited until afterward to tell me he was marrying you today." Tears fill her eyes, despair replacing her anger. "He doesn't want to," she says scathingly, swiping at her cheeks. "He's only doing it out of misguided loyalty to your stupid brother."

Vanessa's words cut into me, and I recoil, stumbling back. For a moment, my world collapses all over again; it feels as if my heart splinters. But I think about Nyx's words of love to me and mine to him. Those confessions were soul-deep and true. He would not, *could not*, allow me a glimpse inside of him and then turn around and betray me. Never in a million years.

I'm not sure how Vanessa knows him, though my guess is it has something to do with his job since Brandy is involved.

Checking my urge to commit violence against this delusional female, I turn away, stomping over to a concrete parking stopper, then plop down on it. My dress and my hair are already ruined. "Unless you intend to shoot me and dump my body among the garbage, I will sit and wait until Nyx finds me. *Or* you can leave. Let Brandy take me to my wedding, and we forget this ever happened."

Vanessa flies at me, shoving me with all her might. When I attempt to brace myself, I land hard on my arm. Pain streaks through me, making me cry out. She kicks my thigh, and so help me, I want to rip this chick to shreds.

"Stop!" Brandy orders. "Are you out of your fucking mind? Nyx will kill you and me if you hurt her."

"Oh, shut up," Vanessa snarls, rounding on Brandy. "He shouldn't have thrown me over."

"He didn't throw you over," Brandy snaps. "You and I both know he never gave you the time of day. Same reason why you were transferred. I can't believe I let you talk me into this. I felt so sorry for you before."

"Soon, she won't be any of our problems. I called Trickster."

The sound of approaching motorcycles backs up those words. Vanessa draws her gun from the holster at her side. But Brandy finally realizes we have company speeding toward us and glances toward the street. Just as Vanessa pulls the trigger, I lunge and knock her down. The bullet misses Brandy by inches. She scrambles out of the way before Vanessa can take aim again.

Three members of the Iron Palms race into the parking lot and circle us like vultures on carrion. Rowan and a few of the other members I met didn't own a motorcycle, so I've never considered them to be a biker gang, just a dangerous street gang. The rotation of the tires grips and grinds the ground, kicking up dust and pebbles.

My eyes slam closed as I cover my head with my hands to try and protect my face. The circulating air lifts our hair and flutters my ruined wedding gown, the hot exhaust warming wherever my skin is exposed. I'm not sure how long they circle like fucking sharks, but it eventually stops, leaving only the purr of idling engines.

Slowly, I drop my arms. Immediately, my gaze lands on Trickster's rancid face, and he offers a checkered, triumphant grin. "Hola, puta." Every other tooth is missing. When he notices my attention on him, he lifts his gun, shooting Vanessa right between the eyes.

I scream.

The three evil bastards laugh.

I don't want to give them any satisfaction whatsoever in seeing me upset, so I try my damnedest to calm myself. Tears still streak my cheeks as I glance around wildly. I don't see Brandy anywhere. She did me dirty on behalf of her friend, but she shouldn't pay with her life. Yet, I wonder if Trickster or one of the other two has already mowed her down, and I've missed the carnage.

It's official. The happiest day of my life will go down as one of the most awful. *I pray it isn't my last.*

Chapter 13

Alex Grayson

Greer

I STAND FROZEN, MY gaze locked on Trickster. My heart rackets around in my chest, playing an unsteady rhythm, and my lungs ache because I can't draw in enough air. Fear rushes through my system as I think about everything that could happen next. As tough as I've claimed to be to Nyx, as independent as I said I am, I'm fucking *terrified* right now.

Nyx! In my head, I scream the only person's name I feel confident can get me out of this mess.

I don't know how he can be, though. He doesn't have any idea where I am. Hell, for all he knows, I could have ditched Brandy and run off to avoid marrying him. And besides, maybe he'll be secretly pleased when I don't show up wherever this secret spot is we're supposed to be saying 'I do.'

I'm fairly certain the Vanessa bitch was lying when she said she and Nyx had a thing. It hurts too much to believe he would actually leave me right after we made love to go be with another woman. Especially one as vindictive as Vanessa.

It's in the tiny piece of doubt, a mere one percent, that is niggling in the back of my head. The part which, if I allow it to grow, will destroy my soul.

The man I used to know eight years ago would never do anything to hurt me, but eight years is a long time. Has he changed completely in all those years? I don't want to believe he has, at least not in that way. Especially because of how he's been since he came back, but when it boils down to it, I don't know him well enough to confidently say.

However, I do believe he will protect me from any threat. He'd never willingly allow Trickster, or the Iron Palms, to get their hands on me. He'll give up his life if it means saving mine, but he doesn't know about this situation.

What will he do when I don't show up for our wedding? Will he believe I've left on my own and, in turn, breathe a sigh of relief he's dodged a metaphorical bullet? His actions since he came back into my life indicate otherwise. His confession of love last night seemed genuine, but maybe it's just my desperation to believe him that makes it feel real.

My mind spins with the possibilities, making my heart skip beats at each one not in my favor.

I'm pulled out of my thoughts when Trickster swings his gun in my direction. He's pointing it directly at my chest, right over my heart. His ugly-ass grin widening as his gaze flicks up and down my wedding dress-clad body.

"I'll say, the trouble of finally getting you away from Nyx has been worth the wait," he says, his voice deeper than I remember it being. It's been a few years since the last time Rowan brought him to the house. Even back then, he gave me creepy crawlies. "But I never expected you to show up in a fancy get-up. It's fucking poetic how I'm stealing you away from your wedding when it was your brother who gave you to me years ago."

My eyes widen at his words. I must have heard him wrong because there's no way Rowan would have done something as insane as he's claiming he did.

No fucking way.

"You're lying," I argue, holding my ground as Trickster takes a step closer to me.

A couple of his gangbanger friends, one I recognize from the coffee shop, shift away from him, going wide to surround me. Intimidation has been used for years as a fear tactic. I may be scared out of my mind right now, but I won't allow this bastard to see it.

"I'm not," he replies, lifting a single shoulder in a shrug. "But it doesn't matter if you believe me or not. The fact remains, you're mine. And I appreciate your dress. It'll help make what happens next more official."

I don't want to ask because I fear what his answer will be. Or what he believes will happen next. I'd rather shoot myself in the head than tie myself to this man.

"And what's that?" I question, making my tone as strong as I can, when in reality, I'm shaking on the inside.

"A wedding, of course." He says it like it's a foregone conclusion, as if there's no choice at all in the matter.

Locking my knees, I straighten my spine and push away the disgusting shivers racing down my back at the thought of being with this vile man in any capacity. I have to play ignorant to give myself more time to come up with a strategy to escape. Or to give Nyx time to find me. If he's even looking for me.

"So you plan to take me back to Nyx, then? I appreciate the effort, but it might be better to just let me go to make my own way. I can't promise you'll live through the encounter if you do it yourself."

His smile turns lopsided, and if it weren't for the missing teeth, messy and oily hair, the pure maliciousness in his eyes, or even on any other man besides this one, the look might be cute. "'Fraid I can't. I don't give away shit that's mine. We typically don't marry the whores we allow in, but for you, I'll make an exception."

"Lucky me," I remark snidely. "Why in the hell would my brother ever give me to you?"

"He wanted in with the Iron Palms. Initiation is to take a woman by force and to make it as nasty as possible. He refused the task and instead offered you. Fights broke out and throats were slit over who would get you. I came out the victor."

He moves closer, his gun still pointed high on my chest. I match his steps with two backward ones. I don't want this evil asshole anywhere near me. I can barely control my gag reflex as it is.

I refuse to believe Rowan would do something so evil, but I still ask, "Then why haven't you attempted to take me until now?"

I move, backing up another foot when he inches forward.

"Rowan had some deal with the boss, and the boss said I had to wait. Rowan's dead, along with the deal, so my wait is over."

"Why in the hell would you ever want me?"

His gaze rakes slowly up and down my body, stopping to linger on the bodice of my wedding gown. When I put the dress on earlier and saw how it offered a tantalizing glimpse of my cleavage, I was excited to see how Nyx would react. Now, having Trickster's eyes on me, I only feel dirty and exposed.

"You're disgusting," I spit. "I'll never let you touch me."

"You'll have no choice, puta." He laughs, like raping a woman is great fun. "The things I plan to do to that pussy of yours. Mmm... You'll coat my cock with your blood so prettily."

Bile rises in my throat, and I almost don't manage to hold back a gag.

I'm done. I can't be here anymore. I need away from this man and the vile things he plans to do to me.

The car we arrived in is off to my left, but I don't think I can get to it safely without a bullet being plugged into my back. The tall piles of trash and debris are another option, but again, when you're racing against a bullet, your chances are pretty much zero. I glance around, continuing to take everything in. I keep hoping and praying for an answer to get myself out of this, but find nothing of use. Pure desperation has my breath speeding up, along with the pounding of my heart.

When Nyx finds out I've been taken, and I didn't leave on my own, he'll come for me. By then, however, it'll be too late. He still has to realize I've been taken in the first place and then find me somehow. The destruction Trickster is hell-bent on causing will have already begun. I don't see this dirtbag being patient. He seems like the instant gratification type of guy.

I have no doubt before we leave here today, he plans to rape me and possibly pass me along to his two friends.

My legs itch to run. Anywhere, so long as it's away from here. My muscles tense, ready to take action and a chance, when something hard presses against my back. For the briefest second, I imagine it's Nyx behind me. He's here to save the day... but I quickly realize the thought is stupid.

Trickster is right here, in front of me. He would have seen Nyx approach. No, this man must be one of the Iron Palms. In fact, I now notice the third guy who came with Trickster and the one from the coffee shop is missing. Or he was, until he appeared behind me.

Fear clogs my lungs as a pair of hands grab my wrists, making me cry out in pain when my arms are twisted too far behind my back. Hunching forward, I attempt to relieve some of the pressure on my joints. What I feel next, pressed against my ass, has vomit threatening to make an appearance as nausea swirls through my stomach. The Iron Palm's member is *hard*.

A moment later, I'm grabbed by the throat, forced to stand up straight. I rear back against the man behind me when Trickster gets in my face. His breath is rancid, smelling like something has withered up and died in his throat.

"I see those wheels spinning in your head," he says. I try to turn my face away to get away from the awful smell of his body odor and breath, but he holds me steady. "No one is going to rescue you. Nyx has no idea where you are, and once he does, we'll be long gone." He leans forward, laying the flat of his tongue on my cheek, running the revolting thing up my face. "But don't worry, you'll get your chance to see him again." A harsh hand is shoved between my legs, and even through the dress, I feel violated. "I'll make him watch as I tear through every hole of your body."

A loud bang reverberates from somewhere, then a split second later, I'm jolted forward, and something wet sprays the top of my head. I blink several times to clear away the fogginess of the sudden jerk. Just as my eyes focus back on Trickster, he's spinning on his heels and bolting toward his bike. I don't miss the splatter of blood on his face and shirt as he goes.

The sounds of his and the other guy's motorcycle speeding away from the scene wipe away my dazedness, making me realize the offending weight at my back is no longer there. I spin around, my mouth dropping open when I find the third guy lying on the ground. He's on his back, decorated with a huge hole through his forehead. Blood, brain matter, and bone fragments cover his face.

What in the hell just happened?

"Greer."

I stiffen when my name is called.

That voice.

The one I never thought I would hear again. The one I've grieved over for weeks and cried uncontrollable tears for.

Slowly, I turn around. I'm terrified my brain is playing a cruel joke on me. Because the person behind me could simply not be the one I just heard call my name.

But it is.

My brother stands ten feet from me... wearing black cargo pants, combat boots, and a T-shirt, with a bulletproof vest strapped over his chest. He looks the same as he did the last time I saw him alive, but he also seems different. Maybe it's because I've believed he has been dead for weeks.

"R-Rowan?" His name comes out in barely a whisper. I sway on my feet as black spots dance on the edge of my vision. "How?"

My body sways to the side, and he darts forward, catching me before I can hit the ground. It isn't until his familiar scent hits my nostrils that I realize this is real. My brother is truly standing here in front of me. It's not some vicious trick of the mind or a dream I may be having.

The same eyes I've looked at since the day I was born peer down at me, sadness and remorse filling them.

"Y-you died," I say through numb lips. "How are you here?"

"I'm so sorry, Greer," he apologizes, and the sorrow in his tone proves his words true.

"What?" I shake my head, disbelief still lingering. "I don't understand. You died, Rowan. *I saw your body in a casket.*"

His jaw twitches. "I had to die. In order to protect you, I had to die."

I push against his chest, needing some breathing room to try to understand what he's saying. He's making zero sense. "What in the hell are you talking about?"

He allows me to take a step back, but his frame is tense, as if he's ready to spring forward again if my body gives out. Like he may be expecting it to give out with whatever he's getting ready to say.

"I've been undercover since the day I joined the Iron Palms."

Chapter 14

Morgan Jane Mitchell

Nyx

MY BEST MEN FOLLOW me out the door, but I take the wheel. With the urgency beating in my chest, I floor it. Greer's gone, kidnapped on our special day. Of all the insane times in my life, this one takes the cake. It would've been nice if we had actually cut our heart-shaped wedding cake.

I make a silent promise to myself and her. *I'll get Greer back and say our vows before Valentine's Day is over. We'll slice that goddamn cake.*

Her ring's tracking device is leading us about three miles past the outskirts of town. Not all the way to the gang's warehouse but pretty close. I'm grinding my molars, hoping she's okay.

"Why, Brandy? Why the hell would she betray me? She's part of my team. Or she was," I ask Ace and Bug as I barely keep between the lines.

"Maybe she has the hots for you, too," Ace answers.

"Vanessa," I say through my teeth as the horrible fact dawns on me. Bug said he sent her packing, and I know she'd want revenge. Crazy bitch thinks she owns me when I've never returned her affection. Brandy, though? What did I ever do to her?

Suddenly, I spot a figure sprinting along the side of the road, red hair whipping around her face. Speak of the devil. *Brandy.* My rage flares. I slam on the brakes, dust clouds billowing as we slide to a stop. She scrambles over, her eyes huge, and wrenches open the passenger door. Ace climbs to the back as she hops in.

"You better start talking," I shout the moment she's in the seat, slamming the door behind her. "Where's Greer?"

Brandy's voice shakes. "I messed up, okay? I thought Vanessa only wanted to crash the wedding, pull some dramatic shit, and maybe sabotage you two. Look, I owed her one. Do you know how many times she's saved my life? She's seriously psycho, Nyx. I swear I didn't know." She chokes down a sob. "Vanessa turned on me when I tried to stop her. Then the Iron Palms showed up. I had to make a run for it."

My blood feels like molten steel in my veins as I hear what I already know. "The Iron Palms? You're telling me you left Greer with those bastards?"

Brandy nods, tears streaking her cheeks. "They're just ahead in the parking lot. Vanessa tried to kill me. I ran, or I'd be dead."

I don't trust her right now, but she might be my only lead to Greer. I stomp on the gas, and my SUV fishtails. Less than a minute later, we're reaching the clearing, braking hard. At first glance, the concrete slab looks deserted. Then, as I get out, I see two bodies sprawled out on the oil-stained pavement.

My heart stops as I scan over their lifeless forms. One's Vanessa, her once mischievous eyes open, a bullet hole sunk between them. I gnash my teeth so hard it hurts. I'd never liked Vanessa's obsession with me, but I never wanted her dead. The other body belongs to a bearded Iron Palms member. Shot as well, he's lying in a pool of his own blood.

Fuck. There's no sign of Greer.

Brandy steps out and points to the ground where the scuffle must've happened. Bug and Ace are taking it all in as she recounts every detail. I notice the tire marks, footprints, and a bunch of scattered bullet shells.

"Looks like there was a fight," Bug mutters.

"No shit," I retort.

"They must've taken Greer. The warehouse is only a few blocks from here," Brandy chimes in.

"You fucking think?" It took everything I had not to grab her and shake her.

I'm itching to move, chase them down, find my bride. I hurry back to the driver's seat. "Let's go," I snap at the others. They climb in, and I'm about to peel out when I hear the motorcycles approaching.

Shit. Looks like the Iron Palms are back.

I spin the wheel, preparing for a showdown. Within seconds, a crew of bikes rolls up, their headlights cutting through the dusty air. The leader, a large man with a bold streak of gray in his long dark beard, skids to a halt, blocking our way. I rev the engine, threatening to mow the gangbanger down, but he one-ups me by flashing his oversized gun.

My hand hovering over my weapon, I jump out and move close enough to scan every face. "Where's my bride?" I bellow, "Where is Greer?"

The thug lifts his chin. "Don't know what you're talkin' about, boy. "'Bout to ask you the same." The patch in Old English on his beanie reads: Hog.

Weapons drawn, Hog's members circle the vehicle to threaten my crew. They disarm me but only take the Glock in my holster, the one I'm drawing attention to, and fail to pat me down.

Fucking amateurs.

Hog steps so close I can smell the whiskey on his breath. "Where you hidin' the girl?"

I've seen his sidekick before. Trickster, the skinny meth head with greasy hair, shows off his two teeth, answering his leader, "Rowan got her."

What? My mind falters. "Rowan's dead," I spit. This has to be a sick trick. "Where's my girl?"

"Her brother made a deal. Offered his little sister up for initiation." Trickster smirks. "The cost of joining this *family*."

I know what their initiation methods are, one of them being rape, and it makes me want to shoot them all for being evil fucks. A sick reminder of why I chose this line of work in the first place—to fucking bury these street thugs.

"You think I don't know that?" I lie. Here I'm under the impression my old best friend had simply gotten in over his head in his deals with the gang, and the Iron Palms were ruthless enough to go after Greer because her brother owed them a debt. Now, I find out he fucking knowingly offered her up on a silver platter to these monsters? Fucking Ro. How could he? I'm seething. Regardless, I state the facts: "Not going to happen. Not now. Not ever."

Trickster shrugs, "Deal's a deal."

His weapon's steady, pointing straight at my forehead, Hog narrows his eyes. "See your friend over there?" He means Vanessa, and she's not my friend. "I'll ask one more time before I make a matching pair. Where's the girl?"

Trickster answers him before I can argue, "You're barking up the wrong tree. I told you, Rowan showed up and shot Blister dead and then took the *puta*." He gestures over to their member covered in prison ink who's laid out in a puddle of blood.

Come again? "No way." I gasp at the ridiculous notion.

Their leader sneers. "Fuck, Trickster. You sure you aren't high and seeing things again?"

"Rowan can't come back from the grave. I saw him in his coffin," I state the obvious, talking more to myself than anyone.

"As did I," Hog says. "Stiff as a board." Then he orders his crew, "Search the SUV."

The guys go in and drag Brandy out, kicking and screaming. They throw her to the ground but refrain from frisking her.

Brandy's armed to the teeth, so it's to our benefit. We exchange a look that would've comforted me before today. Too bad I no longer trust her to have my back.

"I swear it was Rowan. Looked just like him." Trickster won't shut up about my dead best friend.

"Give it up. He's dead. Girl is ours now. We're owed," Hog grunts.

Red-hot fury explodes behind my eyes. "Over my dead body."

Hog snorts, sounding just like his namesake.

Trickster leers at me. "If burying you is what it takes, I can oblige." He cracks his knuckles. "Puta's my property now. I won her fair and square."

My breath comes in short bursts as my lip curls. This gang thinks they can swap my fiancée like they do their illegal weapons. Rage warps my vision, and I see nothing but red. I'll be damned if I let these no-good criminals have her. Greer is mine, heart, soul, forever.

I stand my ground, stepping forward. "If any of you laid a finger on her—"

Trickster advances, rolling his slender neck. "You want a fight, pretty boy? You got one."

A fight, one-on-one, is just what I need to distract these hotheads. "Who you calling a pretty boy? Just because I have all my teeth doesn't mean you can come on to me." Reaching up, I rip off my bow tie and fling it to the ground.

Trickster sputters, "Now, hold up. I'm not coming on to a man." He's taking the bait. "What you trying to say about me?"

Hog lowers his piece, but the rest of the Iron Palms members move in like a menacing circle of muscle and grit.

I shrug. "Pretty pitiful you can't get your own woman. Can't even fight your own battles."

Trickster sticks out his arm, gesturing for his brothers to hold off. "I'll whip your ass myself. Maybe if I deliver your cold, beaten corpse to her, the girl will learn who's boss. See what awaits her if she disobeys me."

The mention of this loser laying a hand on Greer does it. I lose my tux jacket. Fists up, I sink into a loose stance, ready for anything that comes my way. "I don't care if it costs me my last breath. You're never taking Greer from me."

We size each other up while the others fan out, waiting for any invitation to join in. Running my mouth, I'm trying to buy my team more time. All the while, I'm remembering Greer's bright smile, her laughter, the way her eyes used to sparkle with mischief whenever I caught her slow dancing all by herself. I can't wait to hold her in my arms for the first dance at our wedding, twirl her around like she used to dance on her own. I think about how I should be lifting her veil right now, about the heart-shaped cake decorated with all the sweethearts, and how I hope she'll get a kick out of it. Hope she'll finally agree she's my sweetheart. Then, I think about the ring on her gorgeous finger.

The ring. Fuck. If I can only get to my phone, I can check her location again. I will know if these assholes are lying.

Of course, they're not telling the truth. Rowan, alive? I am no fool.

Trickster moves in, taking the first punch.

G<u>REER</u>

I'm trembling as Rowan drives his blacked-out SUV like he stole it. In complete shock, I blankly stare at my engagement ring, then lower my gaze. My shoes are all scuffed. Some thug's blood splattered my beautiful wedding gown that's now torn at the hem. Letting my head fall back, I fight the urge to be sick. When I shut my eyelids, my life cracks open, and every shocking truth crawls out to mock me. Not only am I a witness to a bullet striking Vanessa between the eyes, killing her in front of me all over again, but my own brother, presumed dead, suddenly appears, saves me, and whisks me away.

My eyes pop open, and I snap my attention to him. Rowan glances over at me from behind the wheel. My brother's serious, but I can also read the guilt in his eyes. As much as I'm happy he's alive, I can't help myself. "You should feel guilty," I declare.

"I'm sorry," he murmurs again, for the fifth time since we've pulled out of the abandoned lot. "I never wanted things to go down like this."

"You're *sorry*?" My throat burns with unshed tears. "You promised me, your little sister, to the Iron Palms. I knew you were a thug, but this... this..." I have no words. "And you faked your death, Rowan," I screech.

He curses under his breath, fingers flexing on the steering wheel. "Yes. I was embedded in the Iron Palms, undercover. Believe me, it wasn't a choice I made lightly. Yes, they demanded more than I was willing to give. Yes, your name got tossed around."

"Tossed around?" I parrot him. "How could you trade me like... like a... like a Pokémon card?" Rowan's my brother, and I can't think of anything else in his whole life he's traded.

He winces. "I didn't *trade* you. The gang insisted on having you. I delayed them. I concocted excuses, stalled, made half-promises I never intended to keep. For eight long years, Sis, but then my time ran out." His voice drops a whole octave. "I thought you'd have married Nyx by now, or at least you would've found someone else to settle down with. I thought you'd be far out of their reach, or I would've never made the bet I did. Hell, Sis, you've been in college for over six years."

The start of a headache pulses as I press my fingers against my temple. "I changed majors, you know that. What bet?" I shout before I catch myself.

"The leader of the Iron Palms is a betting man. We made a bargain. Well, I kept a secret for him, so we made a deal. His crew couldn't have you until the day I died. If you were already married by then, the deal was supposed to be off."

"What kind of a bargain is that?" I nearly scream.

"A risky one. One dicey enough for him to love the odds. Said if he ever wanted me to pay up, he could just kill me."

"So, why did you fake your death?"

Rowan shakes his head. "It's complicated and confidential."

"I... I can't believe you're alive," I whisper before the anger takes over again. "Do you have any idea what Mom and Dad have been going through? And me?" Tears well up in my eyes when I think about burying him, or someone who looked a whole hell of a lot like him. I open my mouth to ask, but I'm not sure I want to know. A chill crawls down my spine.

He sighs, saying, "It kills me. Believe me, it does. The good news is I've gathered enough intel on the important members to bury them." He clears his throat, then continues, "I just need a bit more time."

"Why did you show up today?" I ask.

His brow furrows. "We have their warehouse bugged. Vanessa's been in contact with them, so I heard you've been fighting Nyx. I had no choice but to act." He makes eye contact with me briefly. "Like I said, Sis, I need more time to take the Iron Palms down. You must marry Nyx as soon as possible. He's willing, and it's the only way to sever the gang's claim on you."

I sit up straight at his words. "Marry Nyx because I have to?" Anger flares in my chest, but it fades into a warm resolve. "You think I was running away from him? No, I decided to accept his proposal before I was kidnapped, Rowan. Because I've always loved Nyx."

My brother's expression softens at my truth. "I know. I always knew you were in love with my best friend. I noticed it in your eyes when you two were teenagers, the way you lit up around him. I saw how he looked at you, like you were the only girl in the world."

Tears threaten again, but I blink them back. "So, you allowed the gang to think they'd get me?" I shake my head. "God, Rowan... I don't know if I can ever..."

He cuts me off, "Don't say it, Greer. Don't say you can't forgive me. I had no choice; I swear I was stalling for time. I can't bear that they got anywhere near you. I called Nyx to protect you when I knew I'd be out of the picture. I was certain he'd guard you with his life. More importantly, I was aware he could."

"About Nyx... You know his secret?" I channel our old sibling rivalry. "If you truly want me to forgive you, and to not tell all your deepest, darkest secrets, you'll spill it."

"Sis, Nyx's business is for him to tell you."

I huff with disappointment but then stay quiet. Rowan's funeral turning out to not be real, my lonely nights of missing my brother, my parents' grief... all the heartbreak still feels fresh. However, Rowan is right here, in the flesh, alive and well. And by all accounts, as soon as I say '*I do*,' all the problems I have with the Iron Palms will supposedly go away.

Things are looking up.

I'm grinning from ear to ear as we arrive at the wedding venue. Darkness lingers outside, but lights illuminate the steps. I've always imagined my wedding would be full of guests, flowers, and music, but at least my brother can be here with me now.

"Go on inside. Mom and Dad are waiting," Rowan orders, shocking me.

"Really?" That's a pleasant surprise. Nyx must've made amends. My smile broadens, my mind wandering to thoughts of thanking him on our honeymoon.

"They'll be so happy to see you," I reply as I gather up my torn dress, preparing to get out of the vehicle.

"I'm not going inside. They can't see me," he explains and exhales, his expression seemingly haunted. "It'd put them in more danger. You, too, if anyone were to find out I'm still alive. I'm not even supposed to be here."

I shoot him a desperate look, my heart hurting all over again. "They'd be overjoyed to see you breathing, Rowan. *Please*. We thought you were..." I can't bring myself to mention the word at this point.

He shakes his head as he takes my hand, firmly stating, "No. I can't. I have what I need now to start taking the gang down for good. But I'll never be a hero, Sis... I already have another job lined up, and it's twice as dangerous. Gotta keep my cover; I shouldn't have shown my face, even to you."

His words sting, but I try to make sense of them anyway. "Those gangsters already saw you, Rowan."

He almost smirks. "Only Trickster, and he's the biggest liar alive. Nobody believes a damn word he says. They'll assume he's spouting nonsense again."

Reaching for the door handle, I hesitate. "What about Nyx? Can I tell him?"

His gaze drops with regret. "I'll reveal myself to Nyx in my own time. I owe him a hell of a lot of explanations." He rakes a hand through his hair. "But not yet."

The lump in my throat could choke me if I allow it to continue to bubble up, so I swallow it down, knowing how significant this all is. Nyx deserves to know

Rowan's alive, but I can't betray my brother. Not when he's the person who saved me tonight.

I brace myself and crack the door open. Rowan's phone vibrates, and I glance back at him one last time. I can't help but wonder if I'll ever lay eyes on him again, and the question is just as heartbreaking as it is healing, knowing he's alive and well.

His knuckles whiten around the device as he listens. "Yeah?" His eyes drift to me and enlarge, making me pause.

A muffled voice crackles through the speaker, but I can't make out the words.

"Wait," he hisses, raising a hand to stop me from leaving.

Rowan's face is pale when he ends the call. "Change of plans, Sis."

A nasty knot twists in my gut. "What? What happened?"

"The Iron Palms have Nyx."

My heart plunges into the deep. Of all the things going wrong today, this is the worst. I slam the door shut. "Rowan," I almost growl. "I have got to get him back."

"You need to go inside."

I shake my head, pursing my lips. I point my finger and threaten him, "No. If you don't take me with you, I'll tell Mom and Dad you're alive... and that Spot didn't break Grandma's urn, you did."

Rowan hits the steering wheel, a scowl painting his mouth as he shifts into drive. "Damn it, you win. Buckle up and hold on tight."

Chapter 10

Shannon Myers

Greer

"WE'RE DOING THIS NOW? Are you fucking kidding me?"

I look over at my brother, who is pissed as hell, but I have no idea what's going on. We are speeding back the way we came from, and while I am scared to death to be anywhere near the Iron Palms again, I have to go. I need to get to Nyx.

"Yes, sir." Rowan grips the steering wheel so tightly his knuckles are white. "Greer's with me."

"What the fuck do you mean your sister is with you?"

Damn. I heard that loud and clear.

"She was with me when I got the call about Nyx," he responds quietly. The person's reply is too low for me to hear. "Yes, sir."

I bite my lip when Ro hangs up, holding my breath, worried he is going to turn the vehicle around and force me to go back to the venue and wait with our parents.

"That was my boss. He said the timetable is moved up on our op." He grits his teeth so hard, I swear I hear them grinding together from over in the passenger seat. "I don't have quite everything I need, but I have enough to move forward."

My chest is burning with anger; I ask, "You sound upset about it, Ro. Would you rather leave Nyx to fend for himself? *To die?*"

"No!" He slams his fist against the wheel. "I'd rather you two had gotten married when you should have been married, so none of this ever fucking happened!"

"Well, excuse me!" I snap, glaring over at him. "I'm sorry if someone freaking kidnapped me before I made it to my own damn wedding. I'm sorry they've gotten to Nyx when he obviously tried to save me. I'm sorry we are ruining all of *your plans*!"

I am so livid right now, and on top of it, my heart is breaking at the thought of what the Iron Palms are doing to the man I love. Gangbangers are ruthless. They shot Vanessa without thinking twice. I have no doubt they will do much worse to Nyx if given the chance, torturing him endlessly before finally pulling the trigger.

Tears fill my eyes, then stream down my cheeks. I swipe angrily at them, refusing to fall apart. My man needs me.

My man. I've waited too long to be able to call Nyx mine. And now, there is a chance he can be taken from me before we ever exchange our vows.

"Not what I mean, and you know it, Greer." Rowan sighs. "Look, we're meeting my team at a building we use as our headquarters right now. It's a few miles away from where they have Nyx. When we get ready to infiltrate the warehouse, I'm going to need you to stay behind."

"No." I am not sitting around in some building, waiting for them to bring Nyx to me. I'm going to be there so I'm one of the first things he sees when he's rescued, so he knows how much I love him.

"You don't have a choice, Greer. Unless you want to fuck up the entire operation."

"I don't care about your operation, Rowan. I need to be there for Nyx."

"You don't understand how big this thing is, Sis. How far it all reaches. This isn't only the Iron Palms." He glances over at me. "Trust me, Nyx will want you to stay behind and wait. Not just because of how he feels about you, but because you could interfere in something that has been in the works for years."

"Ro, Nyx wouldn't be in this situation if it weren't for those bastards wanting me. If I go in there and..."

"Don't be a fucking martyr, Greer. You go in trying to negotiate, and they will take you and kill him. The Iron Palms are ruthless. They do not negotiate with anyone. I would know; I've been with them for eight long, miserable years." He reaches over, placing his free hand on top of mine. "Let us handle this, please, little sister. I promise I will bring Nyx back to you. Wait where I tell you to, so I know you're safe."

I make no promises, turning my head to stare out the window at the barren landscape as we head outside of town. I don't want to mess anything up for them, whoever the hell Ro works for, but I have to make sure Nyx is okay.

A soft sob leaves me. I need to make sure he's alive.

A few minutes later, we pull up outside of what appears to be an abandoned building. A garage door slides up, and we drive inside, where I see there are several other vehicles. People are moving around quickly, placing things in the vehicles. Others are donning what I assume are bulletproof vests.

"Let's go."

I open the door, hop out, and follow Rowan from the SUV. We head over to where a man wearing a thunderous look on his face stands, waiting for us. He scowls at me, but when he goes to open his mouth, Rowan steps in front of me, crossing his arms over his thick chest. "Not gonna happen, sir."

I freeze as I peek around my brother to see the man's face turn a dark red in rage. To my surprise, he takes a step back, breathes in deeply, and nods. "I apologize, Ms. Ellis, but this situation has me more than a little on edge. Bringing you into the mix right now is not helping. It's my job to keep the men and women who work for me safe. I can't do so if we are worrying about you being hurt while we are trying to save the others who have been taken."

"Others?" I ask softly, slipping around Rowan to meet his boss' gaze.

"I shouldn't be telling you this." The man lowers his head to look at the ground, then brings his clear blue eyes back to meet mine. This time, the anger has been replaced with worry, but also determination. "Nyx isn't the only one who's been taken by the Iron Palms. Three of the people on his team were captured as well. They were looking for you, and it seems the gang was too."

I nod, swallowing hard as I fight back my tears. "I was on my way to our wedding with Brandy, but she took a detour to meet with some woman named Vanessa. I'm still confused over what it was all about, except it seems to have something to do with Vanessa being jealous of my relationship with Nyx. The gang pulled up, and then Trickster shot Vanessa in the head. He told me I was promised to him, and he was taking me."

"Yeah, from what I hear, it seems Vanessa had a thing for Nyx—feelings he did not return. He had her reassigned to a new team effective as of last night, but it didn't go over too well."

Obviously not.

"My brother saved me, but I don't know what happened afterward."

"What happened is the fucking Palms showed up, jumped my goddamn team, and took them."

I turn, watching as a large man with salt-and-pepper hair stalks our way. I have no idea who he is, but the suit he's wearing says he must be someone important.

"Nyx works for you?" I ask, lost as to who any of these people are to Nyx and his team.

"You don't have a clue, do you?"

I slowly shake my head at his incredulous voice.

"I don't have time for this shit." Shaking his head, the man rakes a hand through his thick hair. "I'm Agent Stevens. Yes, Nyx works for me. Right now, that's all you need to know." Raising a hand, he motions to someone, and I catch my breath when I find Noah rushing over. A familiar face is welcome while I am in the middle of this hell. "Go with Noah. She's staying back with you. Get yourself cleaned up and into a change of clothes. Nyx will lose his ever-loving mind if he sees you with blood and gore all over you."

"Wait," I cry out when he turns to leave. He looks back at me. "I want to come with you. Please. I need to be there for Nyx."

"Why? So you can get him killed?" he asks bluntly. "You'll be nothing but a distraction to everyone there. You are not going." His voice softens as he places a hand gently on my shoulder. "Trust me, I'll bring him home. I'm bringing them all home. They are mine."

I lock eyes with him for a long moment before I finally nod. "Thank you, Agent Stevens."

A muscle ticks in his jaw before he gruffly responds, "Name's Sebastian." Without another word, he's gone.

N^{YX}

I grunt, wincing at the pain pounding through my head. My mind's groggy, making me feel sluggish, as my entire body aches. Slowly, I let my eyes open, squinting at the bright lights in the room as I try to remember where I am and what happened.

Pushing against the cold cement I'm lying on, I swear as sharp, excruciating pain stabs through my side. My chest heaves while I fight through the agony.

"You okay, boss?"

I raise my head to look over where the gravelly voice came from. Ace is sitting up against a concrete wall, his head leaned back, blood trickling down from a wound at his temple. He doesn't open his eyes or glance in my direction, and I can tell he is hurting fiercely.

"Yeah," I mutter, my voice gravelly. Pushing myself back, I lean against the wall behind me. No, I am not okay. Not even close, but I'm not telling him that.

"I'm sorry, Nyx. *So sorry.*"

I don't bother replying to Brandy. She's screwed everything up, and she knows it. When we get out of this, and we will, she's gone. I don't want her on my team or anywhere near us. Hell, I don't want her in the same fucking state as Greer. She's put my woman in danger, and because of her actions, we are all sitting wherever the fuck we are, waiting to find out what's going to happen next.

Trickster, the asshole, managed to get the jump on me. Well, not him specifically, but his buddies had taken what should have been a fair fight between the two of us and changed it to five-on-one. When Ace and Bug attempted to help me, the rest of the gang that was there stepped in.

After kicking our asses, they brought us here, to what I assume is their warehouse. We are all together in a cell, sporting bruises and probably some broken bones.

Except Bug. I don't see him.

"Where's Bug?" I growl, pressing my hand against my aching ribs. Hopefully, they are only bruised, but I don't hold out hope for it. I have a feeling a couple of them might be broken after the way Trickster kicked the shit out of them with his heavy boots.

"They came in and took him a little bit ago," Ace replies quietly. "Bastards are having a nice little torture session, if the screams we've been hearing are any indication. Went on for a long time. Now, there's nothing."

"Those motherfuckers!" I pound my hand against the hard floor, not caring when more pain slams through me. Let it hurt. Make me furious, fuming with rage, because all it's going to do is bring out the devil in me. Something no one wants to see.

They are going to die. All of them.

"Ya know, I never wanted to do what we do," Brandy whispers, whimpering softly when she shifts positions to lay down on the floor. She's holding her arm, and for the first time, I notice it looks like it's broken. There is also some bruising on her face and other arm.

"No?" Ace grumbles, still not opening his eyes.

"No. All I ever wanted when I was growing up was to be a dancer." She moans as she switches positions slightly. "My entire life changed focus when my parents were murdered right after I turned eighteen. Instead of dancing on a stage, I picked up a gun." She's quiet for a moment. "I wish every day I'd chosen differently."

"There's still time," Ace says, just as there is a large clanking sound, and a door is opened to the main room.

"No," Brandy answers softly, "there isn't."

Before I can ask her what she means, the cell door is opening, and Bug is shoved inside, hard. He stumbles, dropping to his knees, blood flowing from deep cuts down his bare chest. As he falls forward, I notice similar cuts down his back.

I struggle to his side, helping him as best as I can to lean against the wall. He hisses when his mutilated back hits the cold concrete, groaning deeply before his body eventually slumps over. I manage to catch him, cursing at the pain it causes, and help him lie down so he can rest on the floor.

"I got you," I grind out, wanting nothing more than to fly through the cell door and take out every gangbanger in the building.

There's loud laughing, and I glance over, finding Hog and Trickster watching us. "You're next, pretty *puta*," Trickster says, giving Brandy an evil grin. "We're gonna have some fun, me and you."

Brandy slowly pushes herself up into a sitting position, glancing over at me, panting softly in pain. "Your woman saved my life, Nyx. Vanessa held a gun on me, and right before she pulled the trigger, Greer jumped at her and knocked her over." Her eyes fill with tears. "I paid her back by running. I left her there, and I ran." She pauses, her gaze going to where Trickster and Hog are still making lewd comments. "I'm not running now."

I stiffen when I see the glint of a blade in her hand. Brandy is good in a fight, one of the best I've seen, but she's weak and injured right now. There's no way she can take on both men by herself and prevail.

Slowly, my gaze lands on Trickster, who's just slipped into the cell with Hog right behind him. I slide my hand down my pant leg to my ankle, a dark grin crossing my face once I feel the hilt of my dagger poking out of my boot. If they did a body search before throwing us in here, they never found it. Although, I doubt they even looked.

Brandy struggles to her feet, her body trembling from fear as she stares down the two men coming for her. "Please, tell Greer how sorry I am."

She takes a deep breath, then lunges forward. The blade of her knife embeds deep into Hog's neck. His eyes open wide with shock, a gurgling sound emerging. His hands move to grasp the hilt of the knife, attempting to pull it out, but he can't. With a full-body shudder and a deep groan, he sinks to the floor.

"You fucking *puta!*" Trickster is on Brandy in seconds, grabbing her by the hair and slamming her face-first into the steel bars, over and over again. The cell fills with her screaming, and she tries to pull away but is no match for his hostility.

"Shit," I huff out as I fight down the agony in my side and manage to stumble to my feet, yanking my dagger from my boot at the same time.

Ace yells something, but I don't hear the actual words while gritting through the pain. I know Bug is trying to rise up off the floor, but my total focus is on the son of a bitch who wants to claim my woman as his own; who would rape her and torture her on a daily basis.

I'm not going to allow that. There would be no prison. No escaping. Greer would be terrified the rest of her life if I kept him alive. It isn't something I can live with.

Coming up behind Trickster, I grab his greasy hair, yanking his head back. He shoves Brandy away from him and tries to turn around, but I don't allow it. Running my blade across his throat, I stare in twisted satisfaction as blood flows out and down his chest. I step away from him, watching dispassionately as his body drops to the hard concrete.

Glancing around, I take in the carnage filling the small cell for a long moment before leaning over and wiping my blade against the scumbag's pants. They're dead, and I'm sure I'm going to have some explaining to do, but I don't care. I only want to get back to Greer.

"How about we get the fuck out of here?"

As the words leave my mouth, the outer door slams open, the room flooding in with agents. I release a grateful sigh, allowing myself to slide to the floor, a small smile on my face. The cavalry is here, which means this shitshow of a life I've led for the past eight years has to be over. There's no way they would have brought in so many agents if the investigation were still ongoing. They must have enough evidence to take down not only the Iron Palms but also the Mexican Cartel's drug ring.

I've never been so happy, except for when Greer agreed to marry me.

"Hey, brother," a voice says, one I never thought I would hear ever again. "Let's go. My sister is really worried about you."

"Ro." I have to be dreaming. I open my eyes to see his face. My best friend is in front of me—alive and well... and dressed like a motherfucking government agent. How can this be? "What the hell is going on?"

He grins, sliding an arm around my waist and helping me to my feet. "We got a lot to talk about."

I shake my head, frowning in confusion. "Later. It can wait. I have a wedding to get to."

"Hell yes, you do," my boss thunders, striding into the room. "I promised your woman I'm bringing you back, and that's what I'm going to do. She's had enough crap in her life lately, let's give her something to be happy about."

I release a low laugh, my ribs screaming in pain, as I shake my head with amusement. "Yes, bossman."

Epilogue

E.M. Shue

Greer

MY KNEE SHAKES AS I bounce my leg. The nervous energy in my body is almost overwhelming. I've showered and seen a physician. I'm only bruised everywhere and have scratches, but nothing is broken. It could have been so much worse. My arm from when I fell is sore, but the doctor says it's going to be sore for several days. I'm worried about Nyx, though. Something tells me he's not going to get away as lucky.

Will he be alive when they finally get to him?

It seems like it's been days instead of only a couple hours. Those words from his tattoo, *Remember, you must die,* roll through my mind. We all must die, it's true, but what do those words mean to him? Why did he put them on his skin?

That's when it hits me... Part of me *died* before I found him again. To have our life together, I had to let the anger go to give him the chance. Trust him. It's a form of death to the former me; I didn't trust and only focused on getting away from my old life, along with his betrayal. I want to marry Nyx. Will I lose the man I've loved most of my life now, when we've finally found each other once again? When I've finally pulled my head out of my ass and figured it all out?

I don't care about his secrets anymore.

I only want him.

There's a loud metal grinding sound filling the space, and I can't stop the tremble of my body as fear consumes me. Noah stands up, as do I, and we watch the doors open. Several SUVs enter...

I immediately notice it's not as many vehicles that had left earlier, and it has my heart dropping into my stomach. Before they come to a stop, one of the back doors opens, and then Nyx is standing on the running board. The SUV comes to a stop, and he jumps down. He cringes, and then my feet are moving, pushing me faster as I rush toward him.

"I didn't run! I want to marry you," I hurriedly explain as I slam into his body. We both groan from the impact, but it doesn't stop him from wrapping his arms around my body and pulling me in close.

"Sweetheart, I know. God, Greer... if Vanessa wasn't dead already, I'd kill her for putting you in danger." His bruised knuckles slide along my cheeks, then his large hands push into my hair. Tipping my head back, I peer into his eyes as he leans down.

"I love you, Nyx," I whisper before he takes my lips in a deep kiss. I open, and we fuse together, our bodies so close *nothing* can get between us. My hands fist his damp hair. We kiss as if it's been weeks instead of only a day since our lips last met.

I'll never tire of his mouth on mine.

When we finally part, Nyx leans down, sweetly pressing his forehead to mine. "I love you too, Greer. Will you be my Valentine?"

"Yes. *Always.*"

"Good. We have a wedding to get to." He turns, pulling me toward the SUV.

I glance down at the sundress Noah gave me to change into. It's simple but perfect for us. The soft floral pattern with the cinched waist and bustier-style top accentuates my fuller breasts. My hair is hanging down my back in its loose chestnut waves. Nyx is in a pair of slacks and a black button-down shirt. They must have had him clean up before he came to me too, just like they had me do. It makes me wonder what he must've looked like before, but then I shake my head, getting those thoughts from my mind.

"I'm ready," I smile at him.

An hour later, we're standing next to a heart-shaped cake with several small pastel candy hearts decorating it, all saying 'sweetheart.' Nyx has called me the pet name over and over. I stare up at my husband, my lips tipping up in another soft smile for him. "I'll be your sweetheart," I give him the words I know he's been wanting from me.

I'll let him call me sweetheart any day.

We have a small, intimate ceremony with my parents and the few members from Nyx's team that could make it. Unfortunately, Rowan wasn't with them when Nyx came back. The only explanation I received was him saying we'd discuss it later. Bug is still in the hospital being treated for his injuries. Ace wouldn't go to the hospital but instead got treated by the same physician I saw. He stood next to Nyx as his best man, while I asked Noah to stand with me.

I never needed a big ceremony… only Nyx and myself.

Holding my hand over Nyx's on the knife, together we cut the cake. When he slips a small, delicious slice onto a plate, I can't stop the evil grin from taking over my lips. Grabbing my slice, I mouth *'I love you'* as I smoosh it onto his face, smearing it along his lips and chin.

"Oh, sweetheart, you'll regret that," Nyx chuckles as he cleans his face off. He pulls me into his arms and holds his piece of cake over me.

"You wouldn't. Please don't, I didn't get you too badly."

"Yes, you did. You got me *really* good." He touches the piece, frosting first, to my nose before he leans down and kisses it off me. He whispers in my ear, "I'll be eating this cake off your body later."

My core clenches and my cheeks heat.

"Okay, we're done!" I yell and try to leave, but Nyx stops me again.

Music starts and he pulls me into his body, slowly starting to sway. "I want to dance with my wife before we leave."

NYX

After I twirl Greer around the dance floor, I lead her over to where her parents are to say goodbye to them. I don't like Rowan ditching out on our wedding, but I only have one priority, and that's Greer. He said we'd talk soon, and I'm holding him to the promise. He has *a lot* to explain.

I wanted to give Greer the wedding she deserves. She should have been in a big, frilly, expensive gown, her favorite fresh flowers everywhere, and the rest of the works. But I won't regret the fact that she's mine now. In the end, it's what matters most.

When we finally get into the SUV, Ace is sitting in the front seat, even though I can tell he is hurting as much as I am. I keep Greer pressed into my side, not wanting to let her go. I've made reservations at an exclusive hotel in the penthouse to celebrate our night, and no amount of pain is going to stop me from making love to her again or getting my mouth on her pussy.

"What happened to Brandy?" she asks suddenly as she gazes up at me in the darkened interior. I hate giving her this information, but now that we are married, I can be more honest with her. I promised her I would.

"She told me to tell you she's sorry. She felt she owed Vanessa for her saving her life. She didn't know Vanessa had already betrayed her." I pause as I look deeply into her green-gold eyes. In the darkness, they're so pale. "She's in the hospital and they aren't sure she'll make it. She tried to attack Trickster and Hog by herself. Trickster beat her badly before I could stop him."

I draw in a deep breath, then exhale before admitting something that could change how she sees me. I squeeze her hand in mine and adamantly claim, "He'll *never* come after you."

"Oh my god." Her eyes fill with tears, and as they slide down, I wipe them away with my thumbs. On the way to the venue earlier, I'd told Greer about Vanessa. I had explained about the drive-by at her parents' house and talked them into being at our wedding. How I never went to Vanessa's, as Greer told me she said. Greer believed me about Vanessa, and I'm glad I didn't have to fight that bitch's lies. I hated that she had to die, but it's the least she deserves for putting Greer in jeopardy.

The SUV comes to a stop, and I glance out the window. We aren't at the safe house or even the hotel I asked to go to. "Ace?" My voice is hard as I question him, but after today's betrayal from Brandy, I'm leery.

"It's okay, boss. I was asked to bring you here." The passenger door opens, and Rowan climbs in as Ace steps out, leaving us alone.

"Ro," Greer leans forward through the seats, wrapping her arms around him.

"I had to see you one last time. You were a beautiful bride," he says as he kisses the top of her head. "I *have to* go away, but it will be okay. Don't worry about me."

"No," she begs him.

"Yes. I have a lot to atone for. I shouldn't have allowed your name to be mentioned. I shouldn't have made the deal; it's one of my greatest regrets. However, this job, I can do. I can stop assholes just like the Palms. Today with Nyx, we not only brought down the Iron Palms, but we also brought down the Mexican Cartel cell here. There are still more gangs and thugs out there, and I signed up to do this." I understand what Ro is trying to explain, but Greer is fighting it.

"How long?" is all I ask.

"A couple more years," he starts, but I hold up a hand to stop him.

"No, how long have you been under?"

"Since I joined the gang. You?"

"Since I left. I watched how they jump in people, and all I could think about was it would be done to Greer one day, so I flipped."

"I had to do it after they made me make the trade for Greer."

"Wait, what do you mean?" Greer flicks her eyes between the both of us. She doesn't know it, but both her brother and I did what we had to-to make her safe. However, I was quicker in the process and was able to keep her from their main focus.

"They rape young girls. It's what your brother has been protecting you from," I slide my hand along her neck and pull her to me. "I left to protect you too. They knew I liked you. It was only a matter of time before they would have made me rape you or make a similar deal your brother had too. I wasn't going to allow them to use you against me."

If only Rowan had left with me, Greer would have never been given to Trickster in the first place.

"Really?"

"Yes." I nod slowly as I lean our foreheads together. I start to move in for her lips to kiss her again.

"Not in front of me, Nyx," Ro mutters, making us both chuckle.

"It's our wedding night, bro." I laugh as my ribs pull with pain.

"I don't want to hold you up anymore, but I need you to keep my secret, Greer."

Her gaze meets his, and she nods. "I will."

He doesn't say anything else as he steps out of the SUV, and Ace opens his door, getting back in.

"Are you going to have to leave too?" Greer turns in my arms, staring up at me. There's fear and pain in her expressive eyes, pulling at my heart.

"No, sweetheart. I'm done."

"You're done?"

"I am. I told my boss I'll consult on cases, but I'm out. You and our family we're going to make are my top priority."

"Thank goodness, because I wouldn't have been okay with you walking away from me again. I wouldn't want to bring kids into a situation like that, either."

"I didn't want to leave the first time; you need to know that."

"I do. I love you."

I kiss her long and deep. *She's always been my forever.*

5 Years later

I STARE DOWN AT the cake I had made in pink, with strawberries across the top. Pulling out the heart-shaped candies, I start pressing them onto the edge and smile at the effect. It looks almost identical to the cake we had on our wedding.

A cry comes from the monitor on the counter, and I glance at the camera, finding my son standing in his crib. He starts to pull his leg up to climb over, and I take off down the hall to get to him before he falls and hurts himself.

"Rowan Bennett," I say his name loudly, and he peers up at me with mischief sparkling in his green-gold eyes. The little turkey is going to need to go to a toddler bed because at almost three years old, he thinks he's a monkey and climbs everything. He has no fear, and I know it scares my wife.

"Did I hear my little man?" Greer's voice comes from behind me as I lift Ro out of the crib.

"I was getting him. You have an article to finish." I pull her in with my other arm. Looking down at her lush body, I see the slight rounding of her stomach where our daughter is safely nestled.

Every day I'm shocked this is my life now. I've killed men and have blood on my hands, but I'm a stay-at-home dad now, only doing consultant work, while my wife is an award-winning journalist. I don't let her go far from home, and I'm always with her or my new team is. I've lived a dangerous life, so I know my family deserves the best protection. I lace my fingers with Greer's and pull her along as I take her out to the kitchen.

Her eyes land on the bar, making her gasp. "Oh, Nyx, it's just like our wedding cake!" She's got tears in her voice, and I tug her, pulling her into me, holding tight. Our son leans in to hug her also. My family, safe and loved, filling my arms is all I need to make me complete.

"Happy Valentine's Day, *my sweetheart.*"

~ The End ~

~ Flynn & Sutton ~

Chapter 1

Avelyn Paige

Flynn

"I HATE THIS PLACE!"

Dropping my head, I inhale deeply before squaring my shoulders and setting my pen down. I push up from the chair and circle my desk, my heart pounding against my ribs at the thought of facing my daughter. Taryn is the light of my life, *mo chroí agus mo anam*, but she inherited her mother's temperament and my ruthlessness. Add in what I've been told is typical eleven-year-old attitude, and I might as well be facing a firing squad with her at times.

Thank you, Aisling, *God rest your soul*. Your mini-me has become a mini hellion.

"Bad day at school?" I ask when I step into the kitchen, where she's got her head shoved in the pantry, no doubt looking for a snack.

Shit! I forgot to go to the grocery store.

Taryn whirls around, a scowl on her face that would rival that of all my enemies back in Ireland combined.

"First," she begins as she sticks a finger up to tick off her grievances. "You move me away from the *only* home I knew. And if that wasn't bad enough, you bring me here. Second..." Another finger goes up. "... You enroll me in the *worst* school imaginable. Third, I finally find a teacher I *love*, and today she announced that her last day is in two weeks." Taryn takes a deep breath before thrusting up a fourth finger. "And fourth, you didn't even remember to get me more Doritos!"

She stomps around the large island, but before she can make her angry escape, I grab her and lift her onto the counter. Taryn huffs out a breath and crosses her arms defensively.

"First," I say, leaning close to look her in the eyes. "We left Ireland after Mam died because it wasn't safe for us anymore. You know that. Second, you're in the best, most expensive private school around, and you loved it when we took the tour. Third, which teacher is leaving?"

Tears spring to my little girl's eyes, and she tries to turn away to hide them from me, but I gently grip her chin. "Baby girl, you know you never have to hide your emotions from me," I remind her.

Her chin wobbles, reminding me just how young and fragile she really is. "Mrs. Snopes, the art teacher."

Ah, so that's what's really going on.

"Aw, Tary," I say, using the name her mam and I have called her since she was a tiny infant. "I know how much you like Mrs. Snopes. But maybe the new teacher will be as good. Hell, maybe they'll be better."

"You owe a dollar to the swear jar," she counters, her voice small.

Sighing, I shake my head. "I'm not going to have any money left to send you to college."

Taryn giggles, and the sound is so reminiscent of Aisling that it's like a fist squeezing all the blood from my heart. "We're rich," she says matter-of-factly. "You'll never run out of money."

"That's what you think." I lift her from the counter and set her on her feet. "Go get changed, and we'll buy you those Doritos."

Taryn takes off running, and I slump onto a stool, my mind racing back in time.

"I won't allow you to leave Dublin."

I clench my fists at my side and stare down my father. Killian O'Reilly is a family man, but when it comes to the O'Reilly crime family, otherwise known as The Faction, he's as hard as can be.

"Taryn deserves better than this," I counter.

"Better than what? Better than being surrounded by family and people who love her?"

"No, Da. She deserves more than a life of looking over her shoulder, wondering if whoever killed her mam is coming for her."

"Aisling has only been gone for two weeks," he reminds me unnecessarily. As if I could ever forget. "You shouldn't be making any major decisio—"

"My mind is made up," I snap. "We leave for the United States in a week."

More specifically, we're heading to Boston, Massachusetts, but I'm hesitant to share that particular information. The less my family knows, the safer Taryn will be. What they don't know can't be tortured out of them.

"If you do this, you'll be severing all ties to The Faction."

I take a deep breath, making sure to maintain eye contact and drive my point across. "That's what I'm counting on."

"And you'll have no more financial connections."

"I know."

He stares at me a moment before heaving a sigh. "I love you, son. But this is a mistake. Mark my words, there's going to come a time when you need us, need the family's support, but you won't have it."

"Will I have yours?"

"As Ceann an Teaghlaigh or as your father?" he asks carefully.

"As my father."

He hesitates for a split second. "I don't know."

"Da!"

Shaking away my thoughts of that day, I smile at Taryn as she stares at me expectantly. "Yes, Tary?"

"I'm ready," she states. "Let's go."

She turns on her heel and races toward the front of the house. I rise to follow, laughing slightly when I see the door wide open. Never underestimate my daughter's love of Doritos.

As I walk to the car, where she's already waiting in the passenger seat, movement catches my attention from the neighboring property. A woman is pounding in a 'For Sale' sign near the curb. When she's done, she pulls her phone from her purse and starts snapping pictures of the house.

I turn away from the car and cross the lawn.

"Hello," the woman greets cheerfully. "You must be Mr. O'Reilly."

"Depends." I shake her hand. "Who told you that?"

Her smile falters slightly. "Oh, um… When I met with the Braxtons, they said that you and your daughter are great neighbors. I consider that a huge selling point when speaking with potential buyers."

"Well, then, yes, I'm Mr. O'Reilly," I confirm, purposely leaving out my first name. There are a lot of O'Reillys in Boston, and on the off chance this lady is not who she says she is, I don't want to give her too much info that can be used to link me back to *The Faction* in Dublin.

"It's wonderful to meet you," she says. "I will do my best to find you a great new neighbor."

I nod. "Have a good day."

With that, I head back to the car and slide into the driver's seat.

"What was that all about?" Taryn asks, her tone full of bratty pre-teen.

"Braxtons are moving."

"No!" she wails dramatically. "They promised to let me swim in their pool next summer!"

Just fucking great. Not only do I have to help Taryn get used to a new art teacher, but now I'll have to kiss the ass of whoever moves in so my daughter can swim in their pool.

Sutton

"See ya later, Miss Matthews."

I continue sorting through the art pieces that were selected to be displayed at the art show this evening but smile as my students make their way out of class.

"Bye, Sarah."

When I was hired to be the art teacher at the public high school, I wasn't sure I'd like it. For as long as I can remember, I've wanted to teach art, but I always envisioned teaching at an elementary or middle school level. Molding the minds of young people and helping them to find their artistic passion is my passion, but I've enjoyed my time here. It hasn't stopped me from sending my resume to dozens of other schools around the country, though.

I pull my cell out of my desk to check if I have any missed calls, and my heart skips a beat when I see I have one from a number with a Boston area code, not that I've memorized the area code or anything, since it's the location of the private school at the top of my list to teach at. I hit the button to dial my voicemail, eagerly listening to the message.

"Miss Matthews, I'm calling in regards to an opening for a teacher in the art department of our private middle school in Boston. I received your resume, and I have to say, I'm very impressed with what I've read. I hope you don't mind, but I did a little digging and saw that you have an art show tonight featuring some of your current students. I've taken it upon myself to come to Providence so I can meet you in person and see you in action. Please feel free to call me if you have any questions; otherwise, I'll see you this evening."

Staring at my phone, I inhale and exhale several deep, calming breaths before I return the woman's call. I can't believe she's here in Providence, but I guess it's a good sign. She wouldn't come all this way from Boston if she weren't really interested in offering me a job.

Right?

I glance down at myself and realize I'm in no condition to meet a potential employer. Paint splatters my standard outfit of overalls and a T-shirt. Teaching art is messy business. Groaning, I grab my purse and head out the door. I make my way through the halls to the exit leading to the teachers' parking lot.

As soon as I'm in my car and my cell connects via Bluetooth, I press on the call icon so I can talk to her while I drive.

"Hello."

"Hi," I greet. "This is Sutton Matthews, returning your call."

"Miss Matthews, it's wonderful to hear from you. My name is Gail Stanley, and I'm a member of the school board of one of the most prominent private middle schools in Boston."

Gail goes on for a few minutes about the school and the new position available, and I ask several questions. By the time the conversation is wrapping up, my excitement has built to an almost uncontrollable degree.

"And you don't mind me coming to the art show tonight?" she asks.

"Of course not. I'd love for you to be there. Not only will it give us a chance to meet, but I'm very proud of my students, and any chance to show off their work is a win in my book."

"That's what I like to hear. Well, then, I'll see you in a few hours."

"I'm looking forward to it."

Ten minutes after disconnecting the call, I arrive home, and an hour and a half later, I'm back at the school, freshly showered and dressed to impress.

I bypass going to the art room and opt to go straight to the gym. Several of the students are working diligently to get all the artwork displayed, with the assistance of a few other teachers.

"Where have you been?" the assistant principal asks as he rushes to my side.

"Sorry. I had to quickly run home to change. I want to make a great impression on the parents tonight," I explain, using the one thing I know is more important to him than me being on time: parents and potential funding sources.

"That makes sense," he comments. "I think we have everything pretty well set up for tonight."

I glance around the gym, a grin spreading across my face. "It all looks wonderful."

"Indeed."

A student waves at me from across the room. "Excuse me a moment. It seems I'm needed," I say, nodding in her direction.

"Of course."

Time passes quickly, and before I know it, parents, students, and other community members are arriving. I'm swept up in mingling and gushing about all the talent in the room that I don't notice the smartly dressed woman approaching until she's standing right next to me.

"Miss Matthews?"

I turn to face her and smile. "Yes."

"I'm Gail Stanley," she confirms, thrusting out her hand to shake mine. "It's so nice to meet you."

"You, as well."

Ms. Stanley sweeps her gaze around the room. "You've got some incredibly talented students."

"Thank you. I'm very proud of them."

Her demeanor shifts, becoming more matter-of-fact. "This is a public school, no private donors?"

Immediately, my hackles rise, but I force myself to remain calm. "It is, you're correct."

"I mean no disrespect," she says, clearly reading my horribly disguised annoyance. "I simply ask because it's truly amazing what you've managed to accomplish with these kids despite what I imagine is a very minimal budget."

I relax a bit because she's not wrong. "I utilize everything I can at my disposal. The kids shouldn't have to suffer just because funding isn't available."

"Good for you," she praises. "*But* imagine what you could do with a budget that's backed by numerous wealthy donors as well as portions of students' tuition. I'm talking the kind of money that far exceeds what the budget for this entire school is per year, and that's just for one program."

"The possibilities are endless," I admit.

"We also have the full support of local art galleries around the city of Boston, and each year they offer scholarships to two incoming students for the cost of tuition, as well as two graduating students to cover the full tuition of an art school of their choice."

I can't stop my brows from rising. "Wow, that's... amazing. What's the catch?"

Ms. Stanley chuckles. "I like you, Miss Matthews."

"Please, call me Sutton."

"Sutton, then." She slips her arm through mine and ushers me toward a corner for privacy. "The catch is this: the position starts in two weeks. I'd like you to do a video interview with my fellow board members tonight, after the show concludes. If they like you, you'd have a follow-up interview with the superintendent and principal tomorrow. And if they think you're a good fit, which I know they will, an offer will be extended. You'd need to accept quickly and relocate to Boston immediately."

"Oh, um... that's a lot."

"It is. And because it is, we'd cover your moving expenses and assist you with finding suitable accommodations." She reaches into her purse and pulls out several folded sheets of paper. "In fact, I brought a few listings with me to get you started."

Breathe, Sutton. This might be a lot, but it's what you've wanted since the moment you received your college degree.

"Thank you, Ms. Stanley. I rea—"

"It's Gail," she says. "I'm hoping this is the beginning of a long working relationship."

"Thank you, Gail," I repeat. "I will absolutely do the video interview tonight."

She claps her hands excitedly. "I just know this is all going to work out. You're exactly what we're looking for. Now, I'll let you get back to your students, and I'll come find you once everyone begins leaving."

Before I can respond, she turns and walks away, leaving me speechless. I quickly glance through the listings she's brought with her and stop when one house in particular catches my eye. According to the document, it was put on the market merely a day ago, and if the big, bolded sentence at the beginning of the description is any indication, it might be the perfect fit.

GREAT LOCATION IN A QUIET NEIGHBORHOOD. NEIGHBORS DESCRIBED AS A DREAM!

Maybe, just maybe, my life is going in the direction I always imagined it would.

And the added bonus... a pool!

Chapter 2

Winter Travers

Flynn

"Dammit," I growl, glaring at the cars lined up on the street blocking access to not only my driveway but several of my neighbors' as well. The house for sale beside mine is having an open house today, and people have been in and out since it started this morning. It seems like it is finally starting to thin out some, but none of them show anyone any damn respect with where they park their vehicles.

If this were Dublin, I'd shoot their fucking tires out, but I'm not in Ireland anymore. Instead of being part of one of the biggest crime families in the city, I'm in Boston, where I own a security firm called Clover Security. Which means I can't just go around shooting things up. Not in public, anyway. I'm on the other side of the law now. The one that serves and protects the innocent. I frown. That isn't fully true. Some of the people we protect deserve a bullet between the eyes more than us keeping them safe, but money is money.

"That's another dollar for the swear jar, Da. That makes three today."

I glance over at Taryn and raise an eyebrow. She just gives me that sweet, sassy grin that's an exact replica of her mam's. I bite back another curse as the doorbell rings for what has to be the tenth time in the past two hours. Since when did the possibility of buying a house mean you introduced yourself to everyone on the block to make sure it was a good 'fit' first? The crazy realtor, Cindy something or other, from next door's words, not mine. Right before the mob of people began to show up, she so helpfully came by to let me know people may be stopping over periodically for a meet-and-greet.

A fucking meet-and-greet. At *my* house.

My house isn't the one for sale, and I shouldn't have to meet every possible purchaser for the one that is being sold. It's ridiculous and is starting to piss me off.

The doorbell rings again, and I'm honestly contemplating not answering when Taryn yells, "Da, are you going to get that?"

I rub a hand over my face in frustration and stalk over to the front door. Yanking it open, I freeze as I stare down into a pair of the most beautiful, clear-blue eyes I've ever seen, which widen with a look of surprise when they meet mine. Thick, raven-black curls frame a small, pixie face. There's the cutest little nose with a light dusting of freckles across the top and plump, pink lips that are opened slightly on a gasp.

I blink as I take in the puffy, pale blue coat she's wearing that's unzipped so I can see a bright yellow T-shirt covered by a pair of... what did they call them in America? Not dungarees. *Overalls.* Overalls that have several different colored butterflies from the knees down. There are dark brown boots on her tiny feet. She's small but curvy, and the top of her head meets the middle of my chest.

"Da, who is it?" Taryn comes to stand beside me, and I briefly glance down to find her cocking her head to the side while she studies the woman.

The visitor is now staring at us both with a tentative smile on her pretty lips. Her tongue peeks out, wetting the bottom one, and I have to stifle the groan that wants to break free at the sight. *Fuck.* That should not look as sexy as it does, especially because I am positive she has no idea what she's doing to me right now. It's been a long time since I've reacted to a woman this way.

"Hi! I'm Sutton Matthews, and hopefully, I get to be your new neighbor. I put an offer in on the house next door, so now I'm waiting to see if the sellers accept it. I thought I'd come over and introduce myself in the meantime."

I let my gaze wander over her again, more slowly this time, as I rest a hand on my daughter's shoulder. She looks so young. In her early twenties, I would guess. I'm struggling to figure out how she is going to afford to buy a house on her own, not that it's any of my business.

"I'm Taryn O'Reilly, and this is my da, Flynn."

I stiffen as I look down at Taryn and give her a slight shake of my head. She knows better than to jump into introductions this way. We have to be cautious around new people. We have no choice, especially with our accents giving us away so easily. Not that our names won't come out sooner or later if Sutton does buy the house next door, but for now, first names would have been more than enough.

Taryn bites her lip as she gives me a worried, guilty look, but I just squeeze her shoulder gently. There's nothing we can do about it now, but we will be having a talk after Sutton with the sunny personality leaves. There are rules that have to be followed for a reason.

"It's so nice to meet you!"

"Um, you have something on your shirt," Taryn says, reaching out to lightly touch what looks like a pink stain on the collar. That's when I notice that Sutton isn't much taller than my daughter.

Sutton laughs, her cheeks turning a becoming shade of light pink that matches the stain almost perfectly. "I have to admit, most of my clothes are like this. I'm an artist, and I can't seem to keep anything I own stain-free."

Taryn smiles shyly, something I don't tend to see with her. She's normally outgoing and a little feisty, which seems to get her in trouble more often than not. "I like art."

Sutton's eyes light up even more, if possible. "That's great! What's your favorite thing? Painting? Pottery? Drawing? Crafting?"

"Drawing and painting. I've never done pottery before."

Just when Sutton goes to reply, the realtor calls to her from next door. With a wide smile, Sutton says goodbye and then makes her way back over to the other house, turning to wave before going inside. Meanwhile, I am just now realizing we had an entire conversation with the woman where I didn't open my mouth once.

"I hope she buys the house. She's nice. I bet she'd let me swim in her pool."

I sigh, shaking my head. There's no doubt in my mind the woman would let Taryn come over to swim. The question is, will I allow it? There is something about her that makes me want to run in the opposite direction. Part of it is her youth and innocence that I could spot a mile away. The biggest thing, though, is how hard she made my cock in the short five-minute timespan she was standing at my front door. It's been a long time since I've gotten so hard so fast, and I couldn't do a damn thing about it.

It wasn't like I could push her to her knees, take out my cock, and slide it in her mouth so I could see those pretty, plump lips stretch around its girth. No, I couldn't. However, I sure as hell *wanted* to.

Slamming the door shut, I lock it and tell Taryn to get her coat, which is on a hook by the door to the garage. There's an opening in the front of my driveway, finally, and I am taking full advantage of it. There are things I need to do today, and it doesn't include thinking about a pretty pixie with bright blue eyes and a smile that took my breath away.

Sutton

"They accepted your offer! The sellers declined the last two that I sent them because they were low-balled, but you offered the listing price, and they jumped on it. Isn't that exciting?"

Exciting and terrifying.

I can't believe I'm really doing this. I'm moving all the way to Boston. To a place where I don't know anyone, for a job I found out about a few days ago. I'm leaving the position at the high school I've been at since I graduated college, one where I know I have job security, and am stepping into the unknown. I'm nervous, but there was never any other outcome once I met Gail Stanley. Things moved quickly from the first night, and I found myself signing a contract with her fancy private school soon after all of the interviews were completed.

And now, here I am, getting ready to make one of the biggest purchases of my life.

"It's great that the house is vacant, so you can close pretty much anytime. We can do the home inspection within the next couple of days, and as long as everything is to your satisfaction, close on the day you've requested. Since you're paying cash, there won't be any holdups with waiting the usual thirty days for a lender to get everything ready on their end. We'll get your contract signed, and you in your new home before you start your new job, so the move won't be too stressful."

The real estate agent keeps talking, but I'm no longer listening. Instead, I'm thinking about the reason I can pay cash for this beautiful home I'm purchasing in the first place. The death of my grandmother, the loving, free-spirited woman who raised me since I was three years old, has hit me hard. Cancer is utterly evil and stole away the only person who ever cared about me right after I graduated from high school. I have no other relatives on my grandmother's side, and since my mother is deceased as well, all of my gram's savings and life insurance money have been left to me. The only things I've used some of it for were her burial and a small portion for college that my scholarships didn't cover. The rest I have saved, which is going to help me substantially now.

"I can ask for early occupancy if you would like?"

The realtor's question brings me back to the present, and I shake my head with a smile. "I need to go back to Providence to pack my things and finish out the week at the school where I teach. I'll be here next Friday to sign any additional paperwork we can't email and scan so I can move in that day."

"Sounds wonderful! I'm glad you came today, Sutton. Soon, you will be in your new home."

Glancing around, I take in the gorgeous, wide-open living room with the picture window and wonder why I seem to think I need a three-bedroom, two-bathroom house with a two-car garage and a huge sunroom off the back corner. Not only is it big, but it costs over twice as much as my yearly salary at the public school. Walking through the living room to the kitchen, I stride over to the sliding glass doors that lead out into the backyard, and a slow smile crosses my lips.

Right there is one of the best reasons I can come up with, I think to myself as I stare at the large inground pool taking up a big portion of the backyard. It's currently covered with a dark, custom-fitted pool cover that automatically retracts at the touch of a button, but even covered, it still calls to me. My two favorite things in the world are art and water. The only thing better than having a pool at my new house would be moving near a beach.

"Did you want to take another look around before we go?"

I turn, glancing at the realtor, a small smile resting on my lips. "No, I'm good. I was just thinking about how I can't wait for it to warm up so I can try out my new pool."

"Oh, yes! You should have a housewarming party."

A housewarming party? I have no family. No friends in Boston. Well, to be fair, I don't really have friends in Providence either. More like co-workers and acquaintances who I don't even grab a bite to eat with after work. Not only that, but it's cold as balls out right now. It's not like I'm going to be able to take advantage of the pool anytime soon. But I love the mere thought of having it.

I don't explain any of that to Cindy McPherson, realtor extraordinaire, though. She doesn't care about who may or may not visit me. Once the sale is final and she gets paid, she'll be on to her next house sale, and I will be nothing but a distant memory.

"Thank you for everything, Cindy. I'll see you next week."

As I walk outside, I can't keep my gaze from going to the house next door. Flynn and Taryn O'Reilly intrigue me. Taryn seems to be around ten or eleven years old, with pretty emerald green eyes and auburn-colored hair. She has the cutest accent to her musical-sounding voice too. *Definitely Irish.*

And Flynn O'Reilly, with his golden-brown eyes, held me captive from the moment he opened the door. I could tell he wasn't exactly thrilled to see me. He didn't smile once when I was there or talk to me. Not one word. Come to think of it, he wore a scowl on his face the entire time.

I grin as I walk to my vehicle, feeling a bit mischievous. Mr. O'Reilly obviously isn't going to go out of his way to be friendly. He doesn't seem to want much to do with me. Unfortunately for him, I've already decided he doesn't get a choice.

Challenge accepted.

Chapter 3

Dawn Sullivan

Flynn

THE 'FOR SALE' SIGN next door was removed two weeks ago. And when the sign was removed, so went my peace. I'll never admit to how many times I catch myself looking out the window or checking the footage on our security cameras—that happen to be pointed at the neighbor's house. I'm toeing the line of *stalking*. I've convinced myself it's for my daughter's safety. After all, Taryn is expecting to swim in this woman's pool as soon as it gets warm. Not that I don't already have a thorough background check on Miss Sutton Matthews. Again, she's going to be living next door, as well as being Taryn's new art teacher. Safety. This is all about the safety of my daughter.

This woman isn't good for me.

She's too young and *sweet*.

I've observed how she waves and smiles at fucking everyone. From our neighbors to the school drop-off line. She's barely moved in and already carved a place in the neighborhood and school. Taryn is beside herself that Miss Matthews is her neighbor and already her favorite teacher. It certainly didn't take long to replace Mrs. Snopes. The good news is Taryn now *loves* living here. All because of Miss Matthews.

I'd be grateful to the woman if I wasn't so pissed at myself for the thoughts I keep conjuring up when *I* see Miss Matthews. I feel like such a fucking pervert. This woman is forbidden. One, she's too young. Two, Taryn adores her. And... seeing as I haven't been in the mental capacity to have or want a relationship, I only want to fuck Miss Matthews. Then, she'd *hate* me. Probably distance herself from Taryn, and that would destroy my daughter.

I'm going to have to do my best to ignore the beautiful woman with the shining personality living next door. Which is going to be harder to do than expected since she's fucking singing outside my window.

"What is she doing?" I mumble to myself as I peek through the blinds. It's freezing outside, yet Miss Matthews has taken it upon herself to remove her shutters. *Doolally.* A little voice is telling me I should offer to go help her. Any decent man would. But I'm not a good man. Seeing her struggling outside my window already has my cock hard. Come to think of it, it's been a while since I've had a good lay. I don't have time for a woman. I'd certainly never mess with one so close to my home.

Suddenly, I hear Taryn's giggling. I watch in horror as she goes skipping toward Miss Matthews. Thankfully, she's bundled up, but she's forgotten her earmuffs. Cursing, I push myself from the window sill to chase after her and bring her inside before she catches her death.

As I round the house, my heart becomes lodged in my throat as I hear Taryn's sweet voice harmonizing with Miss Matthews. She used to sing with her mother. It's been a while since I've heard her like this. It both makes me grateful and angry. What if this woman leaves? My daughter is getting too attached, too fast, to this strange woman.

"Taryn. It's freezing. Please get inside, *a stóirín*," I tell her as I place the earmuffs on her.

"Daddy! I'm helping. It's cold for Miss Matthews, too. But if we help, she'll get done faster."

Miss Matthews' nose has already turned an adorable pink. She smiles brightly. "That's okay! You've already made this job more fun, which is the biggest help.

Go ahead on in." With a wink, she turns her attention from Taryn to me. "That was beautiful. What did you say? If you don't mind me asking, of course."

I do mind. However, before I can tell her that and lift Taryn up to carry her back to the house, my daughter speaks. "He calls me his little treasure. It's Irish."

"Gaelic," I sigh. "It can mean treasure or probably more like what you Americans would use for 'my little darling.'"

Her eyes widen. I realize she's never heard me speak, and certainly never to her. Taryn tugs on my hand. "Help her, Daddy."

"Oh, that's not necessary," Miss Matthews tells me.

"Please," Taryn insists.

I need my daughter to go inside and out of this bloody cold wind. Looks like the only way it's going to happen is if this maddening woman goes inside with her. I hold my hand out for the hammer. "You two go inside. I'll remove the shutters and place them in your garage."

"Really, that's not—"

Her mouth closes when I take a step toward her, invading her personal space. In a low voice, I growl, "Taryn needs to get out of the cold. She's only going to do that if *you* get out of the cold. So, you're going to stop wasting my precious time by handing over the hammer and allow me to take down these blasted shutters."

"Excuse me." Her eyes blaze with anger. Damn it, if that doesn't stir something inside of me. "I don't recall asking for your help, you overbearing leprechaun."

"Like I haven't heard that word thrown at me before. Tell me, do you Americans know anything else about Ireland besides magical little men?"

"Angry, little men. Looks like that stereotype checks out."

A dark chuckle escapes me as I lean down to whisper in her ear. "Angry, yes. Nothing about me is little. Now, get inside before I decide to stop playing nice."

"This is you playing nice?"

"Yeah. If I have to ask you again, I'll throw you over my shoulder."

"You wouldn't."

I lean forward, ready to pick her up, but she helps and jumps back.

"Here. Oh, my gosh." She hands me the hammer. "Taryn, sweetheart, what do you say to some hot chocolate?"

"That's a good girl," I mumble to myself, but the snarl Miss Matthews gives me lets me know she's heard me too.

It takes me about an hour to get all the shutters off. As I'm removing the last one, I notice through the closest window that Taryn and Miss Matthews are laughing together while crafting at a table covered in pink and red glitter and construction paper. Of course. It's February, and Valentine's Day is approaching. I need to get something special for Taryn.

I wonder if Miss Matthews has a date? I'm only concerned she would bring some creep into our neighborhood. Surely a woman as young and beautiful as her won't be alone on the most romantic holiday of the year.

I rip the shutter off with more force than necessary, then go to work carrying them all to the garage. Inside, it seems as though Bob Ross and Tinkerbell have had a rager in here. Canvas, easels, paints, glitters, paint supplies, fabrics—it's all here as it appears the woman has her own damn craft store.

The door leading to the house opens, and Taryn rushes toward me with a folded paper covered in glitter and lace. "I made you a card! And so did Miss Matthews!"

What? She gives me a shy smile, and I can't decide if I enjoy her blushing or smirking more. I wonder which one she'd do if she were on her knees.

"I wanted to say thank you." She offers over the handmade card.

When was the last time a woman made me a card? Before accepting it, I stare at her angelic face, making sure to keep my tone cold. "You could've just said 'thank you.'"

"I know." She arches a brow as if daring me to actually accept the card.

I snatch it and order Taryn to tell her goodbye. It's not until we reach our house and I send Taryn to take a warm shower that I finally pause long enough to look at the card. It's red, with a pink glittery four-leaf clover made out of hearts. I open it and read what she's written in lovely penmanship. Everything about her is so feminine.

"You're worth your weight in gold. Irish to show you how much I appreciate your help. Let me know if you're ever in need of a little luck."

Did she just offer to fuck me?

Luck... Fuck...

Does she mean if I'm ever in need of a little fuck, since I told her nothing about me was little? I'm baffled. Is she insulting me or coming on to me? The woman is maddening. She has no clue who she's toying with. The sweet, innocent little thing next door has probably never encountered a man like me—one who could devour her. I'd have her on her hands and knees before me, with her ass up in the air with my handprint marking her. The image sends a jolt of lust down my spine and straight to my dick. Dragging my palm down my face, I pace like a caged animal around the room. My attention is drawn back to the security camera feed on my screen aimed at the house next door.

Taryn comes into the room, freshly dressed and in her pajamas. I quickly close out of the browser window before she can see my screen. "I think I'm starting to like it here. I'm sorry I was so mad before."

"Don't apologize. It's a big adjustment." I take her in my arms and hold her close. I'll always protect her. She'll always come first. Which is why no matter how much I want to fuck her hot new teacher—who happens to be my neighbor—I will not. I need to settle this between us. Whatever game she's playing, it ends.

"Taryn, I need to walk next door to ask Miss Matthews when she plans on putting the shutters back up."

"Really?" The way her little face lights up has my heart breaking. Why does she suddenly care so much for this woman? And why does she seem shocked I'd help anyone? To be fair, I never socialize with our neighbors. It's safer.

"Yes."

"Okay! I'll go finish getting ready for bed and read. Don't worry about me!" She's far too eager for me to visit the woman next door—which makes me suspicious. But my desire to clear the air about the card wins the battle, so I leave.

Two knocks and a ring of the doorbell before the door flies open. Miss Matthews stands before me in a pink, silky button-up top and the tiniest silk pink... are those shorts or underwear?

"What the fuck are you wearing?" I growl.

Her grin stretches across her delicate face. "Well, hello to you too, neighbor."

"What did you mean with that ridiculous card? If I'm ever in need of a little *luck?*" I arch my brows and make a point of looking her up and down. I pretend as though the idea repulses me. Biggest lie I've ever told, and I was in the mafia. Every time my eyes meet hers, even for the briefest moment, it sends shivers over my skin. From the way her nipples are pebbling through her top, I'd bet she feels the same way. She's so close. I could easily have her at my mercy. It's been a long time since I've felt this wild rush of desire. However, I need to crush this. I'm a father, and my daughter comes first. Her needs before my own.

"Ew. Listen, grandpa—"

"Grandpa? Excuse me?" This *doolally* seriously gets off on irritating me.

"Oh, I'm sorry. Are you hard of hearing in your old age?"

"I'm not that old. But—" I raise a finger as soon as her pretty little mouth opens. "I'm glad we're in agreement that I'm too *mature* for you."

Her teeth sink into her bottom lip as she shakes her head. "I meant that I was lucky to have you come help me. And I'm happy to return the favor. Not a sexual favor, you dirty old man."

Her look is knowing. *Shit.* She caught me staring at her body. "The only favor I ask is that you don't hurt my daughter. If you're not staying, don't allow her to get attached. Be there for her at school."

"I'm not going anywhere," she tells me right before the door slams in my face.

Was that a threat or a promise?

SUTTON

Maybe I push my grouchy, psycho neighbor a bit too much. I can't help myself when it comes to pushing him. He's too easily riled, but he still hasn't completely lost control. The fact that he's a total asshole, yet he's also a complete teddy bear when it comes to his little girl. She is absolutely precious. I feel fortunate that not only do I get to have her as a student, but also an awesome neighbor.

The bell rings, and I dismiss my class, waving bye and telling everyone I'll see them tomorrow. It's recess, so I have twenty minutes before my next class arrives. I love it here. My classroom is beautiful and fun, full of bright colors and all the glitter. It's happening. My life is *finally* coming together.

A loud slamming door has me about to go into cardiac arrest. I look over to see Taryn's back pressed against my door as a river of tears stains her cheeks. Her sweater is tied around her waist, and my first thought is: Flynn is going to have a stroke, as it's still freezing outside.

"What's wrong?" I rush to her.

"Everyone saw."

"What? Did you trip and fall on your face? Been there. Did you run into a wall because who hasn't?"

She shakes her head. Her bottom lip trembles as she unties her sweater ever so slowly. Okay. She must've had an accident. This once happened to me at a friend's sleepover. Laughed so hard that I peed myself. We just have to laugh it off, and everything will be fine.

Or not.

Taryn isn't wet between her legs. She turns around, and then I see it. A red stain. "Taryn?" My voice is gentle. "Did you start your period?"

"I don't know." She sniffles. "I stood up, and a boy yelled out that my butt was bleeding. I ran to the bathroom and... I saw the red. My teacher came looking for me, but I ran away. Can I stay with you?"

I give her a single nod. "Do you have any family I can call? Other than your dad." That's an awkward conversation I don't want to have. He might blame me for Aunt Flo's arrival.

"No." She whimpers. "My mommy is gone. None of my family lives here; it's just me, daddy, and... you."

Me? Well, I'm alone here in Boston, too. If Taryn wants me, then I'm happy to be included. The bell is about to ring. There's only one thing to do.

I gather my things and take Taryn to the office to call Flynn. I tell him what's happened, and it's a miracle I don't snort into the phone when he asks if she needs to go to the doctor since it's her first one.

"But she's so young!" he had bellowed into the phone. I roll my eyes again, thinking about the conversation we had. She's not *that* young. There's not a set age for it to hit. I asked him if he'd be okay with me bringing her home so we can go get supplies. What I didn't tell him is we're also getting supplies to celebrate.

A few quick trips, and then Taryn and I are walking into my house. I hand her two bags full of shower items, lotions, sanitary pads, and a new pair of comfy jammies. "Go take a hot shower, and you'll instantly feel better. I'll put on my matching jammies and get our snacks ready."

I've barely pulled the cake out of the oven when Flynn comes storming into my house. "Where have you been? Why didn't you call as soon as you got here?"

"Oh, like you didn't see us pull in the driveway." I roll my eyes.

"Did you bake a cake?"

"Yeah! It's Taryn's first period cake!"

Flynn blinks two times before he turns and walks back out the door. I see where Taryn gets her dramatics for slamming doors from. While the cake cools, I begin preparing our veggie and fruit tray, popcorn, chocolate platter, and chips and dip. Taryn walks in and already seems in better spirits.

"Go pick out a movie. I'm going to show you the proper way to spend the day while on your period."

Her eyes widen in horror. "Am I going to have to go through this again?"

Oh, sweet girl. "You'll get used to it."

"No... I don't think I will."

"Probably not, but let's make the best of it." I take the cake and begin working on decorating it. Sure enough, Flynn enters the house again. At least this time he seems to have more control over himself.

"Hi," he grumbles.

My, my. He even looks sheepish. "I'm glad you came back. For Taryn. It's been a day."

"I know. I feel like such a failure. I never talked to her about this. I thought we had more time. And... I panicked."

"You're here now. Perfect, since I need an extra pair of strong hands." There are several dirty jokes running through my head, but I'll bite my tongue. This guy is already on edge. "Carry these into the living room to the coffee table."

He eyes the cake in horror. "Why are you using red icing?"

"It's a *period* cake."

Flynn's eyes squeeze tightly shut and then open again. Yup. The cake's still here. I go back to work and can feel his stare on me.

"You're really talented."

"Eh. I do all right. Drawing with icing isn't exactly my specialty. I mean, cake decorating is art, is it not? Don't sound so surprised."

"I'm not," he says, the words intimately close. The warmth radiating from his body is drawing me toward him. I want to lean against him.

"Daddy!"

Thank goodness Taryn appears. I was about to do something stupid like spin around and wrap my legs around him. Possibly find other uses for this icing.

"Oh, wow! Sutton!" Taryn claps in excitement at my finished product.

"Sutton?" Flynn snarls. "She's still your teacher. Show some respect and call her Miss Matthews."

I hate the way he says Miss Matthews. It causes heat to pool between my legs. Why won't he call me by my first name? Afraid it'll be too personal? I think back to his warning. He's terrified of Taryn forming an attachment to me and then me leaving.

I shake my head at Taryn. "We're besties. You only have to call me Miss Matthews at school." I turn to Flynn and whisper, "We're blood sisters."

His skin turns a lovely green hue with my words. Taryn grabs the bowl of popcorn and begins munching on some. Around a mouthful of popcorn, she asks, "Why does it say congratulations on womanhood?"

I smile at Flynn. "Wanna tell her, *Daddy?*"

His eyes flare with heat, but I'm not sure if it's anger or lust. Maybe both. He clears his throat twice before he finally speaks, and his voice still comes out hoarse. "This is a sign of maturity. Your body. Maturing."

That was both painful and adorable. Taryn's little eyebrows pinch together. "Huh. Okay... Can we eat it now?"

"Absolutely," I cheer. As Taryn takes the bowl of popcorn back to the living room, Flynn and I both hang back. I dip my finger into the icing and lick it off. "You, however, don't get to call me Sutton. It'll be Miss Matthews to you."

Flynn dips two large fingers into the icing and surprises me by bringing them to my lips. "Suck, Miss Matthews."

This motherfucker. My muscles liquify, and I'm too weak to deny him. I part my lips to allow him to slide his fingers between them.

"Good girl." He takes a step closer to me. "Thank you for all that you've done for my daughter. However, the warning still remains. You hurt her, and you'll learn who I really am. You won't like it." He pulls his fingers out and then places them in his mouth. Sucks. "So sweet." He utters it like a prayer. Next, he picks up some of the trays and carries them into the living room.

My panties are soaked.

Flynn is undeniably hot but seriously unhinged. This hot-and-cold routine is becoming annoying. I can't believe I allowed that psycho to stick his fingers inside my mouth. If Taryn wasn't here after having a traumatic day, I would kick him out. But she needs her dad. It's fine. I'm going to prove to Flynn that he isn't the mature adult here; I am.

I'm going to pretend like nothing happened. In fact, I'm going to pretend like he doesn't even exist.

Maybe I'm not that mature... Eh. Being mature is overrated.

Chapter 4

E.M. Shue

Flynn

"DAD! DON'T FORGET ABOUT my school conferences tonight!" Taryn yells as she bounces into the kitchen.

Sighing, I set down the box of pre-made frozen pancakes. The last thing I want to do is go to a parent-teacher conference. In fact, I think I would rather be shot and left in the dark streets of *Dublin*, waiting for my men to find me as I bleed out, than go to a parent-teacher conference. Especially one that Miss Matthews will be at.

Do you even need a parent-teacher conference for an art class?

I already know Taryn is talented. I don't need to sit through a meeting. That is a complete waste of time to hear something that I already know. As much as I love to hear praise about my daughter, I don't need it to come from Miss Matthews.

Last week was a mistake. I was thrown off by my daughter starting her cycle. I apparently was in denial about it happening so soon. Add in a curvy woman with fire in her clear-blue eyes, who has quickly become the bane of my existence, bringing over a fucking period cake into the mix, and I'm bound to be thrown off my game.

Any man would.

"How many days in a row am I going to have frozen pancakes for breakfast? My friend Kara, at school, says her mom makes her eggs every morning." She babbles on, oblivious to my annoyance at being reminded of tonight.

I'm happy she's making friends. Taryn is a fairly outgoing child, but you never truly know. I think there's always a small fear in the back of a parent's mind that their child will be alone. Especially after the major life changes she's been through recently. I couldn't be prouder to call her my daughter. She's taken every fucked-up thing life has thrown at us better than some of the men in the family. She's definitely an O'Reilly.

"I'm sure there's a recipe online. I'll look it up on my lunch." I try not to let her comments about my cooking get to me because I know she doesn't mean any harm, but that doesn't stop them from hitting a spot that I know her mother used to fill.

"For eggs?" she asks, her face scrunching up in confusion.

"For pancakes and eggs."

"I think you just crack an egg into the pan and mix some batter with water. It isn't rocket science, Daddy," Taryn says with a mouth full of pancake.

I should scold her for that smart remark, but I find myself smirking instead. Aisling's attitude shines through more and more the older Taryn gets.

"Finish your food, *a stóirín*. We're going to be late."

For once in my life, my day passes by too quickly for my liking. It might have something to do with dreading tonight. I need to create a boundary with Miss Matthews. Let her know nothing remotely physical or romantic can happen between us while also staying friendly enough so she lets Taryn use her pool in the summer.

I hate not having my head together. I strive on being composed; it's what got me where I am today. Not a lot rattles me, but Miss Matthews? She gets under my skin.

Here I am, driving to Taryn's school, quickly trying to think of what I'm going to say to her when I should have been doing it already all day. I wasn't expecting to get called into the field today, but it happens. As the owner of Clover Security, I attempt to delegate and only work on the more... threatening cases.

Sliding into the last available parking spot, I cut the engine and pull out my phone. I remember a schedule being sent of room numbers and times for each of Taryn's teachers when she started. The only positive thing about tonight is each slot is thirty minutes. If I can finesse it, I may be able to cut each meeting in half.

I can't help but roll my eyes as I scroll through the "We're so happy to have your child as a student." As if they're doing this out of the goodness of their hearts, and I'm not paying them a small fortune to educate my child.

"You have got to be fucking kidding me," I groan to myself, my head slamming back against the headrest.

Miss Matthews: Room 110 at six p.m.

Glancing at the time on my phone, I realize I barely have ten minutes to get my shit together and be in her room. It's okay. It'll be better this way. I can tell her what I need to say and not have to think about it throughout the rest of the night.

I find her room fairly easily, as it's not that far down from the entrance of the building. Rapping my knuckles against the doorframe, I step inside and stop dead. I thought the inside of her house was bad. But this?

Her classroom looks like Lisa Frank threw up a glitter bomb. The bright colors and glitter covering almost every inch of the room are nauseating. I can't even look at the same area for too long without little dots peppering my vision. I only know about this maddening Lisa person because my daughter insists on having all the bloody folders and notebooks from the store when we have to make a stop.

"Well, if it isn't the overbearing leprechaun," a silky voice sounds from the front of the room, making my molars grind. "Please, have a seat. And while you're at it, you can pick your jaw up off the floor. It's just an art room."

"This is not an art room. This set-up would give any right-minded person a headache," I grumble, glaring at the too-small chair, obviously meant for a child. "You can't be serious."

"It's the only chair available."

"The seat is purple glitter."

"Don't worry. There's a clear coat over the top, so it won't stain your fancy pants."

My scowl deepens as I grab the back of the chair and slide it out before taking a seat. It takes everything in me to not wince and lose my composure as the damn thing creaks so loudly that I'm surprised it doesn't break.

Sutton

I hate that all I can think about as I watch his large hands grab the back of the chair is what his fingers felt like in my mouth. How rough they felt against my tongue for the brief moments he let me have a taste. It makes me wonder how demanding they'd be in other places as well.

I need to remember that I'm the mature one here. He doesn't get to control the situation this time. I do. This is my classroom, my turf. From now on, the only way Flynn exists in my world is as Taryn's father and my neighbor. My grumpy, overbearing, and too attractive-for-his-own-good neighbor.

"Sutton—"

"Miss Matthews," I swiftly correct him. Did he forget?

Flynn inhales deeply, locking his golden-brown eyes swirling with heat on me. Or is it anger? I bet angry sex would be out of this world with him. All of his pent-up frustration he tries to keep a careful lock on comes to a boil and explodes as he flips up the abstract, flowy dress I have on, bends me over the desk, and fills me with his thick, hard cock.

That's what I'm manifesting.

I know the universe wouldn't give a man built like that something small.

"Miss Matthews, let's get this started. As you know, I have many other teachers to see tonight," Flynn cuts through the tense silence, breaking me from my thoughts.

Oh, so it's like that.

I refuse to let this man have the upper hand. Guess you just bought yourself a full thirty-minute meeting with a high possibility of it running long. I have nowhere to be, so I've got all night.

"Oh, absolutely, Mr. O'Reilly," I reply, adding a bit too much enthusiasm in my tone, even I want to cringe when I hear it. "I know these nights can be so long for parents, especially a single dad like yourself."

Mute Flynn is back in action, but I don't let the silence deter me. "Taryn has a fantastic eye for art. We've recently finished up our unit on painting. She's amazing at using different stroke styles, as well as brush sizes, to get her desired outcome. She's a natural."

I motion to the far wall, widening my arm like I'm a game show host to feature the area covered with paintings from the students. "For the final project, we did a little something I like to call *painting in the moment*. Basically, I show them one of my completed paintings and tell them how to do it *stroke by stroke*. Where the student places that *stroke* on the piece of paper is on them. That's why every piece looks slightly different but is still beautiful at the same time. It's all about the different *strokes*."

"Stop saying the word *stroke*," Flynn demands, his voice low and growly.

"I'm talking about a brush stroke, Mr. O'Reilly. Are you insinuating I mean otherwise?" My eyes are dancing as I know I have him right where I want him.

"Every time you say that *goddamn word*, all I can think about is bending you over that desk and fucking you so hard, every person in this school will hear you cry out my name. So, knock it off."

My breath catches in my throat as that deep, sexy voice of his skirts over my skin, leaving pebbles in its wake. The sexual tension that's brewing between us is almost too much to take.

"Would that be such a bad thing?"

"Yes." He looks torn at his admission, but it's enough to make me feel like he's poured a bucket of cold water on me. "We can cut the bullshit. We both know Taryn excels at art. I don't need to see a painting that makes me wonder if you took *MDMA or any other hallucinogenic substance* before assigning this project. What I've come here to talk about is boundaries. The incidents that happened just now and the other night can't happen again. It's a mistake to cross that line with you. I would appreciate it if we can be civil without you further antagonizing me."

It's a mistake to cross that line with you.

This man really knows how to drive the knife in. No one enjoys hearing they're a mistake. "Understood," I respond, but he's already halfway across the room. I'm not even sure if he's heard me.

The rest of the night drags.

I have to force myself to act happy and excited when showing off each student's final project to their parents. I've *never* had to force myself to be excited about art. And I hate that he's making me feel this way. I'll give myself the night to sulk, paired with a good cheesecake I made on a whim the other day. Mr. Hot and Cold can't keep me down for long. I'm determined to not let him win.

The parking lot is mostly cleared out by the time I finally leave the school. Tonight has drained me, to say the least. The only two cars left are mine and a shiny, expensive-looking blacked-out SUV. It puts my measly Honda Civic to shame, but it's not an uncommon occurrence with all the wealthy parents coming and going on the daily.

I throw my work bag in the backseat before climbing into the driver's seat. I'm beyond ready to get home, to the point I can practically taste the cheesecake in my mouth already. My mind races at the sound of my engine turning over, but not actually starting.

"Please, God. Of all days, do not let this be the day my car doesn't start," I whine aloud. Maybe if I lightly rub the steering wheel, it'll turn on. I try it.

Nope. Damn.

Delusion quickly takes over my thoughts as I sit here for another five minutes, continuously turning the key, thinking it will magically start. During my break of resting my wrist from holding the key, knocking on my window has me jumping and screaming with surprise.

"You've got to help her, Daddy!" I hear the sweet, familiar voice of a girl I'm growing to love say outside my car.

"I knocked on her window, didn't I?" The deep timbre from someone I would rather not see right now answers back.

Sighing, I open my car door to Flynn and Taryn.

"Taryn, get in the SUV," Flynn orders. We both watch as Taryn climbs in and shuts the door before Flynn turns his attention back to me. "Your car won't start?"

"No, I'm going to call a tow. You two enjoy your night; I appreciate you stopping," I respond and point my smile toward Taryn, wanting the frustrating man beside me to get my message and leave me the hell alone.

Flynn's expression is conflicted as he looks from my car to the black SUV. "Get in," he finally says.

"I'd rather wait for the tow truck."

"Have you called one yet?"

"No."

"Tow trucks have ridiculous wait times. The last thing I want to do is hang around in a school parking lot for hours until one decides to show up."

"That's funny. I don't remember asking you to wait with me."

This man has the audacity to seem annoyed with me as he claims, "I'm not letting a female wait by herself in the dark."

"Then I'll call a cab."

"Don't be stupid," Flynn growls.

My mouth drops open. "Did you just call me *stupid*?"

"Yeah, I did. Do you know why? Because it would be stupid to get into a cab alone at night. You're asking to get kidnapped and murdered. Now, I will not say it again. Get in the fucking SUV."

I shoot him my worst scowl as I grab my bag out of the backseat and make sure my Civic's locked up. I hate the fact he's right. I've watched enough true crime to know the statistics and further argue.

The ride to our neighborhood is brimming with tension to the point it's practically *smothering* me. If Taryn weren't in the car with us right now, I would have Flynn's cock out and in my mouth as he drives us home. The thought of him losing control and speeding his way through Boston as I take him deep in my throat has my panties *soaked*.

However, it's not like that, unfortunately. Mr. Hot and Cold doesn't seem as if he knows what to actually do with the heat between us, but for some reason, he keeps stepping in the damn kitchen. One of us is bound to get hurt if whatever this is continues on the path it's currently on.

Sighing softly, I sneak a quick glance over at Flynn. My eyebrows lower in confusion as I take in his fists, gripping the steering wheel tightly, and his eyes dancing between the road, rearview mirror, and the side mirrors.

"Is everything okay?" I whisper, trying to keep the tremor out of my voice so I don't alert Taryn.

"I don't know. The car behind us has been following us since we pulled out of the school parking lot. I'm sure it's nothing."

The edge in his voice doesn't do a very good job of convincing me it's nothing. Looking in my side mirror, I notice the headlights moving closer and closer. It's obvious they're driving faster than we are at the speed they're approaching.

"Flynn…" This time, I'm unable to stop the tremor in my voice. "Are they going to rear-end us? It doesn't look like they're slowing down."

"Hold on," he deftly orders before making a sharp right turn. The SUV's tires squeal on the blacktop as we straighten back out.

The car behind us follows suit.

"Daddy, what's going on?" Taryn asks, alarmed from the back. She's sitting up straighter, eyes wide. No doubt she heard the noise and is aware it's not normal, especially on a would-be relaxed ride home.

"We're taking a little detour, *love*. Stay buckled up."

The car approaches again, only slowing down with inches to spare between us and them. Flynn steps on the gas, slamming us back into our seats as he maneuvers his way through Boston. He's skillfully whipping down every back alley and side street in an effort to lose our tail.

"Sutton, breathe," Flynn murmurs as his hand comes to rest on my thigh. "I think I lost him."

I'm sucking in gulps of air I didn't realize I was depriving my body of while Flynn is also trying to soothe a crying Taryn. Neither of us utters a word as he pulls into his garage. The only sound that can be heard is Taryn's quiet sniffles. I gently squeeze her hand before grabbing my bag and getting out of the car. I look back when I've covered half of the distance between my house and Flynn's, seeing him watching me, wearing a hard expression.

Who is this man, and what in the hell have I gotten myself into?

Chapter 5

Andi Rhodes

Flynn

ONCE I GOT TARYN settled down and put to bed, I dragged the closest straight-back chair from my office and placed it dead center between the picture windows overlooking my front yard and my laptop. I have it open and connected to four monitors. I can easily flip through whatever I need to-to remain vigilant. They're currently glowing in the dark while I sit and stare out the window, Glock in hand. I have all areas of our property covered, so what I can't see in the darkness, the security cameras will catch with their night vision.

Every five minutes or so, I glance toward Miss Matthews' place to make sure whoever it was that'd been ballsy enough to follow us from the school's property hasn't decided to hit the easier target out of the two of us. She's a single woman without anyone watching over her, and for some goddamn reason, I've decided to pick up that task as if she is one of mine. I have no fucking idea if she has any type of security measures in place, but that's something I'll need to investigate since she was seen entering my SUV tonight by whoever happened to be watching us.

Every headlight that streams down our quiet residential road has me sitting up straight and pushing the curtains aside. I keep my firearm clasped firmly in my hand as paranoia has me momentarily strangled in a chokehold. It's hard to breathe through the rigidity of my suddenly too-dry esophagus when I know the type of people who may be gunning for us. Taryn is my number one priority. She's the reason I've left the family and Dublin in the first damn place. I don't want a life where I have to teach my daughter to look over her shoulder at all times.

After tragically losing Aisling, I've vowed my sweet girl will never know that type of fear a day in her life. Today's events could have taken my self-declared protection away from her. If anything had happened to her, I'd never forgive myself. Hell, I'd never be able to live with myself.

Whoever the piece of shit is that's scared my little girl is going to drown in his own blood once I slit his throat. You can take the man out of *The Faction*, but you can't take *The Faction* out of the man. I was raised with hardnosed criminals, ones whose fucks given were busted long before my da knew what his balls were used for.

A black-on-black sedan does a slow drive-by, and I inch closer to the window to see what details I can memorize at first glance. With my eyes on the vehicle, I shift my free hand to the laptop and use the camera facing the front driveway to zoom in on the nondescript vehicle. There's nothing particularly memorable about the car, other than you can't see inside of it. No scrapes or dents in the paint sticking out that'll make it easier to trace in the future. No decals, no license plates. All I manage to make out are two dark shadows of figures sitting in the front. The fact that there are no identifiable markings on it has the hair on the nape of my neck standing on end.

My finger shifts slightly, ready on the trigger, as I head toward the side door so I can sneak my way around the front of the house undetected. My nerves begin to fray, and I cringe as the floorboards beneath my feet echo throughout the quiet house.

Technically, I know nobody outside can hear the creaking of the hardwood flooring. However, that detail doesn't negate my fear that there's a listening device of some sort allowing them to hear me, nor does it keep my heart from palpitating to the point I'm afraid it's going to beat its way out of my chest. If we were back in Ireland, I'd be calmer, knowing I had my family and the rest of my brothers from *The Faction* to back me up.

Here, I have me.

Taryn is a light sleeper, but thankfully, her bedroom's upstairs and far away from any noises the house is making. Right now isn't the best time for my little hellion to open her eyes and investigate. Her curiosity is an instinct she gets from me; it's the *O'Reilly* ingrained in her DNA. The need for everything to be in its place and know there are no boogeymen waiting in the shadows. She's brave. Far braver than any little girl should be when her family has ties to the Irish Mob.

When her own grandfather sits at the top.

I shut down the *Da* part inside me that wants to bundle up my daughter and make a mad dash for parts unknown. Instead, I put his fear to rest and evoke the stone-cold killer residing inside of me, inviting him to come out and play. Once my mind is clear and my mob mask is securely in place, I hit the panel near the side entrance, quickly entering the code to keep my house alarm from alerting. It beeps, the signal letting me know it's disengaged. I open the door until it's slightly ajar, barely wide enough for me to slip through unnoticed.

Stealthily, I stick to the shadow of the house, crouching down as I go. I make it to the front corner, using the bushes lining the front side of my house as cover. The idling car is *still* there.

My gaze narrows, silently daring them to make a move and leave the safety of the vehicle. I need them to step out of the car before I can get an accurate assessment of the situation. Is this my past coming for a little payback, or is it something having to do with *Clover Security*? It's a toss-up because both could be just as dangerous and life-threatening as the other.

Who am I to judge another's lifestyle? My clients don't always rest on the right side of the law, some straddle that line. Most of them are shady motherfuckers.

I have a reputation in the industry—I don't fuck up on jobs, and neither does my crew. We're all trained with military-grade precision and accuracy. We do our homework and don't put ourselves in situations where we'll be caught if our job crosses man-made laws. This country is nothing like my homeland. In Ireland, we govern ourselves more or less. It's the eye-for-an-eye lifestyle during times like this that I miss. But it doesn't mean I won't execute anyone who's a threat.

I need to lure them onto my property first, which isn't really doable with Taryn nestled in her bed. If I can bait them and have them follow me inside, I can use the stand-your-ground law to my advantage. The act was put into place so homeowners can use deadly force in self-defense of their home and the protection of their family.

Fuck. If I can get them into my front yard, I'll drag them into my house. Once they're close enough to be considered a reliable threat, I'll shoot them between the eyes and neutralize my prey before they ever get a chance to become the predator.

I stare at the vehicle, taking in every detail I can find. Again, there's nothing standing out, nothing blaringly obvious to help me locate it later when Taryn and Miss Matthews are in a safe location. I'll have to go back through the video recording later and see if there's anything about it I haven't been able to make out. My eyesight is good, but even I can't see clearly through the veil of darkness. The neighbors around here seriously need to take their safety into consideration and use their fucking porch lights. I guess this is what happens when you live a cushy life; you never worry about someone storming your property, eager to bury you.

The person driving is no stranger to stakeouts. Whoever they are, he's skilled. I can say this with confidence, seeing as he's stopped and positioned himself between streetlights, so I can't make out much past it being a nondescript black car. Deciding I need to get closer, I start maneuvering myself to stand. I'll have to momentarily expose myself, unfortunately, so hopefully, they don't shoot my ass.

As I stand, the sound of the garage door opening next door steals my attention. It instantly has my protective nature roaring to life. An audible growl escapes my lips as I realize Miss Matthews is coming outside, wielding a baseball bat. The woman is positively maddening. She's lost her bloody mind.

"What the fuck!" I thunder, running in her direction. I swear, this beautiful, infuriating woman has a death wish.

"Who are you? What do you want?" she yells, peppering the questions one directly on top of the other. I'm both pissed and impressed she's twirling the bat around in her hand as she faces off with potential hit men.

She has no idea the people in the car may kill her. Why must I be attracted to a woman with a fiery personality, filled with enough stubbornness to make me want to spank her curvy *arse*?

The idling car shifts into gear and *revs* its engine.

Before the driver hightails it out of here, and I get the opportunity to stand in their way, the passenger's window lowers. My body wars between running for the vehicle or for Miss Matthews to shove her to safety. It momentarily glues me in place, and my brown eyes meet hazy blue ones in the open window.

Familiar ones.

The irises of my *enemy.*

A scream unlike any I've heard before releases. A howl of rage and sorrow all wrapped into one resonates from deep inside of me and echoes through the air. It's the same man suspected of putting a hit out on Aisling. A *dead* man I've been searching for. Or at least he will be when I get my hands wrapped around his throat.

Arturo Ferraro greets me with a twisted smirk—one I'd like to personally cut from his face. When he lifts up his hand and imitates a gun, pointing at my pajama-clad neighbor, I recognize that Sutton Matthews has now become my problem. Permanently.

As they speed off, I lift my Glock, firing a warning shot. I realize before the bullet releases from the chamber, it won't hit its mark. But this way, they'll know I'm armed and ready for battle. That I'm waiting and wishing, planning on them to be my next kill.

I've thrown down the gauntlet and challenged them now, which means I need to level-up and prepare for the bloodbath that'll be lining the streets. As the car's taillights disappear from view, I swivel around, giving Miss Matthews a 'what the hell' look.

"Do you know what you've done?" I rumble, knowing damn well she hasn't a clue.

"No. What?" she asks, placing her free hand on her hip and popping it to the side.

"You just invited the *devil* into your life," I warn, my tone low and menacing with the reality of my words. "You've laid down a dare to the type of men who'll do things to you that you're too naïve to even comprehend."

S<u>UTTON</u>

The joke I want to make about how naïve I am dies on my tongue when I notice the malevolent expression on Flynn's face. My throat is suddenly parched as my bravado takes a nosedive. When I saw that car sitting between our houses, I thought it was teenagers looking to do a mailbox drive-by or something. I never once imagined that coming outside to scare off a few punks would lead me to a moment like this.

I'm blaming it on exhaustion. I was overwhelmed by today's earlier events, and my mind isn't firing on all of its cylinders. For the moment, I wanted to feel in control of my life since being followed earlier and nearly rear-ended sent me spiraling.

"What... what did you mean when you said I invited the devil into my life, Flynn?"

"I mean, *Miss Matthews*, that you've fucked yourself. It's the price you pay when you do things as stupid as you've done. Do you even think before you act? You know what I believe? That you have a screw loose somewhere!" He ends his tirade in Gaelic, growing angrier with each word.

I'm not sure what his words mean in the end, but I gather it isn't anything flattering. Still, the tone he uses pisses me off. Squinting at him, I huff, hand firmly in place on my hip. "I don't know what you called me in your language, but stop. Use *English*, Flynn! That way, if you insult me, I can at least know to dish it right back at you." I'm fuming now; I've worked myself up. Whether or not it's due to him not translating or the fact I somehow unknowingly have 'invited the devil' into my life is yet to be determined.

He riles me up unlike anybody I've ever met. Usually, my panties are soaked when I hear his voice, especially when tinged with the Irish accent. Right now, though? I want to ball up my fist and slug him in the nose.

"*Bailigh Icat!* Fuck off with your bullshit, Sutton. You have no idea what your life is fixing to become. What I have to do to protect you."

"Well... *shit.*" I've wondered what my name would sound like rolling off his tongue. Now, however, I wish he didn't know what it was to scold me.

He is beyond mad; he's *furious*. Only I had no idea what I was walking out on. How was I supposed to know those were men, *apparently bad men*, and not some dumb teenage boys?

"Yeah, because that sums it up," he berates me, looking at me as if I'm a sullen child. I know the stare all too well, as I use it on my students when they think my class is an easy A and they don't have to participate.

"Stop growling at me, Flynn! I'm not a child; I made a mistake. I thought I was coming out to stop teenage boys from vandalizing our property. How was I to know those men were here with ill intentions far outside of the everyday spectrum? This is something you read about in books, not experience in real life."

"Do you want to stay alive?"

"What kind of idiotic question is that, *Mr. O'Reilly*? Of course, I want to stay alive!" I shout, my chest heaving from the exertion. Again, I'm asking myself what I've gotten into by accepting this teaching position and moving next door to *Mr. Mission Impossible*.

"Pack a bag, Miss Matthews. You're moving in with me," he commands, leaving no room for argument. I almost think he's joking until the stern, determined expression plastered on his face doesn't budge. He's serious.

"I'm doing what?" I ask, my voice loud and dumbfounded.

"You heard me," he counters, putting... wait a damn minute, is that a *gun* in his hand? Yeah, no thanks. I'm not going to stay with a thug. No way. No how.

"Nu-uh," I respond, shaking my head. "No, thank you."

"No, thank you?" he asks, raising his eyebrows until they damn near touch his hairline. I think I've surprised him. Twice in the matter of a short time is probably not working to my benefit with this one.

"Yep. No, thank you," I reiterate, repeating myself as politely as I can in all this mess.

His long, drawn-out sigh should be my first clue that I'm in trouble. As if I'm watching a movie play out in slow motion, he crouches down a bit and then tosses me over his shoulder in a fireman's rescue. The move is so effortless, it leaves me sputtering in shock.

The audacity of this man!

"Put me down," I yell, dropping my bat in the process and switching to pound on his back in protest. "This is kidnapping, Flynn!"

"No. This is me protecting you, since you have no self-preservation. I will not allow another woman my daughter has grown to love be murdered."

Murdered?

The horrific word has me losing steam, my body surrendering to lay on his shoulder. All the fight and anger dissolve as I attempt to process what he's just shared.

His daughter loves me.

And the last she loved... *died.*

Chapter 6

Gail Haris

Flynn

THIS WOMAN WAS GOING to be the death of me.

Sutton's reckless determination to throw herself headfirst into danger had my patience fraying at the edges. Sure, she had thought it was a bunch of teenagers bashing mailboxes, but even then, she shouldn't have come barreling out of her house like she had.

If I didn't spell it out for her—in excruciating detail—what exactly she was messing with, she'd get herself *killed*. And I wasn't about to let that happen.

"Put me down, Flynn," she whispers, her voice soft but carrying that stubborn edge I've come to expect.

"Yeah, I will," I grunt, shifting her weight slightly to get a better hold, "once we're inside."

Arturo might have driven off, but that didn't mean we were safe. As long as Arturo was out there and drew breath, the threat lingered like a shadow. She needed to understand that. I'd drag her kicking and screaming into safety if I had to—and tonight, it looked like that's exactly what I was doing.

"I can't think like this," she protests, squirming in my arms.

"Then don't think," I shoot back. "Just do what I say."

The front door looms ahead, and I adjust her again to punch in the security code. The lock clicks open, and I push the door wide, stepping inside. The beep of the locks engaging behind us is a small comfort, but I know I need to stay on edge.

"Do you think you can put me down now?" she asks, clearly frustrated and irritated.

I set her on her feet but don't let go. "Be quiet," I warn. "Taryn is sleeping, and I don't want to wake her. She's already been through too much tonight."

For once, Sutton doesn't argue. She smooths her hair quickly, biting back whatever sharp comment I can see dancing behind her eyes. "You have a lot of explaining to do, Flynn," she says instead, her voice low but insistent. "Starting with the last woman Taryn loved being murdered. Her mother?"

I run my fingers through my hair and exhale sharply. "I need a drink if we're going to get into that."

Sutton's gaze sweeps the room, taking in my home. "Well, pour a drink and start talking," she says.

I'm not going to let her out of my sight.

I gently take her by the arm and steer her away from the front door. We move down the hall to my office. I grab a bottle of Bushmills whiskey and two frosted glasses from the shelf, then lead her back to the makeshift surveillance setup I have in the living room. The monitors display camera feeds from outside and inside the house. Each screen is a reminder of how precarious my situation has become.

Sutton's gasp draws my attention as she moves closer to the monitors. "Whoa," she breathes, her hand hovering at the monitors. "What is all this?"

I set the glasses on the coffee table and pour whiskey into both. "This," I say, gesturing to the monitors, "is my life. Welcome to it. You just put yourself directly in the middle of it."

She peers closer, and her expression shifts from curiosity to concern. "Does this have to do with the car that chased us tonight? And that creep who was just outside?"

I nod, grab the glasses, and hand one to her. "It has everything to do with it."

She takes a tentative sniff of the whiskey, her nose wrinkling immediately. "Whoa, boy, that is strong."

Without hesitation, I throw back my drink and pour another. The whiskey burns on the way down, but I welcome it. "Drink it," I tell her. "It'll take the edge off."

Her first sip is hesitant, and she gags almost instantly. A cringe crosses her lips, and she sets the glass on the coffee table. She moves to the couch with a disgusted scowl on her lips as she plops down. "I like my alcohol to not instantly grow hair on my chest, thank you very much," she mutters.

A small, humorless laugh escapes me. "Irish whiskey is something you need to get used to." I move to the couch and sit beside her with a sigh.

"Uh, I will just take your word on that." She turns on the couch and shifts so she's facing me. She tucks her legs under her and stares at me. "Are you going to do a story time, or will I have to drag it out of you?"

I run a hand through my hair and wonder what and where to start. "I can tell you the things you need to know, Sutton. You're already in danger. I don't need to stamp your death certificate by telling you things you don't need to know."

Her lips press into a thin line, and then she whispers, "Ominous." Her eyes lock on mine like she's trying to read the secrets I've buried.

I reach out and brush a finger down her cheek. The softness of her skin under my touch sends a shiver through me. "You're so innocent, *bòidheach*," I murmur, the word slipping from my lips before I can stop it.

Her eyes soften as she leans ever so slightly into my hand. "What does that mean?" she asks.

"Beautiful," I whisper. I would have to be blind not to notice Sutton's beauty. It's not just her face or smile—it's in the way she moves, the fire in her eyes, and the way she challenges me.

She blinks, and her mouth parts slightly. "You're going to give me whiplash," she admits after a moment. The corners of her mouth twitch up in a faint smile.

I pull back an inch and am slightly confused. "Huh?"

"You're hot. You're cold. You're hot again," she answers teasingly but with an edge of annoyance. "You just carted me across the front lawn, pissed off because I came outside, and now you call me beautiful."

I reach out again, this time cupping her chin in my hand. Her skin is warm against my palm as I tilt her face up so she has no choice but to look at me. "Because you frustrate me," I admit, my voice low and rough. "And then, I want to kiss you until neither of us can see straight."

Her breath catches, and she stares at me wide-eyed. "Oh," she gasps, the word barely audible.

"Oh, is right, *bòidheach*," I murmur, my thumb brushing lightly along her jaw. "Right now, we should be talking about how your life is in danger, and instead, all I want to know is what your lips taste like." The words leave my mouth before I can stop them.

Her cheeks flush with my admission, and she surprises me with a breathless laugh. "Can't we do both?" she questions quietly, as if she hadn't meant to say it aloud.

Something snaps inside me. In one smooth motion, I grab her by the waist and pull her into my lap. Her knees press against the couch cushion as she straddles me, her hands instinctively bracing against my chest.

"We're going to talk like this?" she asks, and her voice edges with humor but tinges with something else.

Something that sends a rush of *heat* through me.

I shake my head slowly, my hands settling on her hips. "No talking right now." My voice is quieter now, rougher. "We can talk in the morning."

"Does this mean I'm staying the night?"

Sutton won't be leaving my sight until Arturo is in the ground. "This is the only place you'll be safe."

"Right here, in your lap?" she asks.

I nod and tug her closer. "Right here, with me, Sutton."

Her laughter bubbles up again. "You're running hot right now, aren't you?" she teases, her eyes sparkling as she does.

My fingers trail up her body until I reach her cheek, my thumb tracing the curve of her jaw. As I lean in close, I feel the warmth of her breath against my lips. "You have no idea, *bòidheach*," I murmur.

Her laughter dies away, replaced by something heavier, something *deeper*. Her hands slide up from my chest to my shoulders, her fingers curling into my hair. "Show me."

SUTTON

Flynn's lips are on mine before I can process what's happening.

All my thoughts scatter like leaves in a storm. One second, I'm teasing him; the next, my brain is mush from his touch.

The heat of his mouth.

The rough press of his hands.

The way he takes over every ounce of space around me.

It's almost too much.

I can't wrap my head around how we ended up here. It's like every time I'm with Flynn, I get sucked into this push and pull. One moment, I want to slap him for being so infuriating; the next, I'm desperate for his hands to be on me.

And right now?

Right now, his hands won.

His kiss is overwhelming and all-consuming. It's not soft or tentative—it's pure need, raw and demanding. His stubble scrapes against my skin, leaving a trail of delicious heat. My lips part instinctively, and he takes the invitation as his tongue slides against mine in a way that makes my breath catch.

His hands are everywhere. One grips my hip, holding me firmly against him. The other tangles in my hair, tilting my head back to deepen the kiss.

I can't think. All I can do is feel.

I gasp against his lips. His mouth moves to my jaw, then to the sensitive spot just below my ear. A shiver races down my spine, and I clutch at his shoulders, my nails digging into the hard muscle there. "Flynn," I whisper, unsure if it's a plea for him to stop or to *never* stop.

He groans against my skin, his voice like thick syrup, making me melt even more. "God, Sutton. You drive me crazy."

"Likewise," I breathe out. I try to catch my breath, but I can't because his hands slide under the hem of my shirt, his fingertips brushing against my bare skin.

It's absolutely maddening.

He's unraveling me.

My hips move on their own, grinding down against him, and the reaction I get makes my head spin. His breath hitches, his grip on my waist tightening like he's barely holding himself together. "Sutton," he warns, his voice strained.

I lean back just enough to look at him. His eyes are darker than I've ever seen, and they burn with an intensity that makes my stomach flip. "What?" I ask, though my voice leaves me softer than I intend.

"You're going to be the death of me," he admits, repeating himself from earlier. There's something about the way he says it, half-exasperated and half-adoring, that makes my heart squeeze.

I laugh, though it's breathy and uneven. "Right back at you."

His lips curve into a faint smile, but it disappears quickly as he draws me back to him. "We need to get you to bed."

My mind reels. Were we not just making out as if our lives depended on it? And now he's saying I need to go to bed?

"Uh, what?" I mumble; my voice barely audible.

"It's late, *bòidheach*. You and Taryn both have school in the morning."

I pull back again and blink at him. I mean, he's not wrong, but I can be a little tired tomorrow if we get to kiss a little longer. Before I can argue, he lifts me off his lap and stands.

"Let me show you where you'll be sleeping." His tone leaves no room for debate.

What on earth is going on? One minute, I'm wrapped around him like a second skin, and the next, he's acting like a responsible chaperone.

It's dizzying.

He grabs my hand and leads me up the stairs. We pass two closed doors on the right before stopping at an open one on the left. "Taryn is directly next door. I'm at the end of the hallway," he explains as he flips on the light.

I step inside, and he doesn't follow me. The room is nice—cozy even. A queen-sized bed with a pale-yellow blanket dominates the space. A white dresser and armoire line the far wall, and a light blue chair is in the corner by the window. It's simple but welcoming.

"I really don't need to stay the night," I say, turning back to him.

Flynn shakes his head, his expression firm. "Yes, you do. I know we didn't get into it, but you aren't safe anymore, Sutton. There are things happening that you don't understand."

"Then help me to understand," I press, frustration bubbling up.

Flynn shakes his head again, not willing to budge. "Tomorrow."

I thin my lips and cross my arms over my chest. "Do you want me to say okay and go to sleep like a good little girl?" If that's what he's expecting, he has another thing coming.

He steps toward me and raises a hand to cup my cheek. The gesture is so gentle and unexpected, it takes the fight right out of me. "For tonight, please," he says softly. "I promise you'll get your answers tomorrow."

I exhale a deep breath, the tension draining from my shoulders. "Fine." I'm not stupid. I can tell that whatever is going on is big.

Bad.

Serious.

I want answers to what it all is.

Flynn leans in, pressing a tender kiss to my lips. It's a stark contrast to the fire from earlier. "I'll see you in the morning, *bòidheach*."

"Good night," I whisper.

He steps back, heading toward the door. He turns toward the stairs instead of his room.

"Aren't you sleeping?" I call softly, leaning against the doorframe.

Flynn doesn't turn around, but his voice drifts back to me. "Don't worry about me, Sutton. Get some sleep. You're safe."

I listen to his footsteps pad down the stairs and fade away, then lean my head against the doorframe with a huff.

Hot, then cold.

That's Flynn.

It's hard to know which version I'm going to get.

The protective yet distant Flynn, or the man who makes my pulse race with a single glance.

I shake my head to myself and step back into the room, pushing the door closed behind me. Finally, I inhale a deep breath and flip off the light, then sit on the edge of the bed, running a hand through my hair. I replay the evening in my mind and realize there are so many unanswered questions.

With a heavy sigh, I lie back against the plush pillows and pull the yellow blanket over me.

Today was unexpected, and something tells me things are only going to get *crazier*.

Chapter 7

Sapphire Knight

Flynn

IT'S A BIT MADDENING having her here. In my house. So fucking close to my bedroom. It took everything in me to put her sexy little *arse* to bed rather than fuck her in front of my cameras. What kind of a man would it make me if I allowed myself to sink my cock inside her tight little cunt after being thrust back into the middle of danger?

"*Fecking shite,*" I murmur to myself, scrubbing my hand over my face. The stubbles there from the day make me feel more of a savage than the respectable man I've attempted to present myself as in this neighborhood. My eyes burn a touch from sleeping poorly last night, yet my adrenaline from the gorgeous lass and my enemies making their presence known has my head spinning. I couldn't possibly sleep right now, even if I were a godforsaken zombie. I have too much on my plate with what Arturo's untimely presence means to me and mine.

I take my seat again, pouring myself two more fingers worth of whiskey. It goes down smoothly, the amber liquid coating my tongue like warm velvet, inviting me to have another. I won't. I can't allow myself the distraction of floating away on a whiskey buzz when I have a feisty woman and my precious child to protect.

Christ, my sweet girl has been through far too much as it is. I got out of the life to help shield her from this mess, and yet here we are, facing down an enemy without the security of having *The Faction* at my back. I should reach out to my da, give him a heads-up about the trash showing up on the driveway and how I may be burying bodies in America after all.

Reaching for my phone, I pause, hesitating as the reality of what he'll say hits me. I know my da better than anyone else at times, and when it comes to business or our enemies, I could quote him word for word. Tonight, he'd huff down the line, not hesitating for a moment in telling me how it was a mistake to pack up and run from the family. He'd bolster, "The O'Reilly clan is strong. We're steadfast, my son. Just take a look in the mirror; the red in your cheeks won't lie. You belong here; you're Irish through and through. Now deal with whoever's coming for my blood, and don't leave them breathing. Ya hear?"

Releasing a sigh, I stuff my phone away in my pocket and hit the whiskey again. I need a little something to help soothe the burn of my da's unspoken words. Every word he'd say would be right, and I have no ground to stand on to argue over it. Flicking my gaze to the cameras, I peer into each screen, managing to spook myself when a possum goes scurrying across the lawn.

Maybe I should've filled Sutton's delectable cunt, it would've helped take the edge off. I have a feeling once I'm deep inside, stretching her to perfection, I wouldn't be able to stop. To get enough. Nah, when I finally take the beauty, it'll be when I have some time to lay her out good. Keep her thighs spread all bloody weekend, tasting and filling her until she's had so many orgasms she's afraid her head won't stop spinning.

The thought makes me chuckle to myself. It's not being cocky if there's weight behind it, and I remain true to my word. I'm going to drive myself crazy all night, unable to stop picturing her naked, writhing and whimpering with need underneath me as I hover my body over hers. Lord knows I couldn't allow her control in the bedroom; the ornery woman has enough sass and bite to her already. I've got to maintain some control between us, or she'd end up completely owning my *arse*.

My muscles are tight, the ache growing in my shoulders until the pressure is nearly suffocating from the stress of it all. I stretch my neck from side to side, then stand. Nothing's come along on the cameras since I've been keeping track, so I'll take a walk through the house to check on everyone, and it'll ease a bit of the tension coiling me up all over. Tugging my phone free again, I pull up the surveillance app I have on my cell and begin my patrol. A text comes through from Jack, one of the guys who works for me, letting me know he's off shift and headed home. Another successful security detail job completed. It'll look top-notch to my references, but it does me a whole helluva lot of no good with my own damn security issues at the moment.

How did Arturo find our location? Everything is registered to our aliases—the house, cars, business, Taryn's school. They think her name is Terry; no one knows her as Taryn aside from our neighbor. My rambunctious daughter beat me to introductions with Sutton before I could cover our tracks with her as well. I'd almost be suspicious of her if it weren't for her threatening Arturo, having no clue as to who he is, nor how truly dangerous and evil the *fecking* prick is. Then there's also the way she is with my girl, treating Taryn kindly, almost as if she were her own. It makes my bloody heart weep a bit for her mam being gone, missing out on everything.

After I check the windows throughout the house, I poke my head in Taryn's doorway. She's sleeping soundly, snuggled under her bedding, looking every bit my wee Irish princess she's always been. Hell, if Da had it his way, she'd be locked up on his property, spoiled, yet treated like one of Taryn's stories she's had me read her more than a dozen times.

I turn the lamp off on the far side of her bed, leaving the one closest to the bathroom on for her. Brushing a kiss on her forehead, I pause to watch her for a beat. Ever since her mam was murdered, I find myself watching her more and more, just taking in the moments I have with her. She's already insanely independent, and I know it won't be too long before she no longer considers herself my little girl anymore.

Stepping back into the hallway, I cast a glance towards my room but find myself drawn to where Sutton's sleeping. I'd love nothing more than to slide into bed beside her, rid her of her clothes, and make her scream my name. I've never wanted someone the way I do her; it's like my very being craves hers—to touch her, kiss her, smell her, and fight with her. She's a sight when she's fired up, ready to give me hell. One of these days, I'm going to shock her little *arse* by putting her over my knee and spanking her until she submits.

I clench a fist, thinking of how blissful it'd be to feel the pop of her skin under my palm. See what I mean? *Maddening.* I'm losing my damn mind with her in my house. It's too tempting having such easy access to her; she's a distraction I don't need right now, and the thought only serves to make me grouchier than I already am.

My feet carry me to her doorway, where I find myself twisting the knob to quietly let myself slip inside. It takes a beat for my senses to adjust in the room; it's dark, with no nightlights or small lamps on like we have in the rest of the house where my daughter may wander to in the middle of the night. There's only the pale stretch of moonlight from the opening in the curtains allowing me to take in my surroundings. My attention instantly falls on the woman whose presence seems to take up every inch of the room.

She whimpers in her sleep, the sound nearly shattering me in the process. Who hurt her enough to make her upset while she dreams? The last thing I want is her lost, spiraling away in a nightmare she can't escape from. Sutton could be being chased down by Arturo or something for all I know. I still for a moment, completely taken with her being so close while she's vulnerable and all mine for the taking. I can give her all of my attention without her coming at me, winding me up inside to the point I come off all growly, sounding like a dick because I forget how to *fecking* think around her. I reach for her, my hand lightly finding her shoulder to give it a shake.

Her eyes fly open, a gasp spilling from her lips when she finds me standing over her. "F-Flynn?" she mumbles, still sleep-hazed. "What happened?"

"You were dreaming. I heard you."

Her teeth sink into her lower lip, her gaze going a touch soft at my admission. "You were checking on me," she states, and there's no room for me to argue; it's the truth, after all.

"Aye," I whisper, wanting nothing more than to release her lip from her teeth so I can suck on it.

"You sounding all Irish only makes me wetter for you, Flynn."

The damn minx! Her words instantly have me growing hard, my cock a thick, heavy brick in my trousers as I flick my stare lower. Her nipples are pebbled beneath her shirt, her bra nowhere to be found.

"Touch me, my breasts are needy, and my pussy aches. I wasn't having a nightmare; I was dreaming of you finally coming inside of me."

"Holy fuck," I choke out, realizing I should've let her sleep, as dream Flynn obviously knew what he was doing and could've left a good impression for me. I only hesitate for a moment before I'm tossing the rest of her covers to the side, wrenching her legs my way and yanking her until her ass is on the edge of the bed. She jolts with surprise at my sudden movements but quickly catches on when I reach for the scrap of fabric too tiny to be actual panties and tug them off. I toss them behind me and drop to my knees, pushing her legs wide.

My stare locks on the juncture between her thighs, her sweet-smelling, perfect cunt. My hands land on her hips, locking them in place so I can take my fill of her. Leaning in, I press my nose to her sensitive flesh and inhale, knowing I need to eat this pussy. My tongue flicks out, running along the length of her slit, gathering up her sweetness as I go. She gasps at the sudden touch, her groin jerking involuntarily before she steadies herself, staring down at me with a mix of shock and desire in her eyes.

Her hands find mine, fingers wrapping around my wrists as her nails scrape against my skin while I continue to lick and suck at her delicate folds. She's trembling beneath me, her entire body responding to the sensations I'm causing, and it's one hell of a powerful feeling. Her taste is like nothing else, a pure honey making my mouth water for more. She moans softly, egging me on, and I respond in kind. My tongue finds her opening, spearing inside, wanting to get deeper, to make her feel me in her.

I'm so hard, my cock may break at this point. I need inside her, to fill her, and claim her. Jesus, I'm losing myself here; it's too easy to get wrapped up in her and allow the world around us to fade away. "Mm," I hum against her tenderness, making her cry out as my teeth nip at her sensitive bud. "I could eat this delicious cunt all night," I comment. My tongue teases, making her hips buck wildly against me. Her thighs start to squeeze harder and harder with each movement, pushing her closer to the edge.

I'm going to come in my pants.

Her wetness floods my mouth as her cries fill the air. It's the best damn thing I've heard all night, my name on her lips. Moaning and whimpering about how good it feels and begging me to not stop. A man could get used to hearing that sort of thing on the daily, and I'm smart enough to realize it's exactly what I don't need right now. Why does *shite* have to be so damn complicated?

She reaches for me as my phone chimes, and I instantly still. It alerts once again, then I'm on my feet, wiping my face and tossing the clothes at her she'd had on the floor. "Get dressed. *Now,*" I order, immediately pulling up surveillance. "Fuck!" I rush out as the house alarm begins to blare. The fire alarm lights I have throughout the house in each room begin strobing. "Now!" I repeat in a growl, yanking her ass from the bed and pointing at her clothing.

I rush to the wall, moving the picture to the side and key in the code to the small wall safe. I have one in each bedroom for this particular reason. It beeps and the lock releases, allowing me to open it and remove the guns inside. "Here," I hand the smaller Smith & Wesson to Sutton once she's dressed, indicating the safety on the side. "Flick the safety off, point at the largest part of the body, and empty more than one bullet in them."

"Holy shit, Flynn! What the fuck is going on? Who's here? Why did you give me this? I'm not shooting anyone."

"Get to my girl. Use the gun if anyone comes for you. You hear me?"

She's in shock, staring at me with her mouth open, not able to say a *fecking* thing in return. I grab her shoulders, giving them a shake, snapping her out of it. "W-who's here?"

"The bad guys, sweetheart. Now get your *arse* in there with Taryn and take her to the safe room. You stay in there and don't let anyone in. Make sure you get Taryn's phone so I can reach you."

"A safe room?" Her brows scrunch as she stares at me as if I've grown a second head. Lord help me, don't make me have to shake sense into this woman for real. I need her strong, especially if Taryn is going to have to lean on her while I handle this *shite*. The house alarm continues to blare, but then a few blasts of gunfire make their way into the mix. I read the panic on Sutton's face before she says anything.

"Her bookcase. Get my daughter, take her to the bookcase. Pull the left side toward you, and it will open. Go inside, there will be a door. You two go inside and be quiet. It's secure, and no one will ever find you there so long as you stay put. There will be a screen there with the security footage. Whatever you do, don't leave the room. Promise me, Sutton. I need to hear the words." I'm talking as fast as I can, pulling her with me down the hall to Taryn's room as I do.

"I-I p-promise. Get Taryn, find the safe room. Be quiet, stay put, grab her phone." She continues to repeat the words in a whisper to herself.

"Good," I praise and press a kiss to her forehead.

I remain in the hallway, watching as Sutton gets Taryn, quickly leading her to the bookcase. Once it's pulled open, I run down the hall.

Toward the gunfire.

Chapter 8

D. Vessa

Sutton

I DART BACK INTO the darkness of Taryn's bedroom, scanning the room as if it were a battlefield. The soft light from the nightstand illuminates the chaos, the remnants of a life that now feels precariously unsteady. My heart races, each beat pounding a primal rhythm that echoes through the silence, urging me to find that phone and return to safety.

As I reach the nightstand, my fingers tremble slightly when they brush against Taryn's phone. It's small and innocent-looking, but it feels like a lifeline in this moment. I snatch it up and turn, ready to rush back into the panic room when—

Beep!

Beep!

Beep!

The alarm still howls, a siren song warning me of danger. With every sound, my sense of urgency amplifies; time is slipping away like sand through my fingers. I glance out into the corridor—dark shadows flit by past the windows, and my pulse quickens at the thought of what lurks outside those walls.

"Flynn," I whisper under my breath, feeling his presence in every corner of this house. A strong protective instinct surges within me as I fight the urge to panic. He'd told me to stay with Taryn, but leaving him out there...

Pop! Pop! Pop!

More gunfire erupts from outside, sounding too close for comfort. I grip Taryn's phone tightly in one hand and take a deep breath before moving cautiously back toward the hidden door.

"Taryn," I whisper urgently as I slip inside the panic room once more. The dim lighting wraps around us like a protective cloak as I shut the door behind me, the heavy thud resonating against the steel frame. Taryn's blue eyes are wide, reflecting both fear and innocence, but she holds her bear tightly as if it could shield her from the chaos outside.

"Did you get it?" she asks, her voice barely a whisper.

I nod, my breath shaky. I squeeze the phone in my sweaty palm. "I have your phone, but we can't let anyone know we're here, okay?"

Taryn nods, her face pale but resolute, still clutching her stuffed bear. Her eyes dart around the tiny room that feels like both a sanctuary and a cage.

I hunker down beside her on the bed, whispering softly to maintain a sense of calmness that belies the chaos echoing outside. "We just need to stay quiet and wait for your dad."

"I want to see him!" she protests, her voice rising slightly in pitch.

"Shh! Sweetie, you can't. You heard the noise out there. He needs us to stay safe while he takes care of things." I brush some curls from her forehead, trying to soothe her with my presence.

I peer up at the monitors Flynn mentioned before. Monitors that Taryn hasn't noticed yet, thankfully. The flashes from the gunfire blur the images. I watch them like a lifeline, praying for a glimpse of Flynn.

The weight of the moment feels unbearable, as if we're suspended in this fragile bubble merely waiting for it to burst. I can hear every breath Taryn takes, quick and shallow, a mirror to my own racing heart. Outside, pandemonium reigns.

Taryn clutches her stuffed bear with white-knuckled determination—a stark contrast to her wide-eyed vulnerability. "Do you think Da's okay?" she asks quietly after what feels like an eternity lost in silence.

I don't know how to tell her that her father is facing a firing squad right now. She deserves the truth, but scaring her to death isn't going to make things any better. I swallow hard against the knot lodged deep within my throat and nod again, though uncertainty hangs heavy between us, a storm cloud ready to pour rain on everything we've worked so hard not to lose.

"I'm sure he is," I reassure myself more than Taryn, despite no real knowledge behind those words. I lean into our shared warmth among growing anxiety, allowing instinctive maternal energy to course through me as I adjust how I'm sitting beside her—the space is small enough she leans slightly toward me, seeking comfort without saying another word.

"I can't lose him, *too*," she whimpers, the words barely audible. Regardless of their pitch, they're still heartbreaking. This poor little girl has been through too much in her short life, and I vow in the moment to be one person who sticks around in her life no matter what. She will always have me to depend on, to lean on, and to care for her.

A distant crash reverberates somewhere beyond these walls, causing both of our hearts to flinch together—one body resonating with fear, yet unyielding resolve coursing beneath skin somewhere deeper where strength is born from love and necessity. My fingers weave through Taryn's locks, creating a barrier against the world outside, and I feel an unexpected surge of determination.

"No matter what happens," I whisper, "we're going to get through this *together*. You and me."

Taryn meets my gaze with an intensity that surprises me. "Promise?" she asks, her voice trembling but fierce, as if she's channeling her mother's spirit.

"Promise," I nod, sealing the vow between us with an ironclad resolve.

The echoes of gunfire flare up again, more intense now, and I instinctively reach for Taryn's phone, my heart racing as it buzzes in my palm—a lifeline and a warning all at once. I'm tempted to dial Flynn despite knowing the risk; every fiber of me needs to hear his voice, to know he's alright. Instinct, however, tells me to wait. To hold steady and let him do what he must.

The monitor flickers briefly, showing a glimpse of Flynn. He moves like a shadow through the attack—a fluid mixture of experience and power—his tattooed arms taut as he maneuvers in a world that must feel foreign to him now. There's a fire in his gold-brown eyes that burns brighter than any threat outside that door.

"There he is!" I say softly, pointing at the screen. "Look!"

Taryn squints at the monitor, her heart swelling with pride mixed with fear. "He looks like a superhero," she breathes, a small smile forming on her lips despite the danger.

I allow myself to smile back at her, but before I can fully bask in that fleeting moment of joy, the monitor flickers once more, and a heavy sound reverberates through the house. My smile stutters, replaced by a deep-seated dread. Flynn's silhouette freezes on the screen, and I can almost feel his eyes boring into me, as if sensing my panic. Taryn's hand reaches for mine, squeezing it like a lifeline, grounding us both in this terrifying reality.

Suddenly, the power cuts off without warning. Darkness envelops us like an abyss, swallowing every shred of light and sound that once offered comfort. The hum of the security system fades into silence, leaving nothing but a growing void around us and the light from her cell phone screen.

"What do we do now?" Taryn asks. "If the power is out, can we get out of here? Aren't we sealed in?"

I bite my lip, the weight of Taryn's question pressing down on my chest. Just as I was starting to feel a semblance of hope with that fleeting glimpse of Flynn, the darkness swallows us whole, a reminder that our safety was simply an illusion, and now we were more vulnerable than ever. "We wait," I whisper, my voice steadier than I feel. "We have to trust that your dad knows how to get us out of this."

"But what if—"

"No," I cut her off gently but firmly. "We're not going to think in 'what ifs.' Your dad is out there protecting us. He's going to come for us, and we need to be ready when he does."

I hope I'm right and I didn't just lie to Taryn. *The reality is, if he's dead, so are we.* Trapped in this panic room with no way to escape.

FLYNN

I can't shake the weight of dread pressing down on my chest as I watch Sutton's face twist in confusion and fear, but there's no time for remorse. Looking into her eyes one final time before she disappears through the doorway, just as a bullet embeds itself into the door trim of the very same fucking door only seconds after she's left.

Every part of me wants to stride after my gorgeous, stubborn neighbor to make sure she's following my instructions. Because let's face it, following orders isn't her strong suit. Not after her charging outside with a bat toward an unknown car earlier tonight. Sutton is fucking unpredictable—a wild card that I do not need in my life—but my daughter's safety is in her hands right now, and that's something I can't ignore.

Another bullet whizzes past me, way too close for fucking comfort, and I find myself grinding my molars together, wanting to rip these *arses* limb from bloody limb. They're testing to find out where I am. To see if I'm still alive. Stupid fuckers.

I take cover under my desk, constantly switching positions as the hail of bullets continues to rain down on me. The sounds of glass shattering and wood splintering echo around me as they destroy my once-beautiful home. I'd done my damndest to make sure this place was welcoming for Taryn, a home she could feel safe and loved in. They're obviously not just here to scare me off... *they want me dead.*

Too bad for them, I'm not easy to kill.

With a swift motion, I pull back the false panel beneath my desk and retrieve the Desert Eagle—a beast with a biting kick. It was a parting gift from my da; he couldn't send me to the States without a weapon powerful enough to remember him by. My heart races, each beat a battle drum urging me to act. The anarchy outside isn't only noise; it's a bloody relentless reminder of the life I thought I had left behind.

I fire a few shots back, trying to keep their attention on this room and away from Taryn's. They open fire again. Dozens of bullets smash into my office, spraying everywhere. The sound of yelling intermingled with gunfire fills the air around me. Gaelic words shouting orders to the other men spread out in my yard, asking if there's movement in the house.

"*Aon chomhartha na gluaiseachta sa teach?*"

Clearly, Arturo didn't bring his best people if they thought that a firefight would be enough to kill an O'Reilly. Fucking amateurs.

Another round of bullets blasts on either side of me, splinters flying from the desk where it's taking hits like an old soldier in its final stand. I fire a few more rounds before I start crawling toward the doorway, praying that the gunfire will cover my sound enough to make it to my bedroom.

As I edge closer to my room, a deafening crash erupts behind me, and I instinctively flinch. I can't afford to think about where Sutton and Taryn are right now; they're safer in that hidden room than exposed out here with me. My mind races as I push myself into a side roll, ducking out of the line of fire as another volley of bullets sends fragments racing past my ear, reminding me of angry hornets.

I scramble to my feet; the adrenaline coursing through me is pure wildfire. My heart pounds in my chest as I reach for the door of my bedroom, urgency thrumming through every fiber of my being. I can't let them breach this sanctum; it's where I store not just weapons but memories, remnants of a life that feels worlds apart now—a life I must protect at all costs. The men outside don't give a fuck who they hurt or kill.

They've already stolen Aisling from me.

They aren't going to take Taryn or Sutton from me... even if I have to give up the air in my lungs, they'll live. No matter if I have to die to protect them, I'll do what

I must.

My fingers hover over the thumbprint lock on my weapon cache. The heated chaos echoes behind me, each shot a reminder of the relentless pursuit that drives Arturo's men. With a deep breath, I press my thumb against the cold metal. The lock snaps open with a satisfying click, granting me access to my arsenal.

I throw the door wide, scanning my inventory for another weapon—anything I can use to even the odds. The walls are lined with racks of firearms, ammunition glistening in their organized rows, reminding me of jewels. My eyes land on a sleek black shotgun, and I snatch it up like a lifeline.

Just as I'm loading it, a crash resounds from the living room, accompanied by frenzied shouts in Gaelic—commanding orders from someone who clearly thinks they own these halls. My blood boils with fury, but there's no time to waste on rage; it could get me killed.

"You think you know how this works?" I mutter under my breath as I step forward into battle mode. Every muscle in my body is tense, poised for action. A low growl escapes my lips—I've come too far for this shit.

To be attacked in my own home. Fuck them. They'll die today.

I ease back into my space by the doorway, positioning myself where I can see down the hallway and the front door. The sound of more shattering glass and splintering wood fills my ears, and I grip the shotgun tighter. My heart thrums like a drum, the weight of the past colliding with the urgency of the present. I can't shake the image of Sutton's frightened face from my mind, nor can I ignore the knowledge that Taryn may be watching this unfold on the monitors in the safe room. I left that life behind to protect her, and here I am, doing the exact fucking thing I promised Aisling I wouldn't do by bringing her into this mess of a life.

A loud boom hits my front door once. Then again, and again, until the heavy door gives way, smacking into the wall behind it. Gazing through the doorway, I watch the dark figures flitting in and out of view, moving with the practiced fluidity of seasoned hunters. They're circling, still trying to pin me down as if I'm their prey.

I step quietly forward, my eyes narrowing as I anticipate their movements. With a deliberate breath, I brace myself; it's time to remind them who they're dealing with. One of them—a tall man with a scar across his cheek—steps into view just as I take aim. The blast echoes through the house, a roar announcing my presence.

The man flies backward with the impact and drops without a word, a look of shock frozen on his face, forever. The room stills for a moment as they realize I've killed one of their men and shown myself. I can almost hear the hearts of those outside, racing against their will, before mayhem erupts again as they scramble for cover.

They'll come for me now—more bullets will fly—and this time, I won't hesitate. I shift just enough to assess the situation further. My mind races with options; *where's Arturo*? Does he have eyes on me? It wouldn't surprise me if he orchestrated this whole thing from the shadows, like a puppeteer pulling strings while enjoying the show. Just as he'd done with Aisling. The thought sends a jolt of rage through me, igniting my determination to end this once and for all.

My breath steadies as I watch and wait. I peer over at the camera I know is positioned toward my doorway, aware that on the other side of the monitor are Taryn and Sutton. For a moment, it feels like time hangs suspended. If they're watching me, it means they're safe. If they're not, and I make it out alive, Sutton's ass will be meeting with my belt for disobeying me—a hard lesson that I am willing to teach her after this is said and done.

The voices from my living room shift away, fading with each syllable. There's no way that they are still inside the house.

The enemy is regrouping, and I need to turn this to my advantage. Drawing a deep breath, I reach for a flashbang on the shelf beside me. With a firm grip, I yank it free and walk back into the living room, positioning myself behind a sturdy armchair for cover. The adrenaline surges through my veins as my thoughts swim with an unbreakable focus. I pop the pin and hold the device tightly, measuring the patience in my movement as shouts grow more distant.

They won't expect this.

Time to flip the script.

I hurl the flashbang through the broken living room window, its flight a soaring arc until it disappears outside. I repeat the process twice over until I know hell will rain free in a moment. A split second later, a blinding light floods the space, accompanied by a thunderous bang that reverberates through every wall. The power to the house blinks out a second later.

For a brief moment, time seems to freeze with the shock. I take advantage of their confusion—sharp voices drowning in a tidal wave of disorientation—as I leap from behind cover. The shotgun is a bit weighty, yet satisfying in my hands, every ounce of muscle honed for this primal dance of survival.

I step into their fray, finding targets amidst their startled movements. A few stumble backward, disoriented and clutching their ears while trying to shield their eyes from the searing brightness. My finger tightens over the trigger without hesitation as I send another round into the nearest figure—a hulking brute who hadn't even seen me coming.

"Shameless bastards!" I shout, my voice rumbling like thunder against their stunned silence. I reload the shotgun; the movement is so ingrained that it takes me no time at all before I'm pointing it once more. Each word bursts forth with furious energy; I won't let them take Taryn or Sutton from me. They will learn quickly: I am not just some flickering weakling in this game; I am the fucking storm.

The chaos shifts into a blur of movement and sound as I advance, a predator on the hunt. The shadows twist around me, but clarity cuts through—a mix of instinct and sheer will. Each figure that darts into view presents itself as a target drawn on paper, and I become the artist wielding brush strokes of retribution.

A glint meets my eye—a knife clattering across the ground from one of Arturo's men, who has fallen to his knees, dazed and disoriented. It's tempting to lower my weapon, but desperation has taken root in their hearts; they'll regroup any second.

No mercy can be shown.

I keep moving—forward—never leaving a moment for them to gain purchase or retaliate. Distant shouts now feel muffled, like echoes trapped in glass. Adrenaline pulses through my veins with every beat of my heart. I lock eyes with another man trying to recover. He raises his weapon, but before he can pull the trigger, I surge forward, planting my shoulder into his chest with a loud thud that echoes like a drumbeat of vengeance. The force knocks him to the ground, where he slumps down in a daze.

"Where is he?" I snarl, scanning for Arturo's presence among the remnants of his tattered troops. Each furious breath amplifies my resolve. I'll make him pay for everything he's taken from me—from Taryn. "Where the fuck is Arturo?"

A silence descends, punctuated only by the ragged breaths of the men I've taken down. They seem to hesitate, glancing at one another as if expecting their leader to emerge like a specter from the shadows. It's in the silence I feel the heaviness creeping back into my chest—crippling fear for Sutton and Taryn buried beneath my relentless fury.

"You think you can waltz into *my home* and expect me to *cower*?" I step towards the window, where shards of glass are scattered, reminding me of fallen stars, reflecting the destruction outside—a war I refuse to lose.

The bodies of Arturo's men litter my front lawn, an unsavory holiday display. Some still breathing. Others, not at all. The stillness is eerie amidst the backdrop of haze from the gunfire and the ragged breaths of the men still clinging to life.

"Arturo! Show yourself!" My voice booms, echoing through the remnants of my sanctuary. Silence answers again. Was he even here at all?

The distant sound of emergency sirens snaps my attention back to reality. One of my neighbors must have called for help. "Fuck," I curse under my breath, knowing that I only have a few minutes before they arrive. I quickly re-enter the house without a second thought. We can't be here when the police arrive. They'll slap a set of cuffs on me the second they see the trash littering my lawn, leaving Taryn and Sutton both unprotected.

There's no choice. We have to leave because until Arturo Ferraro draws his last breath, the crosshairs will not only be on me but also on Taryn and Sutton.

Chapter 5

Andi Rhodes

Sutton

QUIET HAS DESCENDED AROUND us now, except for the low hum of the security system that's kicked back on. The cameras are down, so I can't see Flynn, and I don't know what's going on out there. A dim, soft light comes from above our heads. Next to me, though, Taryn silently cries. Her body trembles from the sobs, her hand clutched in mine. I wrap an arm around her as her phone lights up near us, bright and almost calming. I know it's him before she flips it around so I can see the message.

Da: It's me.

Clicks and a loud swooshing sound before the heavy door opens. Standing there is Flynn, scraped up and bloody. My legs tremble as I stand, my heart clenching, but before I can say or do anything, Taryn rushes to him, and he lifts her into his arms.

"Come on, we need to get out of here, right now." His husky voice washes over me. I don't know if I want to run to him too or just stand here. My body makes the decision for me.

In the distance, the sirens from the emergency responders let us know they're near, and I shake my head. "No, we need to wait to tell the police what's going on. They attacked us. It's self-defense." The words rush out of me on a gasp.

"We can't. Come on." He tosses a bulletproof vest at me. I catch it, holding it in my hand, looking at it, then back to him. He's trying to put one on Taryn, but she cries and clings to him. "*A stóirín,* let Daddy help you." She calms, and he slips it around her before he sets her on the bed.

He steps toward me next, and instinct has me shuffling back. I don't know this man. I mean, I know him, but do I *really* know who he is? These people are targeting me because of him. He said we'd talk, but we never did. Will he, though?

"*Bòidheach,*" he says in his deep, accented voice. It calms me, and I can't stop the tears as they spring to my eyes. "I need you to be feisty again. I need your help." His palm slides against my cheek and then along the back of my neck. I sigh as he cups the back of my head in his large, comforting hand.

"I'm scared." The confession slips out.

He leans down to kiss my forehead. "I know. I'm going to protect you. Come with me?" It's a question, but something in his golden eyes tells me it's not; it's an order.

My spine straightens, and I'm instantly pissed with the knowledge. How dare he order me around right now. But I also know if I go with him, everything I knew from my old life will change. I'll never be the same Sutton I was before he and Taryn came into my life. However, I won't be whole without them, either.

"Do not order me around! I'm not a part of whatever *this* is." My hand swings around, indicating his now-ruined home, sprayed with bullets and drywall.

"You are now, Sutton. I'm not letting you get hurt. I already told you I wasn't going to allow my enemy to take another woman important to me from us ever again." He takes the bulletproof vest from my hands and slips my arms into it, securing the straps. "Now, carry this." He hands me a nondescript black backpack, and before I can argue, his lips are swiftly, but briefly, on mine.

The kiss reminds me of where we were before the attack, of the fire that burns between us, brighter than it has with anyone ever before.

He pulls away, and I'm left dazed as the sirens get closer. "I can still smell you on my fingers, *ifreann beag*. I'm not letting you go. Now, we have to move." He bends down and picks up the gun he gave me earlier and slips it into the back of his pants. He picks up Taryn, and I snap out of the lustful fog he so easily wrapped me in.

"Did you just call me an idiot?" I call at his retreating back as I follow him out of the safe room and into the destroyed house. Bullet holes mar the walls like pock marks, making me cringe. I start to stop, but his words keep me following closely.

"No, little hellion," he barks as he leads us to the garage.

His SUV is still there and surprisingly intact. I'm shocked that no bullets have hit it, but then I notice they did... His vehicle is bulletproof. Who even is this guy?

I climb into the passenger seat after he buckles Taryn into the back. He slides into the driver's seat and hits a hidden button above the visor. There's a loud pop, making me glance up as the back wall of his garage appears as if it's being cut apart and completely falls to the ground. The missing chunk creates an opening, leading out to the woods behind our houses. This is some straight 007 type of stuff, and it has my mind reeling with everything I've witnessed in the past twenty-four hours.

Flynn floors the vehicle, slamming me back into my seat. I reach behind, and Taryn takes my hand into hers as we drive through the darkness without our lights on through the woods. I'm afraid we are going to run into a tree or something else, but he seems to know exactly where we need to go as he maneuvers the vehicle through the thick brush. I flick my stare behind us as the lights of the emergency vehicles shine through the darkness around our homes.

Will I ever see my beautiful home again?

"I'm sorry you might not." His deep voice breaks into my thoughts, making me realize I said that aloud.

"*Who are you?*" I choke the words out as sobs begin to wrack my chest.

"Those men want to kill all of us, and I'm the one person who will keep you safe. You know me." He turns away from the front, meeting my tear-filled stare.

"Tell me," my voice raises, demanding the truth.

"I'll tell you when we get to safety."

"I have work tomorrow and Taryn has school." It seems like peanuts right now compared to the bigger picture, but I have to remind him we can't just up and disappear into the night without answering to our everyday lives.

Flynn shakes his head, and I turn away from him to look back at the little girl I promised to keep safe and protect. "Thank you," his husky voice causes me to stare at him once more. "You listened to me and protected my child. I'll never be able to repay you for that. She's all I have left."

"I love her." The words spill from my lips, and she gasps. I glance behind me, confessing, "I do. She's all I have."

"I love you too, Sutton," Taryn says as she pulls my hand up to her face and sits forward.

"Lean back, Taryn, there's a big bump coming."

As he says it, the truck hits something hard, and it feels like we are airborne for a moment as Flynn twists the steering wheel, and we slide across the pavement onto a road. I instantly recognize we're a couple blocks over from our homes and in another neighborhood.

Flynn doesn't say anything else as he continues to drive away from everything I've known for the short time I've lived here. I have no one I can call. Certainly no family. I only have this grumpy, sexy Irishman and his sweet daughter.

<u>LYNN</u>

F The moment the safe room door opened and I saw them, my heart settled, finally.

I loved Aisling; she was my wife, after all. However, it has been a long time since she and I were close, and with it, a long time since I've felt the feeling of completeness. Aisling didn't like the life I led before and let me know it. We were still married, but it was in name only at the point of her death. It still hurts thinking of her being gone. I'd promised Aisling I'd protect Taryn; it's why I gave up my life in Ireland.

The pain in my heart when I was battling Arturo's men while Sutton and Taryn were in the safe room almost brought me to my knees. I thought I knew heartache with everything from my past, but I've never felt *that* before. Those *leathcheann* thought they could come into my home and take what is mine from me.

Arturo is going to bleed for that mistake.

I'm going to make him feel the pain I felt when I lost Aisling, as well as the fear from earlier over possibly losing my daughter and Sutton.

I'd set up my home for an easy escape and made sure the trail through the woods was ready should we need it, and thankfully, I was prepared just in case. Flicking my gaze to the rearview mirror, I don't notice anyone following us, my lungs relaxing a bit so I can breathe easier with the knowledge. I need to find out how we were found and get us to safety the second I can. The main part of the city starts to surround us as I continue to drive, trying to get away from the neighborhoods so my dark SUV won't stick out as much.

"Can you tell me anything?" Sutton's soft voice is full of fear, and so help me, I just want my feisty neighbor woman back.

I take my focus off the road for a moment, looking at her. She's facing me, her back to the door, with her long, black hair pulled away from her face, the curls in a riotous mess.

She's beautiful.

"They were sent by the man who—" I pause and double-check the back seat. Taryn is clutching her bear and sleeping, slumped over in the seat, the adrenaline dumping from her system. My poor girl. "—killed Taryn's mother, my wife," I say the words, and my heart, for the first time in a long time, doesn't clench like it used to. I know it's because of this woman. Her blue irises stare me down, and I turn my attention to the road once more, taking the exit at the last minute to confirm we aren't being followed.

"Why?"

"They are enemies of my family." Do I tell her everything now, possibly running her off in fear? Or do I refrain and keep her a little longer? Because I know the same as with Aisling, Sutton's going to hate me for my family, too.

"The O'Reillys," her voice stops me from where my mind is wandering off to.

"Yes."

"Do I need to put two and two together on my own, or are you going to tell me the rest?" The bite in her voice has me flashing my attention to her, finding her gorgeous blue orbs now sparking with anger. There's my woman.

We get into the warehouse district, eventually finding one of the many safe houses I've set up for us. "Put two and two together and tell me what you think. I'm not going to spell it out for you," I mutter, offering her the same attitude she's giving me. I need her to not fold on me yet. I'll comfort her later, but right now, she has to keep her fire.

"You're a mobster."

"Actually," my lips tip up as I share, "I'm the head of a security company. Remember?"

"Are you in witness protection? Are you testifying against those psychos?"

I can't help the chuckle that bursts from my lips. "That's hilarious, *bòidheach.*"

"Don't make fun of me. I'm not beautiful right now. I'm freaking out."

"I know, sweetheart. We are almost there, and then we can talk."

She huffs as she shifts forward in her seat, ignoring me. I drive through a couple alleys and then pass my destination before I double back, making sure it's still secure. It appears Arturo has only discovered my house, and not this place. Stopping in the middle of the road, I pull out my cell phone, keying in a sequence of codes. In the distance, the warehouse lights up, and the fence surrounding the building starts to open. We drive through as it automatically closes behind us. We enter the oversized warehouse, driving inside, and as the bright lights glare around the property, Sutton leans forward, taking it all in. I have a couple more SUVs, along with some cars parked here, should I ever need them. The heavy door of the warehouse closes as soon as we are through it.

"Stay there," I order and step out of the vehicle.

I double-check the system is secure before I move back to the SUV. I'd heard her door open after I walked away, so I'm not surprised that Sutton's standing outside the vehicle waiting for me. "I told you to stay." I press her body against the door and look in the back window. Taryn is still sleeping, safe now, thank God. Tasting Sutton's plump lips again is at the front of my mind being this close to her, and I can't hold myself back from a small sample. I hitch up her leg to wrap around my hip, wanting to take her to my office and have my way with her curvy body, but I have to be patient. I need to get my daughter in bed, then have this woman on my cock before I explode like a *déagóir adharcach*.

As I break our kiss, her eyes open, the deep pools of clear blue sucking me in. I rasp, "I'm going to spank your *arse* until you listen to me, *Sutton*. Then you're going to come on my cock so hard you'll never want to disobey me again."

"Oh, Flynn, you're going to make me want to keep disobeying you," Sutton responds, as my words have the opposite effect on her. She bites her lip, tempting me more. I want to take her right here. Shaking my head, I shift away and move to open the back door, breaking the spell she easily has over me.

Once I get Taryn settled in a room I have set up for her, I close the door. Sutton is checking out the loft apartment that's situated in the middle of the warehouse. It was built this way on purpose; to be the safest option should we ever need it. Turns out, we do. I can tell she's snooping around, so I stalk toward her.

She spins toward me, not backing away. I'm on her so fast, my lips taking hers in a blistering kiss filled with pent-up desire. Her hands push against my chest, breaking us apart enough to murmur, *"Are you finally going to fuck me, Flynn O'Reilly?"*

Chapter 10

Shannon Myers

Flynn

THE VIBRATING FROM MY cell tucked away in my pocket distracts me from Sutton's question. The only people calling right now are important ones, so I can't afford to not pay attention. Tugging it free, I briefly flick my eyes to the ID before hitting *accept*.

"Da," I greet my father. I'd sent him a brief text when we left my house, letting him know we'd been found. I cut ties with everyone, but I'm not foolish enough to believe my father wouldn't want to know if something is going on, not only with his son but also with his granddaughter. He may be angry with me for leaving, but he'd do anything in the world for Taryn. Sutton shoots me a stunned look, but I ignore it, heading for my office.

"It's time to come home. I've had enough worrying over ya, boy. You've proved you can live without us, but I won't have you risking my precious Taryn." His familiar voice makes me long for home. I didn't want to move to the States; I did it because of my wife. I thought I was heartbroken, but as it turns out, I've found the woman who owns me. It's not my wife, and unlike her, Sutton is still very much alive and in danger.

"We don't live there anymore, Da. I left that place to keep Taryn safe, you already know this."

"I'll tell you what I know, boy." The way he says it instantly has my shoulders growing tight. I'm far from a boy; I have been for a long time now. He made sure of it. So for him to use the term, I know he's doing it to prove a point. One I won't enjoy, I'm sure. "I had Aidan look into things." Already, this guy. He moves like a fucking ninja, I swear. "They've got all your locations tagged; you aren't safe anywhere."

"There's no way."

"One of your employees doesn't only work for ya, son. You've been betrayed. Now, get to the airfield so I can protect my family. Do as I say."

Fuck. "Fuck," I echo my thoughts.

"Ta," he grumbles, agreeing. "Get to the airfield. I have a *friend* who owes me a favor."

A friend. Right. "It's not only me and Taryn; I'm protecting someone."

"Kill them and move on. We do not have time for this, Flynn."

"I will bleed out anyone who touches her."

"Christ," he mumbles. "Bring the woman with ya then."

"Promise me no one will harm her if I do."

"Jesus, boy, no one will touch her."

"Fine. They're expecting us at the airfield?"

"I already made arrangements, just get there now."

"And passports? I don't have anything for Sutton."

He chuckles, then hangs up.

Right. I guess whoever is taking us doesn't require it to be legal, and once we're home, I can have papers made for Sutton. I can't believe I'm even considering this, but if what my father says is true, we're not safe anywhere here. Hell, we aren't safe there either, but at least with Da having my back, I'll have the resources and men at my disposal to finally see an end to this. My enemies are forcing me to become what my father has always wished me to be.

Ruthless.

Leaving my office, I find Sutton leaning against the couch, arms crossed. "I'm giving you a pass, only because it was your father," she mutters.

With a huff, I shake my head and reach for her. Taking her hand in mine, I decide to keep the details to myself. "This location has been compromised; we have to go." I press a kiss to her knuckles to hopefully help ease the severity of my words.

"Again? Shit!"

With a nod, I tug her along. I scoop Taryn back up and quickly load her into a dark blue Ford Explorer. It's one of our company vehicles, so it could be anyone who works for me driving it, and hopefully, it'll keep whichever employee that betrayed me guessing. Can't wait to figure out who the traitor is, as they'll be next on my list to get my payback with. Sutton climbs in the passenger seat, and I lean over, buckling her in and closing her door before she has a chance, then I'm rounding the vehicle to my side.

We're damn sure not using the same entrance we came in, I decide, and drive forward toward the back of the building. The overhead door sensor picks up the approaching vehicle, and the garage-style door raises. I give the SUV some gas, the tires screeching against the concrete as I press the gate button and we speed through the opening. Fingers crossed if anyone is parked out here, they won't be ready for us to come flying out the gate like we are, and it'll give us an advantage.

The joke's on me, as a sedan pulls right in front of the gate, attempting to block it. These company vehicles are reinforced with bars in the front and back for security purposes, so I don't hesitate as I plow through the front quarter panel of the silver car. Let them try to follow me without a radiator intact. It'll teach the fools not to give someone such an easy opening at taking them out of the game.

Sutton squeals, reminding me I'm not alone and I need to be more careful. It's not as if I have a choice; I have to get us the fuck out of here as swiftly as possible. "Let me out of this *godforsaken* vehicle, Flynn! You're going to hurt Taryn, damn you!"

Her fierceness over my girl's safety warms my chest. Flashing her a smirk, I argue, "Not going to happen, love. Now hold on while I get us the hell out of here."

"You still haven't told me where we're going."

"Well, it's not back there, that's for sure," I respond, making her huff. She shoots me a glare, but I can only smile. I should dread going home, back to what I left behind, but it has me feeling lighter in some ways. I wish I could tell Sutton, but she'll lose her head if I do. I don't think she has being kidnapped by the heir to the *Irish Faction* on her bucket list.

I tell her what I can and what the enemy already knows. "I found out someone in my company has betrayed me and given up all my locations. I don't know if there are listening or tracking devices, and I don't have the time to check right now. It's not safe to speak about a destination or anything, but when I can, I will." It's basically a lie. I'm waiting until we're on Da's doorstep before I admit to *shite*.

We make it to the airstrip, and I pull to a stop next to the private but very large plane. It's not a typical airport but a privately owned long stretch of dark asphalt. As soon as my father told me he'd called in a favor from a so-called friend, I knew exactly where I was headed. This property is owned by none other than the Bratva, hiding behind a fake company in America.

"Flynn," Sutton practically stutters my name.

"Shh, get out and stay close to me. I've got to get Taryn."

"I'm awake, Daddy," she says with a yawn.

"Come on, then, ladies. Here we go."

Hopping out, I toss my phone to the ground, stomping on it. My father will have one waiting for me on the plane. When he calls in a favor, it's never a small one, so I know he'll have covered the bases, and I can finally breathe easily once we're stepping on Irish soil. Taryn tucks her hand in mine, and I reach for Sutton's.

"Flynn," she leans in, whispering as we begin to walk toward the plane. "I can't leave town; I will get fired."

"I can smooth things over. For now, we have to get on that plane."

"I can't. I mean it, I'm *not* going," she states adamantly as we pause at the bottom of the stairs.

I nod over her shoulder to the man standing behind her. "Nikoli, good to see you. Help me convince her we need to get on the plane."

His head tips back as a loud laugh escapes him. When he meets my stare again, he's wearing a wolfish smile. "Your papa warned me there might be complications." His Russian brogue is thick, making Sutton's eyes widen.

She starts to turn around, but I stop her. Stepping forward, my hand leaves hers to wrap around her waist. I tug her to my chest tightly, still holding on to Taryn with my free hand. My daughter's too distracted with the plane and knowing what it means to notice what Nikoli and I are doing. "No, my darling Sutton, look at me," I quietly order.

Her brow furrows as she meets my calm, stern stare. Then she gasps as the needle Nikoli has in his hand meets her flesh. "H-how could you?" she manages to gasp before her lids flutter shut and she goes limp in my arms.

"Soon, my sweet Sutton, you'll learn. I do *anything* to protect the people I love."

Nikoli grins again as he caps the used syringe and pockets it. "Need help with this troublesome American?" He gestures to the woman I refuse to let go of. I shake my head, and he shrugs. "Then let's go, my new friend, I do not want my pretty plane to get shot up, and according to your papa, it may happen soon."

With a sigh, I release Taryn's hand and pick Sutton up bridal style. "It's okay, Taryn. Grandfather sent the plane."

She gasps, and when I meet her gaze, I notice the fear is no longer present in her irises. It's been replaced with excitement, and I wish I were the one who could've put it there. I've failed in America, and it's a hard pill to swallow. "We're going home? And Sutton is coming too?"

"She is," I agree and follow her as she skips the remaining few feet to the stairs.

Taryn takes the first step and glances back at me, her mouth dropping open when she finally pays close enough attention to the dozing woman in my arms. "Dad! Sutton! Is she okay?"

"She was afraid of flying, so we gave her a tablet to help her relax. She'll take a nap and be back to her rambunctious self when we land." I lie through my teeth, but I'm damn sure not telling her we just drugged the neighbor I've decided I can no longer live without in order to get her to Ireland.

"I hope she sleeps good; she's going to love it when she wakes up. I can't believe we're going to see Grandfather. I miss him. Do you think he'll be there to pick us up? Do you think Skittles missed me?" she peppers on until we're inside and I've laid Sutton down. It's amazing how children can adapt and move on from traumatizing events. I'm sure this entire situation will be dredged up at a later time for her to work through, and when it does, I will be ready to help her every step of the way.

We buckle in and settle for take-off. As the plane climbs in the air, my shoulders fall once more. I managed to get us to the airstrip and onboard, but my fight in this is far from over. Sutton is going to be furious when she realizes what I've done, wilder than Taryn's favorite cat, Skittles, that's for sure.

"So do you, Daddy?"

I nod absently, remembering some of what she said before. "Of course the cat missed you. I bet Skittles is skin and bones without you feeding him cheese and cream all the time."

She rolls her eyes, "Grandfather promised he'd feed him for me."

"Of course he did," I mutter, wondering how she got him so wrapped around her finger when he'd be more likely to chop one of mine off if I were to further displease him.

"I've been thinking about this," she hedges after she's gotten a fizzy soda and some snacks. I've got a tumbler with four fingers worth of whiskey, passing on anything else. I can't eat at a time like this, but my pre-teen daughter doesn't let a good snack opportunity pass her by. She'll be rotten soon enough with the way Sutton enjoys baking, toss in my da spoiling her, and may as well put me out to pasture. "Can I ask you a question? It's serious. Can you give me the truth? If not, I can ask Grandfather."

The way she says it garners every ounce of my attention. She's no longer my little girl; she's growing up, and the fact of the matter is, I don't think I'm ready to give her any truth. About anything. I want her safe, sound, small, and thinking I can take on the entire world should I need to for her. I'm not ready for her to realize I'm not a hero, but just another villain.

"Out with it then, little love," I rumble, worried I may break the glass should she ask me the wrong thing, and I'm forced to fess up to some truth I'm not ready to share.

"Can Sutton be my bonus mam? Can we keep her forever?"

Chapter 11

Kathryn C. Kelly

Flynn

EMOTIONS ARE COMPLICATED. ONE moment, they tangle you up and have you breathless with anticipation. Next, they leave you cold and empty. Other times, emotions will scare you shitless. Like now, for example. Taryn's words wrap around my brain, rendering me speechless.

Terrified.

Emotions are hot and cold. At one time, I could regulate them, maintaining the iciness my profession required. But that's in the past. Now?

Now...

I grimace as I consider my current state. Since meeting Sutton, emotions have *ruled* me. She's right. I *have* run hot and cold. Self-preservation has always been a priority of mine. Well, before I lost Aisling and fled Dublin to protect Taryn. When my wife began to pull away because she hated my world, I closed myself off to her and any possibility of a reconciliation. We limped along for years. Mainly for our daughter, but I knew Aisling fought for *us*. In private, I'd already checked out.

Self-preservation at its finest. I couldn't have my head in the wrong place if I wanted it to stay on my shoulders. Aisling didn't like that I was part of the *Irish Faction?* Then she couldn't be the wife I needed or wanted. I was proud of my heritage and my family. She wanted me to walk away, and it stung.

In front of Taryn, Aisling and I always put up a good front. In retrospect, I wish she'd left; she might have lived.

The thought is painful.

"Well, can we, Da?"

Anticipation brightens Taryn's green eyes. In spite of our harrowing night, she seems none the worse for wear. I'm damn proud of her resilience. My baby girl's light can't be dulled, and I wouldn't have it any other way.

For the entirety of my daughter's life, I've made sure she knows love above all else. I remained with her mam so she wouldn't be a child from a broken home. Unfortunately, loss, devastation, and grief have touched her far too early.

Yet, she *is* young and innocent. Sutton has stepped in as a maternal figure, and all Taryn knows is she doesn't want to lose her. She doesn't understand it isn't as simple as she has worked it out to be.

Sighing, I sip my whiskey, almost wishing she'd asked me something about my life. I cop out and take the easy route. "We have to ask Sutton. She might not want to stay with us forever."

"She does," Taryn insists. "She promised me when we were waiting for you in the panic room." She explains the conversation to me. "*And* she came with us."

She didn't have a choice, but I keep that to myself. "Let us land, Tary. Give Sutton a chance to rest—" And cool down so she won't try to chop off my bollocks for kidnapping her. "Acclimate herself to her new surroundings, then I'll talk to her."

"Fine," Taryn huffs.

I drink deeper. "Rest, little love. You want to be bright and perky when you see Granda."

That instantly settles her down, and she falls asleep within ten minutes. It's been one adrenaline rush after the other, so I'm not surprised. Setting my drink aside, I stand and lift my precious girl into my arms, then take her to the bedroom and lay her next to Sutton.

My heart swells at the image of them, side by side. When I left for Boston all those months ago, I had no intention of finding a woman to let into my life—and by extension *Taryn's*. I definitely didn't think I'd want to keep her as much as my daughter does. But I do. More than Taryn, if possible.

Sutton is peaceful in sleep, serene even. Certainly not the firebrand I know her to be. Raven-colored hair spreads across the silk pillowcase. Plump, pink lips are slightly parted. She's still in the leggings and T-shirt she wore when the night went to fucking shite. The fitted clothes do an excellent job of showcasing her curves. The imprint of her pussy in the thin material makes me wonder if she put her panties back on.

My cock hardens.

Frustrated, I back away and return to the main cabin. Finding my seat once again, I reclaim my drink and finish off the whiskey. The roar of the engines offers a strange comfort. Soon, the land of Nod calls, and my eyes slip closed.

HOURS LATER, I'M IN the back of an SUV, sitting next to my cousin, Aidan. Taryn and Sutton are safely buckled in, taking the middle row. They're both lost in the passing scenery, a far cry from the curses Sutton rained down on my head when she awakened and realized not only was she out of Boston, but out of her country.

The blasted wee termagant.

"You're *losing* your touch," Aidan mutters. "The fact you didn't do thorough background checks on your employees is a massive fucking fail on your part, Flynn."

We haven't long left the airfield where we landed, so the scenery is a mixture of rural charm and country roads with open fields, hedgerows, clusters of trees, stone walls, and glimpses of grazing cows. The tranquil scene doesn't calm me. I want to plant my fucking fist in Aidan's mouth, but that's nothing new.

"Stating the obvious is such a waste of breath," I growl instead. Sutton shifts, tilting her head a touch. I know she's listening. Maybe she's calmed down?

"You could've gotten killed, you bloody fool. And what about Taryn?"

Sutton twists in her seat, glaring at Aidan.

Better him than me.

"Please, tone it down. Taryn has been through enough." She jerks forward again and wraps an arm around my daughter's shoulder.

"She's your mouthpiece now?" Aidan demands, always trying to get a rise out of me.

I don't answer, noticing the route we're on.

We don't merge onto the M4 but follow the road adjacent to the River Liffey, which is a longer route with toll roads. This is a lesson, *a reminder*, meant for me. I can't make it without the might of *The Faction*. I've turned my back on everything that should've been near to me. Instead of immediately seeking revenge for my wife's murder, I took my daughter and left.

Aidan's voice drones on, but I tune him out. I know what's coming, and I sit in stoic silence. Perhaps it's my imagination, but the SUV seems to slow down as we reach *Wrights Anglers Rest*, where Aisling and I were married. The pain and guilt I always believed would overwhelm me the next time I saw it, doesn't flare up, and the realization is shocking.

"It's beautiful," Taryn breathes in awe. "Look, Sutton."

My cross woman takes it all in with a gasp, forgetting her anger as she's swept up in the beauty of the land.

"Still plan to follow in your footsteps and have my wedding here too. If I ever find the right woman," Aidan cuts in.

Fucking dick.

At the sound of Aidan's voice, Sutton stiffens. It isn't his words. He hadn't gotten half a sentence out before she reacted. She doesn't like him.

"You and Mam married there?" Taryn asks as the SUV speeds up and finally passes the establishment. It was one place we never took her to visit, something we should've done long ago when her mother was still present.

"We did," I say, my gaze pinned on the back of Sutton.

I want to talk to her.

No, I *need* to talk to her about so many things.

Top of the list is reassuring her that Aisling is in my past. She, if she'll allow it, can be my future. I'm certain she's not jealous. She's too sweet and sunny for such dark emotions. But she doesn't know what place Taryn's mother held in my life. She only knows Aisling was murdered, and I'm angry about it. I could've been madly in love with her when I lost her.

Aidan had no fucking right to open his trap. Leaning closer to my cousin, it takes everything in me not to grab his head and smash it into something. "You and I are talking, motherfucker," I snarl in a heated whisper.

He smirks in return, putting little stock into my underlying threat.

I'll have my time with him soon, so I don't push the issue. He returns to yapping, which I gladly ignore. Before I left for Boston, Aidan jockeyed for Da's attention. His cunning helped move him up the ranks, but I've never particularly trusted him. He'll stab me in the back if it means attaining the place he wants within the organization.

Every now and then, I point out a landmark to Taryn. Sutton is taking it all in as well, and each time she hears my voice, she reacts. Just when I think she's possibly softening, something must run through her mind to piss her off because her body stiffens once again.

Finally, we're turning onto the road leading to my da's residence. The area is lush and peaceful, offering much-needed tranquility. Our driver pauses at the gated entrance to punch in a code. Once it slides open, he drives down the motor court, swerves around the fountain centered in the circular driveway, and glides to a stop near another SUV.

Not waiting for me, Sutton opens her car door and gets out. Scowling, I slide the seat down in front of me so I can quickly squeeze out behind her. My only consolation is she doesn't know where to go, so she stops short. She stares at the flag proudly emblazoned with the green and gold O'Reilly crest. The lions signify our strength and fierceness. The cross indicates our faith and steadfastness. The bloody hand, our loyalty and justice we demand.

The breeze flutters her hair. She doesn't have a jacket on, and it's chilly here. Not as cold as it was when we left Boston, but enough to make her shiver. I'm glad the sun is out today; she'd turn into an ice cube with the wind. Sutton wraps her arms around her waist, and my heart stutters with the move. I already know she's alone in the world, but this is the first time she's seemed so forlorn. Dark circles ring her eyes. More than likely, she is still suffering the effects of the tranquilizer as well.

Guilt nags at me, but I quickly push it down. It was for the best, no matter how unsavory my actions may seem to her. I'll do whatever it takes, even if it means she momentarily hates me in the process.

We're out in the open, and for some reason, the hairs on my nape stand on end. Considering the second-floor balcony of the nearest house is barely visible over the stands of trees and the stone fence separating the properties, I sigh, chalking it up to paranoia.

"Flynn!" Da's voice cuts through the silence as he steps outside. His white hair flaps in the wind, but he's still robust and barrel-chested. He sure as *shite* doesn't look near seventy. Two of his trusted lieutenants follow in his wake. I nod to Cahir and Breandán, as we've always been on friendly terms.

Once, when Da expected to hand the reins over to me when the time came, I was cultivating relationships to build my own loyal lieutenants.

Aisling's murder changed much more than I realized.

"Where's my granddaughter?" Da asks, his unreadable gaze falling on Sutton. She straightens, stiffening her shoulders, and narrows her stare, her mouth set into a grim line. Surprise flares in Da's eyes, his expression quickly shifting to amusement.

"Granda!" Taryn squeals, flying out from the other side of the SUV and into my father's waiting open arms. He hugs her tightly, lifting her off her feet. "You've met Sutton?" she asks, disentangling herself from his embrace and backing to the woman in question. She takes her hand.

"A pleasure, Miss Matthews," Da says. "I'm Killian."

Sutton's lips tighten further, but she slides a glance at Taryn, then pastes a smile on her pretty lips. "The pleasure is all mine."

Da laughs, "It sounds anything but."

"Sutton's still tired from her nap," Taryn volunteers. "She needs to rest after I introduce her to Skittles."

"Skittles misses you, little one." Da waves in the direction of the house. "Cat's been sunning in the garden."

Taryn kisses Da's cheek again, then takes Sutton's hand again, dragging her inside the house.

"Bloody woman," I grumble. "She hasn't strung together more than twenty words since she awakened."

"Apparently, she had more than enough to say to you then," Da comments dryly. "Nikoli found her highly amusing. *A miserable leprechaun?*"

Tame compared to some of her other names, but I leave that detail to myself.

I scrub my hand over my face. "She's thawing," I mutter. "Hopefully, by Valentine's Day, she will have forgiven me completely. I want it to be special for her."

Da lifts a brow at me. The others around us snicker, even the driver whose name I still don't know.

"I want to visit the family jeweler," I continue. "I'm not sure what unique piece I can buy her with only seven days left before the holiday, but I'll see what they can do."

"I'm sure we can convince him to help you make it a memorable Valentine's Day for Miss Matthews," Da responds. "But we have more pressing matters at hand for the time being. Arturo, for starters."

"I haven't forgotten him," I bark. I'd briefly pushed the fucker aside. To keep Taryn and Sutton calm, it was imperative I tuck him away until I could form a plan of action. The time has finally come. A noise catches my attention, though no one else seems concerned. I glance around, see nothing. Squinting, I try to peer through the trees to the barely visible balcony.

"Is the Byrne place still vacant?"

Breandán nods. "Just as it's been for the last two years."

"Why?" Aidan demands with a knowing look.

I glance in the direction of the balcony again, wishing I could lay eyes on it. "Just curious."

"What's gotten into you, boy?" Da asks, annoyed. "You're more skittish than a woman."

I ignore the dig. "I want no harm befalling Taryn and Sutton," I reply sharply. "We're out here like *fecking* sitting ducks."

"We each do circuits around the perimeter, Flynn," Cahir says. "We did a sweep just before you arrived. Nothing out of the ordinary."

"Come inside and have a drink." Da indicates the open door. "Let's discuss everything in my office."

I nod, and he turns to go inside. Something hot whizzes by me in the next breath, and before my father's able to take another step, he stumbles forward. A pained noise leaves his throat as a deep red spot blooms against his stark white shirt on his shoulder. Panic flares within me, and I whirl around, quickly searching for the threat.

Cahir, Breandán, Aidan, and the driver all react immediately, closing ranks in front of my father as they pull their weapons. I grab my Glock and—

A hole opens in the driver's head. He drops where he's standing. Cahir takes a shot to the throat. I dive for cover. Aidan falls on top of me and goes still.

Fuck!

We're being ambushed!

SUTTON

If I wasn't so exhausted, I'm sure I would be happier to be with Taryn and Flynn. Now that my outrage has receded and the danger is behind us, I am thinking a little clearer. If Flynn had any other way to keep us safe, he wouldn't have upended my entire life and taken me almost four thousand miles away from my home. He would've given me a choice, the chance to gather mementos from my past with my grandma. Photos, cards, *memories*.

I'm still slightly groggy, very grimy, and terribly hungry, none of which is helping my mood improve. I hate that I can't find happiness at the moment when it is so desperately needed, but my world feels upended all over again. Kind of like it did when I lost my grandmother and I felt adrift.

No, scratch that. It doesn't feel upended; it has been upended. Just as I was settling into my new life, I became the unwilling heroine of a B-rated action flick.

"Skittles!" Taryn squeals.

She's hustled me through a breezeway to the other side of the house and out another door into the backyard. A tuxedo cat lounges on gray stone that covers a small patio. It rolls into a manicured lawn with tall stands of trees. My tense muscles unlock as I bask in the peaceful surroundings and bracing air.

Taryn drops down, pulling the cat onto her lap. His ears twitch, then slide backward in a show of annoyance. She doesn't notice. "I've missed you so much!"

The cat wriggles free and scampers away.

"No, wait!" Taryn calls, attempting to catch him. He's quicker and starts to climb a tree but sees something. The hair on his back stands up and he screeches, then sprints into the house. "Something spooked him," Taryn says to me, frowning.

Since I don't know much about Ireland's fauna, I opt for safety. "Maybe we should go inside until your dad is ready to leave."

"Or we can walk to our old house," Taryn argues. She points behind us. "It's this way. Granda usually keeps Da busy for a while. We'll be waiting *forever*," she adds with a dramatic flair.

I laugh.

"We can shower and find clean clothes like you want."

"We don't have any."

"I didn't take all my things when we left. Neither did Da. If none of my clothes fit you, maybe one of his T-shirts will."

Lewd thoughts invade my brain at the idea of wearing his clothes. It would be even better if the material carried his scent. "Let's tell your dad first, so he doesn't worry when he can't find us," I suggest. After all, we have no cellphones now, and he isn't a mind reader.

"Okay, but hurry. I want you to see my room."

I smile and settle my arm around Taryn's shoulders, turning her toward the house. We step inside, and the long breezeway greets us. It's finally appointed with works of art on the walls and heavy pieces of furniture on each side. It has an antique beauty, but combined with the dark décor, it creates an oppressive environment that has my skin crawling. Pastels would work wonders to brighten the place, to infuse it with liveliness it's sorely lacking. Maybe add a little glitter in the paint to give it a bit of sparkle.

Pop!

Pop!

Pop!

We're halfway to the front door when the loud noise startles us. I wasn't well-acquainted with the sound of gunfire before last night. Now it's a sound imprinted in my memory. I'd know it anywhere.

For instance, *now*.

"Da!" Taryn cries, starting to run toward the sound.

"No, stay here!" I order. *She's* the priority. She must be protected at all costs. I'll never forgive myself if anything happens to her.

"But my da!" she cries.

I pull her to me, wrapping my arms around her in a quick hug, refusing to recognize my own fear or how my heart is banging against my chest. "Stay here. I promise I'll return as soon as possible."

Pop!

Pop!

Pop!

I take off in a run, but before I reach the door, I see Flynn's father slumped against the doorframe. There's blood on his shirt, and his labored breathing instantly has concern washing over me. "Get in! Get in!" I screech, not sure if he can do so or not.

One of the men who came outside with him earlier stumbles in, blood and gore coating his white shirt. Like Aidan, he has stark black hair. He grabs Killian O'Reilly under each arm, somehow managing to drag him into the house with him.

"Where's Flynn?" I demand.

No one answers me.

Pop!

Pop!

Pop!

I reach the front door just as Flynn shoves Aidan aside. Four men are scaling the high stone walls like a scene from a medieval war movie. Our driver and one of Killian's men are beyond help. I'm not sure about Aidan. He's bloody and unmoving.

The next moment, I'm forcefully jerked back, the move sudden enough I can't fight it. "See to Taryn," Killian's rescuer demands. "I'll cover Flynn."

"But—"

"Go!"

"Don't let him die!" I order, then turn on my heel. I run back to Taryn, who is thankfully still where I've left her. She's kneeling next to her wounded grandfather with her arms around his neck, her shoulders shaking from her sobs...

Chapter 12

Alex Grayson

Flynn

"ARE YOU ALIVE?" I ask the dead weight lying on top of me.

I may not fully trust the guy, and he can be an asshole to epic proportions, but he's family, and to the O'Reilly name, blood means everything.

We're chest to chest, with Aidan's head lying just above my shoulder. His face is turned toward me, but I don't want to move to look at him. I need to keep as still as possible. If the *arseholes* currently shooting up the place think I'm down and out, they'll move slower. I need as much time as I can get to come up with a plan to get out of this situation.

A low hiss meets my ear that's closest to Aidan, and I feel a barely perceptible twitch on my side down near the waistband of my jeans.

He's alive.

Thank fuck.

Rustling off to our left draws my attention, and it takes everything in me to not look over and see what's coming for us. There's no question it's Arturo's men. How many are there, and how in the fuck did they manage to go unseen by the guards who frequently walk the perimeter? Not to mention the cameras that are placed all over the property.

Anger boils in my blood—a rage Aidan no doubt feels because it makes my body fucking shake with it.

I left this place, leaving behind everything I knew, to protect my daughter. To keep her safe and away from my father's business. And this is the third time she's been in danger in only a matter of days. When I get my hands on Arturo, and I will, there won't be anything recognizable about him. He's fucked with me and mine one too many times.

My only saving grace is that Taryn and Sutton are in the house. Or they were when the shooting started. Knowing my hard-headed daughter and crazy-ass fucking neighbor, they both dashed for the door when they heard the first shot.

Low murmurs come from the direction I heard the rustling. Arturo's men are closing in, and once they get to us, Aidan and I are both dead. "Under my back," I say as quietly as I can.

Thankfully, when I feel fingers slowly inch their way between my back and the ground, I know Aidan's heard me. I don't know what condition he's in, but from the warmth I feel seeping into my shirt, he's been shot somewhere. I have to hope it's not a fatal wound. I need him to get the gun and pass it to me as discreetly as possible.

The lump digging in my lower back from my gun shifts and disappears. A moment later, the cool metal touches my fingertips. I curl my hand around the grip of the Glock and flick my thumb over the safety. I've got a full magazine, so seventeen rounds to get this shite done.

When I hear the telltale thumps of boots landing on the ground, I move quickly. Using one hand and my elbow on my other arm, I shove Aidan off me as hard as I can. He lands beside me with a grunt, sprawled out on his back. I barely spare him a glance as I jump to my feet.

Four men in all black military-style gear are over by the stone wall. I pop off a couple of rounds, both landing between the eyes of two men, before the other two notice me. I dive for cover behind the fountain, away from Aidan, hoping they won't notice him still alive on the ground. The ricochet of bullets hitting stones pings in my ears, and fragments of concrete blast past my face. Lucky fucking break. Those bullets were inches from blowing my head off.

I peek around the fountain, spotting one of Arturo's men as he crouches down behind the blacked-out SUV we arrived in. I don't know if the fourth man is with him or if he's hiding somewhere else.

Flicking my gaze in the direction where I left Aidan, I find him still lying there, motionless. Blood coats his white shirt, covering most of his torso. The only thing that moves is the slow rise and fall of his chest. Fortunately, he's behind a concrete bench, so he's not in the direct line of sight of the shooters.

Unfortunately, I'm going to have to leave my position to get closer, putting me momentarily in the line of fire. It's a risk I have to take because these fuckers are not getting in that mansion.

Just as I'm preparing to roll and dash, a zing whizzes past my head, and a split second later, the shooter behind the SUV falls out of his hiding spot. His face is turned the other way, but there's no missing the hole in the back of his head.

Seconds later, there's another zing, followed by a heavy thump down at the other end of the vehicle. I'd bet my right nut it was the fourth shooter.

And I'd bet my left nut it was Fiona in the attic with her sniper rifle.

Whereas I don't fully trust Aidan, I trust his twin with my life, as well as the life of my daughter. And now, Sutton.

Turning, I tip my head back to glance up at the small set of windows at the top of the mansion. Just past the panes of glass, I see the shadow of a figure before it steps out of view.

I'll hunt down and thank Fiona later. Right now, I need to check on Aidan and then find my girls. The hunting down part will be easy. Any time she's here at the house, it's more than likely she can be found in the attic. It's getting her to accept my gratitude that will be the problem.

Quiet, reserved, and a mystery to most, Fiona is as deadly as a vicious viper, and she doesn't get along well with others. She sticks to herself and prefers to stay in the shadows. She's the complete opposite of her twin, and if someone suggests otherwise, they'll end up with a bullet in their cranium.

With a shake of my head, I turn toward Aidan. Just as I take the first step, the sound of the front door opening fills the now stark silence. Breandán comes running out of the house, gun raised, eyes darting around.

"Taryn, Sutton, and my father?" Fear clogs my throat as I say the three names.

"The girls are unharmed and safe in the house. Your da took a bullet to the chest. Doctor Moore is already on the way."

My shoulders sag in relief, and I turn my attention to Aidan. His face is pale, his breathing labored. Setting my gun on his lower stomach for easy access, I locate the wound and apply pressure to stop the bleeding as best as I can. Breandán remains standing, eyes alert while his attention continues casing our surroundings.

Aidan's eyes crack open. "Fiona?" he wheezes.

"Are you surprised?" I ask.

"No." He grunts when I apply more pressure to the wound. "*Uncail?*"

"Shoulder hit."

His eyes slide closed, and his head barely moves with his nod. "Glad... you're... home," he says before passing out.

I grunt, not taking his words as he meant them to be. Aidan and I have never been close. He's always wanted to take over the family when it's time, and he hates that I'm next in line. Me taking Taryn and getting the fuck out of Ireland gave him the perfect opportunity.

The question is, does he want the position badly enough to stab his family in the back. Going so far as giving the enemy inside information?

Because one thing's for damn sure, this was an inside job.

We have a traitor in our ranks.

THE MOMENT I STEP foot in the house, a small body slams into me so hard I stumble back a step. Closing my eyes for a brief moment, I send up a prayer, not for the first time, that my Taryn is okay.

Bending down, I scoop up my little girl into my arms. She's eleven, too big to be carting around, but she's not the only one who needs comfort right now. Her legs go around my waist as she wraps her arms around my shoulders, burying her face in my neck.

"I was so scared for you, Daddy," she cries. "And Granda was shot!"

"I know, baby girl, but he's going to be okay. The doctor is going to check him over."

"You promise?"

"Promise."

I'm going to be pissed if I break a promise to my daughter.

She pulls her face from my neck and looks at me with wet eyes and red, splotchy cheeks. I hate seeing her so upset. It's happened way too many times lately. "And Uncle Aidan?"

"The doctor is with him now."

Something catches my attention over Taryn's head, and my gaze meets Sutton's. She's down on her knees beside my father, pressing a white cloth against his shoulder. Da's eyes open a mere slit as he says something to her, but she's not paying him any attention. Her stare is fixed on me and Taryn. Her eyes are glassy, like she's barely holding back her tears while her bottom lip trembles.

"Breandán," I call to the man who's just walked in the door behind me. "Can you take over for Sutton?"

"You got it." He walks over to the other side of my father and gets to his knees. It's like she doesn't even know he's there when he removes her hand from the cloth being pressed against Da's wound.

I set Taryn down on her feet. "Tary, will you get Granda a glass of water, please?"

She sniffles. "Okay." After giving me another tight hug, she turns and races out of sight toward the kitchen. The only reason I let her go is because I have a direct view of the room she's heading toward.

I walk toward Sutton, who's still down on her knees beside Da. Grabbing her hand still covered in blood, I tug her to her feet. The moment she's standing, she launches herself at me. She nearly strangles me with how tight her arms wind around my neck.

"Oh, God, I thought you were going to die!"

"Shh... I'm okay," I say, running my hands up and down her back. "I'm right here."

Walking us backward a few steps, I give us a bit of privacy but still keep the kitchen in view. I hold Sutton for several seconds before I pull us apart. Grabbing her cheeks, I drop my head, laying my lips against hers for a brief kiss. When we break away, I keep my palms on her cheeks, swiping away her tears with my thumbs.

"I'm so sorry, baby," I whisper. "So damn sorry you were dragged into this."

She reaches up and wraps her fingers around my wrists. "Well," she sniffles, "it was kind of my fault too. As you said, I shouldn't have come out of the house, bats a-blazing."

"True, but it never should have come to this. It's exactly the reason I took Taryn and left the family behind."

"I'm just glad you're okay." She looks over her shoulder toward Da. "Is he going to be okay?"

"Yes. It's not the first time he's been shot. He's a stubborn son-of-a-bitch. It'll take more than a bullet to the shoulder to take him out."

"And the others?"

I grind my molars together. "Two dead. The doctor is with Aidan right now. They're stabilizing him before they bring him into the house."

"Doesn't he need to go to the hospital?"

"Due to the nature of the family business, we try to stay away from hospitals as much as possible to avoid questions being asked by the authorities. If the situation is dire enough, they'll transport him."

Taryn comes back into the foyer, carefully carrying a full glass of water. She notices us but goes straight to her granda, instinctually knowing, even at such a young age, that Sutton and I need a moment. She drops to her knees, and while Breandán keeps a firm hold on the cloth over the wound, she holds the glass to my da's lips.

"I'm so sorry you lost people today," Sutton consoles, pulling my attention back to her.

Instead of saying anything in return, I press my mouth to hers again. The kiss is short, a simple press of lips, but I use it to reassure both of us we're safe.

And I'm damn sure going to make sure that remains so.

Chapter 13

Alex Grayson

Sutton

MY CHEST IS STILL tight from the gunshots earlier as I suck in a breath, attempting to force my heart to settle. My eyes drift around Flynn's bedroom. If you can even call such a grand space a mere bedroom. I attempt to take it all in so I don't freak out. I've never set foot in a mansion before, let alone one in Ireland. Trying hard to focus on the art of it, I attempt to forget the violence I just witnessed.

Tall windows, framed by floor-length velvet drapes in an extravagant emerald green, let in slivers of moonlight. It glimmers over the dark mahogany panels lining the walls, their surfaces polished to such a sheen that I catch my shaky reflection. Delicate Celtic knot carvings twist around the edges, craftsmanship that makes my inner art teacher's soul ache with admiration.

A massive four-poster bed takes center stage in the room. Each post is carved with intricate shamrock designs, and I reach out and trace the lines with my fingertips. My gaze travels to the headboard, where the ornate family crest from the flag I saw earlier is emblazoned. The thing feels ancient, older than anything in my world.

A plush Persian rug sprawls at the foot of the bed, with muted greens and golds swirling together. There are two antique armchairs by the window, begging me to sit down and imagine I'm in a safe place. I find a crystal decanter of probably aged Irish whiskey on the table, and the glass is sparkling just like the gold crown molding above it.

Boy, do I need a drink.

Pouring myself some liquid courage, I bring the vessel to my lips and sip carefully.

To hell with it.

I throw the whole thing back, then stick my tongue out, momentarily scowling from the harsh burn. My eyes flick to an imposing armoire with beautiful brass fixtures, and I can't help but wonder what secrets Mr. 007 is keeping tucked away inside. Tailored suits, weapons, or something else entirely? My breath hitches as I notice the revolver glinting on the nightstand. A sudden, chilling fear grips me at the sight, making me refocus on the rug's swirling patterns.

I'm an artist at heart. I try to lose myself in color and shape, in texture and shadow, anything to blot out the fresh images of death. Despite all the luxury, this place feels creepy, like something dark and dangerous is lurking here. I focus on the fancy chandelier and shiny floors, hoping they'll distract me from the fact this guy keeps a gun within arm's reach.

Still wet from a shower, I'm lounging in Flynn's robe, admiring his rug, when he walks in. I leap up but stop myself from running to him.

Flynn's a large man, but he moves as quietly as a mouse. His dress shirt is torn at the shoulder, and there's a fresh scrape on his chiseled jaw. I get a queasy feeling remembering how perilous the past day has been.

A quick nod precedes his calm, low voice, which I've come to recognize. "Taryn's asleep," he says. "She's alright."

I let out a sigh of relief. His precious daughter was my main source of worry the moment I realized I'd been whisked halfway around the world with an Irish mobster. Thinking of Taryn's bright little smile, her sketches of flowers and houses, is exactly what I need as I'm flooded with unexpected warmth. Perhaps it's the fact that, out of everyone in this nightmare, she reminds me of myself. After all, in America, she only has her father, and I only had my grandmother. I turned to art to heal a void within me. Perhaps unbeknownst to her father, so has his little girl.

Flynn stands firm, not rattled from the shootout that just rocked the mansion grounds. Blood has dried into a rusty streak on his sleeve, Adian's or his father's. I try not to think about whether the men will make it through the night. A strained look crosses his face as his eyes fall upon the gun on his nightstand.

"What now?" I hear my voice come out in a hush, a bit shaky but resolute.

"You're brave," he responds, his lip twitching at the corner.

I snort because it's far from the truth. "I'm not brave. I just need answers."

He groans, stepping closer until I'm surrounded by his warm scent of cedar and gunpowder. "Now, we keep you safe. Guard Taryn." His voice trembles slightly with more emotion than I've ever heard from him. "I'm sorry about... everything."

An apology?

I'm amazed, but I don't gloat. Maybe I'm more astonished at how much his words soothe me. It hits me then; I'm no longer furious about being drugged and flown to Ireland against my will. In the grand scheme of what we've suffered—the gunshots ricocheting, the blood and death—Flynn's protective disposition makes a twisted sort of sense. Glancing up at him, I take in the dark circles under his eyes, the way his hair is all messy like he's been raking worried fingers through it.

My mind drifts to our time back home. We were starting to get close, and by close, I mean we were about to fuck. The man's fingers had been deep within me. Then everything changed so unexpectedly. My life, our reality, bent around a secret I never saw coming: Flynn's ties to the *Irish Faction*.

He's searching my face for a reaction to his apology, but his shoulders are stiff with what appears to be guilt.

"Is Taryn safe here?" I ask the obvious, allowing my concern for his daughter to guide the conversation. My gaze darts to the door, where, past it, I'm sure his men are still on high alert.

He nods. "Yes, as safe as she can be. Now that the family has gathered, all of them arriving after they've heard about Da. My family's watching over her. And you."

"I'm alright," I assure him, noticing a gash on his shoulder. There's dried blood, and it worries me sick. I surprise us both by reaching out to rest my fingertips on the torn fabric of his shirt. My actions are too intimate, unlike our previous heated encounters. "You're hurt."

He shakes his head like it's nothing. "*Feckers* only grazed me. I've endured worse. It's you I'm concerned about."

Outside the door, the sounds of footsteps in the hall carry to us, along with distant voices speaking in hushed Irish accents. It reminds me again this is not my world. But, for the moment, I'm stuck in it.

I swallow hard, gazing around the lavish bedroom one more time, suddenly grounded by the swirl of emerald velvet, the gleam of brass, and the Celtic carvings on the walls. I try to sound brave as I ask, "So, what's the plan? Because I can't spend the rest of my life holed up in your mansion in Ireland, no matter how beautiful it is. Even if it could stand to be brightened up a bit... And it's Valentine's Day next week. It might seem like nothing compared to everything going on here, but my students put so much work into decorating for their party. Taryn is especially excited. This is her first dance."

A shadow passes over his features, making me realize I've never seen him appear so unsure. "I'm trying to flush out a *fecking* traitor within the family," he says between his teeth. He glances at the door as though he can feel the presence of foes even through the thick wood. Then, with a breath, he softens again. "With everyone here, it won't be long until I get to the bottom of who is working with our enemies. I'll do whatever I must to stop them. So you and Taryn don't have to live in fear."

His determined voice suddenly sounds so sweet to me. He's a protective guy, even if he's a little more intense than your average dad. I can't forget he's a mobster, involved in an extremely violent world. However, right now, I can't ignore the passion in his tone, nor how desperate he looks.

I give a small, unsteady nod. "I trust you," I whisper.

"Thank you," he murmurs, dipping his head closer.

For a second, I remember my classroom with its smell of paint and sparkle of glitter, everything I ever thought I wanted. It feels so far away, and I don't give a damn. Not when we stand there quietly together, the stress melting into something gentler.

Flynn squares his shoulders, breaking the moment. "I need to meet with my family's men, assess the situation," he states. "Stay here. Lock the door. I won't be long."

He turns from me, and, on impulse, I reach for his hand. My grip briefly squeezes to get his attention and let him know he's not alone in this. His rough fingers curl around mine in return, the contact sending a jolt of lust straight through my tired body. He glances my way again as I stand barefoot on the plush rug, his robe dwarfing me. Then he releases my hand and advances to the grand armoire with fancy brass fixtures, his expression flickering with a hint of hesitation.

"I'll find you something to sleep in," he offers, pulling open the double doors.

First, I'm not sure what I'm seeing. Rows of elegant blouses, dresses, and skirts, each hanging neatly on padded hangers. After a beat, realization settles into my chest. These are a woman's clothes, obviously not his. My heart sinks as I recall Flynn's history, how he left this life behind after his enemies killed his wife. The pang of empathy hits me hard, and I press my lips together to keep from blurting out an apology I'm not sure he needs.

He flips through the garments with quick, efficient movements, but I can't help to notice the stiffness in his jaw. As a soft sweater brushes his knuckles, there's a slight tremor in his hand.

My throat tightens, imagining the memories these clothes must carry. A single tear escapes before I can stop it. I don't make a sound, but he turns around anyway, his golden eyes sharp with concern. He's beside me immediately, gently brushing my tear away.

"There's something you should know," Flynn says quietly, his gaze momentarily drifting back to the clothes in the armoire. "Before Aisling died… we were practically estranged. We only kept up appearances for Taryn. As much as I once loved her, we were distant when they…" His voice catches, and he exhales a ragged breath. He laughs a bit, shaking his head. "In fact, I think she'd taken a lover. Somehow, that only makes it worse… not her moving on, but the fact we weren't speaking."

I swallow hard, my heart aching for him.

He pulls a simple, oversized T-shirt from the armoire, handing it to me. His eyes linger on my face as he offers, "This is mine."

I clutch the garment to my chest.

As he quietly closes the wardrobe, I catch one last glimpse of delicate lace and floral prints. Then he's returned to the threshold, ready to slip back into the corridors of his family's dark business. I crumble, sitting perched on the edge of the bed, still trying to catch my breath from everything that's happened tonight. It feels like another lifetime has passed since we were merely two neighbors who shared the love of his daughter.

Suddenly, Flynn hesitates. He releases the doorknob and half-turns toward me. His features are all raw conflict, captivating me. "There's something..." He speaks in a hoarse whisper that somehow makes his heavy Irish accent more pronounced. "I need to do first. Something I've wanted to do since I first laid eyes on you."

Before I can even speak, he crosses the room in two quick strides and pulls me up into a fierce kiss. I grab his biceps, entirely forgetting the mansion, the shootout, the danger swirling outside the bedroom walls.

He breaks the contact only long enough to lift me and toss me onto the bed. His golden stare on me, his voice husky, he confesses, "I know this is the worst possible time, but I can't keep pretending anymore. I need you."

Chapter 14

Morgan Jane Mitchell

Sutton

"FLYNN, I... I'VE WANTED this, but everything's so..."

He brushes a strand of hair behind my ear. "Shh, Miss Matthews. I'm going to fuck you," he murmurs. "My enemies can wait." He leans in and kisses me properly, nearly devouring me. I can't believe we're doing this here... after everything that's happened. But, of course, I want him, too.

Tenderly cradling my face in his big hands, he says, "We've been running on fear and adrenaline, but I promise, I'm not fleeing this. Not from you." His voice is soft as he leaves kisses along my jaw.

I offer, "You're hurt. Let me..." I aim to help him undress, not like it'll be any hardship on my part.

He smiles at my concern. "I'm fine. I just... I need to know you're safe. This... this reminds me exactly why I have to end all of this madness. Maybe I should go?"

Oh, hell, no.

Taking his shirt, I jerk him closer, my breathing ragged. Closing my eyes, letting the moment overwhelm my senses, I plead, "Stay with me. Even if it's only for now."

"I'm here," he murmurs, his voice shaking. "I'm here."

My inhale echoes in the luxurious space as he opens the robe and descends upon me. *"Bòidheach,"* he whispers against my ear, making a shiver run through me. A heartbeat later, he's pressing his lips to mine with renewed urgency. I can't stop my hands from roaming into his pants, finding his cock, hard and ready.

All thoughts of violence, of the Irish Mafia's hold on him, and on us, evaporate as I stroke his cock. My student's father, the single dad, my grumpy neighbor who always seemed so guarded, yet gentle when he spoke about Taryn, is up on his knees stripping off his bloody shirt. My eyes flit over him, his tattoos. I've seen the full sleeves of ink on his arms but suddenly spy the family crest spanning his back as he twists to lose his pants and shove away his boxers in the process.

Just hours ago, my reality flipped into something unrecognizable as I was drugged, dragged across the ocean, and then nearly caught in the crossfire of a family feud I never knew existed. Now, I'm face-to-cock with a gloriously naked Irish mobster, the biggest cock I've ever seen, surrounded by soft hairs matching the reddish tufts on his head. Glancing up at him, I lick my lips, but then reach up to tangle my fingers in his hair, pulling him on top of me.

I want this man inside me, now.

However, Flynn has other plans as he dips down, leaving a trail of rough kisses to my breasts. His teeth take a nipple, and I whimper with delight. He grins, hearing me, before continuing his sexy attack. Kissing and nipping his way down my body, he's savoring every inch like it's the last thing he'll ever taste. When he reaches my core, he spreads my thighs wide with his large hands. I can feel him exhale deeply as his hot breath tickles my wet sex.

As much as I'm excited, I'm keeping my expectations in check. I watch the entrance, waiting for some trouble to show up and ruin our fun like all the times before.

His lips move lower, continuing their sweet assault, and I grab the sheets, hard. *Can this actually be happening?* Soft moans flow from my lips as I feel his breath hit my most intimate place. Flynn spreads my folds with his skilled fingers, teasing me as he circles my clit with his tongue.

"Flynn," I squeak.

"Yes, Miss Matthews," he growls against my pussy. "I'm going to make you scream my name."

His claim gives me chills in all the right places, but his tongue makes me squirm with delight. Every lick brings more and more ecstasy until it's almost unbearable. Just when I think I can't handle any more, his fingers slip inside me, curling and searching for the right spot. Moaning his name, I grab his hair again, this time holding on for dear life.

My hips buck against his open mouth, inviting him deeper into me. "Flynn… Flynn," I repeat, each word a breathy huff as he pushes me closer and closer to the edge.

He suddenly withdraws, the move leaving me frustrated when he notices me flicking my stare from him to the door. He squints for a beat, finally coming to the conclusion that I'm keeping watch. Waiting for us to be interrupted, again.

With a low growl, he moves closer, positioning himself by my entryway. "The door is locked. And *nothing* will stop me. Not this time. I promise. Do you trust me, Miss Matthews?" he asks, his large, throbbing cock knocking at my entrance.

"Yes," I manage, my eyes fluttering.

He mumbles something in his foreign tongue, his voice raw as he grabs my thigh to widen me. Then, with one hard thrust, his cock fills me. I gulp at his girth as my body trembles around him.

"Say my name," he commands, his furrowed brow hanging over me.

"Flynn," I barely breathe.

"*Bòidheach*," he responds in return, his voice all gravelly. "Feck. You're tight, *bheag*. So wet and tight."

And he moves.

"Flynn," I cry out.

He grunts back, eyes blazing. That's all it takes to really get him going. Each move is powerful, almost too powerful. Fuck. My hands cling to his shoulders, my nails poking into his back as my cries ring out through the room. He leans in, demanding, "Who's a grandpa now?" He groans through the sensations as he makes me completely unravel underneath him.

I have no words, can't form a coherent thought to counter how wrong my jab about him being older turned out to be. Only unintelligible pants and sounds manage to surge from me as he nearly breaks the headboard.

Sweat glistens across his forehead, and there's an emotion I can't quite place in his intense stare. It's like he's looking deep into my soul, searching for something. Quietly, he utters what he said moments before, and I'm able to make it out this time, *"Mo ghrá."*

"What does it mean?" I pant out.

"My love," he admits, and even though he's spoken those words before, suddenly, they signify *so* much more.

The warm and fuzzies take over. The walls of my heart seem to disintegrate as he continues his rhythmic assault. A different kind of pleasure wells up within me. *Flynn isn't merely fucking me; he's making love to me.*

He speeds up his pace, his muscles tightening against me. "Oh, Christ," he bellows, deep.

"Mo ghrá," I whisper in return, repeating his words.

His expression darkens, and somehow, he drives even deeper.

Fuck. I cry out his name again and again, my impending climax doing all the speaking for me. Us finally together, like this, is everything. I've needed him, to feel him everywhere.

My name is on the tip of his tongue until it finally falls with a bellow, "Sutton!"

Hearing my name on his lips in his sexy Irish accent makes me lose it. Fuck. My toes curl, my nails scoring against my palm, as my chest heaves from drawing in gasps between his powerful thrusts. It's too much; the sensations are ripping me up inside, but at the same time, I can't seem to get enough of him. I don't think I ever will.

His breath is hot against my ear as he tucks in close, his sensual voice teasing again. *"Tá grá mé dom."* Then, he explodes into me, his body shuddering with the powerful release.

I hold onto him tightly, needing his nearness and weight to help anchor me as my orgasm takes me up and away.

The pleasure.

The connection.

The soul-deep feelings.

We lie tangled in his soft sheets, catching our breath, and I endeavor to gather my thoughts. However, it's no use, my brain is mush. Flynn shifts beside me, easing out of me, and I hate it. I watch him stand, then begin to dress. The strain of recent events lingers on his tense shoulders, but his expression is now softer, more open than before.

He looks at me, resolve burning in his eyes. "I've lived with this life on my heels for too long. Taryn deserves better. So do you."

Propping myself up on my elbows, I ask, "What happens now?"

He inhales sharply, shrugging on his torn shirt. "I'm going to find another way. Whatever it takes. I don't wish you to be trapped in Ireland or in this family's mess. And Taryn... she can't grow up like this, always looking over her shoulder as danger knocks at the door." He glances over to where I'm sitting, clutching the covers around me. "I can't stay in Ireland forever, either. I have a business to run. My family thinks I will take over someday, but it's not my plan." His hands pause at the buttons. "I only want one thing now—two things, really."

His voice goes gruff at the end, and I realize he's talking about Taryn... *and me.* My heart bursts in my chest.

He picks up his gun from the nightstand. "We'll find another way," he vows. "A means for you to go home safely. And a way for Taryn to have a life far from this violence."

I'm about to cry because for all Flynn's swagger and self-assurance, I can see how deeply he wants out. How desperately he needs to keep Taryn, and now me, from living in constant danger.

He comes over to the bed and gently lifts my chin, his gaze earnest. "I'm serious."

I lean into his palm, letting my eyes close for a moment. "I believe you," I say, and I mean it, too. "But please... come back in one piece."

His lips brush mine in a gentle kiss before he straightens, tucking his gun away. "I will," he promises. "Wait for me."

"I trust you. Just... don't shut me out. Promise."

Flynn cups my face in his hands and plants another tender kiss on my forehead. "I promise, *mo ghrá*."

For the first time since this whole mess began, I dare to hope for a future without fear. Where Taryn can grow up drawing sketches of flowers and houses, safe from any looming threats. Where Flynn and I can have a chance to see where this is heading.

He steps into the hallway, and then he's gone, leaving me swooning.

F LYNN

When Sutton begs me, "Stay with me. Even if it's only for now," I know I want to make her mine more than I've wanted anything in a long time. It's not only how her dark hair frames her voluptuous naked body or how her hands grip me like I'm the only man who can save her. It's in the way she looks at me, bright blue eyes full of trust and acceptance when I promise I won't leave her.

For a moment, as we lie in each other's arms, everything else fades, the gunfire I barely escaped earlier and even the shadows of my family's world.

I stand at the bedside, continuing to buzz inside from the sensation of Sutton's curvy body quivering beneath mine. My breathing is ragged; the shirt I put on remains bloody and tattered at the shoulder. Though I wince in pain, I continue to feel the heat of her soft skin against mine. Taste her juices on my lips.

I take one last look at her now. The sheet draping over the gentle curve of her hip, along with the sight of her bare breasts, makes my dick hard all over again. She's beautiful in a way that leaves me feeling reckless. She makes me feel... almost human. Given my experiences, that's anything but insignificant.

Her words echo, "I trust you. Just... don't shut me out. Promise."

And I did vow.

"I promise, *mo ghrá*," the words drum in my head as I move toward the door. I glance at her face, peaceful for once, and close my eyes, fighting the urge to crawl back into bed and lose myself again in her sweet pussy.

Reluctantly, I make my way into the hallway. Instantly, the hush of the homestead presses in on me, centuries of power plays and betrayals. I grip the doorknob behind me, making sure it's locked. My father's mansion looms around me, thick with secrets and the memory of carnage. If I stay here much longer, I'll be sucked right back into the life that's been destroying me.

I'm about to continue on when a figure emerges at the far end of the corridor. A woman. For a moment, I almost don't recognize Fiona. I haven't seen my cousin outside of the attic in ages. She's always the cautious one, the one who takes no risks, but as she showed earlier, her ways can pay off. Her face looks just like her twin, Aidan. However, it's tear-streaked, pale, and trembling at the moment.

My stomach twists.

The fact she's here now, in full view, can only mean something catastrophic has happened. Her cold fingers close around mine, and the despair in her swollen eyes is all the confirmation I need before she has a chance to speak.

"Aidan?" Did my cousin succumb to his wounds?

Fiona shakes her head.

My world tilts. She tells me my da—my father—is gone.

Just like that.

Gone. Cold. Dead.

I'm too shocked to react, remembering how I left him with the doctor earlier. I was sure he'd pull through, yet again, like every time before. I promised Taryn he'd be okay... how foolish of me. There's no time for sorrow, though. My first terrible thought is of betrayal. Did someone kill my father? Is there truly a traitor among my own flesh and blood?

Fiona's tears drip onto our clasped hands as she bows her head in deference, acknowledging me the way our people do for the head of the family.

I've never wanted this.

She mumbles a shaky thanks, grateful I'm here. *"Ceann an Teaghlaigh,"* she uses the title we reserve for those who inherit the mantle of leadership in this dark, twisted clan. I can't bring myself to say anything back. No words fit the magnitude of losing the man who has shaped my entire life, for better or worse.

Her reverence is troubling.

A sickening mix of grief and vengefulness does its worst, carving a bottomless pit in my stomach. The memory of Sutton's breathy voice is the only thing keeping me remotely grounded. With my father gone, the vow I made to protect Taryn and now Sutton becomes even more urgent.

Fiona's still bowing, calling me the head of the family. I can't ignore it, no matter how much I want to. My mind's a mess. My heart is silently breaking. Nevertheless, someone needs to take charge to keep the peace from collapsing into more bloodshed. Taking control is exactly what my father would have expected of me, or rather demanded, more likely. But all I can picture is Sutton lying in my bed, trusting me to keep her safe, and Taryn asleep peacefully in another room, blissfully unaware that her granda is gone.

Taking one last steady breath, I force down the shock and meet Fiona's tearful gaze. I seal my fate by assuring her, *"Is mé anois Ceann an Teaghlaigh."*

I am now the Head of the Family.

Chapter 10

Shannon Myers

Flynn

I SIT AT DA'S grand mahogany desk, a throne I never wanted to inherit. My new role as *Ceann an Teaghlaigh* presses down on me like a thousand stones. My mind races with nothing but dark suspicions, knowing a traitor is lurking in our midst.

The green and gold O'Reilly crest mocks me from its framed position on the wall opposite the desk. While the lions signify our family's strength and fierceness, the bloody hand at its center around the cross represents loyalty and the importance of our family's justice.

Our legacy, *our burden*.

Da always said heavy is the head that wears the crown. I feel that weight now, settling on my shoulders like a leaden cloak.

But it's not just my own neck on the line. My wee girl, who's growing up too fast for my liking, and the raven-haired hurricane who's stolen my heart are facing the gallows with me. I have to shield Taryn and Sutton from this life, from the ugliness that comes with our family business.

I run a tattooed hand over my fatigued eyes and exhale a frustrated breath. A mere two days in, and the responsibilities of this role already threaten to suffocate me. I'm a man of action, more at home dodging bullets and cracking skulls than navigating the tangled web of mob politics. But I can't falter now.

Not when a snake is lurking somewhere in the O'Reilly grass, coiled tightly and ready to strike.

A soft knock at the door jolts me out of my spiraling thoughts. "Come in," I bark out, my voice rough with the whiskey I've been nursing.

Sutton slips inside, carefully closing the door behind her with a soft *snick* before approaching. "You missed dinner again, so I brought you some food."

I swallow hard, my throat tight with emotion I can't afford to show. "Thank you, *mo ghrá*," I murmur as she sets the bowl on the desk. The corner of my mouth lifts in amusement. "Bangers and Colcannon? It's not Saint Patrick's Day already, is it?"

Her lips lift into a smile not quite reaching her eyes. "Taryn insisted. Said it was your favorite."

My chest tightens at the mention of my daughter. I've barely seen her since... everything. "How is she?"

"Worried about you." She passes me the bowl of food before perching on the edge of the desk, brushing her fingers over my cheek. "To be perfectly honest, we both are."

I lean into her touch for a moment before pulling away with a heavy sigh. "I'm fine."

Sutton's vivid blue eyes narrow on mine when I push the bowl aside, concern etched into their depths. "You're running yourself ragged, Flynn. When's the last time you slept?"

I offer a noncommittal grunt, not wanting to admit it's been days since I've had more than a catnap. "I'll rest once I root out the bastard who's betrayed us, *mo chroí*."

She slides off the desk and into my lap with a huff, her delicate fingers reaching out to trace the dark circles beneath my eyes. "Before or after you collapse from exhaustion?" she asks, her voice soft but determined. "I'm not leaving this room until you eat something."

"Is that an offer, Miss Matthews?" I ask, quirking my brow suggestively. I shouldn't be thinking of spreading her across the desk and feasting on her sweet pussy when there's a traitor to catch, but she brings out an almost feral need in me.

Sutton's cheeks flush, but she stands her ground. "Nice try, but no. I meant the actual food, Flynn."

"Fine," I relent, reaching for the bowl when it becomes clear she won't be swayed. Stubborn lass. "Only because you went to the trouble."

I grab a forkful of colcannon, shoveling it into my mouth to distract myself from the temptation of her body. Christ, it's good. I can't even remember the last time I ate.

She grins, clearly pleased, as I devour the entire meal like a ravenous beast. "See? That wasn't so hard," she teases, running her fingers through my hair.

Her touch soothes some of the tension coiled between my shoulder blades, and I set the bowl aside before pulling her closer. "Thank you."

"Any progress today?" she asks, nodding to the papers strewn across the desk.

"Nothing but more questions," I admit with a sigh. "I've known most of these men my entire life. I can't imagine any of them betraying *The Faction* or our family apart from Aidan."

Sutton's fingers are still in my hair. "You truly believe Aidan's behind all of this?"

My jaw tightens, and I shake my head. "I don't know anything anymore. He's the only one with a clear motive, but he also took bullets for the family. Had one of those shots been a millimeter to the left, he'd be six feet under right now."

Like Da.

Not that the bullet wound to the shoulder killed my father. It hadn't even been life-threatening. No, Killian O'Reilly, who'd wanted to go out in a hail of bullets, had been taken out by a trauma-induced heart attack. Were he given a choice in the matter, I have no doubt he would have chosen something a little more dramatic.

I swallow past the sudden lump in my throat, refusing to give in to my grief. Not now. Not when my family needs me to be strong.

Her brows furrow as she mulls it over. "Aidan's a total asshole, but at the end of the day, he's still your cousin. Besides, he doesn't strike me as the type who would take a bullet for show. It's too risky."

"Aye, which is what makes this so *fecking* complicated," I say, feeling a headache blooming behind my eyes. "Either this traitor covered their tracks better than the J2, or I'm missing something."

Sutton shifts in my lap, her soft curves pressing against me. "Maybe you need to look at it from a different angle," she suggests, going back to stroking my hair. "Like an artist would."

I raise an eyebrow, intrigued despite myself. "How do you mean?"

"Think of it the way a painter would. A single brushstroke on its own is nothing to look at," she explains, her eyes lighting up with the spark of creativity I've come to admire. "However, when you connect it to others, a picture begins to emerge. Maybe you need to step back to see the bigger picture."

Her words strike a chord. "The deeper motivations," I murmur, grudgingly impressed. "That's... not a bad idea, actually."

"Know what else is a good idea?" she asks as she leans in to drag her lips along the stubble on my jaw. "You taking a break to clear your head."

Her soft lips against my jaw sends a jolt of electricity through my body. I groan, my cock swelling instantly beneath her curvy *arse*. "Sutton..."

"Shh," she whispers, peppering kisses down my throat. "Just relax."

God, I want to. I want to lose myself in her, to forget about traitors and murder, and the crushing weight of responsibility for a few blissful moments. My hands slide to her hips, gripping tightly as she grinds against my erection.

"Let me help relieve some of your stress," she breathes against my ear before dropping to her knees between my thighs. "Let me take care of you."

My breath catches as her nimble fingers work my zipper down. I know I should stop her, push her away. There's too much at stake to indulge in pleasure right now. But when she frees my aching cock and wraps her small hand around the base, all rational thought flies out the window.

"Christ," I hiss through my teeth as she traces the vein along my shaft with her tongue before swirling it over the precum beading at the tip. My head falls back, eyes closing in bliss when she takes me into her hot, wet mouth.

She pulls me deeper, hollowing her cheeks, and I'm lost to the incredible suction of her mouth and the feel of her throat spasming around me.

Nothing exists outside of Sutton's gorgeous, plump lips stretched around my cock. No traitors. No ambushes. No responsibility. Only pure, mindless pleasure.

Guilt begins to creep in, poisoning the moment. My family is counting on me. Everyone is counting on me. Yet, here I am, getting my rocks off instead of hunting down the person who murdered my da.

What kind of leader am I?

"Stop," I rasp, gently pulling her off my cock. "I-I can't. Not right now."

Hurt and confusion flash in her blue eyes as I hastily tuck myself away before getting to my feet, needing to walk away before I change my mind. She swipes the back of her hand over her mouth before rocking back on her heels. "Flynn, you need to relax—"

"What I need is to find this traitor before anyone else gets hurt," I snap, harsher than intended. "I can't afford distractions."

She flinches at my tone. "Is that all I am to you? A distraction?"

Christ, I'm *bolloxing* this up. "That's not what I meant, *mo chroí*. I just... I can't let my guard down. Not for a second."

"You won't eat. You won't sleep. You won't even leave this office to comfort your grieving daughter," Sutton states, anger bleeding into her tone. "Have you stopped to consider what you're doing to her? She's lost one of the most important men in her life, and now you're pushing her away. I'm spending every waking moment with her, but it's not me she needs, Flynn. It's her dad!"

"I'm doing this *for Taryn*!" I shout, bringing my fist down on the desk. "For all of us! I can either be the family man, or I can keep you all safe, but I can't do both."

She places a hand on her hip, straightening to her full height, bringing her level with the middle of my chest. "So, what?" she challenges. "You're going to keep pushing us away? I'm right here! You don't have to take all of this on alone. Let me help."

For a moment, I'm tempted. The weight on my shoulders is crushing me, and the idea of sharing the burden is so bloody appealing. However, I can't. I won't put her life in any more danger than I already have.

I laugh, the sound harsh and bitter. "What skills could you possibly bring to The Faction, eh? Glitter bombs?"

The moment the words leave my mouth, I'm immediately wishing I could take them back. Sutton recoils as if I've physically slapped her, pain etching across her delicate features.

"If I'm so useless, why'd you bother drugging me and bringing me here in the first place?" she demands, biting down on her bottom lip.

"For your *fecking* safety." I run a hand through my hair in frustration. "Something I'm still committed to, even if it means tearing this entire family apart to find the bastard responsible."

Sutton's eyes shimmer with unshed tears as she turns to leave. At the door, she pauses. "What if there's no family left by the time you're done?" She doesn't wait for a response, the door closing softly behind her. The silence in her wake is deafening.

I slump back into the chair, hating myself for hurting her. *Christ, I'm a right bastard.*

How did Da make this look easy? Forty-eight hours in, and I'm already failing everyone. With a frustrated growl, I yank open the bottom drawer of his desk, hoping a bit more liquid courage will dull the pain. Instead of the bottle of whiskey, my hand brushes against a thick manila folder buried beneath stacks of paperwork.

I pull it out, my breath catching when I see the name scrawled across the tab in Da's messy handwriting: *Aisling*.

Why would my father have a secret file on my dead wife?

Photos spill across the polished wood, and my heart stops.

Aisling, laughing as she walks hand-in-hand with a man who is decidedly not me. Aisling, pressed up against a wall, locked in a passionate embrace.

I was right. She had taken a lover.

My cousin Aidan.

Rage clouds my vision, every fiber of my being screaming for his blood. I storm out of my office, nearly taking the door off its hinges before thundering down the stairs two at a time. I find him in the parlor, lounging on the sofa with Fiona hovering nearby. His bandaged torso is a stark reminder of the bullets he took, but I no longer see it as a sign of loyalty—just another deception.

This lying, two-faced bastard has been playing us for fools this entire time.

Chapter 16

Shannon Myers

Flynn

"IS IT TRUE?" I growl, my fists clenched at my sides.

He takes one look at me, and his face pales. "Flynn, I can explain—"

I don't give him a chance. My fist connects with his jaw, sending him sprawling back against the sofa. "Explain what?" I roar, spit building up at the corners of my mouth like some rabid beast. "How you're a backstabbing piece of *shite*? How you betrayed the family? How you got Aisling killed?"

Fiona shouts in alarm as I haul her twin up by his dark hair before repeatedly striking his torso. Pain flashes across his face as the blows land against stitches and bruised skin, but I'm beyond caring.

"Tell me, you fucking bastard!" I demand.

I pull back to hit him again when Fiona steps between us, pressing her hand to my chest. "Flynn, stop! You're tearing his stitches!"

"Grand," I snarl, struggling against her grip. "The traitor deserves worse."

"I'm not a fucking traitor," Aidan croaks, wincing as he presses a hand to his side. Blood runs down his chin from where I split his lip, but it's not enough to calm the storm brewing behind my ribcage.

I push past Fiona to slam him against the wall, sending picture frames crashing down around us. "Their blood is on your hands!" I spit, holding my forearm over his windpipe. "Aisling. My da. How many more?"

"Enough!" Fiona screams, her grip surprisingly strong as she grabs my arm. "You're going to kill him!"

"Maybe I should," I growl, but I loosen my grip slightly.

Aidan gasps for air, his face red. "I didn't... betray anyone," he chokes out. "I loved her!"

The admission only fuels my rage. "You loved her? She was my wife!"

"You need to cool down before you make an even bigger *arse* of yourself, Ceann an Teaghlaigh," Fiona hisses before nodding behind me.

I turn to follow her gaze, swallowing hard when I discover Sutton standing at the bottom of the stairs, her blue eyes wide with shock.

"I heard shouting," she says quietly, her knuckles white against the banister.

Shame washes over me as I realize what she's just witnessed. I release Aidan, who slumps against the wall, wheezing loudly.

She stumbles back a step when I start toward her, holding up a trembling palm. "Don't. Please."

The same woman who went after an Italian mobster with a baseball bat is staring at me like she's—

Christ.

She's *afraid* of me.

The realization hits me harshly, a sucker punch to my gut. I've become the very monster I swore to protect her from. I watch helplessly as she escapes up the stairs, my heart sinking. How did everything go so wrong, so fast?

Fiona helps Aidan back to the sofa, checking his bandages before clapping an iron hand against my shoulder. "Your da's office. *Now.*" Once we're behind closed doors, she rounds on me. "What the hell were you thinking?"

I pace across the office, feeling every bit of a caged animal by my own doing. My hands clench and release at my sides as I ask, "What was I thinking? That the bastard has betrayed me!"

"Everyone knew your marriage was in name only," she counters bluntly.

"Jesus, Mary, and Joseph, Fi. You knew about this?"

She pinches the bridge of her nose with a heavy sigh, likely regretting her decision to leave the attic. "Of course, I *fecking* knew. I have eyes and ears everywhere, cousin," she admits with a humorless laugh. "Not as if I needed them. Only a fool could have missed the way they looked at each other."

The implication I'm a fool has me bristling. "You didn't think to mention this before now?"

"Wasn't my secret to tell," Fiona says, lifting her shoulder in a shrug. "But acting the maggot and beating my brother half to death isn't going to solve anything."

"Acting the maggot? *He was fecking my wife!*"

"Ah, here, a wife you barely acknowledged," Fiona says, her gray eyes sparking with anger. "You and I both know you were never there."

"No, our marriage didn't work because Aisling didn't like that I was part of The Faction," I argue, though the words sound hollow even to my own ears. If it were the case, why would she go to Aidan?

"It wasn't The Faction Aisling didn't like, you *eejit*. It was who you became because of it. A miserable *shite* who shuts out the people who try to love him."

The truth washes over me, and I collapse into Da's chair, the fight draining out of me. I sit in stunned silence, Fiona's words ringing in my ears like a judgment.

"Christ," I mutter, rubbing my temples. "I'm *bollixing* everything up again."

Her expression softens slightly. "Then stop, ya *gobshite*. You're not your da. You don't have to do this alone," she says, echoing Sutton's words from earlier and reminding me of the fear and hurt in her eyes.

I scrub a hand over my face, feeling the stubble that's grown unchecked. "I moved to Boston to keep Tary safe. Now, I'm right back where I started. Only the target on our backs is even bigger than before."

Fiona sits down on the desk and crosses her legs. "Aye, and you're pushing away the few people still willing to help you shoulder the burden."

Her words hit too close to home. I think of Sutton's face as she fled up the stairs, of how I've neglected Taryn in my obsession to find the traitor. "I don't know how to do this," I admit, staring at the family crest again. "How am I supposed to keep them safe if I can't figure out who has betrayed us?"

"You start by trusting your family," she says firmly. "Aidan may be a right *arse* at times, but he's no traitor. O'Reilly blood runs through his veins the same as yours and mine."

I want to believe her, but doubt still gnaws at me. "If not Aidan, then who? Aisling had no connection to the Italians, so why kill her unless she overheard something she shouldn't have? And who would she have heard it from, other than the man she was sleeping with?"

Fiona shakes her head. "Think, cousin. What information could Aidan have possibly passed to the Italians? He wasn't high-ranking enough to sit in on most family meetings until after Aisling's death and your move to Boston. He didn't have access to the kind of intel Arturo was getting. Do you truly think the great Killian O'Reilly—" She pauses to make the sign of the cross before continuing, "God rest his soul, would have allowed Aidan to remain part of *The Faction* if he thought he was a traitor? Don't be an *eejit*."

"So, we're back to square one. Why kill Aisling?" I ask, pushing out of the chair to pace the length of the office, my body coursing with anxious energy.

My cousin taps her fingernails against the mahogany, deep in thought. "What if you're right? What if Aisling did discover something she wasn't supposed to... but not from Aidan?"

I freeze before cutting my eyes over to her, the pieces slowly shifting into place. "You think she might have uncovered the real traitor?"

"And she was silenced to keep it from coming out in the process," Fiona finishes with a grim nod. "The person who betrayed us likely knew about Aidan and Aisling's affair and set my brother up to take the fall."

"Clever bastard," I mutter, snatching the list of names off the desk. "Not many would have known the things the Italians do, which should narrow this down considerably."

Fiona leans in to study it with a pinched, tension-filled expression. "Someone high-ranking enough to have valuable information but not so visible we'd immediately suspect them."

I press my fingertips to my bleary eyes as one name blurs into the next. "Narrows it to half the inner circle."

"Aye, and every one of them served the *Ceann an Teaghlaigh* for years," she agrees with a heavy sigh. "Any of them could have turned."

Like a painter connecting brushstrokes, we pore over the names, crossing off those who don't fit the criteria. After an hour of debate and analysis, we're left with four possibilities:

Cillian O'Reilly

Darragh Quinn

Eoghan Brady

Rian Balfe

Fiona studies Da's computer screen, her fingers flying across the keys. "Cillian was traveling back and forth to Kilcornan in the month leading up to Aisling's murder. His da had a stroke."

I rub my temples, trying to stave off the worsening headache. "I remember. He barely had time to sleep, let alone pass family secrets to Arturo while dealing with his da's health crisis."

"Darragh's been with the family for over three decades and was there the day you were born," she notes, pulling up another screen.

"Aye, and he's been like a second father to me," I reluctantly agree. "But we can't rule anyone out based on sentiment alone. What about his finances? Can you get access to those?"

Her dark brow arches up. "Cousin, I can get access to anything."

"Then how do you not know who's behind this?" I grit out.

"Simple. I wasn't looking. Women have never had much of a place within *The Faction*, so I've kept to myself in the attic," she replies after a few moments of rapid typing. "No large deposits or unexplained withdrawals. He checks out."

"What about Eoghan? He's angling for a bigger role in the organization, last I heard. Maybe he thought selling us out to the Italians would give him leverage."

Fiona points to the screen. "Well, it looks like Rian's been struggling with gambling debts. The kind of payday Arturo could offer would be tempting, although you'd think he would have settled them by this point."

Too restless to stand still, I begin pacing again. "Not if he's trying to throw off suspicion. He stays on the list, along with Darragh and Eoghan. We know who has the means and opportunity, but which one had the motive? Which one of these is the bastard who stole Taryn's mam from her?"

"We'll get there, cousin," she consoles, coming over to squeeze my shoulder. "For now, you need some sleep before you keel over."

"I will, yeah," I tell her, a phrase meaning the exact opposite of what it does in America.

Her eyes narrow to slits, and she jabs a finger into my chest. "I mean it, Flynn. You look like absolute *shite* and are no good to anyone in the state you're in."

My body betrays me with a jaw-cracking yawn, forcing me to concede. "Fine, for a few hours. Then we get back to work, and wake me if you find anything in the meantime."

"Aye, now off with ye," she says, shooing me toward the door.

Feeling every one of my thirty-five years, I drag myself to my bedroom, stripping down to my boxers before collapsing onto the bed. Sutton stirs beside me, her raven hair spilling across the pillow. Even in sleep, there's a furrow between her brows.

It strikes me how little I truly know about her. Taryn previously mentioned Sutton not having any family in Boston, but does she have any living elsewhere?

I've taken family for granted, I realize—there's always been someone I can call, whether it be Da or a cousin. Thinking it over now, I can't recall Sutton ever mentioning her family, and it doesn't seem like she has many friends. Or any, for that matter.

My throat tightens at the thought of this woman being alone in the world. She's brought the light back into mine and Taryn's lives, and in the last week, I've ripped her away from a job and life she loves, minimized her, and have made her feel worthless. All for what? To 'protect' her? Some protector I've turned out to be.

Sutton's sapphire eyes flutter open, fixing on my face. "I can feel you watching me," she murmurs, her voice thick with sleep.

"Aye," I confess softly. "I was wondering if you have any friends or family you've left behind in the States."

Her chin trembles, and she darts her tongue out to wet her plump bottom lip before coolly replying, "I don't. Gonna point out how useless I am at that, too? Or maybe throw me into a wall like you did with Aidan?"

"I deserve your anger," I admit with a wince. "I've been treating you abominably, *mo chroí*. There's nothing useless about you."

She rolls onto her back, staring up at the ceiling. "Could have fooled me."

"Sutton," I whisper, reaching out to brush a strand of dark hair from her face. She flinches away from my touch, and the small rejection stings more than I care to admit. "Please look at me."

Her eyes eventually cut to mine, wary but attentive.

I press on, despite my exhaustion, desperate to make things right between us. "The night my da—" I swallow past the sudden lump in my throat, finding I can't say the word. Voicing it aloud will make it real, and I'm nowhere near ready for that. "You asked me not to shut you out, and it's exactly what I've done. What I've always done, if I'm being honest."

"Why?"

Raking a hand over my face, I exhale heavily and admit, "Because it's easier than letting people in. Safer. At least, it's what I thought, but I don't want to be that man anymore. Not with you."

She props herself up on an elbow, studying me for a long moment. "What's changed since dinner?"

"Everything," I reply with a huffed laugh. "I've made a right *hames* of it from the start. Then tonight, I saw the look in your eyes when you came downstairs and realized how close I am to losing you permanently. I need you to know you never have to fear me, Sutton. *Never.* You understand?"

"I'm not afraid of you, Flynn. I'm afraid *for* you. You've been so different since..." Her voice trails off, but I know exactly what she means.

Since I became the head of this godforsaken family. Since I took on a role I never wanted, a responsibility already changing me for the worse.

I press my forehead to hers, breathing in the comforting scent I would recognize anywhere as hers. "I know," I murmur. "But I'm still me. Still yours, if you'll have me. I want your input. I need you to feel you can come to me with anything. Big or small."

A ghost of a smile tugs at her lips. "Even glitter bombs?"

My face heats at the reminder of my cruel words. "Especially those. I've been doing this on my own for too long, but you make me want to be better. You challenge me in ways no one else ever has, and I... Christ, Sutton, *tá mé i ngrá leat,*" I murmur before rolling back against my pillow, struggling to hold my heavy eyes open a second longer.

"What does that mean?" Sutton asks, curling into my side.

It means I'm in love with you, Miss Matthews.

I think I say the words out loud, but exhaustion claims me before I can be sure. My eyes slip closed, and I drift off into a deep, dreamless sleep with the woman I love nestled against my side.

HOURS LATER, I JOLT awake when an agitated Fiona bursts into the bedroom. "What's wrong?" I ask, instantly alert despite the fog of sleep still clouding my mind.

She's muttering to herself, pacing back and forth. "We missed someone. How could we have *fecking* missed him? He was right there under our noses the entire time."

I bolt upright, my heart racing. "Who?"

Fiona stops, her steel-gray eyes locking onto mine. "Breandán."

Da's most trusted lieutenant. The one person who would have had access to everything. Every meeting. The intel on Aisling and Aidan. He was present for all of it.

"*Jaysus*," I mutter, throwing back the covers and hastily pulling on the clothes closest to me. I slip my feet into my shoes and turn to her, now wide awake. "What are we waiting for? Let's go nab the bastard."

We thunder down the stairs, moving from room to room, but there's no sign of Breandán. I find Aidan in the study, having his stitches checked over by the family doctor.

He jerks back with a hiss of pain when he sees me coming and throws up his arm. "Not again."

With a shake of my head, I flick my gaze toward the ceiling. "Not here for you, ya *gobshite*. Where's Breandán?"

Aidan lowers his arm slowly, eyeing me warily in the process. "He gave Sutton and Taryn a lift into town. Said they wanted to get decorations for Valentine's Day."

My blood runs cold. "What?"

"Aye, left about an hour ago," Aidan confirms, wincing as the doctor prods at his bruised ribs. "Why?"

"Fuck!" I roar, losing my temper and slamming my fist into the doorframe. Pain radiates up my arm, but I barely register it through the panic clawing at my chest.

Breandán has Sutton and my Tary.

The traitor who's murdered Aisling and Da now has the two people I love most in this world.

Chapter 17

Andi Rhodes

Sutton

"WE *need* to be heading back."

I smile at Breandán, who's been kind enough to drive Taryn and me all over town to find decorations for Valentine's Day. Having no clue what we're doing for the holiday, let alone what country we'll be in, I'm making do.

"One more stop," I tell him. "Promise."

He opens his mouth to reply, but his cell phone rings, momentarily distracting him. Breandán speaks to the caller in hushed tones, and I watch his face in the rearview mirror. He's an odd one, but if Killian and Flynn trusted him, then so do I.

"Aye, we'll see you soon, boss," he says just before he hangs up.

"Was that Daddy?" Taryn asks excitedly.

"It was." He clears his throat. "He's going to meet us for lunch."

Happiness flows through me. Flynn is finally going to take a break from all the crazy.

"Where are we meeting him?" Taryn asks, her eyes bright for the first time since her granda passed.

"Just across town," Breandán replies.

Taryn claps her hands, and I wrap my arm around her shoulders. I love seeing her like this. The sullen girl from the last few days is slowly disappearing, and I'm grateful.

"I'm afraid we don't have time to stop at another store, Miss Matthews."

"It's Sutton," I correct him with a smile. "Miss Matthews makes me feel like I'm in the classroom."

Breandán nods. "Yes, ma... I mean, yes, Sutton."

"Would we be able to stop at the last store after lunch?" I ask, still wanting to get a few more decorations.

"Uh, we should be able to, yes."

Breandán turns the radio up, making any further conversation challenging. I don't mind, though, because it gives me some much-needed time to think. From the moment Gail Stanley left the voicemail about a new job, my life has been tossed into the center of a tornado, and the funnel hasn't released me.

Meeting Flynn and Taryn has brought a lot of stress and pain, but the two of them have also filled the hole in my heart I thought would be impossible to fill. It dawns on me then, I wouldn't trade them for anything, even going back in time.

"We're here," Breandán states, pulling me from my thoughts.

I glance around and scrunch my nose in confusion. The only building around is a large brick one that looks more like a warehouse than a restaurant. There're no signs or other cars to even indicate this is a place of business. "Where is here, exactly?"

Rather than answer, he gets out of the SUV and moves to stand in front of it. I open my door, but before I can step out, two more SUVs pull in behind us. Fear dances down my spine, and I quickly slide into the backseat next to Taryn, locking the door. Reaching beyond the driver's seat, I press the button to lock the rest of the doors as well.

"What's going on?" Taryn questions, her voice wobbly. "Where's Daddy?"

"I don't know," I admit, pulling out my cell. It's then I notice several missed texts from Flynn. I was too engrossed in making the day special for Taryn, I didn't hear the notifications.

Flynn: *Where are you?*

Flynn: *Are you with Breandán?*

Flynn: *Answer me!*

Flynn: *Breandán's not who we thought he was. Weapon in locked box in glove compartment... 4834. Get it, and get away from him as soon as you can!*

My blood runs cold, and I open my contact list so I can call Flynn. Pressing the phone to my ear, I listen as it rings while simultaneously climbing over the center console to the front passenger seat. I open the compartment, punch in the code, and grab the knife right as the call connects.

"Sutton, where are you?" Flynn demands, his Irish accent thick with rage and worry.

Glass shatters around me, and I curl away from the window as an arm reaches in and snatches the phone from my hand. Taryn screams, and I turn to face her. Her eyes are wide, with tears sliding down her cheeks. As inconspicuous as I can, I shove the knife in her direction, silently begging her to take it.

"Ow!" I shout while I'm yanked toward the broken window by my hair.

"What are you going to do now?" a man sneers.

"I'm going to hunt you down like the animal you are and rip your heart out through your throat," Flynn bellows, and I realize he's been put on speakerphone.

"Ah, ah, ah," the asshole taunts. "Is that any way to talk to the man who holds the lives of these two *bellezze* in his hands?"

"Sutton!"

I try to turn my head at the sound of Taryn's scream, but the grip on my hair only intensifies, and then I'm being dragged through the space where the window was. Jagged glass slices through my flesh, sending pain skittering across my nerve endings.

"Take her inside and shut her the hell up," the man orders.

Footsteps crunch on the gravel, and it's only a few seconds before Taryn's cries for help are muffled because she's in the building and out of my sight.

"Arturo, leave them alone," Flynn snarls.

"I don't think you're in any position to be giving orders," Arturo snaps before disconnecting the call, tossing my cell to the ground and stomping on it. All hope of Flynn tracing the call and finding us vanishes in an instant. "Ah, much better." He hauls me to my feet and leans in close to my face. His breath smells of stale cigarettes, and it's all I can do not to vomit. "It's hard to concentrate with him blabbering on, don't you think?"

"What do you want?" I ask, my voice shakier than I'd like.

An evil smile spreads across his face. "What do I want?" he repeats. "What do I want?" Arturo grabs me by the arm, his fingers digging into my bicep, and urges me toward the building. "I want to show Flynn O'Reilly the Italians always have been and always will be better than the Irish. I thought killing his wife was enough," he continues, sneering at me. "But obviously, he bounced back."

That doesn't sound good.

He shoves me through the door, and when I attempt to yank out of his hold, his grip tightens. Arturo walks me down a long corridor, leading us to a large open space. Every muscle in my body, including my heart, tenses once I see Taryn bound to a chair with duct tape over her mouth.

Sliding my gaze to Breandán, my stomach plummets. Any loyalty he may have once had for the O'Reillys is long gone. The knife he's holding next to Taryn's head is proof of that.

The knife I gave her to protect herself.

I don't know the full story here, but I do know I'm going to need to tread carefully. If not for myself, then for Flynn's little girl. "Let her go," I plead. "You can do whatever you want to me, but just le—"

The sound of flesh against flesh reverberates through the space, my cheek stinging harshly where Arturo's just slapped me. I taste copper, the blood from my split lip slipping into my mouth. Taryn's crying and whimpering increase, but

I'm doing my best to put it out of my mind. I can't let my emotions cloud my judgment if I want to have any chance of getting her out of this.

Maybe Flynn's been doing things right.

"Give me three good reasons to let the brat go," Arturo begins. "And maybe I'll consider it."

"Seriously?" Breandán scoffs.

Arturo shrugs. "Never let it be said I'm an unfair man."

"You're making a mistake," the Irish traitor accuses.

"And it's my mistake to make, or have you forgotten who bought you out of your debt?" Arturo shifts his attention to me, pushing me to the floor. "Three reasons."

I blurt the first thing coming to my mind, "She's a child."

"Two?"

"You won't do well in prison if you're a child killer."

"That's assuming I go to prison."

The ego this man has is insane. "Do you really think you'll get away with this?" He nods, and I continue, "Let's assume you do. You manage to accomplish everything you want here today. Great, good for you. But you're forgetting one thing."

Arturo raises a brow. "And that is?"

"The O'Reillys aren't going to let anything you do today slide. Taryn dies, I die, Flynn dies. Okay, yeah, you've made people suffer. However, there are dozens more out there who will seek revenge. You'll never truly be free... behind bars or not."

He looks from me to Breandán. "Is it true?"

"Unfortunately for both of us, yes."

"Fine. What's number three?"

My thoughts tumble and twirl around in my skull as I attempt to come up with a third reason Arturo will go for. He doesn't seem to be a stupid man, but maybe he's too smart for his own good.

"If you let her go, you'll have the upper hand," I finally respond, silently praying I can somehow articulate this to make sense to Arturo, even when it doesn't add up to me.

The prick throws his head back, laughing. When he sobers, he squats down so he can look me in the eyes. "Please, explain that one to me."

"Think about it. Flynn is expecting your worst, is no doubt plotting and planning a way to get to his daughter." I take a deep breath. "When he succeeds—because let's face it, he will not rest until he finds Taryn—he'll have the upper hand. But there's no way in hell that you letting her go is even a blip on his radar. It'll throw him off his game, which means you'll have the upper hand."

"You don't think he will bring the same heat for you alone?"

My heart skips a beat because, honestly, I don't know the answer to his question. A large part of me believes nothing will stop Flynn from finding me, *dead or alive*. However, I'd be lying if I claimed there isn't a small piece of me wondering if I matter enough.

"He'll still come for me," I admit. "No doubt he'll come full force too, but he'll be rattled."

"I don't need O'Reilly to be *rattled* to take him *out*."

"Maybe, but what if you're wrong? Do you truly want to take the chance?"

Arturo straightens to his full height, glaring at Breandán. I follow his line of sight, watching as the Irishman nods slightly.

"Take the girl outside," Arturo instructs.

Breandán's brows knit together. "And do what with her?"

"Let her go."

For the first time since we've arrived at the warehouse, I witness a glimpse of the Breandán the O'Reilly family has trusted for so many years. Relief mixed with a dash of regret flashes in his eyes as he sighs and carefully unties Taryn from the chair. He reaches for the duct tape, but Arturo stops him.

"Tape can wait until she's out of earshot," he snaps. "I don't need to hear her whining."

"Yes, sir." Breandán lifts Taryn into his arms.

She struggles against his hold, but he's too strong. Eventually, she relents, allowing him to carry her across the gigantic space toward the exit.

"Thank you," I whisper.

Arturo hauls his leg back, then kicks me in the ribs. "I didn't do it for you!" he shouts right after landing the blow. "Now, get up." I roll to my side, clutching my midsection while gasping for air. It pisses him off enough to kick me again, in the back this time. "I said, get up!"

It takes a minute for me to gather my wits, let alone the strength to stand. Turning to face the man who is likely going to take my life, I do my best to square my shoulders. The false bravado becomes a little less false as I stare beyond him in the direction Taryn was carried.

Breandán is walking backward with his hands raised above his head. Flynn, along with several other armed men, is following, hot on his heels.

Without giving it a second thought, I lunge at Arturo. He's a large man, and a strong one at that. I don't manage to knock him off his feet, but I do startle him just enough to give Flynn and his men another advantage.

I guess the luck of the Irish is a real thing, after all.

Chapter 18

Dawn Sullivan

Flynn

MY HEART POUNDS WILDLY in my chest as the call goes dead. No Arturo spouting his venom. No more screams from my little girl. *Nothing...* except a silence that sends terror crashing through me.

"Find them!" I roar, slamming my fist into the dashboard in front of me. It cracks, the plastic slicing through the skin on my knuckles, but I don't give a *shite*. My baby is out there, with the woman who holds my heart, defenseless against a man who is the devil himself. He will murder them, the same way he did Aisling, and not think twice about it. He has something against me or the *Irish Faction*, but I have no idea *what*. I've done nothing to deserve his wrath, and neither had my father, as far as I'm aware.

"Almost there," Fiona promises, her fingers flying over the keys of her laptop she has somehow hooked up to her phone so she can log into anything and everything she needs to track down my *taeghlach*. I don't give a damn how she does whatever the hell it is she's doing; all I care about is that she finds them. My family. My daughter and the woman I plan on making my wife, just as soon as she agrees.

I groan, rubbing a hand over my face in frustration, fear of the unknown swamping me. What is he doing to them? Why does he have such a damn hard-on for the O'Reilly family? As far as I know, we have never been a threat to the Italians. We have our faction, they have theirs.

They don't mess with us, and we don't mess with them.

Well, we didn't until Arturo put a bullet in my baby girl's mam.

"Fuck!" I yell in rage, hitting the car again.

We'd left the house as soon as I found out the fucking traitor, Breandán, took Sutton and Taryn. Aiden insisting on driving, no matter the condition he's in after our altercation earlier. Fiona is in the middle with her toys spread out around her. Two other cousins of mine who showed up after Da passed, Rory and Declan. They're in the very back of the SUV.

Behind us is another SUV full of my da's men… my men now. Members I don't want to be in charge of, who now call me *Ceann an Teaghlaigh*. I don't want this fucking life anymore. I'm done. Once I get my family back, we are leaving Ireland and never coming back.

"Go left!" Fiona suddenly shouts. "Now!"

Aiden turns sharply, then takes a quick right at Fiona's directions, hitting the brakes hard when Fiona snaps, "Stop!"

"What the hell?" Aiden growls, glaring over at his sister. "You trying to *fecking* kill us?"

"According to this, they are two blocks that way." Fiona points northwest. "We have no idea what the situation is. We could get Sutton and Taryn killed if we rush in like a bunch of damn *eejits*."

"What do you suggest?" I demand, staring at her computer where a dark red dot stands out on the grid, unmoving.

A slow smile tilts the corners of Fiona's dark red lips as she shuts the lid on the laptop, placing it beside her on the seat. Reaching over, she picks up the sniper rifle case she's brought with her, then opens her door. "Give me five minutes. Then, go get our *taeghlach* back."

Our family.

Here I've been thinking of Sutton and Taryn as *my* family only. But they aren't; they belong to all of the O'Reillys. The entire *Faction*. Because when I do leave, and trust me, I am going to, they will still be here and be my family. At least, I hope they will.

I glance at my watch, attempting to wait, although impatiently, until the precious minutes Fiona demanded are up. It crawls by slowly to the point it feels more like hours, but finally, it hits the full five bloody minutes. Aiden has the vehicle in gear and is tearing down the street again before I have the chance to say anything.

Soon, we come to a stop outside a red brick building where one of our vehicles sits, the same vehicle Fiona was tracking to get us here. There are two SUVs behind the car, and no less than six bodies are littering the ground, bleeding out around them.

My cousin has impeccable aim.

"Let's go," I command, slipping out of the vehicle and palming my Desert Eagle. I'm almost to the front door, my cousins and men at my back, when it opens, and Taryn runs through, rushing toward me. My chest rumbles with a deep growl of anger at the sight of the tape across her face and the tears streaming down her cheeks. Beyond her, I find Breandán watching us closely as he takes a step back. The look in his eyes says he knows he's majorly fucked up and is about to die.

Scooping my little girl into my arms, I hug her tightly before turning and handing her over to Fiona when my cousin appears beside me out of nowhere. As much as I want to hold Taryn close, I need to get to Sutton. I place a kiss on Taryn's forehead, my gaze meeting Fiona's. "Go!"

The second she's gone, my eyes lock on Breandán. "I trusted you," I snarl. "My da trusted you!"

Breandán nods, his jaw hardening. "Sometimes we're forced to do things we don't want to. There was no other choice... I need the money."

"There's *always* a choice," I bite out. "You made the wrong one."

"I was going to die anyway," he admits. "At least now when I go, my mam and sister will be free to live their lives."

"What the hell does that mean?" I don't have time for this.

"I owed people some money. I had no way of paying them back. It's done now."

"You should have come to us," I snap. "This could have all been avoided." I shake my head. "Too fucking late now. You endangered the most important people in my life. You were dead the second you decided to deliver them to that monster."

"Hands up," Aiden orders, stepping forward to stand beside me, backing me up even though he has to be in pain after the beat down I gave him earlier. "Keep them there."

I stalk toward Breandán, raising my gun and aiming it directly at his head. He backs up, his hands in the air, a look of resignation on his face. As we enter the building, I glance over to witness Sutton throw herself at Arturo. She doesn't manage to knock him down, but he's distracted enough that he doesn't notice us coming up behind him until it's too late.

Sutton pushes away from where they are tangled up on the floor, crawling quickly away from his reaching arms. Before Arturo can grab her, I aim and shoot, putting a bullet in his leg. He screams, grabbing his calf, his chest heaving as he glares at me.

"I'll fucking kill you! All of you!"

"Seems you aren't the one in control right now, Arturo Ferraro."

No, the fucking prick isn't in control. I am.

Arturo glances behind me, his face lighting with excitement as his eyes settle on something, or someone.

"Your men are all dead. You have no one to come save you. You will die today."

A slow grin spreads across Arturo's face, and he throws his head back, laughing, before glaring at me with a gleam of satisfaction in his dark stare. "Oh, really? I don't think so. Not today."

"Lower the gun, cousin."

I freeze. The voice behind me is one I never thought I would hear as my enemy. My hand shakes slightly as I turn, already knowing who I'm going to find.

Fiona.

She stands just inside the door. She has one hand holding tightly to my daughter's arm, the other pointing a Glock at her head. The one family member I thought I could trust with anything is betraying me.

Fiona moves across the room, squeezing Taryn's arm harder, causing her to cry out in pain. "I said, lower the gun."

I peer down at the coward at my feet, gritting my teeth as he laughs. A crazy, maniacal laugh. It grates on me, making me want to squeeze the trigger of my gun still pointed at his head.

"Fiona, my *piccola*. I've been waiting for you to arrive and join in the fun."

I frown, my gaze going from Arturo to my cousin. "Fiona, you are with this bastard?"

She bares her teeth at me, her eyes bright with fiery anger. "Of course not."

Arturo sputters out another laugh. "That's not what you were saying in my bed last night, piccola."

Fiona raises a delicate eyebrow. "You were a means to an end, Arturo. Nothing more, nothing less."

Before he can say anything else, Fiona moves her gun away from Taryn's head long enough to point it at him and fire. Screams come from my girl, muffled by the tape that still covers her lips as Fi points the gun back at Taryn's head.

A hard, calculating gleam enters Fiona's eyes as she looks at me, then at the members who surround us—my cousins and my da's men. I'm about to find out who is loyal and who isn't. I have no idea at this point what to think.

"Breandán, good to see you again. Family doing well?" Breandán stiffens but nods. "I'm glad everything's worked out since I put you in touch with Arturo." She laughs softly. "Come here. Show them who you truly follow."

"No," I growl. "Don't you move a *fecking* inch."

When Breandán ignores my order and begins to close the distance between him and Fi, I don't think twice. I send a bullet between his eyes.

Fiona cocks her head to the side, watching as Breandán's body falls to the ground, then turns her cold, hard eyes my way. "I'm still ahead with the body count."

"You killed Aisling," Aiden mutters quietly. She nods, but there's no remorse whatsoever on her face. "You killed her... knowing I loved her."

"Well, technically *I* didn't pull the trigger. That was Arturo."

"You gave the order," I claim, confident it's the truth. I have no idea who this heartless woman in front of me is, but she's definitely not the cousin I've known and loved all my life.

"I did."

"Why?" Aiden rasps, a look of tortured agony on his face. "Why would you do that, Fi? Why hurt me? Why go against the family?"

"Once again, she was a means to an end."

I speak up, "She did it to try and weaken *The Faction*. To weaken *me*." I know it's true. Somehow, I'd gotten it all wrong before. Aiden wasn't the twin I should have been worried about. It was Fiona all along.

Taryn whimpers, fighting to tug her arm from Fiona. My cousin refuses to let go. She digs her bright red nails into my daughter's skin, causing her to cry out in pain.

I try to ignore the fear I see in Taryn's eyes. I can't let myself be consumed with fear for her right now. I need to figure out a way to get her away from Fiona. The woman is lethal and seems determined to destroy us.

A thought comes to me. "It was you, wasn't it? You did something to my da. You murdered him."

Fiona shrugs. "It was easy to do. When you have money, you can get pretty much anything you could ever want or need off the internet."

Pain fills my chest, my heart clenching in dark agony. She killed my wife. My da. And now, she has my child in her sights. The Glock still presses to Taryn's temple, making my stomach clench and twist in worry.

"So, what exactly is your endgame here, Fi?" Rory, our cousin, interjects. He is younger, a mere twenty-five, but is climbing the ranks of *The Faction* quickly. "What are you hoping to bloody gain out of all of this?"

Fiona's eyes narrow on Rory, shifting the gun to level it at him. "What the hell do you think my endgame is, cousin? I ordered a hit on Flynn's wife to weaken him. It got him to leave Ireland. Arturo's men would have gotten rid of both him and his brat in Boston, but he ran home to his da instead. I had to switch up my plans." Her dark red lips twist into a sinister smile. "Arturo hit him hard when he got home, but I could only allow it to go on so long before I had to play the heroine and save all of you."

"You almost killed me," Aiden hollers, his voice thundering around the empty building.

Once again, Fiona gives another casual shrug. "You didn't die. Suck it up."

"What is your plan now, Fiona?" I ask, interrupting them as I watch Sutton moving slowly out of the corner of my eye. She's been crawling steadily toward a chair in the center of the room a few feet away for the past couple of minutes, just a gradual inch here and there. I'm not sure what she's doing, but I don't want her to draw Fiona's attention her way.

"I thought it was obvious, cousin. Maybe you aren't as smart as I thought you were."

"I know you want to take over *The Faction*," I state. "What I don't understand is how you think you are going to do so with no followers."

"They will have to follow me," she responds, aiming her Glock at me now, "because after I kill you, there won't be anyone else to take your place."

"Actually, if I die, Aiden will move into the position as head of the family." I may not like the man, but he has definitely earned the right, and he is next in line.

"No, I am the eldest. I'm next!"

Fiona and Aiden were twins, but she was older by three minutes. Three *fecking minutes*.

"Aiden has proven himself over and over. He will lead if I die," I insist.

A calm, blank expression flits over her face, and I know what she is going to do before she lifts the gun from me. Her twin stares at her in horror as she turns to him. "Sorry, brother."

"Fiona, don't do this," he whispers hoarsely.

"I am sorry, Aiden, but I've spent my entire life working toward one goal. To be the head of this family. I refuse to let anyone stand in my way. *Even you.*"

Before I can say anything to try and stop the delusional woman from taking her own brother's life, Fiona lets out a cry, her eyes going wide in shock as she drops the Glock to the ground. One hand goes to her throat as she falls to her knees, gasping for breath. She moans and tips over to her side, blood pooling around her body. A large knife protrudes from her back, stuck directly through to her heart.

She draws in a broken, ragged breath, then another, before she has no more breaths to take. Her unseeing stare left open widely in her death.

Sutton's standing in the spot directly behind Fiona, her hands cupping over her mouth. Her eyes shine, full of tears, as she shakes her head in denial as to what she's done. My beautiful woman, with the sweetest soul, had to take a life.

Immediately, I run to Fiona, kicking her gun out of the way, even though I know she's gone. In the next beat, I'm lifting Taryn into my arms and moving to slide an arm around Sutton. I hold her close, needing to feel her against me.

Finally, I have them both in my arms once again.

I'm never letting them go.

Epilogue

E.M. Shue

Sutton

One year later... Valentine's Day

IT'S AMAZING HOW MUCH has changed. You know what they say, "A lot can happen in a year." For me, that's the understatement of the century. A year ago, I wouldn't have believed any of this possible, but here we are. The year brought lots of new and big changes, along with a couple of firsts.

New town.

New house.

New job.

Visited a new country – Ireland.

First abduction.

Committed murder for the first time.

Not my proudest moment, but I don't regret it. I'm still trying to process the fact that I ended a person's life. She threatened the people I love, and I turned feral. *That* part I'm kind of proud of: finding my inner badass and saving the people I love.

I wasn't expecting to give my heart to a tiny little angel and her lunatic, head of the *Irish Faction,* father. That was definitely not on my bingo card, but moving next door to them might've been the best decision I ever made. Because now my heart is so full, and I've never been happier. There's still a small part of me afraid they'll go back to Ireland and leave me behind. Even after we got back and settled into a routine, Flynn has to fly back and forth on occasion. Sometimes he takes me along, and we have a mini vacation. But how long will the clan allow him to go back and forth? And when he finally goes, will he take me with them?

The real question is: could I leave after I've finally gotten my dream job and house? I suppose they need art teachers in Ireland. I stand in my classroom surrounded by bright colors and glitter. I do love it here. Maybe I'm worrying for nothing...

The bell rings, and I dismiss the kids, wearing a big, genuine smile, and wish them all a *Happy Valentine's Day.* It's my prep period, so I'll get to have some time to myself. As I walk to my classroom door to close it, I hear a giggle and a low chuckle. I peek my head out to find Flynn standing and talking to one of the other teachers. She places a hand on his strong bicep.

I've cut a bitch before...

No, no. That's not me. I'm not one of those crazy jealous girlfriends. She throws her head back and laughs, and I don't miss how her fingers flex on his arm.

He's not that hilarious.

I internally cringe. Deep breaths. I'm better than this. I will not harm a co-worker over laughing and groping. Technically, I think what she's doing could be considered groping, bordering on sexual harassment. Frowned upon by most sane individuals. Unlike me, who is going crazy. I hate that he makes me so possessive and brings out my jealous side. And it's not even his fault. He's probably discussing Taryn. She's probably telling him something funny or adorable she did. Meanwhile, I'm over here foaming at the mouth for no other reason than being a woman who is obsessed.

My eyes lock with his, and I jerk my head back inside my classroom. I try to shut my door, but a black boot slides in the way. *Shit.* I slowly look up and see Flynn's handsome face through the square glass. How'd he even get over here so fast? Did he sprint down the hall? I could inform him that running is against the rules, but I doubt he's going to care. Now's the time to decide if I'm going to feign surprise at seeing him or own up to watching him share a chuckle with the music teacher.

I'll own it.

I release the door handle and casually stroll back toward my desk with all the confidence and not a care in the world. I pretend to be busy, shuffling papers as I speak. "I wasn't spying. I was coming to close my door."

"Didn't say you were, Miss Matthews."

I don't look up, but I hear him shut the door and then slide the lock in place. *This is taking an interesting turn.*

"Although I do enjoy seeing your claws out." I can hear the smile in his voice, and that does have me raising my head and—as he's put it, '*my claws coming out.*'

"You're ridiculous. *I do not* have my claws out, sir. And I'm far from the jealous type. But I can show you what it looks like for them to come out."

He gives a low chuckle, and then his voice comes out raspy. "Aye. I've experience with your claws... *on my back.*"

My face heats as I take in his knowing grin. Can't argue with him there. "Anyways, what brings you here?"

"Came to see my Valentine. I left a teddy bear in the office for Taryn."

"Aw. She's going to love the gift. It's so cute seeing all the kids get excited. I can't wait to hear if she got a Valentine from Ash also." His eyes widen at the boy's name, so I quickly say, "Ashley. Her new bestie."

"I'm her Da; of course, I'm going to get her something." His voice takes on an edge to it as he continues speaking. "And, until she's twenty, I'll be her *only* Valentine." When I nod, Flynn narrows his eyes. "Is there something I should know?"

"Nope." I pop the p.

May the good Lord be with the brave soul who comes to ask Taryn for a date. I won't be the one to tell Flynn how Taryn is hoping for another Valentine. He's a scrawny little boy with a big smile named Ash. He's a good kid. She's told me all about him, and she's hoping for a special card from him.

"This isn't off to a good start. I know you're hiding something, but we'll circle back to that later." Flynn inches closer toward me. "I came to ask you something. It's *shite* location and timing, but I'm tired of waiting for what seems like the right moment. I'm no good with this kind of stuff anyways."

I make a show of batting my eyelashes and smile. "Did you come to ask to be my sweetheart?"

"Not your sweetheart. I want to be your forever." He takes my hand and places it over his heart. "I promise when I do make a mess of things, I'll admit I'm a dumb *arse*. I promise when I don't measure up to whatever romantic *shite* you women expect, I'll make up for it in the bedroom. I promise to protect you with my life, even if it might be some of mine and my family's bullshit that put you in danger. Not a single day will go by where I won't be a devoted husband and father. I'm completely, hopelessly, madly in love with you, and I'll spend forever loving you." Flynn lowers himself to one knee. "Sutton Matthews, will you do me the honor and marry me?"

There's no doubt in my mind he's telling the truth. I was worrying over a possible future without him barely twenty minutes ago, but now that he's confessing his love and devotion, I'm slightly overwhelmed. If I marry him, I'll be in the Irish Mafia. I'll be the boss man's wife.

That does sound kind of cool... and dangerous. I'll get Taryn as a daughter, which would be amazing! Could I ever walk away if I wanted to? But why would I? I love this man. I love his daughter. *This feels right.* It's been a whirlwind of events leading up to this moment, but I know without a doubt.

"Yes! Yes!" I throw my arms around him. "Yes! As long as Taryn's good with it, yes!"

"Are you kidding? She's the one who's been on me to propose."

"Wait." I push him off me. "Did you only propose because Taryn wanted you to?"

"What? Are you mad, woman? Of course not. I wouldn't marry just because my daughter asked me to! Hell, we've been warming each other's bed for a year now. Christ, you're positively maddening."

His eyes catch my lips twitching as I try to fight back my smile. He looks even sexier when he's all riled up. I love his Irish temper.

He hoists me on top of my desk and leans over me. "Just so we're clear, I was only asking as a nicety. *You're mine, Miss Matthews.*"

"*If* we get married, will I keep my last name? You seem to enjoy calling me Miss Matthews."

"Hell no. I'll enjoy calling you Mrs. O'Reilly even more." His lips claim mine in a hard kiss, his tongue plunging into my mouth, meeting mine, to dance. A large hand grabs the nape of my neck and holds me firmly in place. Not breaking our kiss, he shoves me to the edge of the desk so he can bring his body against mine. Grinding against me, I sigh into his mouth and wrap my legs around his waist.

Flynn's lips move to my jaw first, and then he whispers in my ear. "Is that a yes, or am I going to have to make a mess on your desk?"

My desk. I push him back and straighten myself up. We could easily get caught.

He raises his hand to inspect it. "It seems to already be a mess. Fuck. I've got glitter all over me. Do you go around dumping it everywhere?"

"Speaking of glitter," he rolls his eyes, and I continue, "I read about this product that's basically like a glitter bomb for your vagina. It's called *clitter.*"

"The fuck..." He shakes his head. "Nope. Nope. Nope."

"What? I can't remember if it's flavored. Seems like it was. They have edible glitter for cakes, so why not my—"

"You didn't..."

"I didn't. Because I was more concerned about getting an infection since it has to be inserted and then dissolves. The idea of my pussy juices sparkling does sound fun."

"It sounds horrifying. Listen, your pussy glistens just fine the way it is. It tastes heavenly. I don't want to fuck anything that shimmers or sparkles. Honestly, it sounds a bit disturbing."

"Really?"

"Do you want to?"

"You can't tell me Tinker Bell isn't hot? Edward Cullen? I can think of plenty—"

"The only person you'll be thinking of is me. And my dick doesn't glitter... and it's not going to get covered in glitter." He pauses, narrowing his eyes. "Or my arse."

The bell rings, and I hurry to stand. "Shush! Kids will be coming."

"I locked the door."

"There's a window!"

He looks over, frowning. "You don't have blinds on the bloody thing?"

"No." I laugh and shove him toward the door.

"So, yes?"

"I already said yes to you. I was only riling you up."

"Same. Like I said, I only asked to seem like a gentleman." He holds up his left hand, where I notice a fresh tattoo on his ring finger. *Sutton* is in a beautiful and intricate Celtic font. The thin black inked lines weave a stunning design. I'm impressed with how they managed to fit my name and the design to loop around his finger.

A part of me wants to call him a cocky bastard, but the other part of me is absolutely *swooning*. I hear the kids in the hallway, and the door handle jiggles. I hurry over to the door and open it for my next class to file in.

Flynn comes to stand next to me with a smug smirk until Taryn comes charging in. "Daddy!" Hearing and seeing her, the cocky Irishman is gone and replaced with a lovable, protective father.

"Did you ask her?"

"I did."

"Well? What'd she say?"

Flynn glances at me, and I nudge him to continue. He releases a heavy sigh. "She said only with your approval."

Taryn beams. "Yes! More than anything!"

She leaps into my arms. "I love you so much, sweetheart."

"I love you! Does this mean you're really going to be my new mommy?"

"Yes," I tell her. My hug is cut short when Taryn wiggles out of my arms and announces to the whole classroom that I'm engaged to her father.

"Miss Matthews is going to be my mam! She's going to marry my dad!"

The classroom goes wild, erupting in cheers. I lean into Flynn and whisper, "I guess I'm going to need to get my first tattoo."

"Is that right?"

"Yeah. I want your name on my finger, too."

"Don't you worry. You'll have my name soon enough." He winks and then walks over to Taryn to hug her bye.

I PULL MY CAR into the driveway and immediately feel something is off. Taryn usually runs out to greet me. Before I can swipe my phone to call Flynn, a text from him pops up.

Flynn: Come inside

Slowly, I exit the car and listen. *Nothing.* I key in the code to my front door and enter the house, then immediately come to a stop. The entire living room is covered in white burning candles, floral arrangements, and... people. There are people in my house. My eyes connect with Flynn's across the room, and immediately I relax.

He smiles and walks over to me. "I'm doing it proper this time." He takes me into his arms and brings his lips to mine. I melt into him as people cheer, but I barely register them. "I love you," he whispers in my ear.

Flynn releases all but my hand. He leads me to the center of the room where he goes down on one knee. "Sutton Matthews, will you marry me?"

"Yes!"

Another round of cheers fills the room. Flynn stands and I pull him toward me. "I notice you didn't make all your promises? Too many witnesses?"

"I'm ready to speed this along for the other plans I have for you, which are more intimate." He growls and gently pinches my hip.

I finally take in who is here. Most of the faces I barely recognize, and then I see him. *Aiden.* "What are you doing here?" I ask in surprise as I wrap him in an embrace.

"Making sure this *fecking eejit* doesn't blow it. If he did... and you like the luck of the Irish, well..."

I laugh and hug him tighter. Flynn isn't as amused. He gently pulls me back and tells me, "One more surprise." He leads me into my kitchen, where there's a makeshift tattoo station set up. I shouldn't be surprised, but I am. Flynn turns to me, his face serious. "I'm needed back in Ireland. My clan, *The Faction*, needs me. I want you to come home with me and be there as my partner, wife, and queen."

He's asking me to move to Ireland with him, which is probably why everyone is here. This must also be his way of declaring me as part of his clan. I don't have any family, but I've made a few friends. I do have a life here, and it's going to be hard to leave it all behind, but my heart is with him and Taryn.

"You forgot a title."

"Sweetheart?" he guesses, frowning at the word I'd teased him with earlier today in disgust.

"No, you *eejit*. You forgot, mother."

"God, I love you." His lips claim mine again in a passionate kiss, stealing my breath away. When we pull back for air, we only look at one another and nod. I walk over to get his name tattooed on my finger because I know in my heart it'll only ever be him.

This Valentine's Day is *everything*, as it marks the beginning of our *forever*.

~ THE END ~

Thank you for reading Not Your Sweetheart!

We hope you loved both stories and will consider leaving a positive review. Each review and recommendation helps us spread our love of writing great stories!

-MMM25 Authors

Have you read the other MMM25 multi-Author collaboration stories?

Read it here: https://books2read.com/NaughtySantaDaddy

Please read on to learn a little bit about some of our Authors and where to find more of their books.

About The Authors

Sapphire Knight is a Wall Street Journal, USA Today, and Amazon International Bestselling Romantic Suspense Author with over 60 novels that reflect on what she loves to read herself. She's a Texas girl at heart who's crazy about football, Dr. Pepper, Doberman Pinchers, and has always possessed a passion for writing. www.authorsapphireknight.com

Alex Grayson is a USA Today bestselling author of heart pounding, emotionally gripping contemporary romances, including several series and multiple standalones. Originally a southern girl, Alex now lives in Ohio with her husband, three cats, and one dog. www.alexgraysonbooks.com

Wall Street Journal and USA Today Bestselling author Winter Travers is a devoted wife, mother, and aunt turned author who was born and raised in Wisconsin. Winter spends her days caring for her family and her nights writing happily-ever-afters. www.wintertravers.com

Andi Rhodes loves creating MC romance stories with a generous helping of suspense, chaos, and happily ever afters! When she's not writing, she's living her own HEA with her husband & their boxers. www.andirhodes.com

USA Today Bestselling Author Morgan Jane Mitchell takes you on wild rides you won't see coming with her stories packed with twists, drama, angst, secrets, revelations, and those panty-melting hot moments we all crave. From her epic paranormal sagas to gritty motorcycle club series like Asphalt Gods MC and Royal Bastards MC: Nashville, TN these tales are not for the faint of heart. www.morganjanemitchell.com

D. Vessa is a romantic suspense author who loves a morally gray alpha, the color black and a good Aperol Spritz. When she is not writing she spends her time running from her problems, and wondering what color to dye her hair next. www.authordvessa.com

Shannon Myers is a native Texan who loves writing dark and gritty romances filled with clever twists. She resides in the west Texas desert with a posse of men (nothing like she'd imagined in her fantasies) and a plethora of fur babies. https://shannonshaemyers.com

Avelyn Paige is the creative force behind gripping romantic suspense, motorcycle club, and mafia romance novels that land on the Wall Street Journal and USA TODAY bestseller lists. She calls a cozy corner of Indiana home, where she lives with her husband and five furballs. www.authoravelynpaige.com

Kathryn C. Kelly lives in Texas and writes romance across several genres. www.katckelly.com

Dawn Sullivan loves writing Paranormal, Suspense, and Witchy Romance with strong, badass women and the men who would do anything for them. She has a wonderful, supportive husband and three amazing children she enjoys spending time with when she isn't lost in the worlds she's created, spinning new tales of romance and suspense for her readers. www.dawnsullivanauthor.com

Liberty Parker is a USA Today Bestselling romantic suspense Author who specializes in bringing readers happily ever afters that'll rev their engines one page at a time. She spends her days drawing inspiration for her next novel from her amazing family, friends, and her precious furbabies, past and present. https://www.bookbub.com/authors/liberty-parker

E.M. Shue is an Alaskan award-winning romance author. She writes in many different sub-genres but always features badass heroines in gritty situations. www.authoremshue.com

Acknowledgements

Cover Designer— Ct Cover Creations. Thank you so much for not only one, but two, absolutely stunning covers for this unique collaboration!

Editor— Shelby Limon. Thank you for your support and willingness to work on such a tedious project. You are awesome!

My Collab Friends— All twelve of you. I love that we could come together to create two unique, happily ever afters. Your professionalism and willingness to put this project first speaks to your dedication as a fellow businesswoman, and I've enjoyed working with you chapter by chapter. - Sapphire

Our Blogger, Bookstagrammer, and TikTok Friends— YOU ARE AMAZING! You take a new chance on us with each book and, in return, share our passion with the world. You never truly get enough credit, and we're forever grateful for every share and review.

Made in the USA
Middletown, DE
20 February 2025